THE GINGER JAR

The Ginger Jar

Kathryn Purnell

Contents

1 Chapter One 1

2 Chapter Two 12

3 Chapter Three 25

4 Chapter Four 49

5 Chapter Five 79

6 Chapter Six 93

7 Chapter Seven 104

8 Chapter Eight 144

9 Chapter Nine 159

10 Chapter Ten 237

11 Chapter Eleven 258

12 Chapter Twelve 267

13 Chapter Thirteen 311

14 Chapter Fourteen 329

About The Author 341

Title: The Ginger Jar

Author: Kathryn Purnell (1911-2006)

First published in 2025

Copyright © J R Garran 2025

ISBN 978-1-7642584-0-1 (Paperback)
ISBN 978-1-7642584-1-8 (Ebook)

A catalogue record for this book is available from
The National Library of Australia

www.trove.nla.gov.au

J R Garran Publishing
Sydney
www.garran.au

How long will it take
to fill my virgin spaces:
will it take all my life
to occupy these places?

1

Chapter One

It was during the hot tiresome days of Ramadan that I broke the ginger jar. In Cairo the month of Ramadan is a hard month to endure when it comes at the end of summer. The long, lazy days of dust and fasting eat into your equanimity, so that your senses are acute to notice every hungry man who falls in the street and the round, swollen stomachs of the beggar children who will not eat until sundown no matter how insinuating the temptation. An unwritten law exists between yourself and your servants, that on their part they will do all the work as usual no matter how many visitors you have and on your part that you will overlook irritability, breakages, even illness itself. At night you cannot sleep for the festivities, the loudspeakers blare forth with deafening defiance of sleep, restlessly you toss, waiting for the sun at dawn. This is the hour your servant creeps back to his bed or curls up on the dirt floor in the house of a friend. You bite your tongue to stillness when you see him in the morning. Yet you cannot resist his sleepy smile. It reminds you of a little boy who has run away at the fair, so sheepish, so relieved to be at home again and yet so proud of himself for running away.

It was my custom to try to get everything done in the morning, before the urge to sleep overcame the household. While the cook did the shopping I dusted the precious things and changed the water in the flower vases. On that morning when Hassan came in with the mail I had just arranged a compact mass of brilliant, tangerine geraniums in the blue of the little ginger jar. It fell from my hands as I turned at his touch and smashed into pieces on the tile floor. It should have been funny. The astounded face of Hassan with his half-sleepy eyes and his wide-open mouth under the white turban was humorous enough. His thick, black hand extended towards me holding the letters, displayed incongruously at the wrist, the cuff of an old fawn sweater he insisted on wearing all through the heat of summer, beneath the spotless white of his gallabiyah. But I was not amused. I drew in my breath. I found myself so furious that I began to tremble and my eyes filled with tears. I walked straight past Hassan and his incredibly surprised face and sat down.

All of my sadness about Egypt plus all the irritations of Ramadan welled up inside of me. But I did not cry after all. I just sat. Behind me, Abdul the cook berated Hassan as he cleaned up the broken fragments. Then, with the closing of the kitchen door, there was silence.

From the long veranda I could see the Nile. A felucca drifted past with the top of the sail so high the tip of it appeared above the many-storeyed flats on Mazhar Pasha. Across the water in Bulak a café was packed with clients from which came the bizarre monotonous drone of an Arab song. It came to me in mournful beats, punctuated with the sound of traffic on the bridge.

With one hand, Abdul put a small table beside my chair. With the other he put down a small tray. In the centre of the tray was one part of a three-piece, handmade, lace duchess set which he had special instructions only to use on my dressing table, because my mother had made it. On it was one of the best coffee cups, and beside it a small plate with a piece of sticky Ramadan pastry and a pink biscuit. Under the plate were the letters. Abdul put a cigarette box on the table too and an ashtray, before he said

"Hassan is very sorry, Lady. He did not mean to break something. He is very stupid boy, Lady. He is on back steps."

"Tell him to come in, thank you, Abdul. It was not his fault. I broke the jar. It was very old anyway."

"How many years, Lady?"

"All the years since my childhood."

"Then it had many journeys."

Then it had many journeys! From North America to Europe, eastwards again to Malaya, south to take temporary root in Australia, home again to Canada, east again to Egypt. Now it would mingle with the dust of the Pharaohs, a small blue and white jar, one of millions made in the land of China as a suitable medium to export ginger. A small blue and white ginger jar for which Charles Gilbert paid fifteen Canadian cents.

***

I was in my sixteenth year on that Friday in June when I met Charles in front of the Hudson Bay store in Vancouver. He was coming out and I was going in.

"Charles!"

"Hello, what are you doing? No school today?"

"I've been to the dentist and Mummy said I might as well have some lunch before I go home."

"And have you?"

"No, not yet. I was going up to the Hudson Bay Cafeteria."

"How uninteresting. Come with me. I'm going to eat with a friend of mine in his café."

"Oh, Charles. You don't think he would mind?"

"No, he owns the place. He'll be pleased."

"Where is it?"

"You'll see."

We started to walk. He went so fast I could hardly keep up.

"Charles, shouldn't you be teaching?"
"I came down early today to order books."
"Do you like it there?"
"No. Well, I don't mind it but I guess I'd rather be further from town."
"Oh?"
"Well, it is neither urban nor rural, neither one thing nor the other."

He walked in long strides as if he were on an open country road.

"You're going a little bit fast, Charles."
"Sorry."

I didn't like the street we turned into. It made me apprehensive and excited. The shops were boarded up in front, like a secretive and sinister face with half-shut eyes.

"Are we in Chinatown, Charles?"
"Yes."

Mummy wouldn't like it. I didn't think Daddy would like it either. I knew Mother would be furious. Nobody knew Charles was even in town. If anything happened to me they would not know where to find me. People disappeared in Chinatown. Chinatown was not the place for young girls to have their lunch. I felt nervous. I suppose I lagged. Charles took my arm.

"Haven't you ever been in Chinatown before?"
"No."
"Haven't you ever eaten Chinese food?"

"No."

"Then it's high time you did."

"But, Charles, I don't think —"

Charles wasn't even listening. He steered me down a little lane.

"Down here,"

The door into the narrow hall was just a few yards from the street. At the end of the hall we climbed a flight of stairs which led into a large, almost empty room, arranged with plain board tables and chairs. A short, fat lady in a Chinese dress with split skirt stood up behind one of the tables near the door. The only other people I could see were two Chinese eating rapidly with clacking chopsticks at a table at the other side of the room.

"Mister Charles!" the Chinese lady said. "Mister Charles. Nice to see you. And who is this frightened one you have with you whose eyes are so large."

"This is my cousin, Kit, who has come to have her first Chinese meal. And it better be a good one."

"Sit down, my friend, sit down at the table by the window and I will bring Chang."

Charles bowed to the two Chinese eating at the table and they rose to their feet, folded their hands across their chests, bowed, and sat down again. We proceeded to the table in front of the window. I grew tense with a new fear because Charles was at home here, which made him a person not known before. I looked at him as he sat down opposite me after ceremoniously pulling out my chair. He had an amused sardonic look on his face and his eyes seemed almost shut, making me feel I did not know this man at all. I found myself wishing my father was with me. There was a dignified padding of feet across the floor but I was too scared to look up. I was telling myself that if this was all right for Charles, it must be all right for me, but the magic formula would no longer work.

"Chang," Charles was saying. "This is my young cousin, Kit."

"Who has come for her first Chinese food," said the softest voice I had ever heard in a man. "Welcome, Missy Kit. You are my friend and my guest in my house as the friend of my friend, Mister Charles."

I took a quick glance up at the face above me. Mr Chang was bowing to me and to this day I have retained only one impression. The eyes in his fat face were no larger than two black shoe buttons yet they shone with such a glint of humour that I had the impression that they were not black but silver. There was absolutely no trace of a smile on his face which seemed as impassive and still as the face of a stone Buddha.

Then began a discussion the like of which I had never heard concerning food. Mr Chang and Charles discussed fish and fowl, duck and veal, bamboo, pineapple, asparagus, birds' eggs and sharks' fins all mixed up with sing-song words in Chinese. The little fat lady stood behind to giggle and squeak while the voices of the two men rose and fell so rapidly that it almost sounded like a serious argument, except that I happened to realise that Charles was enjoying himself.

Quite suddenly the Chinese gentleman clapped his hands and disappeared as quietly as he had come and the Chinese lady put a little pot of tea and two bowls in front of us. I found myself alone again with Charles.

"Well." I said and let out my breath.

Charles said. "We have tea first." and began to pour it from the teapot into the little bowls. "This is a real tea. No sugar, no milk, just tea." He lifted his bowl and began to sip.

I lifted mine and sipped too. "It's a little like soup," I said, "but not quite."

"Soup," said Charles, "will come at the end of the meal."

"Charles," I said. "Do you often come here?"

"I do whenever I can. Not often enough."

"It's a bit creepy, Charles."

"Creepy! What's creepy about it? What you mean is, that it's different from any other café you've been in. That's what you mean isn't it?"

"Well, not exactly."

"Listen." said Charles and his tone was almost angry. "You wait and have your meal and then make up your mind. Don't prejudge places or people either for that matter. Wait and see first."

Charles had changed or was this a side of him that I hadn't seen before and therefore did not recognise? I felt he was suggesting that I change the subject but I wouldn't.

"How did you meet Mr Chang?"

"His son and I were in the same class at school and one day he brought me home with him."

"Here?"

"Yes, here."

"Is this a house too, Charles?"

"Yes, this is a house too. As a matter of fact it is a beautiful house. There's one room upstairs, full of the most beautiful things you ever saw. Far more artistic but as rich as a museum."

"Then why don't they move into another place and show the beautiful things off better?"

"Well-bred Chinese," said Charles, "do not believe in showing off."

There was a finality in his voice that prohibited my carrying that subject any further. I was being forced to change the subject, but I could not submit so easily.

"I never knew you had any Chinese friends, Charles, you never told me."

Charles looked across the table at me. "The first time I came here was one day after school. When I got home I was licked."

"Licked?" I gasped. "Given a licking?"

"Licked and forbidden ever to come again."

"So now you are grown up you come just whenever you like."

"I always came whenever I liked." said Charles.

"Oh!"

"Oh, what?"

For the first time in my life I was furious at Charles and instinctively I leaned back against the chair as if I were backing away from him. He responded with a long, hard amused look which held me tongue-tied. It seemed we waited hours for that food. We probably did not and I had not then learned that one of the side-blessings to be enjoyed with Chinese food is the wonderful sense of patience one develops while waiting. It has the supreme virtue of always being worth waiting for, a quality that Chinese food shares with the French.

During the interval of silence anger seeped out of me and I decided that whatever the food was I would eat it for Charles' sake. If I had to choke down every mouthful I would make Charles feel I enjoyed it. If I had to be sick, then I would be sick. If I had to be kidnapped then I would be. I half-filled my bowl with rice and helped myself to the chicken that came in the first little platter. Beside the chicken was what looked as if it might be pineapple. I tried a little. Charles suggested that I should sample the bamboo shoots. Our host pulled up a chair and sat down spreading himself comfortably over it with a benevolent air. I picked up a fork, and Charles, with a chagrined look at Mr Chang out of the corner of his eye, a pair of ivory chopsticks. We began to eat. By the time the meal was finished I was more than willing to be kidnapped provided Charles was kidnapped too and our jailers provided meals like Chang.

Chang said to Charles, "You still do not bring your wife?"

Charles said, "Not yet, Chang — give me time."

"I look forward to the day you will bring the little Charles."

"One day I will bring you the Number One Son."

"He will be as my own son."

"You can teach him Chinese."

"It will be my greatest pleasure. Perhaps he will not forget the characters like his father."

"I was too old when I started. Children should learn languages young."

"You had other things to learn for yourself. These you will pass on to your son."

"I hope so, Chang."

"The way is shown to those who desire it." Chang rose. "I will be back before you go," he said, then he turned to me, "You are no longer frightened, Missy?"

I choked, "No, I'm not frightened. This is the best food I ever had in my life. Thank you very much Mr Chang."

"Will you come again?"

Impulsively I said, a little out of my depth, "I would like to bring my father."

Mr Chang said, "Is your father partial to good food?"

"No," I said. "We don't care so much about food, Daddy and I. It's something else."

There was, as might be expected, a considerable silence. I had a dreadful feeling in the pit of my stomach, when I saw Charles' face. It was all crinkled up so that as far as his eyes were concerned he might have been Chinese himself. It was the first time I was to see a Chinese laugh. All of Mr Chang laughed, his eyes and his shaking cheeks, all of Mr Chang that was enclosed in that voluminous black gown. But he did not make a sound. Quietly he turned away on his slippered feet.

I kept my head down and my shocked eyes riveted on to the remains of the wonderful lunch Mr Chang had provided, perhaps the most delicious lunch I had ever eaten. I dared not look at Charles. Mrs Chang bustled up and began to take away the plates. Charles was joking with her and when she replied she giggled. I tried to pass her the little bowls still keeping my head down.

"What a shy one it is you have brought, Mister Charles. I will be telling them in the kitchen. You have brought us a shy dove to be fattened."

"Do not be so sure of that Mother Chang," Charles said.

"With you I am never sure, Mister Charles."

Mr Chang was standing by the table again. "Missy?" he said.

I was forced to look up. When I did, I glanced quickly at Charles. Surprisingly enough, Charles was beaming.

"Missy?" Mr Chang said. "It is possible that you do not know it, but you have paid me a great compliment. I have in my hand a little jar of ginger that has travelled many miles from China to my home. I am going to charge your cousin, Charles, fifteen cents for it, and for his dinner so that indeed you cannot refuse to take it. Perhaps you will one day bring your father here. It would be my pleasure to have him as my guest. If not it will not matter for I am honoured to tell you that I have met him already."

'But," I said. "Mr Chang —"

"Oh, not himself eating here," said Mr Chang. "You yourself have said that he does not go seeking the satisfaction of his stomach. I have met him because he has come in you."

Mr Chang bowed low and put the little ginger jar on the table.

***

How strange it seems to remember that day. The ginger jar is broken now, it has fallen from my hands into a dozen odd-shaped irreplaceable fragments. Yet how can I throw these pieces away without recognition, when the combination of these separate parts made the unity of the whole on which my life is based? Can I ignore the shattered roundness which was my body under the pale white northern skin and the dispersed pattern traced in sapphire which symbolised the wonder that revealed itself through the mirror of my light blue opening eyes? All of us have a ginger jar to focus our understanding. Some of us construct it on a potter's wheel of our own making but others such as I, have it offered to them, modestly, as a free gift of love. I alone knew the price that was paid for my ginger jar. I will gather the fragments together and breathe into them the other life from which they have been detached. The pattern on the ginger jar was painted by my cousin, Charles Gilbert, on two sides, over two summers. One summer at the beach was the beginning and the other, at the lake, the end of my youth.

***

2

Chapter Two

Surprisingly there were not so many pieces and two were large. But the fragments, what about the fragments, those small bits of porcelain broken away in the shattering? Can you mend that which is fragmented?

Abdul, for some reason, had neglected to remove the remains of the ginger jar, leaving the dustpan and even the brush on a corner of the buffet. Ramadan no doubt made him forget it and because I was upset he feared to return. He would slip in later after watching me leave the verandah, hoping I would not notice. Yet I did notice and I fingered the pieces, running my thumb lightly across the largest edge. The ginger jar did not fracture the skin. Only my mind was fractured and suddenly I recovered quickly. The letters! What had happened to the letters?

I went back to the veranda table and picked up the bundle of letters. I should have known the one on the very bottom of the pile would be from Charles Gilbert. Holding it in my hand I sat down again. This time my thoughts would have to go back even further: further than the ginger jar.

***

This is all I can recall, myself in a pink coat and bonnet, lost and terrified. I remember how I came to the place where I stood and looked, and then how I ran on and looked until panic seized my eyes and blinded me. I remember how the din became so chaotic I could hear nothing. Finally my throat seized and I could neither cry nor speak.

I ran past person after person, man, woman, boy, girl, booth, stall, lucky dip, afternoon tea-tables, all wrong, distorted and twisted out of perspective because I was lost, because the dark night might fall and unknown catastrophe overtake me while I was alone and deserted, unable to get home, isolated from my security. After the tea-tables I found myself in the space beyond the bazaar where I ran around the dancing platforms, each one the same, one piper blowing for the swinging kilts dancing high above me beneath unrecognisable re-mote, concentrated faces.

Then suddenly my undirected flight was blocked, to the right, to the left, by an uncompromising pair of large, worn shoes gleaming with ancient dinted silver buckles under plaid socks and the red bony knees so often displayed beneath the kilt of the Seaforth Highlanders. The voice of salvation cracked above me:

"Where'd you come from?"

I knew the harsh school-boy voice at the unreliable breaking point which belonged to the threshold of manhood. It held a recognisable tone of amused tolerance at finding a little thing in pink related to it-self wandering alone in such a big park. I had found a cousin. It was not strange to have found a cousin at such a gathering; all told I prob-ably had ten or even more relations within shouting distance. But I hadn't been able to find them and I was incapable of shouting. Overcome I sat down on the grass and howled. The boy, undoubtedly at his age embarrassed, leaned down and picked me up.

"Gee Whiz" he said. "What's the matter? Where's your ma?"

I threw my little arms tightly around his neck and hung on with only one thought, one idea; determination not to be dislodged not to lose this refuge newly found.

"I got a nickel" my cousin said. "If you want I'll buy you a toffee apple. But stop howling."

I stopped howling but I didn't let go. I buried my face in the lace jabot at my cousin's neck and hung on. We moved.

"If you don't let go how'll I get the nickel out of this fool suit of clothes?" he said.

It seems according to family legend that he carried me to the back of the cake stall, toffee apple and all, and handed me over to his mother, my Auntie Meg, whom he saw first, before my own mother who was busy waiting on the customers.

"Charlie, for heaven's sake, what have you given the child? Her coat's ruined, not to mention yoursel'. I put in a solid hour on that lace. Do you not remember I asked y' to take care, a special care Charlie?"

"I'm sorry Ma. But gee, the kilt's too small Ma."

"I know lad. You're getting pretty gangling" Her voice softened. "Well, make off with yoursel'. We're busy here."

And a big man said in a big voice:

"Hey Bonnie Prince Charlie, can you sell me a cake?"

Charles must have made off. I don't know. I don't think I cared. It was only years afterwards when they teased me about that day, that I knew the kilt had belonged to Davey Gilbert when he was young like Charles before he had gone to the war. After that day I was lost, Auntie Meg put the kilt away in a box and it didn't come out any more at Highland gatherings because when the contingent of Seaforth Highlanders came home to our town Davey Gilbert was not with them. Sometimes my family talked about a battle called Vimy Ridge. I knew the battle was fought in France, that children shouldn't ask about it and somehow I connected it with Davey Gilbert, but perhaps I only imagined that the Canadian Seaforth Highlanders fought at Vimy Ridge.

If I was spanked that day I have forgotten the disgrace as a thing much less terrifying than being lost. But I don't think I was punished. I think that even my pretty coat was washed without comment because years afterwards my mother spoke of the day my cousin Charles took me to get a toffee apple.

My cousin Charles! I don't think I heard him called Charlie after that sports day. But I could be wrong about that too because I was so small in those days, one of the "wee ones" who were minded at home by adults whose minds were centred on the grand lads who were fighting abroad. Four sons my Auntie Meg saw off to France. She was the eldest of my Mother's family and she suffered the most. Twice I was left at home when my father went to see one of the Gilbert boys swing by in a victory march after the Armistice and a year after that in the Gilbert's own house I was lifted up to kiss my cousin Jock surrounded by his brothers who were trying to help him forget he had only one arm and a stump and one brother too few to welcome him home.

One of the wee ones I was, like my brothers, like my nearer cousin Greta, emerging to consciousness, beginning to comprehend.

"Eleanor Jane Marshall, where have you been?"
"That wild youngest of mine took her to buy a toffee apple. Her coat's for the tub no doubt."

Eleanor Jane Marshall, the soft round, curly-headed wee one cuddled and called Kitten, saved for the day by a sugar-dipped apple. But without any possibility of rescue from the approaching perils through school, illness, wonder and the incongruous glittering shafts of growing consciousness about to strike the round bubble head behind the budded glance of innocent blue eyes.

Some undefined childish malady later diagnosed as rheumatic fever assaulted me at the time of Armistice so that I lay an especially pampered patient through all the days of rejoicing. My long convalescence became a burden on my mother's child-bearing years. With the advent of my youngest brother, the new Davy almost at hand, I was despatched to the home of Auntie Meg Gilbert, as much, I am now convinced, to provide for her a girl-child of tender years, as to relieve my mother. The Gilbert house tragically bereft of the eldest son was possessed by other sons thrown back from the cauldron of war in France, boys turned men deprived of youth. They swarmed restlessly around the large family house of Auntie Meg and Uncle Gil, and my Aunt's heart watching them comfortless as she encountered in her sons great silences of angry bitterness and a startling cynicism already past redemption.

My little smocked dresses, my bed in the tiny box-room across from her bedroom gave her a focus to hold her hand steady when her transfigured sons came home without Davey. I was summoned to receive a French doll with a white china face from a kit bag and a black wool poodle named Fifi, soldier's gifts. My gift in return to the Gilbert family was the precious condition of my health.

"Mind the child, lad, she's not sa' strong poor lamb."
"Not in front of the wee one, mind your words."
"That's not the language for the child to take away wi' her, I'm thinking."
"God bless you child. What would I do without you."

This last Auntie Meg would say when I found her in tears, on those odd occasions at night before I slept when she would rush upstairs into her room and collapse like a dress fallen from a hanger into a low chair that stood by her bedroom window. I would get out of my bed and walk stiffly in my little white nightgown into her room to pat her cheek and comfort her the best I knew with favourite verses from my little flower book.

"Oh mistress dear, the daisy said
I'll lay my petals round your head
A crown I'll make, oh mistress mine
Of golden centres plaited fine"

Being a shy sensitive child, inhabiting a particular world of my own I was able to discard as unessential the adult world of stress and strain which otherwise might have made me nervous and uncomfortable. The time I spent with the Gilbert family was a combination of superficial, imaginative dreams and peculiar sensitivity. I sensed that I should never be a nuisance to Auntie Meg so I pretended to be less capable of activity than I was. Long after I knew I could walk steadily and run, I would wait patiently, to the point of exhaustion, fighting sleep, to be carried upstairs. I kept quiet and out of the way so that the family would forget my presence. I developed a secret way of absorbing myself away from the display of war souvenirs and stories which frightened me in some inexplicable way.

My soldier cousins treated me like a rare piece of china and argued acidly among themselves for the amusingly unfamiliar privilege of carrying me upstairs for a bedtime story. I was beginning to read for myself and sensed the subject of their solicitude was really something other than myself. In any case they always forgot in the force of some further argument and it was my cousin Charles who took the burden of my weight on the stairs for he being so much the youngest in the family hungrily hung upon the words of his brothers and yet was somehow relieved by any chance to break away from their company. Perhaps this was why he spent so much time outside so that after suggesting innumerable times that my bedtime had come, Auntie Meg would call him from the back door. When she did I would stand behind her in the kitchen and put up my arms to be carried as soon as Charles appeared. He refused bluntly to read to me but he would condense some story of his own briefly into a few well-phrased sentences or tell me impetuously about a bird or a bear he had seen during his holidays. He was gentle but always diffident and embarrassed as if I forced him by my very presence out of the seclusion of his own thought processes.

Later when I was stronger I played outside in the back garden, an expansive area in which my uncle worked a plot of vegetables surrounded by a border of petunias and lawn. I began to dance a little in my own company under a huge tree at the very back of the yard near the fence behind the vegetable patch. Small flowers, the replica of those weeded and thrown from the beds, had reorganised themselves in a wild splendour of colour. Nasturtiums, forget-me-nots, primroses, pinks and violas were among this company plus lobelia, buttercups and English daisies.

Once when I was dancing there, I discovered Charles with a book above me in the tree. Mutually embarrassed, he recovered first and pointed his hand towards a row of diminishing specks in the sky.

"See" he said, "That's a flight of wild geese. See how they fly in a wedge shape, the first one is the leader. They fly thousands of miles honking like that from North to South.
"How do they eat?"
"They come down to the earth silly."

Uncle Gil was a tall gaunt man with an enormous wrath in his voice that at times silenced even his soldier sons but never seemed to frighten me. Charles helped him with digging vegetables on Sunday morning. They worked together with quiet almost dedicated intimacy calling me over to them when a worm or a beetle came up on the shovel. Lady-birds they pursued for my pleasure so I could hold for a minute in my hand the tickling red wings.

Uncle Gil conversed little but I adored him. There was a remote restfulness about his personality and a comfort provided by no other person except my Father. Every day from Monday to Friday while I was at Gilberts, at five, just before he left his office, my father phoned to enquire about my day. He always finished this conversation with love to Uncle Gil. I delivered the message the minute Uncle Gil came in from work and was rewarded with a sticky gum-baby from a small bag in his pocket or a small peppermint stick. I wondered for a long time why Uncle Gil still had a blue chin under his mouth after he had just finished shaving. When eventually I screwed up the courage to ask him he told me with a chuckle that he had a blue razor. I believed him. To me he was a man beyond doubt. The span of my Uncle Gil's arms was enormous but never once while I lived in his house did he lift me onto his knee or carry me up the stairs. Because he only gardened on Sundays while Auntie Meg was at church my childish conceit led me to believe that he stayed home from Church to mind me, a solution of his presence in the garden which ignored the importance of Charles to dig and carry in the vegetables. Charles played games on Saturday. Uncle Gil and Daddy talked together all afternoon, Saturday being the day my family visited. My aunt Mary brought Greta to play with me, and for supper Wilfred came to fight with Charles. It was Peg who always helped in the kitchen. Greta and Wilfred were next nearest cousins to me, but the three of them, like Charles, were the youngest instead of the oldest in their respective families and though I loved them I felt the gap. Often I sat all afternoon on my father's knee while he talked to Uncle Gil. Greta at that time was too precocious for me and hung around Peg, while Peg, being fascinated to hear the adult talk of her mother and her aunts about the soldier-boys, could not be dislodged from the kitchen. My father and Uncle Gil talked above my head of many things. Their voices droned on and on like the bees among the clover of the summer grass. Their youth came into the conversation and Auntie Meg and houses and gardens and money and something they called higher education of sons.

"I'm glad I stuck to property" Uncle Gil said many times as if finishing a conversation begun long ago. "There'll be enough."

They would observe a silence then and my father would relight his pipe and puff at it mercilessly to make it smoke to suit him. He smoked many pipes with Uncle Gil. Sometimes the smoke fogged his glasses and he allowed me to wipe them on a little round flannel he carried in his pocket.

In September I went home to normal childhood again but with the difference of another home and school and lessons on the piano. Instead of the privileges attached to being so much the youngest, I gradually assumed small duties as the oldest of the very young. From a house where the name of Davey was only mentioned with undercurrents of diffidence or defiant anger I resided in a house where Davey was a name of frequent occurrence and daily demand. Auntie Meg came more often to our house that year than we to the Gilberts. My father went every Friday night to smoke a pipe with Uncle Gil while Auntie Meg visited all her other sisters at our house. I saw little of the Gilbert boys and there seemed to abide in me no special interest in hearing about their terrifying familiarity with guns. With uninhibited regularity I sent my love to Uncle Gil with my father every Friday evening; but if Uncle Gil sent his love back my father neglected to tell me on Saturday morning. There came a time when my father still visited the Gilberts on Friday nights and my mother, taking the baby with her, went too while my cousin Peg or another older cousin spent Friday night with my brothers and me.

For some weeks I didn't see Auntie Meg at all and I had missed her enough to resent her absence long before the Friday night came when neither my father nor my mother went to Gilberts because they had been to Gilberts every other day for the whole of that week. For some unexplained reason that odd Friday was to be spent at home without visitors.

"But if you don't go to see Uncle Gil tonight Daddy, how can you give him my love?" I asked.

My mother said quickly, her voice strangely high-pitched as it was when she was sick or Davey was vomiting his milk.

"Daddy won't be going any more dear. Uncle Gil has gone to heaven."

Astounded, I stared up into her face.

"Why?"

"He was very sick and God took him away."
"Did he want to go?"

My parents regarded one another in strained perplexed silence.
Then my father said,

"Yes, I think he was ready to go."
"Did he fly south like the wild geese?"
"Yes" my father said quickly before my mother could speak.
"Will he have a garden?"
"Heaven is a garden" Mother almost wailed, her voice rising high
and shrill.
"But he won't have Charles to carry up the vegetables and Auntie
Meg to cook them."

My mother put her hands to her face then and went out of the
room. She was weeping again and I knew she had been crying all
week.

"Oh Daddy, Mummy's sick" I said in distress.
"Stay here, dear, like a good girl. I'll help Mummy."
"I hate heaven" I announced and stamped my foot. "I bet Charles
hates it and Auntie Meg too."

My father stood above me, remote and stern, his voice when he
spoke thunderous. I have never forgotten his face.

"Don't ever say a thing like that again. Never again."

I thought he was going to strike me but instead he followed
mother. My face puckered up and I began to cry. I did not mourn Uncle Gil who was in heaven although I did not know then that all my
life whenever I came unexpectedly upon a bed of velvet, white and

felted pink petunias, the quality of their colour would be different for me than that of the other flowers. There is in me some soft memory that makes petunias stand out as infinitely more than just petunias. Instinctively I know the texture of the petals, the unseen stamen and the stems. Petunias flash a light at the back of my eyes that magnifies them creamier white, rosier pink and deeper purple than the same colours in other flowers, holding for me a hidden significance that settles upon me like balm. How useless it was to think that Uncle Gil was dead when petunias continued to bloom every summer in his garden.

On that day I only cried for myself, because my father and mother were angry at me and it distressed me to hear my mother sobbing as though her heart would break.

Yet after the death of Uncle Gil there departed from me the perceptive innocence of childhood where no difference is made consciously between the inner and outer life; where what is seen is believed as reality and what is believed is right or wrong unquestionably. The protective thought processes took over inconspicuously, absorbed from my parents and my relatives, but mostly by experience of their life itself.

"Look, this grub has made its house on a flower"

"It's eating it dear. It will kill the poor flower."

"But the flower will die anyway."

"Riddled with holes, all spoiled. Knock the grub off and kill it, Kit."

"Oh no Mummy the flower is inside of it helping to make it into a butterfly. The flower doesn't mind."

"What a funny little thing you are Eleanor Jane. That grub will never become a butterfly. It is not the right kind."

"Does the flower know Mummy?"

"No dear, the flower is not meant to know. Only people know the difference. Only people can think."

"I don't want to think if a grub eating the flower isn't trying to make itself a butterfly."

"You must think dear because you are growing into a big girl now. You are not a baby any more. But you have to learn to think about things that matter."

"Doesn't the grub eating the flower matter, Mother?"

"The Lord made the arrangements, Kit and it does no good for little girls to question His way."

I knew the Lord who lived up in the sky. He ruled our house and the homes of my relatives and the Church and the Sunday School. He had finished the war on our side no matter who started it. I had great respect for the Lord and would never have dared to argue with His way. The Lord had taken to heaven Aunt Meg's Davey and Uncle Gil so I trusted the Lord as capable of looking after a mere flower and managing a grub. It was quite simple really once you understood the Lord was responsible. There were flowers to be eaten by grubs and grubs to turn into butterflies and flowers to turn into grubs. Little girls on the other hand had to grow up and think!

***

3

Chapter Three

Dear Mother! I have never taken her advice and I know when I open her letter, placed so carefully on the top of this pile, she will warn me again about the different species of my own kind. She does not approve of my leaving my girls in boarding school so I could return to Cairo. I read this message in every air letter. As if I am not miserable enough. As if I do not know that Abdul would place a letter from my girls on top of the pile. Every day he rearranges the post, having learned to decipher the important addresses, the Australian stamp first, Canada second. It is his ritual. It is the way of the world I tell myself harshly, the young must break away little by little but definitely, inevitably. Yet I am comforted by Abdul's solicitude, his kindness and I have forgiven Hassan for the ginger jar if I had anything to forgive. But still I am sad.

***

When I was twelve and we moved to the Avenue, Charles Gilbert was grown to twenty and was finishing his training as a schoolteacher. His holidays were long and he indulged in solitary canoe trips and fishing expeditions. He also built boats, played rugby, planted trees and walked from his mother's camp for miles at the beach on the sea-shore and in the forests. Charles stood out quite suddenly among my elders when he had a poem published - I had just discovered poetry and decided I must love my cousin Charles because he must love poetry too, a characteristic unheard of in my other relatives, even Greta and Peg my closest companions and mentors from whom I learned all family opinion. Except my parents of course but that was different.

Because of his age his activities seemed as removed from me as the stars. Yet for all that at the beach after a swim I asked, and Charles told me with candour, that he wrote the poem because he was in love and temporarily possessed. He was not a poet in any sense of the word, he assured me. Unexpectedly this made no difference to me at all. The die was cast. He had already become my first episode in poetry. He stood out from a large and devoted family circle like a flowering tree on a hill of scrub.

The family called Charles 'the silent kind'. He had never been given to initiating discussion of the personal; the truth was, that which affected him closely could not be easily drawn from him. That he could be rude and unsociable without malice, seemed well understood in family circles by the time I was old enough to notice. But I did not suffer this rudeness, nor, I realised, did his mother Auntie Meg. Perhaps since after the war while my mother was having Davy, I had lived as a little girl in his mother's house, he accepted me, as he did his mother, without particular emphasis or restraint. Without being his confidant, neither was I excluded, an experience which happened to me often enough with the grown members of our clan. For I made of myself a suitable target, sitting in a strangely absorbed silence among adults, like an ostrich with its head in the sand until I was invited to go out and play. It never seemed to occur to Charles that I should be out playing if I did not want to go. If I was present he included me in everything he had to say. When he left he did not bother to apologise. As I grew older he talked to me oftener and left me even more abruptly which I understood for I did not sit so long unwanted because of what I hoped to hear but because I was too shy to make the move to leave. I could never think of an excuse to go, or a parting re-mark to make for I did not want to go out to play even at home let alone at my relative's house. When I was transported to the social life of the house on the Avenue, I had begun to feel that I was unsociable, in an extraordinarily normal and gregarious family.

There were innumerable parties in that house on the Avenue, each the celebration of some cousin's engagement or birthday, too often it seemed to me, the important occasions of those cousins who made me feel uneasy with their glib acceptance and disrespect of my mother's property when she was not about. Wilfred for instance, the hand-some blonde hockey-playing cousin so renowned as a Casanova that he expected to bowl over his younger female cousins, Greta and me, by running his shiny red hands through our hair or pulling off our hair-ribbons while laughing with raucous glee. He told jokes as well which I never understood but which always made me blush, but he never told them in front of my mother whom on party occasions he referred to as his best girl, which I thought presumptuous.

My mother and my aunts, during the parties, fluttered in and out through the swing door between the dining room and the kitchen serving the guests and buzzing like bees in a hive. I never knew where to go or what to do. Often I sat on the wide stairs where I would be constantly passed by black satin pumps under rustling shot taffeta skirts going up and down to my mother's beautiful room with the wonderful mirrors reflecting the rose satin bedspread under lace, and polished maple-wood under the silver appointments in the upper part of the tower.

I sat there one night, feeling fat and itchy in a heavily frilled or-gandie dress specially made by my mother for the occasion of my cousin Robert's engagement to a girl called Beverley Bent. Greta sat beside me temporarily, for she never stayed long in one place. She too was in organdie only her dress was pale green which had the advantage of setting off her blonde hair which she was allowed to wear uncurled like yellow silk straight down her back. I was light-headed as usual with the numberless carefully constructed shoulder length curls surrounding my face like a tea cosy. Both our heads had always been a source of parental pride and joy, mine curly, Greta's spun gold. A vast difference however lay in our attitudes. Great loved her hair and I abhorred mine.

"Fancy" Greta giggled. "Anybody called Bent, naming their daughter Beverley."

"It wouldn't have mattered what they called her" I said nastily. "Whatever her name it could be reversed, couldn't it."

"It sure could, Bent Sue, Bent Mary, Bent Annie, Bent Daisy."

"No wonder she wants to change her name" I said. "She seems quite nice, don't you think?"

"She's not specially pretty." Greta said.

"Well, Robert's not specially good-looking."

"He's not bad-looking." Greta said with formal family pride.

"But he's not good-looking, like Charles, say."

"Charles! Like Wilf you mean or George."

"I said Charles. I don't think Wilf is all that special."

"Well the girls do. He always gets the girls. Did you see the one he brought tonight?"

"Uh-huh."

"Well, she's cute isn't she? Look at her. The pick of them all."

I gazed down through the double doors into the parlour. The girl Wilfred had invited to the party was almost hidden by the ring of her admirers. She was a small dark girl in a long black dress, with a revealing low neckline and a fringed skirt. Her hair sat like a smooth black cap above her white face and her lips were outlined in pure scarlet.

"She's wearing the very latest.' Greta said.

"Well I don't like it. Fancy wearing a dress like that."

"It shows her off." Greta said. She was the youngest of her family and her elder sister was married. I accepted that she knew more than I did about such things and she accepted my homage with knowledge-able pride. "They're going to dance. There's the music."

The dancing was in the dining room but all the girls were waiting in the parlour which we were watching.

"I wonder who she'll dance with?"

"Who?" I enquired, for my eye had strayed to my cousin Peg.

"Why the girl Pat of course. She's new, you know. Her people have just moved back here from California. Her clothes are all American. Trust Wilf to find her!"

"Well she'll dance with him I suppose. He brought her, didn't he?" I said in disgust that Greta should be impressed with Wilf too.

"Yes, it looks like it. He's taking her away."

Nobody was taking Peg away although she was standing right be-side the guest of honour whom Robert, of course, claimed for the first dance. I was filled with dismay the see Peg left standing there.

"Kit Look!" Greta whispered, her voice full of excitement. "Wilf has introduced Pat to Charles and Charles has asked her to dance. I'll bet Wilf is furious. She's his girl and Charles had no right to ask her for the first dance."

"Anybody with any sense would prefer Charles." I said.

With this new development I felt it worthwhile to slither down the stairs to the dining room door to watch the dancing from a better vantage point. Pat danced with Charles. She was flirting outrageously with him and he was looking at her with his eyes half-closed. I noticed

Pat's eyes then for the first time. She had unusual eyes, deep set, black and a little slanted. They gave her face the peculiar fascination of the unexpected. Yes, I conceded. Greta was right as she so often was about such things. Pat was attractive. It seemed perfectly natural to me that she should find Charles Gilbert the most interesting man in the room. It did cross my mind that Charles had a cynical satisfied look on his face which may have meant he had put one over on Wilfred but I was in a nasty mood that night and delighted that Wilf had lost his girl. Wilf had been teasing me about my curls again, which Charles never did. To be fair I scarcely saw Charles at all at the time while Wilf delivered for his father's shop nearly every week. Charles was teaching in his first country school and had come home only because Auntie Meg pressured him not to miss Robert's party.

'But I'll be home all this summer,' he had protested according to Greta as if that made any difference when his mother begged him to come. Out of the life he had I do not think Charles would consider such an episode important. Perhaps if I had been able to ask him, he would not have remembered at all.

He was a tall man, slim, dark and deeply tanned. His was the lean type of face that emphasised the hollows under his cheek bones and made his mouth a straight serious line except when he smiled and revealed his teeth which were beautifully shaped and very white. I remember he had a way of raising one eyebrow and giving me a half-puzzled look. I once mentioned this to some members of our family who looked distressed and did not seem to recognise this characteristic in him at all. I would have liked to think that it was a look he reserved for me alone but I would not be honest if I did. No one else in my family, not even my father, let alone Greta or Peg, could understand what drew me to Charles for they found him politically argumentative. His silences distressed them and his moods they found embarrassing. All of which, because I had decided to love him as a poet, increased rather than diminished my problems.

The Avenue was a big house. It was my parents' pleasure to share it. My cousins held dances and there were musical evenings in the parlour. Informal Sunday nights were held for singing practise as both my parents had choir and solo voices. We children marched around the house as the Victrola blared out from the needle of his Master's Voice, the Pilgrims Chorus and the March from Aida. In the spirit of music I spent hours at the piano beginning with scales and Czerny and finishing up with the Moonlight Sonata. By the time we moved to the Avenue, music and books had already become the companions of my leisure. Only animals and insects set themselves up in competition in a distant, impractical way which was somehow connected with the months of summer.

The time of heartbreak is not when the horizon of adult life appears, it is the time when childhood begins to end. The catastrophe occurs in the no-man's land of sand between the earth and the sea where a raft must be constructed under the pressure of the turning-tide. I think it is true to say that when we moved to the Avenue, childhood departed from me and left a vacuum. I stood in a hollow empty place of infinite magnitude which I sensed I was expected to occupy without any knowledge of how to begin. I was whole but fragmented, a jig-saw puzzle of odd-shaped pieces without either a known filled place or a promise in any pattern into which I felt I fitted. Every essential piece was no doubt present in fluidity, but nothing was fixed so that some parts of me protruded as they grew and some receded; others swam round in a limited area without hope of the expansion required for solid occupation and still others, enormously out of proportion invaded all the cavities in their vicinity. Parts of me poured forth and dried up with equal abruptness. Self-importance and nervous hesitation lived constantly in each other's habitation. Basking blissfully in the acceptance of the concrete manifestations of love and security, I wallowed tentatively in the precincts of its opposite, experimenting with the qualities of hate as a cat experiments with a captured mouse, letting it run only to pull it back. I found myself capable of unexpectedly devastating responses as the recipient of every loving care.

The new house on the Avenue presented me with the opportunity of picking up, as a magnet picks pins, a host of suggestions for the occupancy of my empty spaces, all of which I found unsatisfactory and the rejections echoed my emptiness like thunder in my ears.

Before we moved I had accepted my Sunday-school teacher's version of life, death and sin as presented in the Shorter Catechism of the Presbyterian Church. After the move we entered a new society of religious affiliation called the United Church of Canada. My father took pains to explain to me that essentially there was no difference except that we were taking the opportunity to accept the broad rather than the narrow view of Church participation. But I knew my Sunday-school teacher had elected to be continuing Presbyterian so that had we not moved to another district, we would have changed our place of devotion in any case. My Sunday-school teacher cried when she said goodbye to me and gave me a small white copy of the catechism and I suspected her tears were not for me but somehow for herself so sadly left behind.

It may be that it was for this reason that the attraction of independent thought intruded itself into the previously unchallenged domain which categorised without question the definitions of God and sin and made me see death for the first time as a personal menace. I found myself stuck without warning on the first verse of the catechism, 'Man's chief end is to glorify God and enjoy Him forever.' I loved this verse and lulled myself to sleep with it night after night in the new house, until one night, it clashed in some subtle way with my prayers. I tried repeating 'The Lord is my Shepherd' with no better success. The God in the first verse of the Catechism and the Psalm was poetry and the God of my prayers the judge of heaven and hell, almighty, powerful, omnipotent, the force behind the wages of sin which was death. Death rose up and stared me in the face!

Since my illness at the end of the Great War, I had been considered delicate. My youngest brother was bronchial and as the two children in the category of those who had to be specially watched, we had shared the same room before we moved to the Avenue. Davey's bed was in the huge boy's room at the Avenue but he shared the new white double-bed in my pink and white room nearly all the first winter we spent in the new house because along with the first cold I shared with him, we suffered together mustard plasters on our chests, swallowed the gruesome mixture of sulphur and molasses by the tablespoonful and cod liver oil as we underwent that continuous process known to adults as 'building up a child'. The final indignity, before the spring of my thirteenth birthday was sharing the fumes of a vapour lamp with the small hot body of my brother, who was remarkably adept at kicking me in the stomach and flinging his elbow into my face unconsciously as he slept. He was a loveable little fellow which made me feel morbidly mean and inferior when I declared I would not put up with him anymore.

Yet the fact that my parents accepted my request in a mild 'to be accepted manner' aroused my suspicions. Obviously they were quite willing to put me into some new position in the family which entitled me to the sanctuary of my room to myself as a right instead of a privilege. When I was sick I was to be allowed to be sick alone and my door could be shut if I wished it shut and the boys were not to be allowed in without knocking.

This was more than I had visualised; much more than I had anticipated or bargained for. I began to feel somehow isolated in a very large and formidable house. Nevertheless I closed my door out of pride and learned how lonely one can be in a room by oneself in a house full of people. I discovered how black the lightest, most beautiful room can become in the dead of night when you can't sleep and there were times when I screamed in terror and brought my mother to me and other occasions when I only thought I screamed and no one came at all. I contemplated the possibility of death by choking for breath with asthma or an even more appalling death by heart failure and devised a series of small schemes which involved unusual methods of waking my parents and procedures which kept my door open while it outwardly appeared shut. I practised certain small dishonesties such as offering out of apparent kindness to sleep in a small brother's room when my parents planned to visit a neighbour for the evening.

There were periods when I preferred to be a boy with a separate bed in a shared room, so I stole marbles and hid the glory of coloured glass at the bottom of my bureau drawer as my brothers did. I also tried to strengthen myself further with wildlife adventures stolen from the Boys Own Annual substituting this happy ending literature for poetry and verse which concerned itself with death even more than I did. But though the stories fed me they did not fill. My own inventions had greater if more terrifying substance.

Until suddenly, or so it seemed to me, I began to grow up. My body matured and I accepted the inevitable with a sort of shy excitement and observation combined with secrecy.

In that first year of our residence in this big house there were first mentions without number thrown out in general as threats, hints and superior wisdom by girls in my class at the new school and in particular by one of the girls from the neighbourhood whom my mother encouraged on the principle of kindness and whom I detested because of the fear of some startling disclosure she might make. Her tittle-tattle populated my life with haemophilia and other sorts of bleeding; with the fertilisation of seeds and the differences between boys and girls who mysteriously changed at my age into men and women. Swellings and pains were expected and a new glorious beauty of face and figure that exuded a luring scent of attraction to the opposite sex. Harriet, the neighbour's daughter, told me all of this and all I could think of when she said it was dogs and cats. I kept running away from Harriet, which mother said was rude. I sneaked out of school lest she should accompany me on the way home. What she was so anxious to tell me, I wanted to hear, if hear it I must, from someone else, my mother or Auntie Meg whom I loved, or my father. But among my closest intimates there seemed to be a conspiracy of waiting, which was not to my advantage. There seemed to be a secret world of which they would not tell. My father had always presented animal life without explanation as a wonder of God but there seemed to be no connection with wonder in Harriet's furtive insinuations and the games she suggested we play in our basement.

I didn't want Harriet but she hung around and my mother encouraged her partly because she was lonely and partly because she thought I must be too and she was anxious that I make new friends. All I really needed for friendship was the passing of time. New at the school, the girls that appealed to me most were already well acquainted and ensconced in an intimate group.

The doctor's daughter, Helen Farson and her friend Margaret Cuppets kept smiling at me but I was shy. Neither Harriet and the group of her associates nor the new Canadians from the Settlement were encouraged to join the company of these two girls.

I made friends with a girl from the Settlement who was called Inga. Almost silver blonde, learning English with amazing rapidity, Inga was to me a refuge from Harriet and I clung to her during school hours. Harriet whispered that I should not take up with the settlement people. Dagos and Towheads she called them. They were a filthy lot and lived in unfinished shacks without bathrooms. What was worse, they married cousins and produced idiots.

It would not be fair to say that Harriet was responsible for my introduction to race discrimination but she highlighted it because she was jealous of my friendship with Inga. Inga was not allowed by her own parents to come home with me or to visit anybody else either after school. When she invited me to her house one Saturday afternoon when I had known her for nearly a year, my mother who had not met her refused to let me go. If it was a tea party why wasn't Harriet invited or any other girl who lived around us? I argued with my mother for a week, pointing out to her that Inga did not like Harriet, and that all the other girls in our immediate vicinity were either two years older or two years younger than I was and therefore did not know Inga. But mother said no and I felt it was the settlement that I was not allowed to visit because I remembered an Italian girl, Alicia Moreno at one of our parties who shocked me violently showing off her beautiful figure, who flashed her black eyes and white teeth and had said with bold bravado 'look me over and see what my mother made.' Yet Inga was not her so I sobbed my heart out on Friday night. My pillow was soaking wet when my Father came in to say Goodnight.

On Saturday morning at the breakfast table my father handed me a dollar.

"Even if you can't go to your little friend's birthday party, I think it would be nice if you bought her a present anyway" he said.

"It's not her birthday Daddy. It's much more important than that. It's her grandmother's birthday. Inga's share was only four, three friends and herself. She asked two other girls and me."

"Which two other girls?" Daddy said.

"Helen Farson and Margaret Cuppers."

"Well" Mother said taken aback, "I shouldn't imagine Dr. Farson would let his daughter go."

"He is. He is driving her over. He loves Inga's grandmother. He is going to drink her health himself. Inga told me."

"Is Inga disappointed you can't come?"

"I haven't told her I'm not coming."

"You haven't told her!" You were to tell her days ago. That's very rude, very rude indeed."

"I'm not going to hurt her feelings" I muttered staring sullenly at my plate. "I was going to phone this morning and say I was sick again. She'd understand that."

I began to push my chair back in preparation for the dash to my room for the coming tears.

"I'll take her round Mother" my Father said firmly, "and I'll pick her up."

My chair half tilted back, I halted, watching wide-eyed and breathless the duel of eyes between my father and my mother.

"What about Harriet?" my mother asked. "I asked her for tea this afternoon to make up for the party. What about her feelings?"

"Of course she accepted - always hanging around. I hate Harriet and I love Inga."

"Be quiet" my mother snapped.

Having gone so far I had to clinch the argument. I was underhand and unkind but also desperate.

"Harriet tells dirty stories" I said in a loud whisper knowing only too well that it was not a rare thing in our house to have one's mouth washed out with soap.

"What a thing to say" my mother was shocked. "What a thing to say. Harriet hasn't had your advantages, my girl, with her father killed in the war and her mother working for a living."

"Inga doesn't tell stories and her father and her grandmother lost their house and everything else because of the war. That's why they came here."

"You can go" my mother said, suddenly defeated looking at my father. "This time you can go. When you come home I will talk to you. If there's something Harriet has picked up her mother ought to know."

"Why" I said. "I don't believe what she tells me. I think she makes it up just to make herself important."

"Start the dishes" Mother said and my three brothers sprang from the table in glee and made for the kitchen door.

We didn't have domestic help living-in any more. We only had a daily twice a week in the mornings. I didn't wonder why although I should have because the house was very large and mother had too much to do. She was always bossy and harassed on Saturday morning.

I had a wonderful time at Inga's party but Harriet was right about the Settlement. Inga's house was unfinished and there was no bathroom, only a privy standing out like a sore in the middle of the back yard.

The contrast between Inga's house and mine was thought-provoking and I pondered the differences with sadness and more sympathy toward Inga than was warranted. After the tea party was finished Inga's relations cleared the food away to another detached building called the kitchen house, took down the trestle tables and began to dance on the newly finished board floor to fast music provided on an accordion and a fiddle by two elderly men with long moustaches. Before I knew what had happened a tall fair boy of about sixteen in an open shirt had bowed to me politely seized me around the waist and due to the fact that I had never danced before in my life with a partner and did not know what to do with my feet lifted me completely off them and swung me round and round until I was dizzy. Out of the corner of one startled eye I looked for Helen and Margaret and saw them dancing gaily with great abandon. Everybody seemed to be dancing from the four year olds to the over forties. Only Inga's grandmother and two or three other old ladies with handkerchiefs on their heads sat clapping their hands on the sidelines.

Dr. Farson picked up Helen and Margaret at about seven and had arranged with my father upon my arrival to bring me home as well so I had no reason to explain the dancing to my family. I concentrated on the quantity of the food. My father would not be drawn into a discussion of Inga's house further than to say that it was a disgrace that the settlement was not sewered. 'It's not the settler's responsibility, it's the government's' was his comment! What he told my mother privately, I didn't know of course, but mother let me ask Inga to tea and said afterwards that she was a lovely little girl. There was only one aspect of the return visit which puzzled me. Unlike Harriet, Inga was unimpressed by my room. She admired it politely even to the glass knobs on the built-in wardrobe doors but for Christmas gave me a dresser set embroidered skilfully in a cross stitch design of green and crimson as if she hadn't noticed my walls were rosy pink. I insisted on using the clashing dresser set instead of the crocheted doilies, for it cemented my friendship with Inga which I felt was above envy. The conflict of differences was in myself. It took me some three or four years to resolve it. By the end of that time the differences fascinated me for I knew them to be what they really were, surface variety. I was never troubled by fundamental personality differences between foreigners and myself any more than I was between my fellow Scotch Canadians and others of the English speaking variety. One either liked a person or one didn't. It was simply Inga or Alicia Moreno; myself or Harriet. But when I lived on the Avenue I felt I had far too much more in the way of worldly goods than Inga had in the settlement. I decided the distribution of money was biased, unfair, and discriminating.

After Inga's party, Helen and Margaret widened their fellowship and tried to include me in it. But it didn't work. I wasn't ready. At thirteen the other girls had developed something which I had not. They handled with natural ease the ordeal of mixed company. To me boys were little brothers or older cousins. I was shy to the point of embarrassment with boys of my own age and the parties where smiling parents teased as they supervised games of postman's knock and spin the plate and encouraged the first steps that led to ballroom dancing were to me nightmares of insufficiency. The perfume of attraction which Harriet had led me to expect did not descend on me. With my curls gleaming like my patent leather slippers, in my first party dress of rose and blue shot taffetas, I was a wallflower. There were many boys with faces red from a first crop of pimples who blushed in a huddle in the doorways. But they did not appear to have anything to do with me. I knew no relationship between their case and mine even though one of them, a rugby player of no mean renown in our school, occasionally turned up to carry my books home to the Avenue. At parties I was stiff and dumb and no amount of lavender water made up for my deficiency. The idea of kissing a boy filled me with horror. Kissing boys your own age led to petting and if you didn't look out petting led to 'it' according to Harriet. What 'it' was I had not the slightest idea nor had

I any intention of letting Harriet explain to me although she got so far one day as to connect it with having babies so that on the day my mother hesitantly asked in a hinting sort of way if I knew about babies I hurriedly assured her that of course I did and changed the subject.

One night coming home from a party at Helen's there were half a dozen boys and girls seeing each other home, swinging happily from door to door holding hands.

"You're breaking the chain" Margaret said to me. "Go on take Jack's hand. He won't bite."

Thankful for the dark I blushed to the roots of my hair. That was the stage I was at when I lived on the Avenue.

Physically I wasn't up to much either. In the summer at camp I swam and in the winter sometimes I put on my brother's ice skates with two pairs of socks and with the aid of a borrowed hockey stick skated in solitary contentment on safe ice and the edge of the pond. I could handle a sled by myself but a big bobsleigh that held half a dozen enthusiasts terrified me. My parents didn't encourage my real participation in active sport. I spent enough time as it was in the doctor's care and overstrain was a constant worry to them. In actual fact I had little personal interest in sport as a participant but on the Avenue I grew acutely conscious of the sporting prowess of my relatives. My elder cousins were sportsmen and sportswomen of no mean measure. One played hockey for the Maple Leafs, three played rugby for British Colombia teams, one was pitcher for the big league baseball team in town. They won foot races and diving competitions; they all played basketball, men and women, boys and girls alike. They captained teams and one of my girl cousins was going steady with a boy who was an Olympic long distance runner. There was never a Saturday when one of my cousins was not representing the family in some big match. There was considerable sports talk at our table concerning nephews and nieces and when we visited our relations particularly the home of my favourite Aunt Meg, sport took a definite priority over every other subject. On the strength of free tickets, I ate peanuts in the baseball stadium, stamped my feet in the ice-hockey rinks and ran around the grounds at Brockton Point following the centre-forward in particular if it was Charles. I could score and tally, I could cheer with the same enthusiasm with which I followed a parade of the Seaforth Highlanders. I could cheer and boast but I kept debating inwardly at the Avenue whether that was enough, if somehow I wasn't letting my mother down by not taking up basketball with brilliancy and fervour as Greta was now doing. Sports were healthy, Greta shooting up into a willowy nymph explained to me. According to my cousin, sports were good for the personality, good for the figure, participation in sports developed the spirit of real fair-play, a sense of the value of teamwork, producing an all-round personality with a balanced outlook on life. I knew I could do with these qualities. I was tremendously in need of better health, a charming personality and a good figure.

As a result of my enthusiasm for the by-products, rather than the activity I tried out for the school basketball team and painstakingly took part in the gym classes. But it didn't work. Either I was sick because I had to have an excuse to cover my inadequacy in the chosen field or I didn't make any team and both my figure and my personality continued to bulge in the wrong places.

I resigned myself to being a follower. I hoped my brothers would do better for my mother's sake. My father didn't appear to worry very much. I had one and only one moment of recompense for my aches of inadequacy in the sporting world. It happened at the Gilberts, a favourite haunt of mine. Adoring Auntie Meg with increasing fervour as I grew up, I found my affection returned and she encouraged me to consider her house my second home. I spent many weekends helping Auntie Meg whose household was overcrowded with young adults of unsettled inclinations until their weddings were eventually over and my cousins one by one took root.

The Gilbert boys argued over the dinner table, sport, sport, sport, players whims and shortcomings, team possibilities and failures, big league, back-yard rugby, American versus Canadian rules. They quarrelled and sparred until my Aunt brought her little fist to the table, and spilled the coffee over the tablecloth.

All the Gilberts were good to me but there were times when their affection took a startingly personal turn.

"Heard you missed the basketball team Kit" one of them boomed. "Too fat eh?"

They roared with laughter, every one of them. Except Charles.

"The fat's not all in her head anyway" He remarked laconically, "like some people I could mention" Charles thin and angular was a wiry centre forward but he didn't talk about it much.
"Such as –?" his brother menaced.
"The cauliflower collectors in the scrum."

Wilfred who was present had an ear swollen to the size of a baseball, deforming one side of his handsome face.

"Why you" Wilfred began, and then recollecting where he was reverted to sarcasm. "Just because you manage to keep yourself well out in front."
"Brains, my dear boy, brains" Charles said. "My policy is to score while intact and bloodless, believe me!"

"Looking after your eyes to read to your beautiful class."

This was because Charles was still at Teachers College and Wilf was already launched into a business career with his father.

"Rather that than a butcher."

"Dear me" Wilfred said. "We are getting class conscious aren't we?"

"Look out Wilf, or we'll be in for a political discourse on what's wrong with the world. You won't have a chance. He's got everything lined up from Marx to the Carnegie Corporation."

"And a date" Charles said rising. "Excuse me!"

"Be sure and take a poetry book under your arm" Wilf snickered, "to read to the fair lady. Taking her to the dance tonight?"

"Hardly" Charles said from the door. "She's a canoe."

So Charles thought brains more important than brawn. He read as well as wrote poetry, the only subject at school at which I could safely count on scoring one hundred percent. I felt amazingly light and airy.

Sewing was another inadequacy I suffered. I couldn't sew. My mother and my aunts and all my female cousins seemed to be able to make anything from a boys overcoat to a lace tablecloth. At school I tried to make a pair of pink pyjamas that mother had to take out of my hands, pull apart and restitch into a garment that was presentable at the annual needlework exhibition in the school hall, but of a size far too small to be stretched over my body and was thereby useless as a garment. A blouse I attempted fared no better and a petticoat charmingly embroidered and admired because of my original design failed to fit over my head. I couldn't knit, I couldn't crochet. I couldn't make buttonholes. I even had trouble with blanket-stitch. Yet my fingers could play the piano. With my name printed on the program I offered the Pathetique Sonata to an audience and was applauded until I encored with a little Schumann romance. By the time I was fourteen I was a teacher of youngsters and beginners came to the house to commence their studies with me. I practised four hours a day before and after school and I loved music.

Here then I shone! No indeed. Here then I was ignobly defeated. Here in my own realm I suffered my most outstanding collapse at the Avenue.

Harriet played the piano and Harriet took exams. My parents, my doctor and my teacher, a far superior musician to Harriet's, decided I would be better to avoid the strain of exams. Harriet went through one exam after another with a mechanical precision that astounded me. She had taken exams from the first year of study long before I knew her. Her mother wanted results for her hard earned money. Harriet provided them. As soon as she passed one examination she commenced immediately the studies of the next. Harriet played no pieces save those called for in the syllabus. She did not play for pleasure. She played for certificates. She could not take time to learn an accompaniment because it was time stolen from the next item on the syllabus.

I did not know this at first. I assumed Harriet loved music but was learning it in a different way perhaps, according to her teacher's idea. I was fourteen when I found out that what she wanted from her teacher was merits, not music.

"Of course" she said to me one day, "you're quite right to think your teacher is superior to mine. He is. Look at his fees."

"Oh Harriet, I didn't say that. Your teacher is very good. You pass your exams every year."

"Exactly. But not because she's good. But because I want to. I'm going right through. I want every certificate."

"Do you think it's so important to have the certificates Harriet?"

"I'll say I do. Oh I know you're sick a lot and can't do exams and all that. So your music is just played for your own pleasure. Mine's different. Mine's serious."

"I'm just as serious about music as you are Harriet, only my teacher doesn't believe in the yearly exam system."

"That's because he teaches society girls and all that and gives fancy recitals."

"No it isn't. Lots of his pupils take exams and win prizes too."

"Oh well it doesn't matter. It's too late for you anyway seeing you haven't passed the first exams. You'll always play the piano anyway."

"Well, of course."

"But I'll have my diploma and be able to use it if I want to."

"I don't know what you mean. What's the difference?"

"You are silly sometimes. I'll be a qualified musician, that's all."

"But I will too."

"No you won't. How can you be? You have to have the certificates to prove it. Nobody pays any attention if you haven't got a diploma. I'm not going to do anything I don't get a certificate for. It's not worth it, it's a waste of time."

Shattered I replied meekly. (Why was I always so meek with Harriet?)

"But you said you didn't want to teach music Harriet. You're going to college aren't you to train as a teacher?"

"I am. When I get through I'll have a music diploma as well and I think in the summer I might start taking shorthand and typing. If I have three diplomas, nobody will be able to turn me down for a job, I'll get a city school."

"You mean if you can teach music as well."

"With my music diploma" she said proudly.

"But you said you didn't want to teach music?"

She looked at me with a kind of hopeless disgust. She was a narrow boned thin girl with sandy hair and long straight pale eyelashes. She was dressed that day in a brown pleated skirt and a green cable-stitch jumper she had knitted herself. I knew because she had asked my mother to help her when she got stuck with the sleeves.

So when I was fourteen years old I gave up music lessons and pupil teaching and practising four hours a day. I was very tired, maturity caught up with me at the Avenue and there was no future in music anyway. I could always play the piano, the Moonlight Sonata, several times over if I felt like it; an accompaniment for a friend's violin or a baritone solo. I could sight read the hymns at Church and play for the school gym classes and the local boys jazz orchestra. Some little children were always asking to have lessons with me for fifty cents a half an hour. I could enjoy concerts and recitals and biographies of the great composers. There were even times when I manufactured tunes and studies for myself. But once music as a profession was closed to me the price of a good teacher was a needless expense for my parents whom I had overheard talking of costs in a different way to which I was accustomed.

My parents owned a block of land at the city limit. They spoke of building a house there. It was near an excellent high school and a public school that was small and select. It was an area of new houses, smaller homes, with modern conveniences, the kind of house a woman could manage more easily on her own. There would be space for at least a dozen fruit trees in the backyard, a chicken run and a vegetable patch, maybe even a cow or goat for milk.

One day my parents asked me apprehensively if I would mind another move. In that moment many things fell into place. For the first time I noticed the thick grey hair above my father's ears and the tired, overworked circles under my mother's eyes. My parents came alive as personalities, as worried people, raising a family against odds which I sensed were becoming bigger than I knew. I was no sportswoman nor could I sew. But I could appreciate what I felt, I could love. I need not be a needless expense nor an invalid. Strength flowed through me and began to fill the vacuum. I wasn't much but for what I was, the die was cast. Childhood was going and the sooner the house went with it the better.

"I'd love to" I said. "Do you mean we could build a house on our lot. What fun. Can we all go out and have a picnic there on Saturday?"

They smiled wistfully and so did I. But because they were smiling goodbye to the Avenue which they loved they could not know that I was merely smiling goodbye to Harriet.

***

4

Chapter Four

All spring, if you can call it spring in Egypt, I have been part of a group of foreign women raising funds to send little girls from the streets of Bulak for a two week camping holiday to the shores of the Mediterranean, a distance from Alexandria. Most of these little girls aged between ten and twelve have the same name as an older sister so their fathers can get them married to any suitor who comes along, though they are under the marriage age according to the law.

None of these little girls have seen the sea, nor have they any clothes save the garments they stand up in, nor any sandals for their wide brown feet. Soap, toothbrush and a towel are dreams. So we who are affluent collect these items: cotton dresses, panties, little head-scarves and believe it or not we also provide a shift for a nightgown and sheets for their camp cots. It is a Christian camp, a missionary project but most of the little girls are Muslim and it is necessary to persuade a reluctant father to allow them to go. Deception is attached to the persuasion. Good food will enhance the charm of the child who will soon become a woman. Our attitudes, though never our words, inform the parents that we know the law and are also wise in judging a little girl's years. "So many mouths to feed." he murmurs, "So few piastres for so many children."

Usually on this day I sew, as best I can, the cotton dresses with my team, or rather I should admit, cut out the patterns. But, Ramadan and heat has defeated us all, women and children. So I sit and dream. First of the sea on the shore of Alexandria where next week at the end of Ramadan I will holiday at Beau Rivage where I do not camp but enjoy every comfort, even the enormous golden moon of the Mediterranean. Yet the dream fades as I go back and remember another sea and another camp, less romantic perhaps - or was it?

***

My father believed in camping. Back to nature he called it. Walking, swimming, fishing, bonfires, sun-baking, canvas and creatures he considered God's greatest gifts to children and he would be the last one he informed us to deny his offspring part of this natural inheritance. My mother went along with almost all his views on camping except for creatures which she could not abide.

Fortunately Auntie Meg Gilbert believed in camping too so for years it was the pleasure of the sisters to suffer their camping trials together. Wherever my mother and Auntie Meg chose to camp, one or two other members of the family would hire a site nearby which meant that between our various camps a stream of visiting relations dropped down like migrating birds for a day, a week or a weekend vacation. Auntie Meg who was the power behind the vacation habits of her family preferred to hire a cottage on the pretext that she had to cook for adults, whether or not her sons and daughters and grandchildren erected a tent in the grounds for their beds. My father held out with the same degree of tenacity for canvas on a beachfront that granted my mother proximity to Auntie Meg's cottage.

There were many camps when I was a child before the families discovered Cedar Cove. Thereafter like homing pigeons we returned to it for five years in a row so that when I remember camping a picture arises in my mind of every line of that rock-enclosed beach with every maple and every pine in its familiar place. The details of the last summer we were there under canvas, the summer of my fifteenth year, stands out clearly like the irreplaceable lines in an etching.

I had always agreed wholeheartedly with my father on the blessings of camping, which was strange in a way for I was. in normal urban surroundings, nervous of so many things. I think, even so, I went further than he did and added to his list of outdoor blessings not only the creatures that mother abhorred but trees, moss, flowers, rocks and shells. Before I was in the first year of my teens, I had also added solitude and the night. I had no fear on the forest paths or on the beach for when camping I discovered one could always escape and sit doing nothing, a pastime not encouraged at home. I wandered alone and without scolding to my favourite haunts within a radius of the beach. I considered them retreats for privacy and contemplation. Small brothers and older cousins were always otherwise occupied on the sand, which diminished their nuisance to a minimum from every point of view. My spirit responded to camping. I did extra chores willingly and with speed for the freedom that lay hidden in the rest of the day. Every insinuating intrusion that threatened my inner sanctuary at home at the Avenue was dispelled in the summer when we were camping. I heard the music of poetry flow from the swelling moan of the pines to the sea and in the spasmodic conversation and song of birds. Colour startled my eyes into new alertness and sensitive appreciation. The solitude I gained bored into the vacuum of my mind phrases of expression that attempted to answer the conundrum of life, breeding in me merely an exquisite dissatisfaction that called for interpretation rather than a heaviness that obliterated imagination. I think that from twelve to fifteen there must have been times when I only managed to survive the winter with the hope of summer. In the winter at the Avenue I struggled mightily and stood still; in the summer at Cedar Cove Camp I relaxed completely and standing still, I grew.

This is why I found myself beginning the story of my journey into adulthood in the summer of my fifteenth year. I was on the threshold between childhood and youth. The awareness of growth into a new phase of life pressing upon me could only be revealed in the beloved surroundings of Cedar Cove. Because living was intensified for me at the camp it was natural that Charles would be an instrument of understanding. To leave behind my childhood and step forward I needed those I loved best in a place I adored. My need was to gather in one place, at one time my father, my mother, my brothers, my Auntie Meg, Greta and Charles. All of them must play a part in my debut into maturity and be present for my first summer.

Cedar Cove was an area for ten camps hired as platform sites. Large tents and small tents according to the size of the family were arranged on and around the permanent wooden floors. It was a glorious beach, semi-circular like half a plate with the great Pacific waves breaking in on the white sand to run up to the drifted logs which had escaped the booms and come to rest at odd distances from the water's edge. Beyond the last log where the sand ended and the face of the great rock cliffs rose as a protecting wall encircling the beach the tenting sites were fitted in under the trees that had found a place to send down roots. Above the beach the road ran by on the cliff top and every day we climbed up and over it into the forest to the clear river pools for buckets of water for the camp. All the way to the lighthouse such little beaches had been hollowed out of the cliff face by the pounding of winter. We came in the peaceful days of summer like migrating birds and departed again before the winds of autumn stirred the Pacific to its winter rage.

The Cedar Cove Camp was in some special way an inhabited and yet almost primitive world and when we were young the days went by with a peaceful rapidity of detached unidentifiable joy. The weeks passed in a blur of sand, sea, sun and rain, the collecting of wood; the gathering of sweet wild blackberries, round red huckleberries and bitter salmon berries; in climbing and fishing and swimming and sleeping in the sun. There was also sunburn and lacerated feet, leaking tents and smoking stoves, robberies by bears and stings by bees, but these afflictions have become part of the soft memory, all the sharp edges obliterated like the edges of coloured glass that the sea sand made in to the jewels Greta and I collected for a sea-shore shop when we first went to Cedar Cove. The weekdays I recall now as landscape. The weekends brought exciting episodes.

The men took over the weekend. They arrived amid mounting excitement, bringing the lists of supplies for the mothers and children, unloading watermelon, hot-dogs, corncobs and marshmallow for the Saturday night bonfire, presenting to awed silences the news from the home front. They stripped down for a swim before food, ate heartily in their shorts, took an evening stroll, arranged early Sunday fishing trips, chopped the wood, laid down the law to the boys and spoiled the girls with bags of candy.

Among all the youngsters there was a special interest in the guests who arrived for the weekend only. For girls in their early teens weekend guests provided a thrilling if often unadmitted form of enlightenment. There is more to be observed on the romantic front in one seaside weekend than in a year of normal life at home. Until our last summer at Cedar Cove, Greta and I were the only members of our family group of an age to profit from this observance. All the rest of the relatives were grown up or too young. The married cousins, with broods of babies were pleasant but romantically uninteresting. The single cousins, on the other hand, provided in the company of their guests a limelight of entertainment value out of all proportion to their numbers. Greta and I looked, listened, criticised and surmised in a secret schoolgirl fashion about the amorous intentions of every guest of every cousin, using as a basis for our wisdom our previous knowledge of who accompanied whom to this event and that during the months prior to the summer. From the earliest days of our intimacy Greta proved better informed than I on matters of the heart. I learned to wait for the confidences she saved only for me, for she was usually proved correct in her assumptions whereas I was often wrong enough to have appeared ridiculous had I ventured to speak to anyone else. My mother discouraged what she termed 'tales' and Greta respected my mother, sometimes, I suspected more than she did her own. On occasions Greta fought her mother to go out and won, but in my case my mother fought me to accept invitations. My mother was a woman who discouraged any form of suspicion in herself and her family. Auntie Meg was the same. It didn't occur to Greta to pass on an unfounded rumour to me in the vicinity of mother or Auntie Meg. When she told me a secret it was a secret which when openly revealed or deliberately withheld from us proved to be the truth. I never even tried to find out how Greta knew about everything. I trusted her absolutely for she never told me a lie and unlike Harriet, never on any occasion did she make the kind of insinuations which belittled my intelligence. Greta accepted without question that in some respects she and I operated on different thought levels and she didn't try to reduce or increase mine into line with hers. She had become without my realisation, the friend who counteracted the flattening influence of Harriet. Greta could not stand Harriet and said so.

One weekend that summer after breakfast Charles appeared. He had not gone fishing with the other men.

"Do you want to bring your lunch and tramp up to the Lighthouse with me and come back in the boat?" he greeted me.

I glanced at Greta. She shrugged her shoulders and said she just wants to swim all day. I knew it was alright with her. She was already in her bathing suit, her straight silky hair falling to her shoulders and her nose covered with sun cream. She knew I wanted to go with Charles away over the rocks, up the cliff and into the deep pine forest that led to Point Atkinson. She also knew that I defeated myself in a blue bathing suit of Mother's choice and only wore it as a proper garment to swim in whereas she wore her new black one with the grace of a duchess in an evening gown and gathered compliments on her figure from Sunday visitors. I was not so sure about Mother who often suggested that Greta or one of my brothers join my excursions with Charles. I think she was puzzled that Charles should choose to take a schoolgirl when he could have invited so many pretty girls from the beach. Once when she asked me what Charles and I talked about, and I answered poetry, she looked really baffled, and Greta said that was why she refused the invitation.

"I get enough of that at school," Greta commented.

Since the days of my girlhood I have not walked that lighthouse trail. There may come a day when I will go back. But I do not think I would enjoy the trail as much as I do the memory of it. I am no taller now than I was then but I am sure the forest of pines will be smaller, even if the axe of man has not destroyed one tree. Whatever shoes I put on my feet I will not feel the ground so soft or the pine needles spring under my heels. My eyes acute for the forest trail would hold less sparkle now and I would not subdue my breath to keep the deep silence or call my echo softly from within the woods.

I know why Charles took me on those excursions. It was because we wasted no words. We just went. He had his deep rebellious thoughts and I had mine. It did not matter to Charles that I thought of him as a poet. I did not make the mistake of telling anybody that I thought of him as a poet. There was little he did not know about the woodsman's arts. He knew his Indian signs and his bear-tracks.

He could light a fire with wet wood and bark from the trees. He had handled a forty-pound salmon with a practised ease, and if I chose to ignore the fact that Chrles went hunting and brought home venison because he was an excellent shot between the eyes of a deer, Charles felt this to be no concern of his. On our tramps, canoe and fishing trips Charles treated me as an equal and a companion of such good standing as to respect silences. The equality of course was all on his side. He spent the money on the chocolate bars or our lunch, he lit the fire for our brew of tea, he plotted our progress and took the responsibility for our safe return. When we trawled for salmon he ran the boat, and while I sat as still as a mouse he paddled the canoe. What did I do? I just went. I was company. We were both internal creatures, secretive.

We went up over the hill and the road and into the forest following the path in the bracken until we came to the stream. From that point the climb was steep, over rocks and fallen logs where the rivulets ran fast until we came to the rock pool where we sometimes swam. It was a deep pool, cool and green. The sunlight breaking through the cloudy summer sky reflected the branches of an overhanging pine in clear cold water, a sentinel on the very edge of the pine forest where another path started down again toward the road from which we came. Climbing up the steep way you came suddenly upon the pool and from the rock above it you looked up at solid rock escarpments adorned with little fishbone ferns sparkling like jewels over the green water. It was a silent place of mystery and wonder.

Charles sat down on a boulder at the pool's edge, hanging his feet out over the water. He extracted a chocolate bar from the back pocket of his shorts, broke it in two and handed half to me.

"Sit down," he said, "and tell me about your troubles."

Blissfully unsuspecting, enchanted as I always was with this haven of solitude and beauty after the still climb, I settled myself near Charles, on another rock which offered me the comfort of leaning my back on the rock he had chosen yet providing an equal view of the chill emerald water and the reflected pine. Shifting a little forward I found it was also possible to include the silvery falls in my field of vision. I began to eat my chocolate.

"Well," Charles said, "Tell me about your poetry."

Slowly I finished my last bite, still unsuspecting.

"What poetry?" I said, gazing into the water.

"You are a very strange girl, Kit," Charles said, "In spite of all the poetry I have discussed with you this summer I had to wait until my mother happened to mention you won a prize for poetry at school at the end of last term. You might have told me!"

The pool darkened as a cloud obscured the sun.

"It wasn't anything, Charles, just a competition for the school magazine. Hardly anybody entered. It wasn't a good poem, Charles."

"It must have been good enough to win."

"It wasn't good, Charles. I know it wasn't good. I don't want to talk about it."

"I do. Did they print it on the front page of the magazine?"

"No. In the middle." I shut my lips tight. But Charles persisted.

"Why didn't you send it to me. You've hurt my feelings."

"Oh, Charles, it wasn't worth it, really it wasn't. It wasn't my best one."

"Let me look at them all then, and I'll tell you if it was the best one."

"I can't"

"Why?"

They're lost."

"Lost? Did you say lost?"

"They weren't any good Charles, really."

"What happened to them, Kit."

It was no use. I had to tell him. It was like rubbing a lemon on a burst blister so I didn't look at him in case I might cry.

"I had all my poems copied in a little book and after I won the prize I was so pleased with myself that I took the book to Mr Cox and asked him to read and criticise them for me. He said he had no time just then but he took the book and told me to come back in a week."

"Who's Mr Cox?"

"He's the literature teacher."

"And he lost them?"

"It really doesn't matter, Charles. I must have seemed silly and vain to him. They weren't good poems."

"How did he lose them?"

I gulped. "He thinks they were thrown out with the old examination papers."

"Did he tell you that?"

"Yes."

"What else did he say?"

"That's all."

"All? What did he say about the poems?"

"Nothing."

"Didn't he say he was sorry about it?"

"I don't think so Charles. I was so surprised. I couldn't believe he had lost them. I asked him if he was sure. I shouldn't have asked him that. He said naturally he'd looked through everything and that he thought if I concentrated on literature I had a good chance of topping the class."

"Decent of him I'm sure" Charles said, and I knew he was furious.

A terrible suspicion grew in me that he would want to go to the school.

"Oh, no Charles." I cried out. "You mustn't, please Charles. I'd die if you did. Nobody knows I took the book to him. Nobody even knew I had the book, not even Mummy or Daddy and they were so pleased about the poem in the school magazine. I couldn't bear it if you said anything, Charles! The poems couldn't have been any good. He would have known right away if they were good."

"If he read them," Charles said. "In any case they were your property. And I suppose he calls himself a teacher. It's the Principal I ought to go to or the School Board!"

"Charles!" I burst into tears at last, good tears for they washed the poison out of the wound that still festered. But they were hard tears that choked in my throat, and stung my eyes before they could flow.

"Alright," Charles said, but his voice was still bitterly hard, "Alright, don't cry like that, Kit. I won't go. But only on one condition. You're to promise to write more poems. Will you do that? You're to promise to write and one day when you're ready you're to show them to me. To me, do you hear, not anybody else! You're to bring them to me. And I won't tell you they're good if they're not. I'll tell you how to make them better if I can."

"It doesn't matter, Charles."

But they were possessing me again, those first poems. They were coming back. I could almost remember the one about the pine forest and suddenly I knew the one called the *Shore of the Sea* was there deep down. It was still in me waiting. It had begun to whisper.

"It does matter!" Charles exploded. "It matters a lot. More than you know, thank God! But I know. One day I'll stop being a teacher because of all the Mr Coxs. Don't interrupt! Put there to watch the plant, they bury it, rake it over and hope it will come up again as grass to be mowed into a nice even lawn! I know them! Grass clods themselves, they can't see anything but grass, eating everything out of the soil and spreading grass. You have to be a strong forest tree to beat them. Flowers don't have a chance. Too delicate - flowers! Too beautiful! Too pure!"

I had stopped crying. I must have been staring at Charles, my mouth open, my eyes wide.

"They can't see what stares them in the face. Top of the class for literature, always has been! Ploughing under what might be the best professional opportunity he ever had - the whole justification for his working life - the whole reason for being what he is!"

"I don't understand, Charles."

"No, of course you don't understand. You are one of those who shouldn't have to. But you will! One day you will! But don't try now. Just keep writing poems and anything else that comes into your head. Don't pay any attention to Mr Cox. Just keep writing."

"But Charles, I have to pay attention to him. He's my teacher and literature's my best subject. If Mr Cox doesn't like my essays I'll fail."

"Neither Mr Cox nor anybody else can make you fail. But you will really fail if you don't produce what's in you to produce."

"He marks all the papers."

"And you want to pass."

"Oh, yes, and I'm not very clever."

"Would you like to study literature at the university?"

"I don't have enough brains for that, Charles, even if I could afford to go."

"Don't be silly."

"I'm not silly. You have far more brains than I and you didn't go to the university yourself. You couldn't afford it."

"I didn't care that much. I wanted to be a teacher. Would you like to be a teacher?"

"I don't think so."

"Well, what are you going to be?"

"I don't know, Charles. I'll get a job I guess and keep on with my music"

"Do you want to go in for music?"

"I'm not good enough for that. I'd have to get a scholarship and go away to study for years and years."

"Do you read anything else except travel books and poetry?"

"Of course, I do. That's only my favourite reading. But I read novels and plays as well and books about the great composers. I took a wonderful book on Beethoven out of the library last week. I couldn't put it down. I read nearly all Saturday night and couldn't get up in the morning. Mummy was furious."

"You'll have to make up your mind soon, you know."

"What do you mean, Charles?"

"About what you're going to do."

"Well, not yet. Daddy says when the time comes he'll be able to get me into a bank or something."

"A bank!"

"Well, you see, Dad's best friend in the choir, Mr Johnstone, is on the personnel staff at the Royal Bank."

"The last thing I can imagine is you in a bank, counting out the money."

"Oh, they wouldn't trust me with the money. I'd be a lesser light in some back office, I suppose."

Charles deliberately shut his eyes and held them shut for a full minute. Then he sighed and said:

"Kit, are you going to let other people push you around all your life?"

"Oh, Charles, what a thing to say. Who's pushing me round?"

"You were pretty upset about what Mr Cox did to you."

"It was my own fault. I made a mistake taking my poems to him. They were very good obviously."

"There's nothing obvious about it. Obvious is an overrated word used by the ignorant to cover what they prefer to accept rather than understand. Don't put it in your essays! You don't even know if Mr Cox read the poems before he lost them. The mistake you made was to trust him with something belonging to you. You misplaced your trust. The second mistake you made was not to have kept the book yourself and given him a copy of the poems."

"I didn't think of that."

"Neither of those mistakes need ever be repeated and neither of them have anything to do with the quality of the poems. So it is not obvious that they were good or bad because of Mr Cox. Do you understand that?"

"Oh yes, thank you Charles. I don't mind at all now."

"You should, you've lost the poems."

"I haven't really, Charles. Not all anyway. While we were talking they began to come back again. I can hear some of the words inside my head right now."

"Then write them down quickly."

"Oh, I can't, not yet. They're not ready yet. They're still a kind of rhythm going around and around. I'll write them when they're ready."

"You'll promise to bring them to me?"

"But they may be months coming."

"I'm inclined to think they'll be years coming as you call it. I doubt if I'll be around to pass judgement." he added, tartly and stood up.

It crossed my mind as I looked up at him that Charles would fit very well into a poem himself with the straight profile of his nose and chin, the tanned prominence of his cheekbones and the severe line of his mouth.

Romantically, I imagined he had the controlled intensity of an Indian looking at the dying sun. I should have been frightened of the anger I knew was in him but I sensed the insignificant part I played in it. All I knew was that he had, for the time being, enough of me and my little problems, enough of what I was, and was going to be. I had touched off in him a fury with which he was wrestling by himself. Somehow he deprived me of any part in it. It was a fury that Charles at the moment faced alone.

So he stood there for one long instant with unseeing eyes while I sat silent at his feet, waiting for him to leave me, to stride off ahead into the pine forest. I felt strange, a little heady, drunk with the sudden idea of putting Charles, this immobile Indian-like Charles into a poem, a secret poem that I would not show him with the others he wanted to see when the time was ripe. A wisp of vapor that would be words came between my sight and his face. To catch the essence of it I shut my eyes, blocking out the sun and shadow along with the disappointment over poems lost replacing with the new poem about to begin.

It seemed a long time before Charles' usual voice returned as if a normal previously experienced resignation broke into my reverie:

"Sometimes you have the uncanny silence of a witch."

He swung round before I could reply to walk under the trees that overhang the path. I got up and followed him at a respectful distance; making no effort to catch up or overtake him, keeping the silence between us. Once in a while I had to hurry a little to keep Charles in sight and there were times when he slackened his pace to look back for a moment where the way turned. All the time my mind played with words so that when we reached the beach and Charles stood waiting to take me into camp, I drew abreast of him to smile straight into his face so that I could run ahead of him without speaking and go down into my tent to write the words down.

There were not very many words really. I have them still in my notebook, a few phrases, unbelievably inadequate, forlornly inexpressive of the emotion of that long walk back to camp. The indefinable quality of beauty of being alone with the security of Charles walking into the distance before me was not in those words.

"Alone, absorbed in fury under the dying sun,
He stands transfixed, while the long shadows run
From mauve to purple under the drooping needle-weighted trees
Beneath the forest firs approached by night. Unmoved he sees
The evening kiss of sunlight, bestowed when day is done
To bless nocturnal growth. He has no heart for these."

What made me write those words for Charles? For he who gave me back that day the very soul with which I wrote them. For Charles who taught me to love the shadows and the sun at dusk. For the man who was always moved by the beauty of trees. Why should I have grasped something out of the whole which was his life, that one moment of his fury against the inevitable? I wrote the words quickly, intensely, panic-stricken in case they should escape me.

Then I hated them. They were not Charles at all. I read them over and put down my pen. I would do better than that. But even as I thought I knew that no poem could express Charles' being, that I did not know him at all, that he was a universe of his own, a different world that I contacted only briefly among worlds I scarcely touched,

I could not write a poem that expressed Charles, not one or a hundred. I could only try to express myself, and that tentatively, searchingly, haltingly. That was all I could do.

On those excursions, we talked while we had lunch. When Charles did not want to talk anymore, lunch was over and we got up and tramped on. When we went to the lighthouse we always ate our sandwiches before we arrived. We had a special place high up above the cliff-face looking out to sea. From that point the Pacific stretched before us as far as the eye could see and below, the waves beat on the wild jagged rocks of the point with the roar of thunder. There was a tree in that spot, a twisted crooked juniper and the green mosses spread like a cushion at its feet. To step over the cliff was immediate annihilation, to sit there in the sun was the peace of heaven.

One day at the end of July by the time we were across the first cliff on our way to the forest I knew that Charles was super active and I was tired. There was one particular place on our way where we had to hang over a cliff edge and drop onto a log below. It was only a small drop, six inches at the most. I hung over facing the cliff and then slithered. For Charles it was different, he was so tall that when he went over he almost touched. He always went over first, because I suppose he felt responsible for me. But this day there was a terrible space in time when I felt I couldn't drop. I hung facing the cliff, suspended. Usually Charles waited but this day he was away and off the other end of the log. I sensed his going and clung. He sensed the lack of my presence behind him and came back. Just before he reached me I made the drop. But I was shaking.

"Sit down on the log" Charles said, "You must be tired."
"I didn't sleep very well last night" I said and almost bit my tongue.

I thought I would see Charles' eyebrow raise but it didn't. Instead a hard stony look stiffened his whole face. His straight mouth hardened. He put his hand into his pocket, brought a bar of chocolate and handed it to me.

"Eat this," he said, "while we go along."

We started off again but we went more slowly. Charles did not seem to be with me and yet he kept closer than was usual with us. We spoke little and it was a quarter to noon when we reached our juniper tree.

The sun shone on the sea, the moss and the juniper tree. After lunch I felt wonderful. Charles stretched himself out full length on the moss, his arms above his head. Without looking at me he said:

"And why didn't you sleep well last night?"

It was unexpected and I did not know how to handle it. I had hoped Charles would forget what I said as we had come through the forest. Then I had forgotten about it altogether myself. As I was fast growing towards a woman's size I fell upon women's ways. Instinctively I tried to change the subject by asking another question. I was more woman than I knew.

"Charles" I said "Whose friend is Tony Johns, yours or Wilfs?"
Charles was taken by surprise. This time he did look at me. For the first time in the day his eyebrow went up. "Trumped my ace" he said
"I beg your pardon, Charles."
"Women!" said Charles
"Well," I said vaguely hurt and troubled without knowing why "I was just wondering"

"And sticking to your guns too - unusual for you. He's not my friend."

"Do you like him?"

"No."

"Then why does he come to your place all the time?"

"Because the women want him to."

"No they don't. I heard them talking and they don't."

"Who did you hear talking?"

"Oh, Mother and the rest."

"I meant the young women, the unmarried ones, not the mothers and others" The eyebrow went up again.

"Well, I'm not married and I think he's a nuisance" then I added "but I like his music."

"That's exactly it - they like his music. But I don't."

"I didn't think you did."

"Why?"

Embarrassment flooded me again. Words can so easily escape, simple little normal everyday words. You use them a thousand times and then one day you say them and nothing is the same. You are forced to tell lies or retreat.

"I can't say."

Charles fell into a silence. He sat up and I thought perhaps it was time to go. I had spoiled his day. Perhaps this would be our last trip to the lighthouse. I sat with my back to the juniper tree, my eyes following the rhythms of the white caps far out at sea. The silence held for me all the inadequacy of being half woman, half child. I felt urged to speak and compelled to silence. There is something to say, I thought, but I do not know what it is. I had seen Charles angry. He was not angry at that moment. He was not irritated. Was he hurt? When Greta was hurt she always shrugged her shoulders and deliberately shifted away from what hurt her and began to talk about something else or deliberately change her clothes to prepare to start something new.

There was nothing which Greta did which would fit Charles. Nor my brothers. Nor my parents. Myself then? If I was hurt what would I do? Hide it. Change the subject. Get away from it. Retreat to my imaginings. Escape.

I said 'There are thousands of whitecaps out to sea. Do you think there will be a storm?"

Charles took the time to light himself a cigarette. Then he heaved a considerable sigh which I felt penetrated my inner self. I was a very serious girl.

Charles said. "Don't worry. I won't ask you your secret. All girls have secrets I find. You have yours with Greta don't you?"
"Yes I do"
"Did you know she fights like a cat for you. I often wondered why. Now I know."

A little voice inside tried to tell me that Charles did not like Greta. I would have nothing to do with it. The thing was impossible. Charles did not know her at all. It was only that he must have known she liked Tony, preferred Tony as Charles thought all the girls did. A chill ran through me as I thought of Greta in the night.

"Oh, Charles"
"Don't be so frightened. Now you and I have a secret too. That's all."

Charles was somehow trying to protect me, even trying to warn me. But all he was succeeding in doing was giving me two secrets to carry around like a heavy burden. Adults are like that. They never seem to be sure how young a child is.

"I could keep three secrets Charles."

"Then what is it you want to know?"

"About you and Pat. Is she your girl?"

He countered, "Do you think she is pretty?"

"Not quite. She has a kind of Asian look that isn't quite right because she isn't."

"That's it exactly. And she's got a kind of Asian fascination too and that isn't quite right either. Can you understand that?"

"No Charles."

"No, of course you can't. I can't myself. It's a quality of personality that you can't really get at, but can't leave alone either."

"So that it would be better if she really acted Canadian or really was Chinese."

"She is pure Canadian born and her parents came from England. I asked her once and she was furious."

"Doesn't she like to look Asian?"

"No, absolutely hates it. Some child at school once suggested she might have Indian blood. It took me weeks to get that out of her."

When I said that, a sense of their intimacy embarrassed me. I had the third secret. Charles was in love with Pat.

Charles waited a little and then he said.

"Poor Kit, three secrets that all add up to one big one. You're not interested in boys yet are you."

"No."

"You're lucky. And don't let anybody tell you you're not. Not for a good while yet."

I felt he was getting at Greta again. Greta would be sitting on the beach now, her hair silky soft and wet like a spaniel from diving into the sea from the raft off-shore. Around her there would be an admiring group of boys threatening to throw her into the water, pushing her in play, pretending to argue with her, hoping to be fast enough to race her to the raft.

Charles had said she fought like a cat for me. Suddenly I knew why. She was always telling me how young I was for my age. Often I had wondered how it was that she, who was two years older than I, should choose me out of those she knew to be her greatest friend if it was true that I was so young. So that was why Greta fought for me like a cat. There were some things she would not let people say about me, such as:

"Boys don't like me."

It was out and I was strangely glad it was out. It was almost as if I had had a little ball of string winding itself in my throat getting bitter and bigger that I had suddenly been able to spit out. I had hardly known it was there until that instant, yet the relief was so great when I got rid of it that my eyes filled up with tears and I thought for a dreadful minute that I was going to cry in front of Charles. If I had it wouldn't have mattered for Charles was not looking at me. He was lying on the moss again, full-length with his feet almost to the edge of the cliff.

"Boys don't see you that's all. Silly fools. You're too old for them. I like you don't I? I'm male."

"It's not the same."

"Yes it's the same. All the teenage nerds around Greta. All the eligible females around Tony."

It crossed my mind that I would have much to think of this night on my cot in the tent that I could not share with Greta. Adult things, problems, conundrums. It struck me to wonder that if, as I knew, Greta would not that night be thinking of even one of the teenage herd, who would Tony be thinking about?

"Is Pat like Greta, Charles, I mean did she used to be?"

"Yes she was."

"She's not as pretty as Greta."

"No, she's not. She has always been the centre of attention just the same."

"Then," I said in my new wisdom "she probably didn't want any of the boys who were hanging around her"

"You are right, she didn't. But she won't give up the herd nevertheless."

We had swung back to the present. It was like a seesaw from my problem to his. He did not seem to mind talking about Pat to me. I was proud because I knew that he knew he could trust me.

"Who did she want?" I asked

"I thought that was obvious, me."

"But you didn't want her."

"Not in the beginning, no."

"Why?"

"I was like you, I suppose. I didn't want to travel with the herd. I wanted to find out a few things first. I was scared of women, especially Pat's kind of woman. I still am."

"Like Jimmy Millar."

"Who's Jimmy Millar?"

"Oh, you know, he's Tom Millar's brother. He comes down sometimes. He's my age."

"Who you went fishing with last Sunday?"

The tone of voice had changed. I was being teased.

"You were fishing last Sunday, yourself. You went with the men."

"I got back at 10 o'clock. You were nowhere to be seen. Greta was swimming when I went in and she said you had gone fishing by yourself."

"Well, Jimmy came too. I was going by myself."

"Isn't he the one that works so hard at school, I think Tom said he was the top student or something. That's the one?"

"Yes, the boys all tease him about it. He's terribly shy, Charles. He won't even go swimming with the crowd."

"But he does with you?" teasing again.

"Well, you see Charles, it's just that he is like a boy in your class at school, you know he doesn't care about all that, well, all that sort of talk. He just sits and when the other boys speak to him he blushes. I feel sorry for him Charles, I really do. It must be awful for him. Anyway he hardly ever comes."

"Did you have a good time fishing?"

"Oh yes, he's nice to be with. He's not silly. We caught two rock cod and he took them home."

"Is he coming today?"

"No, next Sunday. He's only allowed to come every second Sunday. The other day he goes to his grandmother's or something. He comes out on his bike and brings his lunch."

"Did he make a date with you?"

"Oh don't be silly Charles. Of course not."

"I mean, did he ask you to go fishing with him next Sunday."

"Oh that. I said I would if I didn't go with you."

"And what did he say to that?"

"Just that he'd be seeing me. Why?"

"Well, I suppose he could come with us, if we go."

"Oh no, Charles."

"Alright, if you prefer to keep the two of us for alternate Sundays."

We began to laugh. We were not given to fits of laughter together. Charles threw back his head and roared. His laughter rang out over and above the sound of the beating sea like a trumpet. I just felt extraordinarily light-headed. I wanted to giggle rather than laugh. I was having my first taste of the wine of the gods, which a few moments before I had felt sure I was denied. It was perfectly true that Jimmy Millar was a very clever boy and only shy because he was so busy learning. And Charles was the nicest man in the world except for my father. Every week there would be one or the other for a whole summer. Yet I was convinced that Charles was frightened that I was jealous of Greta. Poor dear Charles, how could he have been so mistaken. He didn't know Greta very well. But he knew Pat. There was something wrong about Charles and Pat.

Our laughter died away on the wind. Charles was standing up. He began to gather up.

"You might as well know," he said. "I'm going to marry Pat. But keep it under your hat for a while."
"But what about Tony?" I gasped.

I couldn't believe I had heard right. Back on the beach at Cedar Cove there would be a group of teenagers with Greta in the centre. Somewhere a little further along there would be another group all laughing and teasing only in their grown-up way. There would be a centre there too and the centre would be Tony. Tony and Pat. Bewilderment filled me, consternation, anxiety. It wasn't right somehow, not good enough for Charles that he should announce that he would marry a girl who preferred to sit in a circle around Tony rather than walk in the woods with Charles. Every weekend Charles was with us at the beach, walking, swimming, fishing. Every weekend of that summer. Where then, was this girl on all the summer days? What did she share with Charles that he was going to marry her? He had not wanted her when he was younger. But she had wanted him.

"Don't worry about Tony. He won't get her. He only wants what he can't get. He thinks he can't get Pat. If he thinks he can, he won't want her. That will be the end of that." said Charles bitterly and started down the hill towards the lighthouse.

***

That night was calm and quiet. After dinner I had a little walk with my father. We always had a little time together on Sunday night. When we came back my brothers and Greta were already in bed. The camp was still. The husbands departed early on Monday morning, and an early Sunday night enveloped the beach as effectively as a curfew. Surely, I hoped, there would be no sound of the guitar to break the later stillness. Most young people had returned to town. I slipped into the little tent I shared with Greta, and my parents went to sit for a last half hour as was their habit, on a log in front of their tent. The murmur of their distant voices came to me as I slipped off my clothes in the dark.

Greta was not asleep. It was the first night I could remember since we were little girls, that I hoped she would be.

"I wish I was tired," she said. "But I'm not a bit."
"I am, but then I ought to be, all that walking I did."
"And all the sensation you caused!"
"I beg your pardon, Greta?"
"Well, you did, going off with Charles."
"I always go tramping with Charles whenever he asks me."

"You know perfectly well that Charles went right off and left Pat. She wasn't even up when he left. Everybody on the beach was talking about it."

"Why?"

"Don't you know that Charles and Pat have been going together for two years?"

"Yes I know." This was safe, I did know now. "But she never did go on any walks with him. Never."

"Nobody could understand why he should go and ask you to walk to the lighthouse yesterday when Pat was on the beach. It didn't seem right. Auntie Meg said, 'how exactly like Charles.' You could tell they were all furious."

I was stubborn.

"I don't see why." I said. But of course for the first time in my life I did.

I also knew it was really something else they were all furious about. It had nothing to do with me. Greta knew this yet here she was lining herself up with the adults, pretending I was too young to know real reasons again. I seethed at the condescension, yet what could I say? I held three secrets and I scented another.

"What did Pat do?" I asked into the silence "Did she sulk?"

"Sulk!" Greta said. "It's obvious you don't know Pat. No she didn't. She went off with Tony Johns and didn't come back until nearly dark. They expected them for lunch too and Auntie kept the dinner hot. Everybody knew about it. Your Mother and I were up there for lunch. We went after your dad and the boys went for a picnic up to Willis Bay. Then just to finish everything, just as we were leaving, that boy Jimmy Millar turned up. Here."

"Daddy told me." I said. "He went to Willis Bay too."

I waited determined not to say any more, snuggling into my bed. This was getting a bit much for me.

"Your Mother didn't know what to do with him so she suggested he eat with us and then that perhaps he and I set off after your father to Willis Bay. Me!"

"Well," I said, "why not?"

"Why not, because I didn't want to, that's why. I don't know him. And he's only a kid."

"And you wanted to go up to Auntie Meg for lunch. Jimmy couldn't help it. How was he to know?"

"Did you know he was coming?"

"No, he didn't think he could."

"Oh, so he talked to you about it."

"Why shouldn't he?" This was terrible, it was almost as if I was fighting with Greta. I would have to try and smooth it out. She was very angry because Pat had gone off with Tony. I could feel this but I couldn't cope with it, I couldn't understand it. He was grown up.

"Well anyway" I said, "you didn't have to go to Willis Bay did you?"

"No I didn't. Jimmy didn't want to eat with us. He said he had his lunch and would bike over to Willis by himself."

There was a long silence from Greta's bed - I didn't speak but I knew she was not done.

"She won't get Tony."

"How do you know?"

"He only wants her because she's Charles' girl."

"That is mean and horrible. Do you think Tony's mean and horrible?"

"No I don't. I think Pat's mean and horrible. I think they all are. They'll get Tony put off the beach. You heard, didn't you?"

"That's for playing his guitar."

"It's always one of them he plays the guitar for. Do you think it's Pat tonight?"

"I suppose so, Greta. I like his music the best about him, don't you?"

"I don't think it's worth putting him off the beach for."

"Greta," I said "She's after Charles isn't she? Isn't it all mixed up!"

"Yes, it's all mixed up." Greta whispered.

Somewhere on the beach then just beyond the reach of the curling ends of the waves on the sand, just close enough to sing in harmony with them, the music of the guitar began to croon. Silence had settled again in our tent. It seemed superfluous to even say another 'good night'. I settled to listen, to dream and then to sleep.

I awoke in the clutches of cold fear. The shadow of someone was on the tent. There seemed to be no sound. The tide must have been up, and the wind wandering through the firs was friendly, but the chill that gripped me obliterated them completely. In that tense moment between the sleep of contentment and awakening in fear, the shadow moved and crept into the tent. It slipped past me in silence and re-turned itself to Greta's bed. It sighed. I sat up in bed. Greta lay very still.

"You frightened me," I said. "I had begun to shake and quiver and the camp cot shook. Greta slipped over to my bed and put her arms around me.

"Are you sick? What's the matter?" Her face now near mine was glistening, as if with tears "Shall I get someone?"

"I don't know what it was," I whispered. "I woke up so frightened. I was petrified - I was quite cold, quite still. It was when you came in the tent door."

Greta sighed, "I'm sorry I went, anyway." she said.

I was still shaky and a little stupefied.

"Went where?" I said.
"Down to warn Tony."

I was flabbergasted.

"Warn Tony! What did you say?"
"Nothing, nothing at all. When I found him it was too late. He had stopped playing the guitar. I couldn't even see who he was with. It was like only one person on the beach. It was awful. I ran back." The words all ran together out of Greta in a little breathless whisper as if she wanted to cry them but couldn't. Worse than that it must have been Pat that stopped the music of the guitar with Tony on the beach. Had there been two watchers on the sand, Greta and Charles?

***

5

Chapter Five

For me that year started on that weekend in July and continued on into the glorious month of August. All the joys of that time stand out in my mind like the photograph of a pleasant dream. The weather was perfect and everyone who could, spent every minute of time that was possible, at the beach. Jimmy Millar came and pitched a little pup tent every weekend. Charles was there every Sunday. Greta and I spent day after day together talking of love and magic in the last days of her adolescence.

At night under the moon the smelts ran in silver phosphorescent streaks across the cove. Like primitive men we were after them for breakfast, swarming ankle-deep in the water scooping them out with pots and pans and nets and baskets. Afterwards we ourselves swam in the phosphorescent water, glittering streaks of human moonlight, disembodied figures. The seas pounded the beach bringing in the driftwood for our fires and huge onion seaweed, throwing up the buried shells and smooth coloured stones. Sometimes I danced with Greta in a secret place we knew, a little stage with a backdrop of high Hemlock and a curtain of green saplings. It was a ritual dance, each dancing with herself alone. I can still see Greta, her blonde hair straight and silky, her deep-set tan-brown eyes hidden under her heavy lashes, her small, pointed face and her mouth so sweet and soft and young. I wish I had known, as I danced to the far-off music of the pipes of Pan, that Greta danced to the pagan calling of the beach guitar. It might have helped if I had known more than I did. If that year had been one of my years of reality instead of one of my years of imaginative wonder, would it have made any difference? I see now that Charles handed me over that summer to my own age, to a reality my own size that I could cope with. Every Sunday morning Jimmy Millar was at our tent before Charles arrived.

Charles invited him to come along. I remember Jimmy looking at me the first time with the peering anxious look of a dark eyed spaniel. When we set off together. Charles explained precisely to Jimmy exactly how best to paddle a canoe upstream and how best to recover if swamped with water. I thought perhaps I should resent this special instruction to Jimmy for I myself could do these things. It seems that Charles did not expect that I should be doing them alone. I did not know that Charles was abdicating. Conversation with Charles was not of course the same with Jimmy present. It wasn't that Jimmy said much or that Charles talked less. Rather it was that Charles talked more and that Jimmy hung on every word and benefited from watching intently everything that Charles did. I always found the conversations interesting if more detailed than I felt the need for. Jimmy was so anxious to absorb whatever information Charles offered him that Charles often became expansive and very much the schoolteacher I had never known. Charles had always subtly teased me. Jimmy took us both so seriously that Charles felt compelled to explain even his teasing so that Jimmy could join in. This situation usually ended up in both Charles and me teasing Jimmy instead of Charles teasing me. Nevertheless, the three of us enjoyed ourselves so much that I scarcely missed my intimacy with Charles because it was he and I together initiating Jimmy. My relationship with Charles had always been such an ephemeral thing anyway. I wouldn't have expected Jimmy to understand it and if he had not, he would have been worried by his lack of comprehension. Charles was so obviously impressed with the speed with which Jimmy's mind grasped information especially of a practical nature that with Jimmy present Charles became a teacher in the real sense of the word. I was strangely proud of them both, especially proud of having found Jimmy and flattered when Charles so magnanimously referred to him as "your friend Jimmy". Charles always seemed so pleased to be talking to us jointly that I forgot most of the time that he was really explaining how everything worked to Jimmy and that Jimmy somehow kept Charles on the subjects that he wanted to know about the most. As I was always included there were times when they even took great pains to make further explanations for my benefit, vying with one another to make me understand what was obvious. Perhaps I should have learned much that summer. If I did I cannot remember. Memory is a fickle thing. All I remember now is the one thing about which I longed to have their opinion. It was constantly on my mind to discuss a boy called Rupert whose father owned the store. I wanted to know why there was something about Rupert which worried me.

That summer, for the first time in my life, a new menace had afflicted me. A series of words in connection with this boy roamed my head like disconnected phantoms in phrased pairs, little circles, typifying nothing at all and everything. 'Pale eyes - deserted eyes - gone eyes - departed eyes - fish filmed, water drowned, screened fluid, ghost eyes, move away, walk aside, empty eyes, veiled eyes, feared depths, incomprehensible signs. Pale eyes - pale eyes.'

I remember these words as intangible stupidities tangled and inextricably involved in me. The rest is nebulous, the boy's face, the words he spoke. I can do better for others. The first time the boy's eyes were everything: one startling glance followed by another of verification before complete avoidance, before defensive detachment. Rupert was a little boy, younger than me, about the age of my brother Donald.

He was fairish of complexion and, I think, loved, finishing the first cycle of school. Helpful, my family said, useful, willing yet for me a boy in a dream. I walked into his dream, inadvertently sucked in to be abnormally spewed out with the haste engendered by this new and terrifying fascination. I was an unwanted stranger in this unknown terrain to be reached, I discovered, by a single side-step into an air pocket running parallel to my own life, unseen by my accustomed sight, unheard of through my normal hearing. A firm steady path lay in front of my feet yet beside me lay this great void, this waiting emptiness. Pale eyes. The haunting pale eyes of Rupert Thoms. All the time those I loved and who made up my youth, parents, brothers, aunts, uncles, cousins, even Jimmy were around me. They were all there yet in this area of intuitional self I was consciously alone, cut-off, isolated. A palliating part of me was involved with a stranger called Rupert whom I scarcely knew, and with whom I had no cause for connection, not even the attraction of friendship. The merest acquaintance blown up like a balloon in my mind from a mere feeling, from a shadow beyond sense to usurp reality unless I beat it down in my thoughts before sleep. 'Pale eyes, pale eyes.' Instead of poetry under the bent branch of the Douglas Fir, 'ghost eyes, veiled eyes' haunting the road between the camp and the store, hovering over the sea at the gap's edge where the road was cut out of solid rock, leaving instead of beach only crevasses where the most delicate fronds of fern sprouted and a minute jack-pine, like a miniature Christmas tree, clung by its roots to a portion of soil unmolested by the wild wind that shrieked down the rock chimney to the sea.

On Sunday as we tramped back in single file from the lighthouse I thought my chance to speak had come because Charles who was walking in front of me almost in answer to my thoughts gave me the opening I needed.

"We'll be back well before dinner" he announced, "I think there's time to go on down to the store. I want some cigarettes."

"I think there's something funny about Rupert Thoms" I said abruptly.

"How do you mean?" Jimmy asked.

"Yes indeed, explain yourself, my dear Eleanore" Charles flung back over his shoulder.

"Eleanore?" Jimmy questioned.

"That's a poem" Charles replied and began to quote softly.

"The forest flowers are faded all
The winds complain, the snowflakes fall
Eleanore, Eleanore
I turn to these as to a bower
Thou breathest beauty like a flower
Thou smilest like a happy hour
I turn to thee"

"Poetry," Jimmy said, "I don't get it."

"Well, you see, Jimmy" Charles said solemnly "as it is rather a nice poem and as Kit's name is really Eleanor, I sometimes tease her with it."

"I'm sorry" Jimmy said, "I still don't get it." He drew abreast of me and asked quite seriously. "Is your second name Eleanor?"

"Indeed it is not" Charles said, laughing. "Her real name is Eleanor Jane. Isn't it Kit?"

"Don't be so awful Charles" I said but I couldn't help laughing too.

"I still don't get it," Jimmy said.

"What, the poetry?" Charles inquired, his mouth twitching.

"I don't know much about poetry" Jimmy said with finality, "I mean if Kit's name is Eleanor Jane why is she called Kit?"

"The reason should be obvious even to you Jimmy. Only her mother and I thought she looked like an Eleanor. All the rest of her relatives thought she was more like a round cuddly kitten. We have a lot of relatives as you know and their opinion predominated."

"Charles! That's horrid and you know it. The truth is" I said turning to Jimmy, "that my father has always called me Kit and that's all there is to it."

"I see," Jimmy said, "that explains it."

Charles strode off ahead of us down the path, his shoulders shaking. I was suddenly furious with him. It was impossible to bring up the boy Rupert again. If I did Charles would laugh about it and I didn't think it any laughing matter. I turned rather violently on poor Jimmy.

"Explains what" I inquired tartly, "Do you think my name needs explaining?" I dragged out the last word with deliberate emphasis.

"Oh gee no Kit," Jimmy said, "I like it."

He looked embarrassed for some reason and I was glad.

"But you couldn't make a poem out of it could you?" I said sweetly.

"No, I guess you couldn't" Jimmy said. "But who'd want to anyway?"

"Somebody might" I said airily, "someday somebody that liked me."

"If somebody liked you I guess they'd say so, not go wasting time writing poems" Jimmy announced and kicked a stone with the toe of his boot.

I called to Charles, striding ahead of us.

"Are you going all the way down to the store now?"

"That's the idea" he called back.

"I don't want to go to the store," I said petulantly to Jimmy.

"Why not?"

"I just don't, that's all."

"It's not that far," Jimmy said. "I guess we ought to go if Charles wants to."

"Then you go."

I stood still on the road where a path started steeply towards the beach and shouted.

"Charles, I'm not coming to the store."

Charles turned and stood for a moment, then came back.

"I was going to buy you a Vanity Fudge," he said.

"Thanks all the same Charles but I can't be tempted by a chocolate bar."

"You've been tempted before," Charles said.

"Kit's tired." This was an announcement for Jimmy.

"I am not."

"I'm surprised it's important enough to insult both of us," Charles said mildly. "You said something a little while ago about the Toms boy - Rupert. What was it?"

"Only that I don't think I like him very much."

"So what - he's only a kid and a harmless kind of a kid at that. What's he said to you?"

"Nothing. It's just that I don't like talking to him. There's something funny about him, something not usual. It's like he's not there Charles. It's hard to explain. He's talking to you and yet he's not there."

Charles laughed but there was no humour in the laugh, no teasing.

"Well, he's there alright Kit, no doubt about that. Maybe he's shy with girls and that's what you feel."

"No it's not that. He's not shy. I think it's his eyes that are strange. There's nothing in them."

"Ye gods. You've sure got a lively imagination sometimes Kit. Do you mean to tell me you don't want to go to the store because of that?"

I had no answer. What he said was true. I didn't want to go to the store simply because I might encounter Rupert. He might be behind the counter in the store and give me the chocolate Charles would ask for and I would instinctively draw away from him, fearing the blank emptiness of his effect on me. The whole of the previous summer I had found it difficult to remember his name. His personality even then had somehow not registered with me. Yet when I spoke with him this summer or when he stood near me without speaking I was so conscious of this new intangible wall, this barrier. The reality which was the boy himself still eluded me. Yet how could I tell all that to Charles. It was easier to cover my confusion by pretending dislike.

"Well, I can't help it if I don't like him can I?" I said.

"And the poor boy can't help it either if you don't like him" Charles said.

"Oh he doesn't know Charles."

"Then what's all the fuss about?"

"There's no fuss," I said suddenly resigned, "I'll go."

"What's it matter anyway?" Jimmy said.

So, we began the walk down the road past our beach around the great curve of the gorge on to the store. It was not a long walk but usually it was a silent one for human voices could not compete with the violence of the pounding sea on that turn where the road had been hacked out of the solid rock and the waves beat mercilessly on the great boulders below. I walked between Charles and Jimmy, fortified and safe with one on either side. To avoid any car that might drive by we faced the traffic squarely keeping well to the side of the road, a dusty trio after our day's tramp. Rupert was not in the store.

My father, upon whom I usually depended for explanation of strange phenomena was no help to me about Rupert Thoms. Perhaps I was not explicit enough in my questioning, for when I asked Daddy if he thought Rupert Thoms had funny eyes the reply I received was in the negative. Daddy had noticed nothing peculiar and let the matter rest there. My discussion with Mother on the other hand was unexpectedly alarming and final. One day during the week my brother Donald went down to Thoms' store for bread and was late getting back. Mother seemed uneasy about the lateness of the hour. This presented an opportunity too good to miss. Even so, such was the complicated state of my mind, I came at my mother from a different angle, unexplored in previous attempts at discussion on the problem of Rupert, and more direct. As was often the case when I was driven to Mother or my aunts, I got more than I bargained for.

"I wish Donald wouldn't go around with that boy from the store" I said. "He gives me the creeps."

"What boy?" Mother said, still preoccupied.

"That boy from the store - Thoms' store."

"Rupert? Donald likes him. What's the matter with him?" She turned sharply and looked at me.

"He gives me the creeps."

"What do you mean - gives you the creeps? That's a silly thing to say."

"Well, he does."

"I wouldn't repeat such a thing, my girl. The boy is a good two years younger than yourself and it's not like you to say such a thing."

"I only said it to you."

I saw my mother's eyes narrow a little in recollection.

"No, Donald told me you walked away and were rude to the boy now I come to think of it." Mother was looking at me closely, her mind jumping to obvious conclusions. "Was Rupert nasty to you?"

"Oh no, it's nothing like that. I didn't mean to be rude to him. It's just that it worries me to be near him. It's his eyes."

"His eyes, what's the matter with his eyes?"

"They aren't like other people's eyes."

"And why should they be?"

At last what was inside of me came out.

"Mother, he stands right beside you and you don't feel he's there. And he looks straight at you and you don't feel he sees you. It's awful."

"Then it's something else than his eyes you feel. His eyes are quite normal and as far as I can judge the boy is not only normal but a good boy as well and from a nice family. What you are trying to tell me is that for some reason he gives you a funny feeling. Is that it?" She put a hard deliberate emphasis on the 'you'.

"Yes," I said, relieved. "Yes that's it. I don't dislike him, Mother, really I don't, I'm just kind of scared of Donald going around with him."

Mother grew very still. "I see" she said, "And did you ever speak to your father about it?"

"Yes, once I did, when we were coming back from the store around the rock cutting - you know where the road is so dangerous - there."

"What did your father say?"

"Nothing - he hadn't noticed anything."

"And Charles?"

I was unawares and fell straight into the trap.

"The same, and that I had a lively imagination."

Mother responded, very gently I thought, considering she now knew she was consulted last of all. Also, that I had been talking far too much about an unspeakable subject which was to her, mortal sin.

"It's obvious something about this lad worries you Kit. But if your father says the boy's alright, you're to put it out of your mind and say no more about it."

"But I don't like Donald being with him."

"You said that before and you're not to say it again. There's things you have to keep to yourself. I'll tell your father to keep his eyes open, if that will ease your mind. But you're to say no more about it. You'll promise me."

"Buy why?"

"Because it's not the boy people will be thinking strange. It will be you. You'll say no more about it. And you'll promise."

"Well, I'll promise not to say what I think to anybody else but I won't promise not to think it."

"You will do better to stop thinking about it. Thinking will do you no good. You will do better to put it out of your mind."

"I can't see that it's wrong to think about it."

My mother was being extraordinarily patient and I took advantage of it. When she didn't answer immediately I continued the same line of thought.

"Anyway, how can I stop thinking about it when Rupert goes around with Donald all the time."

"That he does not do" said my mother sharply. "About once or twice a week or so he sees Donald, no more, and that only this summer. He works hard that boy doing deliveries for his father. Donald spends most of his time with young Ian when he's here, and his own brothers." Still her patience was not exhausted and I began to wonder why.

"Is Ian coming next week?"

My mother committed herself. "I was thinking I might ask him for the rest of the summer. Still, there's Greta until the end of August." She looked at me hard. It meant another boy and more potatoes to peel. Mentally I made the bargain.

"If he did" I said, "I guess I could forget it."

Did I see relief in my mother's eyes or was it the sun flickering the shadows on the canvas? Anyway, she was suddenly and belatedly angry with me.

"There are times when I wish you were grown-up and times when I think I'll never know what goes on in your head when you do. Your Aunt Meg thinks so too and so does your cousin, Charles I suspect."

"Why?"

"Because you're always putting us in the position of not being able to explain what you shouldn't want to know. Your odd feelings for instance".

"I can't help my feelings," I said.

Mother calmed as quickly as her temper flared.

"No, I suppose you can't" she said, "but I wish you'd realise that at your age I can't explain either. There are things none of us are meant to understand.

"You mean at my age?"

"At any age. You can't explain some things, feelings like you have about that boy for instance. Sometimes experience gives you a kind of answer and sometimes it doesn't. That's all I can tell you."

"Do you think I'm funny to have feelings like I have about Rupert?"

"No, some people have them and some don't"

"Do you?"

"No - but I know about them because you're like your grandmother and she had 'presentiments'."

"Did she tell you about them when you were a girl?"

My mother laughed - "She did not. If there was one subject she would not talk about, that was it."

"Why?"

"I told you before. Time told me why and no doubt time will tell you. But it's a thing you have to find out for yourself. I can't tell you." My mother sighed and walked away from me into her own tent.

I went to a rock I knew beside a little sea pool and sat down. I found myself still left with my feelings which I presumed might now be presentiment and therefore might harm me if I talked about them. My conversation with Mother had certainly ended up on an unexpected note. Contrary to my expectations I was more puzzled than ever. Instead of the answer I had hoped for I had discovered something in our family that my grandmother possessed, as did I but my mother did not. Something more subtle and appalling than curly hair. I wondered if Auntie Meg had it but decided, had that been true, Mother would have sent me to her. I felt that at last I had direct cause to dislike Rupert Thoms. But I couldn't dislike him. It was easier to avoid and forget him. I decided to do this by deliberately pretending he didn't exist and not allowing myself to think he did. This would be easy to do because Greta, who had gone home to go to the dentist, was returning on Friday while Ian was coming with Donald and Charles for a weekend trip. When I had made my decision I felt somehow ashamed and full of remorse, as if I had unknowingly done the boy Rupert an injury or inadvertently discovered a secret he was desperately trying to keep. I accepted this feeling to be what was meant by unmentionable presentiment. I would look up the word in the dictionary when I got home because I thought I better not ask Charles or Daddy what they thought the word meant. Perhaps if I tried to write a poem about it I could get the feeling out of my system. But I didn't want to write a poem. What was the point? I had made up my mind that I would read poetry and talk about it to Charles when he brought up the subject but I wasn't going to try to write it anymore. It was a waste of my time. No, I wouldn't try to write a poem about the feelings Rupert Thom aroused in me. I would simply avoid and forget him.

***

6

═══════════

Chapter Six

The third Saturday night of August at the bonfire, Tony Johns
chose Greta. He reached out of his crowd into hers, offered her
his hand and made a place for her beside himself. I cannot say that he
seemed bored with his own crowd. He just suddenly noticed Greta,
saw she was beautiful, fed up with her own regulars and seemed incongruous as a third to Jimmy and me. So, amid much laughter and
teasing he took over the roasting of her marshmallows. Apparently
nobody except me took much notice. Everybody was having too much
fun.

Later when the beach was hushed and we were ready for sleep
Greta slipped out of the tent to the call of the guitar as swiftly as a
moth flies toward a candle. I was still awake and I pleaded with her
not to go but I knew she would and she knew I would not tell. For
a long time I lay worrying less about what Greta would talk about to
Tony on the beach, than apprehensive as to what I would tell Mother
if she found out that Greta had gone.

Intermittently the strange wistful music floated over the booming
of the waves with a wild exultant throbbing. I resolved to stay awake
until Greta came back but youth sleeps easily under the influence of
the fresh sea air. When I awoke in the morning Greta lay on her
camp-bed, smiling a little as she slept, her face as sweet as a flower in

93

the early light. She did not wake up though I dressed noisily in the tent and the clatter of breakfast plates, water buckets and fishing gear filled the camp kitchen. I left with Charles and Jimmy while she was still asleep.

The following Sunday was the last in August but I did not go to the lighthouse. When Charles came I could only shake my head under my bitten lip. Charles, his face wooden, went away from the test to disappear into the forest by himself. On his way across the sand he looked at Jimmy who was standing at a distance. I saw Jimmy shake his head. Jimmy didn't come any closer to our camp all day but I knew he didn't go with Charles and I think I gained a little strength from his peculiar vigil although I did not have time nor thought to realise it at the time.

I had not saved Greta and that morning we were waiting for her Father to come and take her home. Inside of me there was a great emptiness. I had been sick in the morning and had lost, with the contents of my stomach, a part of my childhood that I would not recover again. I could not eat to replace the one because I knew I could not replace the other. I was a vacuum sitting in space on the bench behind the trestle table. My brothers awed into silence almost tip-toed from place to place gathering their gear. They were being disposed of for the day. My mother clattered as she tidied up. It was not her normal practice to clatter and she did not ask my help. She would not have accepted it. She was not speaking to me. My eyes followed her every movement and every clatter of every pan hit my head like a blow of a hammer.

My father said to her, "I think you are wrong dear. Kit couldn't help it."

"She could have told us. She knew. She knew she went last week."

"Just the same, it was a hard position to be in."

"Not that hard, not as hard as the position I'm in. I've had Greta here off and on all summer, every summer for years for that matter. I have full responsibility for her."

"She never did it before Mother" I cried out.

"And she won't get a chance to do it again either. She's ruined her life, that's all."

"Oh come now Mother it isn't that bad."

The boys stood ready, all ears. Mother said to my father.

"Here, take the boys down to Peg. Here's the lunches. She'll be ready to take them now."

They departed and I felt deserted. I kept saying a little prayer over and over to get Father back again quickly before anybody else came. I felt I couldn't stand anybody else unless Daddy was there. I wanted to be where Greta was waiting all alone in our tent, but it was no use asking.

Mother had put her head into the little tent and told Greta to get dressed and come out immediately. She had told her to dress ready to go back to town and to have her bag packed. She also told her not to expect me to help her as I was not allowed to go in.

Auntie Meg arrived. She didn't look at me but began to murmur to mother in the big tent. They came out and stoked up the fire and put out cups for coffee.

Auntie Meg said. "He's just sitting there. To tell the truth I thought he'd be gone this morning. His type nearly always bolts."

"I can't see what he's waiting for."

"He told Wilf he'd like to apologise to you."

"I don't want to see him."

"Well, after all she did go out to him. She admitted it, didn't she?"

I could stand it no longer. I could see Daddy coming back across the beach. There were three people with him. "She's in love with Tony" I cried out as if that was the answer to everything. Then I burst into tears.

Greta's father stalked in first. We were all afraid of Uncle Pete. He was a severe stiff man. Greta's mother, my Auntie Mary, white and frightened followed after. She was a small plump woman like my mother except that she had the timid soft eyes of a frightened doe.

My father said, "Sit down Pete."
Mother said, "Greta's in the tent."

I expected to see Greta fly out and fling herself at her parents, but there was no sound from the tent. Both my mother and Auntie Meg opened their mouths but it was Father who spoke.

"It's like this," he said. "There's a young fellow who comes here to stay sometimes on weekends. He's a damn nuisance playing a guitar and keeping the whole camp awake on Saturday nights. He also makes trouble with the girls, luring them out. Some of the men decided to scare the devil out of him by sneaking up in the dark with their flashlights. I didn't know about it. Anyway, a couple of our folks went and got more than they bargained for. He had Greta under the rug with him on the beach. We didn't know she was out and Kit was asleep in the tent."

Greta's mother turned then and looked at me. As she did I somehow knew she didn't understand Greta at all and was depending on Mother and me and we had let her down. She didn't say anything but her eyes slowly filled with tears. I ran to her and threw my arms around her.

"She's in love with him." I repeated over and over, "She's in love with him."

Mother said softly, but I knew she was tense. "Why do you keep repeating that? You'd better go down to the beach for a bit and stop crying." Strangely enough my father did not back her up.
"No," he said, "just stop crying and stay here." His voice was a mixture of firmness and compassion. He turned to Mother. "We've let her stay this long so she might as well see it out. After all, the young have their side too."

Greta walked out then. She looked taller, older, and I thought beautiful in her straight green sleeveless summer dress. Though her mouth looked pinched-in, her eyes looked enormous and I knew she had been brushing and brushing her hair because it shone right to her shoulders as smooth as a cap of gold. With her suitcase in her hand she seemed to me as grown-up as Charles.

"I'm ready Mummy and Daddy." she said and then more distinctly, "I'm sorry Uncle and Auntie."
Her father absolutely roared at her "Go and sit down you disgraceful girl and explain a few things and explain them quick." As he spoke he took a step toward her and I thought he was going to strike her. But he didn't and she didn't move. She just stood there all grown up like somebody waiting to go somewhere, tired out and waiting for dallying men.
"Well," her father roared again. "What have you got to say. I'm waiting."
"Nothing," Greta answered. "Except that I'm sorry to have caused Uncle and Auntie and Kit so much trouble."
"And what's your excuse?"

"I have no excuse, not for myself." Greta said. "It was the meanest thing I have ever seen in my life. All these men hunting down Tony just because he made a bit of music on the beach when they wanted to sleep. I'm glad I was with him. I'm glad it was me."

I think I felt Uncle Pete move. I think I heard Auntie Mary whisper, "No Pete, not here." I did hear my father say, "No Pete, whatever the provocation I won't have that."

Then Auntie Meg cried out "George and Tony are coming. George and Tony."

I had been too frightened to look at Uncle Pete and Greta would not look at me. I looked down the beach path and saw two men dressed in their best summer flannels, shirts and ties approaching our camp from the sea. George was bringing Tony.

We waited in silence until they arrived; Greta and I, my father and Uncle Pete standing, and the three sisters, my mother and two aunts sitting on canvas chairs. Face to face with us my cousin George shuffled from one foot to the other before he gulped and said, "Tony asked me to bring him over to meet you Uncle Pete." But he wasn't looking at Uncle Pete he was looking at my father and so was Tony who addressed Daddy directly.

"I wanted to say I'm sorry, sir."
My father said, "I see. Greta's parents have come to take her home."

I think it was then I realised how handsome Tony Johns was. One saw it even in these circumstances as he stood like a trapped animal shifting from one foot to the other waiting for someone to speak. It had to be Uncle Pete whose tone was menacing. "I have just asked my daughter for an explanation. I will talk to you later."

"I told you I had no explanation." Greta repeated in the same flat light voice. "I told you I thought it was disgraceful that grown men should hunt for another man on the beach just to take his guitar away from him."

Tony raised his head and looked at Greta and perhaps in that moment saw her for the first time as a woman rather than the prettiest girl on the beach. She was looking straight back at her father with a kind of patient boredom as if she had heard his expected outburst many times before.

"Stop your insolence."

Tony stepped up on to the platform. "It's my fault sir. I took her to the beach."

Uncle Pete wheeled round on him. "You took her to the beach all right. And what are you going to do about it eh?"

"I think I've fallen in love with her sir. I'd like to marry her if that's okay with you sir."

"Marry her? She's only a child."

"No she isn't sir."

"I'm damned if you will." Uncle Pete roared.

"Then what do you propose sir?"

We were all momentarily stunned. I heard the waves breaking into separate voices at the shoreline. As was to be anticipated Uncle Pete recovered first. Turning he took two steps towards Greta.

"Do you want to marry him? Do you have to?"

"Yes." Greta said. "I want to marry him."

"I asked, do you have to marry him?"

"Yes, I think I have to marry him."

Uncle Pete turned then with such a scathing look at my parents and my aunts that I hated him. When he spoke it was with a decided and purposeful sneer in the direction of his wife.

"So much for your great trust in your family Mary. You seem to have misplaced it. This finishes them as far as I am concerned. Come along."

Tony picked up Greta's bag and addressed her father "Do you mind if I come into town with you sir? There are some things I suppose we will have to talk over." He then asked George to bring his bag up to town. "I'll get it later tonight." Then he added "You can give away the guitar."

"No!" Greta cried out.

And then she suddenly threw her arms around me. I could feel her lips trembling against my wet cheek. She hugged me very tight and I hugged her back with all the strength I had. There was nothing to say. Greta walked out beside her mother. I thought I had come to the end of summer.

Later, outside with my father, I mused to myself: girls are odd creatures with sudden illogical thoughts.

"I always thought I would be Greta's bridesmaid Daddy. She'll be such a beautiful bride. It isn't as if there is anybody else who is likely to ask me like some girls who have sisters."

My father stopped in the road, stooped and picked up a small stone and hurled it with considerable force at the nearest tree. It hit and then clattered down into the bracken fern with a series of muted thumps. In surprise I turned and faced him. There was an expression on his face that quite suddenly reminded me of Charles. Later I realised it was at that moment I knew why Charles had taken himself to the woods all day and departed early that night. There came a time later too, when I understood why Jimmy sulked on the beach, skipping dozens of flat stones on the sea and then picked up his bicycle and departed just as Greta went home with her parents. I had thought it so strange of them both.

"It isn't the wedding I'm worried about Kit. It's that confounded faith you have in people. I don't want you to lose it. I don't want you disappointed, that's all. Anyway, not yet."

"Don't worry Daddy." I said. "Please don't worry. I know it's awfully hard for you. It will be alright. I'll just wait until I am grown up and then I'll see Greta again, just the same as ever. She'll understand.

My father put his hand on my shoulder and we turned and walked back toward the beach. Before we started down the hill I said, "Daddy, would you do me a favour?"

"If I can."

"Would you send her a present and say it's from me? She always wanted a yellow satin petticoat."

***

Charles did not come to the beach again that summer. September came and at the end of the first week there was a great bonfire the night before we packed up to go home. The bonfire was the biggest of the holiday season. The parents attempted to make up to the children for the gloom of the previous week. For me there was no Charles and no Greta. There was instead Jimmy. I do not feel I was good company for Jimmy but he was a shield for me. Without him I would have had to answer the barrage of questions about Greta from the weekend crowd, all of whom missed the one they admired the most. If I was preoccupied, Jimmy did not appear to notice it. He passed out marshmallows and hacked into the new watermelon as the slices disappeared. I was my father's chief assistant.

Home at the end of that summer was a welcome haven after the last week at the beach. At home I made myself forget my relatives. I did not want to see them. I absorbed myself in school and in my music. Yet September would not allow me the isolation I demanded. The beach stayed with me all that month. It was the month of my birth. My parents arranged a wonderful party on the day. I was to be surprised and I was. Family friends came and with them their children. All day long I tried to forget the beach yet only succeeded in remembering it. When I blew out the candles of my cake I found that my wish was for happiness for Greta. Nobody knew my wish, yet a strange fleeting feeling of uneasiness accompanied it. But I would not take it back. Involuntarily it had swept over me and with its ending a feeling of relief that I must wish for it in spite of uneasiness, in spite of anything. I cut the cake and there was laughter and toasting, more food and games. My parents watched me laughing and smiled at each other. They had made me queen for the day and they were glad.

At the end of that wonderful day my father came into my room with a parcel in his hand.

"But Daddy, you gave me a present. Another?"
"Open it." my father said.

It was a petticoat, a beautiful petticoat, the most beautiful I had ever seen. It was a pale pink satin petticoat, heavily trimmed with ecru lace.

"Put it away in your bottom drawer." my father said. "I sent one to Greta yesterday, exactly the same, only yellow. This was the day she chose to be married, so you celebrated her wedding after all."

The days of September moved on. As the leaves of the maples turned from green to red and then to gold, I thought of Greta and of marriage and how it was to be grown up and have a satin petticoat waiting in your bottom drawer. Of all my music I mostly practised the nocturnes of Chopin. At night I read the poems of Edna St. Vincent Millay. I almost knew them by heart. Charles had sent them to me, a slim volume arrived in the post the day after my birthday, the day after Greta's wedding. Charles had sent them to me from Nanaimo on Vancouver Island where he was teaching. Charles who never remembered birthdays and never had time to write letters. Yet it was not the new poems of the new poet that repeated themselves before I slept at night. The new stayed apart that month of September waiting to be savoured, waiting to be understood. My heart still rang with the old, the tried, the safe and impregnable.

***

7

Chapter Seven

The laundry boy is sitting out in the kitchen. He will not go until he has his tip. His own tip had nothing to do with his bossman, the mullah in the mosque at the end of Gezira Island, who runs the laundry business between his calls to prayer. I know the mullah well for he it was who refused Abdul the right to forego the fast of Ramadan until, from the depths of my English language Koran, I discovered and pointed out to him those clauses by which one of the faithful, with legitimate reason, may be excused. As Abdul had diabetes and was using insulin, the necessity was understood.

"As milady is so well versed on the contents of the Holy book, her wishes are mine," the mullah told Abdul, adding sagaciously for the sake of his beautifully presented basket of returned laundry, "you are indeed a lucky man."

But usually it is the boy who works for the mullah who brings the basket and demands, with enormous melancholy eyes in a wizened face, an extra donation of piastres over and above what is expected by the mullah. For himself. He needs it.

"For a new gallabiyah," Abdul explains, "he has no other possibility, lady. He works, assisting the mullah, for his food."

Indeed, it was true, the boy's only garment was in tatters and his feet were bare.

"How old is the laundry boy?" I asked Abdul.

"He has survived sixteen Ramadans, Lady. I give him tea in the kitchen every week with bread, but not this month of Ramadan."

So, for four weeks he will not have had tea and bread at my expense, just his piastres. Suddenly I feel mean and overfed, and over clothed in my thin summer dress.

"Give him five piastres and that brown pullover of my husband's that waits in my mending basket."

We had struggled through the great depression, Jimmy and I, but he will never miss the sweater.

***

So, I passed my birthday. I had wept for Greta and mourned in my heart for Charles but the summer was not yet finished with me. There was still this other thing to happen before Indian summer.

I heard the end of the conversation as I came in from the street after school. Dark had already fallen and the last rains of autumn were as bitterly cold as sleet. My hands in wet gloves were aching yet you could tell outside that the stinging wind would cease and rest a while before it converted the icy rain into falling snow. It was only early October. My Auntie Meg was sitting at our kitchen table, her back to me as I came in. Her voice rose above the warm haze of the kitchen.

"Right over that cliff" she was saying. "I know the place exactly, where the road has been cut out of the cliff face. The driver couldn't have been able to see at all on a night like last night. The first storm in the season is always the worst."

"Maybe the boy had no light on his bicycle."

"Well, it was only five o'clock the paper says."

I stood in the doorway automatically pushing it closed behind me. Mother rose at once and came towards me.

"Heavens, you must be cold, Kit."

I began to wring my hands in the wet gloves.

"My hands" I said, "my hands ache."

"Put them under the cold-water tap."

Then Davy said, "Did the paper say what the boy's name was Auntie Meg?"

"Rupert Thoms" I said straight and clear into the room.

They all turned and looked at me. A blur of faces in a warm room. I began to shake and tears poured silently down my cheeks. My mother put her arms around me but I knew she was staring in horror at Auntie Meg over my head.

"Gee" Davy said. "I remember him. Gee."

Auntie Meg rose from her chair, took charge of us all, even my mother.

"She's frozen stiff. Put her beside the stove and give her an aspirin and a drink. I'll rub her hands." she said to mother and then she added too quickly., 'The paper says Robert Thoms, Kit. It could be another."

Donald lifted a pale and frightened face from the paper he had seized when Auntie Meg had put me in her chair. His young breaking schoolboy voice boomed out at first like a man's and then cracked to end up like a little boy's.

"No, it's a mistake in the paper. It says Robert but that is Rupert's father's name. And he only had two little sisters. It's him. It's Rupert. I know it's Rupert. They didn't come back to town this year. They were keeping the store open. They were going to get a post office. He told me. Rupert told me." He stopped, his mouth open with excitement and awe, then he ended limply, "Gee, I bet they sell the shop now. Gee do you think they will?"

"Time will tell," said Auntie Meg.

I put my face into my hands and began to sob. My mother took a towel to rub dry wisps of wet hair that had escaped my beret.

Auntie Meg said, "If you ask me she's got a chill. She's shivering. She better get into bed right away. I'd say."

From above my head mother's voice spoke harshly.

"Davy, get into the bathroom and start running the bath."
Davy complained. "I wanna read the paper - Don, gimme the paper, I want to   look too. I know that boy. I do too."
Donald said "No, don't you dare touch it."
"Davy do as I say" There was no mistaking the tone of mother's voice. Davy went.
"Donald, close the door after the boy" Mother said, "and give me the paper. We'll hear no more about it."
Donald began to answer. "Do you think?" he began.
"Donald, get to your homework and give me that paper. Do your work, there's a good boy and you can talk to your father after dinner."

A wail burst from me - "Then I'll be in bed."
"What's the matter? You never liked him" Donald said.

His voice was all deep and soft like a man's yet somehow concerned, almost kind. He threw the paper onto the table and my hand itched to pick it up. But I could not. I knew I would never read that paper. By the morning it would be gone to make the breakfast fire, its contents having been re-read, discussed and consumed by every member of the family but me. In this I was alone, isolated - different.

Inside of me a small voice said clearly. "But you do not need the paper. You knew all that was in it before."
I should have asked urgently, "And who are you?"

But I let the chance go by. Instead a sense of relief swept over me. I was suddenly glad to be avoiding the discussion, glad to be having a hot bath, a warm bed and my supper brought up to me. It crossed my mind that I would read one of my favourite poems and think about sad things until I slept. I had an excuse to do that. I felt almost grateful. I was so often ashamed of the time I spent being sad because of a poem, because of a symphony. Tonight I could be sad because of the boy Rupert. But not with fresh shock like poor Donald. Because I had always been sad about Rupert. Before it had been such puzzled sadness. I had not been able to recognise or even to know it was sadness at all. Now I knew why I had been sad about Rupert. For him I had only an honest sadness. The puzzled sadness, the wondering would be for my family from whom I was cut off on this night. Why had I known what they could not?"

Unexpectedly it was Donald who brought up my dinner on a tray. I was surprised that it was him, especially this Donald, a boy who said to me with a quiet deep voice I scarcely recognised as he put down the tray:

"I'm sorry for saying you didn't like Rupert, Kit. I guess it wasn't that you didn't like him."

"No, it wasn't that."

"When I went to do my homework I was thinking about Rupert and I remembered Ma saying that it wasn't that you didn't like Rupert, it was that you just didn't like me going around with him. I asked her why and she said, 'Girls are funny sometimes about things like that'. Gee, Kit I didn't know before, but Rupert getting killed like that I got to thinking."

I didn't know what to say. For the first time in my life I was embarrassed with my brother.

"Yeah, I got to thinking that maybe if I had got to be such good friends with Rupert I might have even been asked for this weekend or something and been with him."

"Oh, Don don't say that."

"Well, I would have fought hard to go if he'd asked me. I liked him a lot."

"I know. I'm awfully sorry Don."

"I never knew anybody who was killed before."

Donald caught his breath and made for the door. I heard him go downstairs heavily two at a time Donald in his turn was now fourteen and much too old to cry.

***

Summer does not end with the first snap of cold in a blast of frosty rain. Winter does not descend in force until the soft alluring seduction of golden weather called Indian summer, which harbours

Thanksgiving and allows a last mellow appreciation of warmth irretrievably past.

My recollection may be less than exact but I think it was the death of Rupert Thoms that made Auntie Meg suggest I go instead of her to visit Charles and Pat for Thanksgiving weekend. She feared my unmentionable intuition concerning Rupert had made one disaster too many to bear for one season. She hoped to keep alive, as a balance, something she knew existed in my relationship with Charles.

"I'd rather you go," she said to me. To Mother, who was sceptical to the point of refusal she added, "You know Jean, if I could afford it I'd go along with Kit, but I'd be bound to go again, for Charles is my son and I'm not abashed by this marriage, sudden and all that it was. I'm just thinking it would be nice for Charles and Pat if Kit is the first from the family to pay them a visit.

"Kit has not been invited, Meg," Mother said abruptly.
"Well, it's better, no doubt, to do away with such ceremony."
"I'm not so sure," Mother said. "If Kit was older perhaps."
"Oh Mother" I put in, "how old would I have to be, for goodness sakes, if that's your only reason."
"You want to go then, I take it?"
"Oh yes, Mother, I'd love to. Charles asked me to visit him on Vancouver Island if he got this job. Long before he was married he told me the forest places were so beautiful that I would love them."
"He thinks so, I daresay" Mother countered, irony coming through distinctly, "but the girl he married is decidedly a city type. I have my doubts how happy she'll be in such an isolated place. I'm not wanting to hurt your feelings Meg, but I'm entitled to my own. There was scarcely a Sunday last summer when Charles was not wanting Kit's company for one of his tramps. I saw no sign of Pat in my camp, the

view I had of her was in another group. The least I should have had was a letter from Charles. I'll not have Kit made use of."

Shocked speechless, I watched Auntie Meg purse her lips.

"You were not hurt more than I, Jean. I've admitted that I cannot understand why Charles took such an out of the way school and decided to get himself married in Bellingham. Pat's parents were angered past speech, so I know it was not a financial matter. But I know Charles, Jean, and he is capable of wanting to be married in a wigwam just to avoid the fuss!"

"Well," Mother interjected, "according to the remarks from the rest of the family such fuss is bread and butter to the girl he married."

"Can you not see Jean, that I have to allow them their reasons. Charles was not of an easy disposition. What's in his heart is rare enough to see. I'm hoping it will be right for him now. The romance may not have been easy for the girl but now she's in our family I'm hoping we'll all give her the benefit of doubt."

There was a minute during which Mother digested this challenge aimed at her Christian charity with all the persuasion of a sister's beloved will. She answered testily.

"I'm willing to do just that. I'll abide by your wishes Meg. But I'm the one to say if such a journey is right for Kit to take at the moment."

"No Jean, you know I'm the first to admit your wisdom with your own, but like the rest of us you're stubborn at times, not seeing what's in front of your face. There's no doubt at all that Kit's the best one to break the ice with Charles."

"There's no need to be breaking ice at all, Meg, as I see it. If Charles wanted Kit to come, to come for such a purpose, he would write and say so. It was you he wrote to, his mother, which was right."

Quickly I interposed "He never writes to me Mother, but I know it's alright because he sent me the books for Christmas."

"Humph" my mother snapped, "I'll thank you to keep out of this Kit. Filling your head with poetry is not the subject I'm discussing with Meg. A fine slew of literature you have from Charles that he might have been wiser to give to his wife, who is no reader I'm told, whereas you ruin your eyes as it is, well into the middle of the night."

"Which is just what I mean" Auntie Meg put in. "For Charles is the same."

"I doubt very much he still will be." Mother commented dryly.

"Why ever not?" I asked brightly. "Now he's married, I suppose Pat will read in bed too."

They regarded me strangely for a moment before they made the fatal mistake of looking from me to one another. Auntie Meg laughed first and defeated my mother to whom the appeal of a joke with her sister was irresistible. Mother's mouth twitched and her eyes flashed between horror at Auntie Meg and consternation that she herself should be so unexpectedly affected. She turned on her heel and flew hurriedly from the room, her shoulders heaving. Seeing Auntie Meg giggling helplessly, I felt an impulsive stupid grin spread over my face, not in appreciation of the joke which I did not understand but because Auntie Meg was infectiously funny with the colour of her face rising from pink to beet red, her eyes watering and her hands fluttering helplessly in front of her face.

"Oh dear me" she gasped convulsively. "Oh dear, dear me."

"Well, I can't think of anything nicer than reading in bed" I remarked affably.

"Oh don't, don't" Auntie Meg shrieked "Oh bless my soul, dear me." And before my startled eyes she hurried after my mother.

I sat down stupefied, to the accompaniment of a renewed outburst of merriment from the bedroom. Well, I thought sitting there, this is something new. They were fighting about me and now they're laughing. Laughing at me, goodness knows why. No, that's not it - laughing at Charles and Pat. Laughing at Charles and Pat reading in bed. No, not that either, laughing at me for thinking Charles and Pat would read in bed. Well really, acting like Wilfred and my other grown-up cousins. My Mother and my favourite Aunt laughing at the sort of joke that makes Wilfred so popular and that I am never supposed to hear. Suddenly, I was reminded of Harriet and filled with a superior and condescending disgust. Would I never come to the end of finding out about people. How disillusioning it was and how tantalising to be deprived and protected at the same time. Surely, but by the time one was sixteen it shouldn't be necessary to go on learning much longer from watching the scenes unfold. Surely it would soon be possible, even for the likes of me, to take a seat on the stage with the others. Did they think they still had secrets? After Harriet, after Greta and Tony Johns, after my association with Charles all summer! Because I withdrew myself, did they think I didn't know the facts of life. How simple I must appear, how incredibly naive.

I shrugged my shoulders and sighed. Like a flash the idea came to me that I could easily do away with the subterfuge and force the issue. I merely had to walk into our kitchen, announce that I knew people made love in bed and on the beach too for that matter and demand an explanation of the joke insofar as I couldn't see what reading at night, in an isolated logging town, devoid of any other entertainment, had to do with it. I played with the thought until the very enormity of it startled me to a new form of indignation which divorced itself from resentment. Was it likely that adult jokes were not secrets at all but umbrellas to cover embarrassment?

Mother and Auntie Meg were embarrassed about Charles and Pat! It was from embarrassment that Mother was trying to protect me and Auntie Meg was putting up an umbrella for Charles and Pat. Their embarrassment had overcome them, caught them out, and dissolved them into pathetic tears of laughter because neither of them could think of any but the sexual attraction between Charles and Pat. All their individual reasoning and painstaking explanation had come to this calamitous conclusion which they refused to admit even to themselves.

This was how it began, Indian summer, russet brown and withered scarlet under the lemon-tinted stillness of an autumn sky. Auntie Meg wired Charles and the reply came without delay.

"WILL MEET TRAIN FROM NANAIMO, ARRIVING HERE 4.30 - PAT"

For most of the trip across the Sound I stood outside on the deck, my salt-stung face turned seaward and the wind raising my hair straight up from my head. The sea rolled drunkenly beneath the steamer, sun-struck under a yellowing blue sky. The mountains behind me on the vanishing shore glowed purple as the maturing grape. I was sixteen years old with the ocean beneath me, foaming and sprawling in grandeur; a receiver of imperceptible treasures, in a profusion of miraculous variety. Inward moving, contrary winds wanton with icy whispering deprived me of no part of the glory of promise reflected in the sea. Imperturbably sanguine, I rode the waves, a figurehead of my own imagination I, Kit Marshall, the chosen one of all the family to visit Charles; my relationship with him acknowledged, my mission no less than to discover and recollect the beauty of his new surroundings and the new happiness of his countenance.

When I got off the train dark was already shadowing the sun in the sky and the air tingled with the threat of frost. I turned up the collar of my trench coat and wriggled my toes inside my flat Oxfords. Pat was on the station huddled in a sealskin coat that reached almost to her ankles. Her feet in patent-leather pumps supplied a ludicrous balance for her head was wound tight in a scarf turban.

"It's freezing cold isn't it" she said. "Come on. We'll get straight home for a cup of coffee. I can't stand cold weather."

"Have you been waiting long?" I said perturbed. "Is it far to the house?"

"Far enough. We have to walk. There's no other transport."

The sky was turning to orange as we started up a long boardwalk leading away from the town.

"What a wonderful sunset" I said.

"It will be gone in a minute. That hill blocks it out."

"Oh, is that the school?"

"Yes, rustic isn't it?" Because of the holiday Monday, Charles let the inmates out at noon today. He's working the extra half day at the mill on his weekend."

"Oh, does Charles work at the mill too? Whatever for?"

"The usual reason of course, the pay's good. The manager's trying to get out all the timber he can before the road becomes impassable."

"And Charles is helping him?"

Pat laughed inside the collar of her coat. I could scarcely see her face.

"Oh yes, Charles and a Russian and an Englishman who all appear to need extra cash as well as each other's company."

"Mother sent her love."

"Oh thanks. Don't walk so fast, I can't."

"Oh, I'm terribly sorry. You're very tiny aren't you, I was forgetting."

"I'm as tall as you are" she said, "only I'm tired and cold and all your family walk too fast. Charles is the worst of the lot."

We slowed to a snail's pace and I had a sudden urge to take her arm. She seemed so out of place on the boardwalk, so ill-fitted to exist in a mill-town surrounded by forests.

"Why on earth did you let Charles come here?" I blurted out. "He's a very good schoolteacher. He could have got a city school."

She stopped in her tracks and faced me.

"Because I'm having a baby - didn't you all guess?"

She must have seen the complete astonishment on my face, for she started walking again before I could find words to speak.

"There's the house" she remarked, "thank goodness."

The path in from the road was stony and rough, passing through an old once-loved garden of a tangle of shrubs and trees turned autumn red and gold that led to a wooden veranda that creaked a little under our feet. Inside the house it was cozy enough and warm with a huge fire in a stone fireplace and another of coal in the kitchen range. One bedroom opened from the living room and another from the kitchen. Pat opened the door off the kitchen and invited me to put down my bag.

"It's not much of a bedroom, you'll see, but all there is," she said. "Make yourself at home while I get coffee."

There was a bed in the room in front of the window, a table beside it and a chair. The remaining space was filled with a great heap of suitcases, hat boxes, crates and even parcels hastily wrapped. I took off my trench coat and laid it on the bed. They hadn't known, my mother and Auntie Meg. They hadn't suspected a baby. If they had, they would certainly have never let me come. Poor Pat, I thought embarrassment was resting on her too. When Charles came home I told myself everything would be alright. He would fill the house with welcome and laughter and Pat would be happy again and I would be glad for them both.

But Charles didn't know I was coming. When Pat heard his step on the veranda, she opened the front door and said "Surprise", just the one sharp word so that it echoed round the room like the agitated wings of a trapped bird.

"My God" Charles said, "Kit. What on earth are you doing here?"
"She's paying us a visit for the weekend, of course. What do you think? Aren't you pleased?"

Charles recovered himself slowly, stiffly in a series of mundane gestures that hid the depth of his fury. He bent to kiss Pat on the forehead and then he brushed my cheek with the cold breath of ice.

"How nice" he said, "we'll have a cheap sherry shall we, to celebrate such an overwhelming surprise."

He brought long thin glasses from a fireplace shelf and poured into them, on the edge of the dining-table, a carefully judged equal measure of sherry.

"Sure it won't upset your meal?" he asked Pat, his voice sarcastically solicitous and smooth as a tiger's purr.

"Not at all" Pat said and sat down like a princess waiting to be served.

She balanced her glass daintily in small thin fingers Her lips smiled as she turned her face up and looked at Charles, but not with her eyes which were half-closed and veiled beneath her lashes. Charles did not look at me when he gave me the sherry. He turned to pick up his own glass with a quick sweep of his arm and raised it to the level of his face.

"A toast," he said. "Welcome Kit. Welcome to the woods, to the wilds, to the nether regions, to the decrepit home of a country school-teacher."

"Dear me," Pat said. "We are modest all of a sudden."

The dry bitter drink nearly choked me and I drank it in sudden sips as if it were hemlock. I had little experience, which Charles knew well enough, for sherry was not served before meals in our house. I managed the meal that followed in less obvious carefully measured gulps.

"If you don't eat more than Kit, you'll waste away" Charles said. Yet there was more on my plate than on Pat's.

"I'm not much of a cook" Pat said. "She may not like the food, Charles."

I was forced by politeness to offer an excuse.

"It's very good, but I have a weakness for candy and I ate a lot on the train."

"It's very bad for a young girl's figure – candy," Pat remarked.

"Whereas one always hopes it has a sweetening effect on older women" Charles said.

They smiled at each other, Pat's eyes lazy and deep with hidden meaning and the eyes of Charles half-closed, flashing fire. They did not want me. It was very apparent that they didn't want me. I didn't mind so much about Pat, I expected nothing from her except perhaps an effort towards friendship for Charles' sake, a sign that she loved him and would therefore welcome communication with his people. But this married Charles was more than I could comprehend, keeping me at a stranger's distance, isolated without a smile or a clue to let me know which was his wit and which his irony, while phrases flowed from his tongue like honeyed caresses for Pat. With anyone else I would have taken refuge in my youthfulness, retiring without obligation to the simpler world of my own size and status. But with Charles it had never been like that, I had been included, not excluded, accepted, never rejected. And this night of all nights, I was strung to high tension, acutely perceptive, excited and almost frightened. I was like an unavoidable shadow in the room, a black smudge between the lamp and the book. I felt my presence resented, yet how could I remove myself? I longed for home but its comfort was far away. I thought of the bed in the room off the kitchen. Surely I could at least go there. Did they want to go to bed? Was it like Mother had intimated? Did they? I watched hopefully. Even by the time dinner was finished any escape would have been worthy, any exit palatable.

They gave me no chance of escape, nor any sign. I was tossed relentlessly between their ambits of conversation. A question about home for Charles and Pat drew him back into her orbit like a magnet. A condescension from Pat and the voice of Charles, sticky again with subtle innuendo, forced her withdrawal from me. They neither moved from the room nor allowed my escape. We sat, all three of us by the fire, until at last in sheer unadulterated desperation I cried out:

"I'm sorry but if I don't go to bed now, I'll fall asleep where I'm sitting."

"Oh, you poor child" Pat said, "One forgets how young you are. Fancy us not noticing. And Charles, fancy you not noticing dear. Why it's eleven o'clock and usually you're bored to distraction by nine. We have so little company you know, Kit."

They both took me to my room. Charles put a lamp by my bed, his eyes turned away from me towards the bags and boxes. Pat turned down the bed and I felt I made a crowd even in that small, restricted space devoted to my comfort. Charles built up the stove in the kitchen to keep me warm during the night and Pat insisted suddenly that I have her hot-water bottle in case my feet were cold.

"After all, I don't really need one do I Charles?" You'll get it to save me running to our room, won't you dear?"

Less than a moment after he went his voice came back to where we stood,

"Pat, come here will you, I can't find it, strange as it may seem."

Both of them came back with it. Charles filled it much too full and fat from the hot water in the kettle. Pat took it from him and put it in my bed carefully, exactly where my feet would be.

"Goodnight Charles,"

I caught his eyes on my face for the first time, full of a strange, unexpected light that might have been pity and could have been tears. Or else could have been simply the full flicker of the little kerosene lamp.

"Goodnight Kit."

"Goodnight Pat."

"Goodnight. Now whatever you do, don't get up in the morning. Charles goes to the mill at a disgustingly early hour. He just stokes up and goes. I'll call you for breakfast when it's ready. You're to have a nice rest this weekend."

I don't know what made me speak at that moment. Some compulsion forced me, some unpremeditated demon of speech unsubdued in my heart.

"Rupert Thoms was killed Charles. He went over that cliff between the store and the beach."

He started, and his mouth dropped open slightly, then closed again into a straight hard line.

"Forget it," he said, "and have a good sleep."

They closed my bedroom door and the kitchen door and then the door that led from the living room into the other bedroom. Before I blew it out, the lamp flickered grotesque shadows on the walls and on the ceiling. In the bed I held the silly bulged hot water bag in my arms. What a cold room it was I lay in, remote and unloving. Some small night creature, a rodent or a bird scampered on the roof and a shiver ran through me like a knife. Tears squeezed out the corners of my eyes and ran down the sides of my cheeks to the pillow as I lay on my back unheeding. Never in all my life had I been so lonely.

Through all the closed doors the voice of Charles and Pat penetrated my consciousness, rising and falling like the distant swell of the sea. The sound of them was like the swish of a rope hitting the face of a drowning man. They were arguing, otherwise I would not hear them. The sound was an explanation. Charles was angry, he had been angry all evening, controlling his fury, disguising it in words I would not understand. I should not have come. Charles had wanted Auntie Meg and because she had sent me instead, would not ask her again. He would want none of us now. Unless I could prove to him that our motives were blind, he would cut himself off from us all. Remorse and responsibility replaced my utter loneliness. Anger in Charles was a personal thing that held no violence and somehow, dreadful as it was, it was better than loneliness and the sound of violent argument, reassuring after black silence. If only he would argue with Pat a little longer, I could sleep.

Pat's dressing-gown was black satin, piped with white, austere as a man's dress suit. But the back, when she turned, was startling with an embroidered lily that swooped up from the hem to open in scarlet glory above the hipline.

"Charles left this book for you to read."
"I thought I'd like to walk up to that hill this morning."
"Go when you've finished breakfast then, seeing you're dressed. It looks like rain."

I fingered the book in astonishment, an old, battered copy probably left by previous tenants in the house of 'Anne of Avonlea'. I had just finished Tolstoy's, 'Anna Karenina'. Charles was playing a school-teacher's game of literature suitable to the age of the pupil.

"I'll wash up for you and then go" I said.
"Suit yourself. But put something on your head. I don't want you to go back with a cold. It's bound to rain."

Under my trench coat I wore a blue scarf. On a sudden impulse in front of the kitchen mirror I whipped it off before I went out and put my hair into it, sweeping the scarf up from the back of my neck, around my face and tucked it in, turban fashion. My reflection sur-prised me; my cheekbones stood out on the oval of my face and my eyes looked enormous and particularly blue. Lobelia blue, my father always said. Pat was dressing so I walked out the door and through the town and back again to skirt the fringe of the gaunt, dark, cloud-threatened hill.

Sitting in the house that Saturday afternoon while the rain beat upon the roof and ran in rivulets down the window, I felt as detached in spirit as I had been walking alone on the edge of the hill. At home I was permanently involved because one member of the family was always concerned with another and through this with the house, the street and the city. There was no centre, only a constant communion of activity, which somehow included sitting, reading, even thinking. Yet here I suffered detachment speculatively as if I were a stranger be-longing outside as part of the tangled rain-swept garden, looking in the window unseen, posing to myself previously undefined, unstated questions.

There was no communion here but there was definitely a centre. Pat was the centre of everything in the house which was trimmed to suit her like a hedge. Yet I felt no pull of gravity. The very opposite was true for I seemed for the first time in my life to stand off and look because I could not feel. For two hours after lunch we had been sitting together in front of the blazing fire, Pat with the latest Vogue maga-zine on her knee while I thumbed through the book Charles had left me. Slowly I realised that I was studying Pat's physical person with in-tense preoccupation which she did not sense. She seemed to me beau-tiful like the glossy picture of a movie star is beautiful or a model or a nameless mannequin, yet I had arrived at the disconcerting conclu-sion that she had no one feature of outstanding distinction, fascina-tion or charm.

I had thought of her as petite in the French fashion, with dainty head and tiny hands and feet, but I discovered her to be merely compact and neat, complete, no part of her too large or small for the rest, nothing casual or unstrung, which was something else altogether. I stuck mentally on the word 'casual' realising part of my analysis must be wrong. There was something casual about her, what was it? After a little thought during which I turned the pages of the book without connecting the words, I stumbled on a phrase of conversation which gave me the clue. Pat's speech was casual, deliberately so, as if part of some plan.

Some plan? That was it. With Pat everything was premeditated. The idea was preposterous but it fitted. The sign of such a self-consuming egotism aroused in me not only wonder but an almost hypnotic fascination. How skilfully designed she was, her skin white against the outlined red lips which were allowed no change of colour for I knew that every hour or so they were renewed carefully in front of one of the many mirrors. Even in this back block of civilization, with only myself and Charles to witness, her eyelashes were heavy with mascara. Heavy eyebrows were skilfully pencilled to the same shiny blackness which distinguished the smooth cap of coiffure from which no hair escaped. She was dressed for Saturday afternoon alone with me in a beautifully cut black jersey suit with a red silk blouse and silk stockings. How strange, how utterly fantastic! She had made herself what she was, black and white and red, startling colours of contrast and line. Amazed at such a precocious revelation in myself, I spoke involuntarily,

"Do you like pink or blue for a dress Pat?"

She lifted her head only so far, having no interest in encouraging discussion, even of clothes, for my sake.

"I never wear weak colours" was her answer.
"Would you like me to make a cup of tea, now?"
"Alright if you want to."
"Will I use the tea set?"
"Of course, why not?"

The bizarre orange and black tea set, the wood table painted stark white, red leather chairs, black and yellow cushions.

"What will you have to eat, Pat?"
"Only tea, black thanks. I hate milk in tea."

I cut myself a thick slice of bread, spread it with butter and brown sugar, then carried it in with the tea.

"Good heavens, what's that you've got?"
"Bread and brown sugar."
"You'll never be a beauty on that diet."

A beauty - she had made herself a beauty and she knew it. A black and white beauty, drinking black tea from an orange cup. This was Charles' wife, the reason for such an extraordinary change in him, and because of whom he had made such an effort to distance himself from me. Charles was the moth that had fluttered too close to the black, white and red centre and could not escape. Charles loved Pat. Surely there was something I did not understand, some facet of personality that I had missed, some depth I was too young to fathom, some secret she shared with Charles besides the bearing of his child.

Like a young savage, I sank my teeth into the bread and wished for cinnamon to spice the brown sugar.

***

Dinner on Saturday night when Charles returned was swift and sickly sweet. Only I was not shocked any more, only impotent as they expected me to be, just a little girl slipping out as we went to a movie in the local hall. Pat had seen the show, not that it made any difference she said, she had always seen whatever they put on anyway and they had to do something special for me. Playing Charles' game with my own rules, I neglected to mention that I had also seen the film in case by such an admission I would have to endure another night in their disturbing company. The movie was no less special for me than a gift from heaven, but my mood being far from angelic I did not fail to notice that whereas the children spared a sideways glance of frank curiosity at the cousin of the teacher, the eyes of everyone else in the hall were centred on the teacher's wife, elegant in her fur coat, a tiger turban on her head, and a matching purse of immense proportions in her small hands. The smile she bestowed on the parents of Charles' pupils was ravishing and she shrugged her shoulders lovingly at Charles as she seated herself between the two of us just as the lights were about to go out. Not that I wanted to sit beside Charles. I knew I had forced myself into an untenable position through counting on an indefinable past intimacy with Charles that could no longer exist since his marriage. I didn't need it spelled out to me in unmistakable gestures by Pat and the forced levity of Charles. My heart hurt dully, with a worse ache than a forewarning of toothache deep down in the jawbone. Had it been possible I would have run away for I was ashamed that I had come, chagrined to have forced my presence where it was unwelcome.

When we came out of the hall, the sky was clear and the wood bathed in clear, crisp light of a full moon riding high beyond the black outline of the hill. The wet boardwalk smelled musty and sweet and the snap in the air cleared my head. I had my first real attack of self-justification. Why should I have been forced to indulge in a morbid examination of my motives in paying a beloved cousin a short visit. I was no eavesdropper on the kind of vicissitudes that fall on a married couple who expect a child before society approves. True, I had wanted to see Charles and make closer acquaintance with his wife, and truer still I had been conceited enough to have considered myself the chosen one for the mission but I hadn't anticipated such an extraordinary radical change in Charles so that his friendship to me could only be patronising, unequal and pointedly unbalanced.

Charles had been kind to me when it suited him. Now he was married it didn't suit him anymore because it didn't suit Pat to encourage his family. The sooner I left the better.

My thoughts were not discouraged by Pat's conversation on the slow walk home. She was talking about the mill manager's wife. Into a silence I asked:

"Was she there tonight?"

"Oh no," Pat said. "She only lives here for the summer. They keep a Chinese house-boy here and the manager goes to Victoria every weekend. They have a beautiful home there." I understood.

"She's mentioned a lot in the society columns of course, their children are at school in Victoria."

"The mill manager wasn't there either then?"

"No, nobody important was there, actually," Pat said.

"Except the schoolteacher, of course," I said ferociously.

"As a matter of fact," Charles said "Matt couldn't come, he's at the mill finishing up the accounts. He's going to Victoria on Monday."

"Oh" Pat said, "you didn't tell me."

"You didn't ask," Charles said.

"We didn't have much time at supper, did we dear?"

At that I walked on in disgust at myself for feeling bewildered again, unjustified in self-justification, strangely anxious and filled with some unreasonable fear that involved me unnecessarily in an adult situation. For I knew then that as surely as the moon shone, I had somehow forced Charles to cooperate with Pat in keeping me isolated from him, a non-participant in his activities, an intruder in the arrangements he was making for his future.

"Doesn't your house look beautiful?"

It rested tranquil under the moon, a house built with wide swinging eaves as a sanctuary against snow. In the moonlight the shingles shone through a filigree of trees, each branch a geometric design of black on silver, an embroidery against the sky.

"Beautiful" Pat laughed. "You astound us, Kit. The house is a wreck, almost falling about our ears."

"It's a mirage, I guess" I said, "the garden has grown now to what somebody hoped for when they planted the trees and shrubs when the house was new. Are you going to make the garden in the spring Charles?"

"No."

"You should. It's worth it."

"It's not worth it," Pat said, "even if we were going to stay. Nothing could ever be made of it. It's disgraceful for the teacher to be expected to live in it."

"I was glad," Charles said, "my predecessor lived in it."

"And died in it. He was here for twenty years."

"Then he must have planted the garden" I insisted.

"His wife did, they tell me. She was the gardener." Charles said.

"If that's a hint darling, it's wasted" Pat's voice was bored with the subject.

I ignored the hint.

"You could make it beautiful Charles. You're wonderful at gardens."

"What a dark horse I have married" Pat murmured. "A gardener now as well as a teacher." Then she spoke up. "We want a new garden Charles and I, a new house when we settle, don't we dear?"

"It takes years for trees to grow," I said. "We found that out when we built. Thank goodness there were a few trees on the land."

"I wouldn't want Charles to waste a minute of his time on this place" Pat said with finality. "I can't think of a bigger waste."

"You're right dear" Charles said and put his key in the lock without a further glance at the shrubs quivering in the moonlight.

But I wouldn't let it go. How persistent we are when we are young - scraping away at trivialities, blowing them into inflations that burst in our eager faces.

"Why you've got blue jays nesting in the trees, Charles. There must be at least three families of them. I was watching them this morning. In that fir outside my window there's woodpeckers and an owl."

Pat put her exotic purse on the table.

"I told Charles to get rid of that owl but he couldn't find it. It's like a ghost in the night. I hate it. So that's where it lives."

Panic stricken, my eyes flew to Charles but he didn't look at me. He stooped instead to criss-cross two pieces of bark on the embers in the fireplace.

Pat went on, "You know Kit, you surprise me. I expected that at your age I would have to dig out our local boys to meet you. Instead,

I find you prefer blue jays. It's just as well you're young for your age as Charles says. I would have been hard put to find suitable company for you in this backwood of a place and I don't suppose your mother would approve of you meeting lumberjacks."

Standing beside Charles as he knelt at the fireplace I handed him a piece of wood. He let me hold it in my hand for what seemed to me minutes before he took it from me without a word and placed it across the springing flame. I reached for another piece and held it toward him, ashamed that my hand was shaking. He spoke then but only to ask if I were cold. It was a way out I realised but even then I did not want to lie to Charles, not even to save my face.

"No" I said, "I wanted to help you, that's all." I couldn't add anything. I couldn't say the fire would warm up the room or make it friendly. I couldn't say I was already hot from embarrassment and shame.

"I'm cold," Charles growled, "chilled to the bone."

"I'll stir up the kitchen fire then, shall I?" I asked. "A hot drink might warm you."

"Oh do" Pat said, her voice metallic and bright, "I'd love a hot drink. The coffee wasn't much, was it? I only had one cup and it was nearly cold." She walked towards the bedroom peeling her coat from her with precision as if it were a second skin.

"Bring mine into the bedroom will you Charles. I'll get into bed. I'll leave the door open so the heat will come from the fireplace."

When the kettle boiled I made cocoa and carried two cups into the living room. Charles was sitting almost on top of the roaring fire which cast great moving shadows around the otherwise dark room. The lamp was very bright in the bedroom making the door an oblong of yellow light.

"Thanks" was all Charles said, "Where's yours? He didn't invite me to sit down nor did he move and all of him was in front of the fire as if carved in stone.

"I'll have mine in bed, I think" I said.

"Sensible child" Pat called out. "Do bring mine in Charles while it's hot. Good night Kit. See you in the morning."

"Goodnight Charles" I said.

He didn't answer. I turned and went back through the kitchen to the little room where something scratched on the window and the owl hooted.

On Sunday morning Charles took charge. I woke to the sizzle and smell of frying bacon and the pounding of a drumstick on my door.

"Come on, get dressed" Charles yelled. "It's a decent day so I'll take you down to see old Beaver-whiskers and his pals."

I didn't bother to refill my jug of washing water. The cold splash on my face tingled on my skin as I opened the door into the kitchen having dressed hurriedly in skirt and jumper.

"Is it far?" I asked, grinning at Charles.

"No, only a bit muddy," This turning his back to me as he broke eggs into the frying pan.

"Is Pat coming?"

"But of course" Pat said entering from the other door rugged up like a wool squirrel in ski clothes, black pants and a red angora jacked. "I haven't met this character Charles visits every Sunday morning. I wouldn't like him to think you were Mrs Gilbert." She seated herself at the table as Charles handed her a plate of bacon and eggs. "Looks good Charles. Do you think you might make the bed darling. It's rather a stretch these days."

My bed was made. The dishes would be my task. I made no other offer and seated myself greedily in front of my plate. The bacon was crisp under my teeth and the fried bread supported two perfectly cooked yellow and white eggs. It was the best meal since my arrival and I made the most of it. Pat did not eat fried bread which resulted in her plate being messy and difficult to wash.

The old-timer woodcutter who had the beaver dam at the junction of two streams running through his five acres, was waiting for Charles. He was an odd old chap with a little breakfast attached to his whiskers and a trace of whisky taken to sustain the occasion of anticipated conversation. He welcomed me with toothless enthusiasm as Charles assisted Pat over a log drawbridge beyond the shack that led upstream toward the beaver dam.

"Me beaver dam is me fortune, me girl, all that is left. Time was when I'd have taken a young 'un like yourself in me gig to the lake. Ain't the same now, though, at the last, nothin' but fancy games there now, ain't nobody serious - like fer fishin' 'cept in them high -powered engine boats, frightenin' fish away if ya ask me, it's all fun-fishin'. An' the road ain't through anymore, got to go round the long way by car. Me life's done now 'cept fer me beavers."

"Aw go on" Charles said catching up. "Matt Mathews takes you over by car to see Jim, and Alex is still a canoe fisherman. You're losing your memory, Beaver Whiskers."

The old man opened his gummy mouth and chuckled with mirth. Perhaps the beavers recognised his laughter for as we approached the dam three or four of them sat up in the water and watched, their two buckteeth giving them a stupid Peter Rabbit expression that belied the shared industry of their ceaseless activity. When we came close they ducked beneath the logs and the old man whistled at them through his two fingers as if they were dogs.

"Come on out youse" he called. "Got ladies to see youse. Ain't youse the limit actin' shy."

"Jim brought Eloise and the baby to see them, he was telling me" Charles said as we waited.

"She loved 'em she did" the old man replied proudly. "Sure did love 'em, fer a foreigner-like. They come out fer her too."

"Eloise" I said. "What a pretty name. Are Jim and Eloise friends of yours?"

"They live at the Lake," Charles said. "Eloise is French."

"Building their own house if you please," Pat remarked laconically. "Log by log, you should see it. I don't know how she stands it."

"It's not finished yet," Charles said.

"But a person like Jim Thompson, a university graduate. Alex I can understand but not Jim Thompson."

"It's his own" Charles spoke sharply then. His own land and his own house, made with his own hands, plus Eloise' of course."

"Is she nice?" I enquired. "Eloise, I mean?"

"I've only been over once," Pat answered. "She only speaks French which I don't understand"

"She was born in Paris" Charles said and abruptly changed the subject. "Do you think your beavers are going to turn us down, Whiskers?"

"Nope" the old man said, "They'll be out again. Like kids aint they? Actin' up. Alex come yesterday."

"Oh, I didn't see him. He didn't work.
"Nope, huntin' agin."

"Who's Alex?"

"A Russian hunting and fishing type who haunts these strange parts," Pat said. "Rather a fascinating man actually."

"You may as well look at the lodge Kit" Charles said, "if you're interested."

"Oh yes. Mr Whiskers have the beavers always been here? Were they here when you came?"

"No Sirree, they weren't no sign of 'em. There was jus' this here timber and one big rock dead centre that stream. They come one night and felled one of them thar poplars and landed it in the water. When I first seen 'em they was strippin' off the branches. Took even the bark off they did, gnawin' an' chewin'. I never let 'em see me lookin' but I wuz lookin' alright, watched 'em putting that poplar across the stream above that big rock. They sure worked them fellers, gettin' it straight. Then they begun building up branches an' stuff up stream there, mud an' rocks an' bark an' even bulrushes, fixin' it all the way they wanted to dam my water up. I sure wuz pleased, didn't need so much water did I, no sirree. I let em dam my stream cheeky little fellers, nearly flooded thimselfes out too, they did, had to fix places on both shore sides to let the water through. After they got it all fixed just right they started fixin' up houses for thimselfes and protectin' thimselfes with more dams downstream. Bin there ever since, me beavers, gittin' tamer an' tamer."

I walked upstream past the dam and peered at the dome of the lodge. I knew how beavers cut logs with their teeth, criss-cross branches into a raft, sink it with mud and stones, sink another raft and then another until a dry island rises to water level mid-stream. Finally they built the apartment I could see above water level, completely snug, clean and dry, bitten out of the boughs and branches and lined with evergreen needles with a door leading to the basement of this dwelling at water-level from which escape channels lead out to the water and the banks of the stream. The whole lodge was as ingenious as a medieval fort and all constructed by animals never more than three and a half feet long, weighing, as Charles said, one third of my own weight.

Standing on a small shore hillock above the beaver lodge, looking downstream past the pool and the dams I saw how the stream dwindled into an open water space of fern and rushes that might have been a sanctuary for birds. The old man's path led down through a beaver's larder of willow, birch and poplar, light against the dark of spruce and cedar. I decided to go down to the sweet air of the ferns, away from the pungent odour of sour water behind the main dam, for it was the end of summer and nearly time for swift snow water to purify the stream.

Charles, Pat and Beaver Whiskers were still standing where I had left them. The beavers had come out again above the main dam, their black noses furry above the water scenting no danger in the smell of man as they swam beneath aspen and birch branches longer than themselves, which they were dragging to underwater winter storage.

The old man was talking to Pat.

"An' I knew Matt long before he met her. She ain't been here but Matt's brought his little girlie more'n once. She's purty too, sumf'n like this Miss Kit, smells things round the forest like, but his missus, there's a beauty for youse, seen her only once, down here in the mill house, Matt givin' me a meal. Meals for any old trout comin' by - that's Matt."

"It's pretty smelly above the dam. I'm off downstream to pick ferns" I said. "What a perfect place for wild geese, Charles"

"Last mallard only left a week or so ago" the old man called after me. Then I heard Pat's voice asking him some question. I suppose it concerned the manager called Matt again and his wife who lived in Victoria.

Leaving Pat corralled in the reminiscences of the old man, Charles walked downstream to stand above me on the other side of the creek.

"Don't fall in," he said. "Whatever you do, don't fall in. It's deeper than you think."

It was the first time since my arrival that I had been alone with him. My head bent above the ferns I spoke breathlessly in case this should be my only chance.

"I didn't know about the baby, Charles. I wanted to come because you asked me last summer. Pat thinks the family knows but they don't and I won't say anything if you and Pat want to tell people later."
"What did Pat tell you when you first arrived, Kit?"
"Just that - well," I floundered for words, my hand trembling among the ferns, but Charles did not help me so I had to go on, "just that you came to this school because of the baby coming."
"I see" Charles said. "Thanks."

I stumbled on, my words like sweat gathering in drops to fall from my lips.

"It doesn't matter Charles. Don't let it matter. I knew you were in love with Pat. You're married. It will be wonderful to have a baby."

Charles drew a deep breath and let it out again slowly between his teeth.

"What else did she - did Pat tell you, since you've been here?"
"Nothing except that of course she's hoping to go back to the city to live. I suppose you'll come back home to teach as soon as you can get a school in town, won't you Charles?"

"I will never come back home to teach. I haven't told Pat yet. I can't until after the baby."

"It wouldn't be fair?"

"No, strangely enough, it wouldn't be fair."

"I don't suppose it's easy having a baby in the country if you're a city girl."

"She's going to Victoria at the end of the month. She'll stay in a rest home there until the baby arrives."

"Until the baby arrives - but that will be…" I could have choked myself.

"Expensive." This time Charles finished for me. "Yes, it will be. She wants it that way. Since she saw the doctors she's nervous, in case anything goes wrong."

"Why doesn't she go home then - to her mother in Vancouver?"

"She doesn't want to."

"Perhaps it is better Charles, if you can manage. She can stay as long as she likes. She'll want to come back as soon as she can. You'll see. It will be wonderful for you Charles, watching the baby grow."

But I felt empty, a vacuity all by myself, a spot in a circle hemmed in by a ring of unknown complexities which I sensed but with which I was inadequately fitted to cope. I felt like a child clutching in vain at the garments of absorbed adults talking in secret whispers. I remembered suddenly being in exactly that position in our living room after what I knew later had been a funeral. Charles had given warning but still I had fallen in and the water was very deep indeed.

Then Charles said:

"How's Jimmy - Jimmy Millar, I mean?"

"OK. I guess. I haven't seen him lately. He sent me a card for my birthday."

"How's the poetry? Did you bring some with you?"

"One or two verses. I thought I might work on them on the boat."
"Give me a copy before you go back."
"But you're going to the Mill tomorrow. I'm leaving at noon."
"You've got tonight, haven't you?"

He saw me loop up towards Pat and the old man who had started to walk towards us down stream on his side of the dam. I stopped to gather up my armful of ferns.

"They just came into my head Charles. I haven't looked at them since."
"All the better" he said and straddled the stream. "It's narrow here, let me help you across. "He put out his hand but I leapt past him lightly and landed with my ferns a little beyond where he stood.
"Give me the poems as they are" he demanded again but I made no promise.
"And what world shaping subject engrosses you two" Pat was ahead of the old man bored with renewed talk of beavers.

I looked at Charles and said nothing. Let him tell her about the poetry if he felt he must. I could not.

"A boy called Jimmy Millar" Charles said. "He's interested in Kit."
"Oh" Pat said in mock surprise. "I didn't know Kit had a boyfriend."
"You must have had your eyes shut." Charles said. "He hung around all last summer."

He added, I thought mockingly:

"Everywhere Kit was, we tripped over Jimmy Millar."
"How devastating for you," Pat said. "I was under the impression that all the eligible young men hung around blond cousin Greta."

"Which shows how wrong one can be," Charles said. "You missed Jimmy Millar who has more of the qualities needed for potential success than anybody who has hit our beach for years."

"Imagine that" Pat said. "Then Kit is to be congratulated on her choice."

The blood rushed to my face and I stammered:

"But I…"

"Don't be modest Kit" Charles interrupted roughly. "You know perfectly well you were his main reason for coming to the beach."

"And you Charles. He said he learned so much from you. He thought you were wonderful."

"What a mutual admiration society you cousins are," Pat said.

The manager of the mill called round less than an hour after our return from the Beaver Dam, on his way to his house from the mill. We were stacking the lunch dishes. When he knocked on the door Charles and Pat left the kitchen to welcome him into the living room. I heard Charles ask him if he had already had lunch and his large booming voice replied affirmatively. Pat offered him a drink and closed the kitchen door for I had started to wash the dishes with a clatter

.

"Come on in Kit" Charles called out and I called back too quickly, "Just a minute."

I did not want to go into the living room but was without excuse. The coffee pot still bubbled. Nervously I added more coffee, more water from the kettle and pushed it forward to the hot part of the stove. I took down the tray, laid out four coffee cups, cream and sugar, and a small bowl of biscuits. Charles, his face irritable and almost angry, put his head in the kitchen door.

"Aren't you coming Kit?" he demanded.

"I thought your visitor might like coffee" I said hastily, indicating the tray.

"Good girl," he said. His voice sounded relieved as he went back again leaving the door swinging wide.

I let the coffee bubble for a moment before I filled the cups and went into the living room with the tray held in front of me like a shield. I might have been the Gilbert's maid. Pat was balanced daintily on the edge of the couch and beside her a huge man sat uncomfortably, like a St. Bernard beside a Pekinese. He rose up when I came in.

"Just what I needed," he announced in his loud voice. "So you're the girl I came to see."

Charles took the tray from me and put it on the table.

"Cream and sugar Pat?" he said.

"No thank you dear. I won't have any more coffee just now, if you don't mind. I have to be careful." Her tones were honeyed.

"Of course," the big man said "so I'll have two. I can do with them."

"There's a whole pot full on the stove" I said.

"Two sugars Charles" he said and with the cup in his hand turned to me.

"I came to see you, young lady," he repeated.

"Did you?" I said uncomfortably.

"Yeah, Charles said you'd dropped in and were leaving tomorrow noon. I thought that if you could be ready by eight in the morning I'd pick you up with Charles and show you over the mill. Then I'll sit you in my office while I sign a few letters. Charles can have a quick cup of coffee with us at eleven and I'll drive you to the boat myself. I've got to go out to the port anyway. What about it?"

I felt like an exhausted swimmer hauled prematurely out of the race to be wrapped in a rug and warmed by the engine of an unexpected vessel.

"Oh, thank you, that would be wonderful." I stammered. I'd love to see the mill. I love mills."

"Alright with you Mrs Gilbert?" The big man turned to Pat.

"Oh certainly" Pat said. I could detect nothing from the tone of her voice.

"My little girl loves the mill" the manager said.

"The sawdust smells so sweet" I said.

"Well, what do you know! My little girl thinks that too."

So it was that I escaped first thing in the morning, squeezed on the front seat of a new Hupmobile between Charles in his working clothes and the wide girth of Matt Matthews. The dust-filmed road was colour splashed on either side with the massed orange red of sumac, yellow gold poplars and stick slender birch. A blue-jay, brilliant as sapphire dived across the windscreen. Chipmunks on nutty expeditions scurried as we passed. Parallel to the car a black bear loped along a path he was following in the bracken.

Charles and his friend made much of my company, encouraging with obvious intent my naturally uninhibited comment on a forest setting they loved. I responded to their banter but my heart ached fully like a forewarning. I was ashamed to have come to be rescued like this, chagrined to have forced my presence where it could not be welcome. Never would I visit this place again, I vowed, never in all my life.

We reached the junction of the road and drove from dust to bitumen.

"Now" Matt announced, you will see forest worth looking at and views as magnificent as any to be found in the world. Straight ahead at the end of this wood is the Lake. I wish I could take you to see it, but we turn off to the mill in a couple of miles. Just the same we will stop at the top of this hill, eh Charles? We never miss a chance to show off our town, Kit, let alone our landscape."

Charles had shown me a landscape. I reflected bitterly that there was for me no beauty in it. But I was wrong. Charles had shown me nothing. From the crest of this hill the forest swept down in majesty to an oval gem of turquoise blue and climbed again in the blazing grandeur of Indian summer, sunstruck on the distant ridges of the rising mountain. I stood entranced. The town I had left was obliterated, having no part of this magnificence. I could dismiss the teacher's house and the silly black knob of a hill that rose beyond it. It was not what Charles meant by the beauty of the island. The revelation of this meaning was centred in the lake that lay before me as a small translucent mirror reflecting the morning light.

"The Indians in the Reservation say the lake is enchanted" Matt said.

"Their ancient legends say a lake spirit is trapped in its fathomless depths. They give it a wide berth because" Charles added "those compelled by a fear of the waters, cannot resist the call and are drawn into the depths."

"Don't frighten the child Charles" Matt said sharply. "Or she won't come back again."

Charles reply was enigmatic.

"There's a difference between fear and pride Matt," he said. "Kit doesn't frighten easily. She has nothing to fear from the waters."

"Then you'll come back Kit" Matt Mathews said.

"Yes" I said, "perhaps I will" and I looked past Charles into the sunlight and added "to the lake."

***

8

Chapter Eight

"It's a dull place Charles has chosen to live in" I reported to Mother attempting to conceal with disdain my hurt and bitterness. "The mill manager's wife mostly lives in Victoria and Pat goes there too every chance she gets. Of course, you know how Charles is about any part of the great outdoors but from where he lives you have to drive miles to get to the nearest lake. I certainly wouldn't call it much of a place to choose to teach in."

After my return it was in this fashion that I countered the interrogations of the family at large, making it evident that I was disappointed in the scene of Charles' withdrawal in order to disguise my consternation over the change in Charles himself. Subconsciously I felt hypocritical and somehow disloyal for though I would never have admitted the cause I was convinced that marriage had taken the shine from him. As subtly as I could I smeared away the possibility of family realisation of this truth by identifying my weekend with the scenery instead of with Charles and Pat. I bored with exact detail the way I spent my time, dwelling on the forest of the beaver-dam on the river until Mother suppressed my pseudo enthusiasm in exasperation.

"Oh well Kit you have made your point, no doubt. There is no need to elaborate on the smell of a beaver-dam which all of us, including yourself, have encountered before."

"There was nothing else to see in the whole town."

"So you've said and no one doubts your word, but that's enough of it"

Yet it was difficult to wend a way carefully through the forest of family opinion and conjecture about the marriage of Charles and Pat. In my youthful vanity I aspired to affect the silence of innocence when motives were discussed, personality values weighed and measured. I kept the secret of Pat's baby. I protected the annihilation of Charles' relationship with me which the family accepted as something unique. But before a week was out a new Charles had emerged which I had never known before, the Charles the family knew, the Charles the family would have preferred. Balanced against the Charles of my childhood was a Charles who was a child himself.

***

My cousin Wilf astounded me.

"You've seen the bride and groom, they tell me" Wilf was immaculate in greys, white shirt, navy blazer, pocket crested in gold, tan and white shoes. He was curious I thought, but off-hand because of vanity still rankling a little I suspected beneath his suave exterior to have been superseded by Charles in the affections of any woman.

"A man doesn't know whether to send a present or not - thought I'd ask you - what do you think?"

"I don't think it would matter terribly to Charles. But send them something Wilf. Something sophisticated for Pat perhaps."

"Sophisticated to the tall timbers - what for example?"

"You're more sophisticated than I. Besides you know your own finances."

"I'd let my head go for old Charles. I wondered about cash."

"Charles wouldn't like cash Wilf." He'd prefer you to choose something!"

"What did our glamorous Pat look like in the woods?"

"Glamorous."

"Impossible! All for old Charles!"

"He's not that much older than you, six months, isn't it?"

"You're going to be devastating darling, when you grow up."

"Oh thanks. But not in Pat's class. She's your type Wilf, you choose the present."

"Easily done for Pat. But my dear girl, my cousin in this case is Charles not Pat and Charles is not my type - what does a man do, if cash is out. Go to a department store and choose the latest cocktail shaker?"

"Why not?"

"Seriously, darling cousin, seriously."

"I am serious. A silver cocktail shaker would be very nice. They have a drink before dinner every night. I don't think they have a cocktail shaker. I didn't see one."

"Go on, you astound me! What kind of place have they got?"

"The schoolteacher's house, old with sweeping eaves but furnished in a modern manner. The tea set is orange and black."

"Shocking the locals, eh?"

"What?"

"Pat, I mean, butterfly in a frog pond."

"Did you know her very well, Wilf?"

Taken by surprise he hedged.

"How old are you now Kit?"

"As old as you'll ever be Wilf."

"Ace" he said and laughed. "Then you'll know as well as I do, my dear cousin, that poor old Charles probably knew her less than any other man she went out with."

"He's the one she married, though."

"More fool Charles to fall for it."

"Insofar as you went after her yourself Wilf, that's a mean thing to say."

"When it comes to the point, I guess I'm Charles' cousin first before a lot of other things. What she's got is not good for Charles. You can get it for a nickel anywhere. I wish old Charles had settled for something that suited him better."

"Such as?"

"A loving little Indian to paddle around in his canoe, or even paddle it for him, wouldn't have surprised me."

"You never liked Charles much did you Wilf, even as a kid?"

An expression fell upon his face that changed it entirely as if his jaw was slipping.

"He never let me. He kept me at arm's length as if what went on in his mind was beyond my reach. He was always so damned self-sufficient and moody and it so happened I wanted to see myself as his best friend for years. I never made it - nobody ever has that I know of, except you perhaps."

Aghast I was forced against my resolution to speak for Charles.

"He makes wonderful friends" remembering in my urgency Mr Chang and a son of his I never met.

"Not among the mundane members of the family" Wilf retorted, "considering there are some who thought for years he preferred me, to all the other male members. Funny how different he is from the rest of us. I never even knew he liked a drink."

Faced with the boy-Charles I had not known as well as the unexpressed depth of the strangely disguised hurt eating like a cancer in Wilf, there was no defence in me.

"Then you better not send the cocktail shaker" I said.
"Sure I will," he said. "It's as good as anything else and God knows Pat will use it or sell it whichever suits her best."

Overcome, a new emotion threatened to strangle my words.

"I'm sorry for Charles, terribly sorry for him."
"Why, is he sorry for himself?"

Taken aback I stared at him, being for the first time in my life somehow sorry for Wilf.

"Why no, I don't think so. After all, he's just married.
"Even you," Wilf said. "I might have known. You're wasting your sympathy Kit. He'll never admit anything. I guess he's got what he deserves - a cocktail shaker."
"He'll hate it." I said.
"It'll be his just the same, oddly enough from me although no doubt he wouldn't think me subtle enough to see it."

Wilf had dropped in to give Auntie Meg a package of ham slices from his father to make the sandwiches for the annual bazaar in aid of her society for orphans. Mother was baking for the occasion at home and I, as the butter spreader, had been invited to lunch. I had left my post at the kitchen table to see Wilf to the car. It was almost a family ritual to accompany one another to the gate. As I walked back I knew Auntie Meg would be waiting for me, for I had not had occasion to talk to her alone since the weekend on the island. Meg, as my mother said, was one to bide her time.

"He's good, your uncle, never fails to send the ham, no matter what," she said as I picked up the spreading knife.

"Well," I said, "he can afford it."

"It's not the rule that those best able, contribute the most, I find. He's a loud man but in his way generous for all that. Was Wilf asking you about Charles?"

"How do you mean?"

"Just what I say Kit. I would not be thinking Wilf the one to miss his opportunity. His father said his few plain words to me when he heard of the marriage. There's not much doubt that the family agreed with each other for once. It was a poor thing Charles did, running away to be married in such a fashion. But I wondered about Wilf. He let his father and mother do the talking while I was there, an admittedly unusual thing for him, you must admit."

"He was wondering what to send for a wedding present."

The large liquid brown eyes lighted for a moment with relief as she glanced at me.

"Wilf was always in front of Charles as a boy. They are of an age."

"Yes, I know."

"It seems it was Wilf who introduced Charles to Pat."

"It was at Robert's engagement party at the Avenue."

"Was it, I hadn't realised that you remember then?"

"Yes, I remember. Greta thought Pat so attractive."

"But you didn't"

"No, I don't think I did then, but I was wrong. She is attractive Auntie Meg." I fell silent.

"That's all then Kit? There's nothing more you can tell me?"

The appeal was forced out of her, drawn from a heart which was aching for some reassurance she suspected I was unable to give for she had heard already of my trip by sea, had sat beside my parents her hands folded in her lap, her eyes on my face while I described Charles' house and the detailed activities of each separate day. She wanted something else, to know that Charles had a chance of happiness that she had been unable to perceive, a new fulfilment of ambition or desire. I could only look at her and shake my head and watch the eyes upon my face fill slowly with tears. She did not of course allow the tears to fall. A queer little smile twisted her mouth, to twitch at her cheek while her hands went on placing ham in the sandwiches. I did not interrupt when she began to talk. Her conversation was at first spasmodic little gusts of thinking aloud in order to clear her mind for some resignation or some new effort.

"You see Kit, Charles was not an ordinary little boy like the others. From the beginning he played a lot by himself. Gil and I used to laugh about the funny solemn things he would say. He was twice as thoughtful as the other boys, except perhaps Davy. Davy was thoughtful too but in another sort of way, but then he was the eldest and somehow you expect more of the eldest and get more amusement out of the youngest. Davy never laughed at any of the odd things little Charles said. He always took him quite seriously and explained what he was getting at to the rest of us. From the beginning Davy took Charles off my hands which were busy, believe me, with six. Charles trailed a bit being by five years youngest. I suppose we spoiled him. The others were at school and he just a baby. He could read a little book at four, Davy taught him. Davy was our family boy, you know Kit. He could make the others mind when I couldn't. Your Uncle Gil never talked easily but there never was a man who loved his family more than he did. The boys were his whole life. He wasn't a man for much outside his home and garden. When the war took Davy, it finished your Uncle Gil. When you're a woman you keep going, you have to for the sake of the others. I never saw such a change in a man as I saw in Gil when the boys went off to war. One after the other they enlisted after Davy until the terrible time came when there was nobody left at home but Charles."

"He was never any bother, at school, at sports, helping at home, he was always a willing and self-sufficient youngster. He didn't ask for any help that I can remember when he was at school. He certainly didn't after Davy went off to France. He was just ten when Davy and Jock enlisted. Then Tom went. Willie and Doug went together two years after. It was a terrible time. Gil said three was enough to give and tried to hold the youngest back. But Douglas put his age up. He was determined to go, Willie waited for him. The night they came home and told us, your uncle cried Kit, cried for the bitter waste. He begged me never to be proud to have raised sons for such a waste.

"I have never known whether I did right by Charles. He is the cleverest son I had which I realised too late. First there he was, the lit-tle fellow being looked after by Davy and then when he was ten the war began and he was the only one at home with his father and me, with the casualties list up every day and our minds distracted. In a way he went through all the awkward stages himself, getting through somehow without asking for assistance, keeping himself occupied, helping me when he could without question, working weekends be-side his father in the garden. He wasn't one for bringing other boys home from school. He hung onto the letters. Davy wrote to him sep-arately. He must have been a lonely boy, Kit for once he ran away to Chinatown. I nearly went out of my mind when I heard. We couldn't understand why he should want to do such a thing and he didn't explain so he was punished. He never did explain anything. If we objected, he just apologised and let it go at that. He read such a lot that I asked his father if he thought he was too serious for a boy, too little with lads his own age, but his father thought it was alright. He understood, he said, why Charles preferred his own company and books to the constant mock battles on the vacant lots. Gil said he was a good boy and intelligent and would be right when his brothers got home. I thought his father knew him best. They spent a lot of time together. Gil took him everywhere on the weekends when the garden was done. Perhaps you can see him in your mind's eye, Kit, as much a part of this house as his father.

"Yes, I can. He used to read a book up in that tree at the back."

"I've kept the house going for him, but he'll not be needing it after all, I see that now. It's a strange thing how wrong you can be about your own. Jock's coming in with me soon and after a bit I'll get a small place for myself. After all, he's my eldest. The war was hardest on him."

"Are Jock and Elsie coming back from Powell River?"

"As soon as he can. Elsie's expecting again. This'll be my fourth grandchild. She'll be glad to come here. Jock's restless and wanting to change his job again. There's more in the city for him and the house will anchor him. In a way it was his house and Davy's."

"But Charles has never lived anywhere else, not really."

"Pat was here once or twice and it's not her house Kit."

"No, it's not her house."

"So he'll not be wanting it will he?"

"But Auntie Meg, it's your house. You've always been here. It's your whole life."

"It's a family house. Since Davy went and then Gil, and now the last of the boys married, what use have I for a family house?"

Silence fell again on the huge kitchen and in the garden a little wind rustled the leaves of the old shrubs. Upstairs a door swung on its hinges and the squeak raucously descended the hall stairs.

"It needs a man's hand, this house. I'm needing a small house now, a little pretty house, with just an extra room for you and my grandchildren. Jock's the eldest son now. Elsie can have the Christmas party."

"She's a wonderful cook" I said for something to say.

"Your mother's lucky" Meg said, "having you. You've been good to me too, Kit, like a daughter."

Her sigh was long and deep. Reflecting the unspeakable because I was not really her daughter, not that little girl christened Sara, still-born between Douglas and Charles, whose small, tended grave was sheltered now by Uncle Gil.

We packed the sandwiches in neat square wax paper packets and filled two baskets with them. Then we made lunch. The aroma of strong fresh coffee filled the kitchen and Auntie Meg produced from the oven of the black wood stove a small dish of corn casserole.

"I'm not expecting you to eat ham ends as well as making the sandwiches" she said. "When I have my little house I'll not be tied to housework, that's a sure thing. I'll see to that. There's things I'm wanting to do."

"Sewing you mean?"

"Some, but I wasn't thinking of that. When I was a girl I painted china a little, you know those one or two pieces inside" she indicated with her shoulder the dining room door. "Some years back now, Charles bought me a book about china-painting. I came across it the other day. There's another book there, on Chinese ceramics he gave me too."

"He gave me Chinese poetry for Christmas."

"I noticed that. It may have been that sent me looking for the Chinese plates. He read so much Kit. Do you think he was not living in this house at all, after another manner of thinking, but away where his books took him?"

"Yes, I think that Auntie Meg."

"He went through school so easily. The principal at High School told me he had the brain to do anything he chose. He suggested the university but Charles stuck to his idea of teaching. It was something to do with the war. The principal told me that, not Charles."

"The lack of teachers, you mean."

"No, the waste. I think what his father called the terrible waste. He thought children should be taught that war was a waste. The principal admired this point of view but he tried to persuade Charles to get the best education he could first, but Charles couldn't wait. Besides I was a widow, you know Kit and the teachers' college was free.

"Who made a woodsman of him?"

"Gil and Davy, I guess. Davy was twelve years older than Charles you know. Gil was like your father, mad on camping for boys so we went for years every summer to Bowen Island, Wilson Sound, White Rock. Anyway, I'm not wanting to depress. Come along and we'll eat."

"It was the best thing to do with six boys. Davy and Jock lived for camping. Davy never minded Charles following him around and I knew Charles was safe with Davy."

"Did Uncle Gil take Charles when the boys were at the war?"

"No, he didn't. Camping was left until the others got home again. You've mostly been with us since."

"It's never been the same then?"

"As with Gil and Davy, no. When the boys came back it was different. They never felt the same. Doug said he got as much exercise out of football. Jock had Elsie waiting all those years for him, but he was so changed. Willie was in and out of hospital and Tom's nerves shot to pieces.

"Poor Auntie Meg. What a time you must have had with them all."

"No time for Charles. Gil never recovered from the shock of losing Davy. 'For nothing' he'd say, and the boys would argue with him, what it was for. He'd bring his fist down on the table with a bang and yell, 'I said for nothing' and the boys remembered such a quiet man and couldn't understand him. The war killed Gil as well as Davy.

"I remember" I said, "he banged the table once when I was here, staying with you when I was little."

"It's a wonder when you were with us. He used to say to me 'only Charles is normal and the little one, God bless her.' If only he could have lived a little longer and seen them settle down. But he saw five fine boys go to war and four men he didn't know come back, one armless, one treating a girl who loved him like a gypsy, one that screamed and shook with morose and unaccountable passions and one who packed up his bag and walked out his home. None of them spoke his language anymore."

"The talk of them Kit - the talk of them" She paused, a knife held upright in her hand above the white slice of bread she was spreading with the dark red of damson jam. Her voice faltered but she spoke on in violent gasps of remembrance: "cock-eyed guns sniping at 'Heinies' - sitting on the gun trail - the baptism of guns - the brotherhood of the gun-pits - as if the guns were friends Kit, as if they loved the guns - the camouflage, the screen over the gun's mouth, the 5-9s coming down and the feeling of isolation of a man and his gun alone - the gun batteries coming suddenly to life - the machine gun-rattle and then the terrible crumping sound that worked back on itself like an echo - and such a profanity, such oaths they had learned in the trenches. They didn't speak Gil's language at all - they talked about 'Fritzies' and duck-walks and horse-lines and Verey lights and asked each other, 'What's the dope?' - 'What's gripin' you?' - 'Didn't you know he got a plunk in the neck that finished him?' - 'How about a rum-up?' Poor Gil scarcely knew what they meant. And they had such a terrifying familiarity with death which no one who had not known the trenches could ever understand. They talked about flattened foot-sloggers in the filthy mud and black ghosts hanging in pieces on the barbed wire and corpses stacked like shell cases at the dugout entrances as if such sights were as common as a daily garbage collection , They talked about other things too, Kit that even now you wouldn't understand. I hope you never will. Things that went on in a place behind the lines they called 'the estaminet' where they drank vin-blanc in the village. But I shouldn't talk like this to you, I don't know why I am, you see they thought their father knew nothing when they first came home, they laughed at his morality and religious faith, scoffed at his ideals as useless escapes from reality. It was like supporting ungrateful strangers in his house. They drank hard liquor openly and then their conversation appalled him. But the silences that came out of the conversations were worse. They left him outside like an old pair of unwanted galoshes. You see they were careful not to shock me but Gil was a man and their father and they included him without thought in a man's conversation but ignored him in a father's capacity, so that he never knew why they acted the way they did. They quarrelled too among themselves, bitterly and briefly like wildcats and we would never know why. It was the same with all the boys just back from the war. The women bided with them and spoiled them but the men resented them for they treated the home front as less than nothing and not worth the heroes of the battle.

"It must have been horrible for Charles."

"Charles, yes. I recall that he was as tall as he is now when he was fifteen. He looked weedy but he seemed adult compared to his brothers. It was as his father said, he was normal. There was no use trying to keep from him how ill his father was. I didn't have the heart to tell the other three boys. It seemed to me they'd been through so much. But Charles said, 'They have to know, Ma.' So I told them at dinner time that their father had a bad heart, that the doctor said his illness was serious. Gil was in his bed upstairs. They looked at each other,

I remember, and then went on arguing among themselves. Charles helped me carry out the dishes and while we were in the kitchen, another row began. I leaned against the sink and began to sob. 'I don't think I can stand it' I said, 'with your father ill, I can't stand it.' Charles turned on his heel and went into the dining room, the door open behind him. 'Shut up' he roared. They turned on him, rising to their feet, staring. 'Dad's ill upstairs' he said. 'So what?' 'So I guess I don't blame him for wanting to join Davy.'

Then he went out. You know the way he does, straight downstairs and out the basement door."

"It was just that the others didn't understand. They were wonderful when they realised, I don't know what I'd have done without them. One after the other they sat up nights with Gil. They got Doug back home. Gil didn't want to go to the hospital and Doug bathed him and changed the sheets as gently as if his father had been a baby and Jock spent hours with him, sometimes talking about pain. He's been through a lot more than I realised, Gil told me when they were all reconciled with him again. Towards the end, except for your father, Gil didn't want to see anybody else but the boys. He saw my sisters and friends who came of course, but only for a minute, as if he felt he couldn't spare time that was in a way making up for the war years. When he died, he was happy Kit."

"I'm glad" I said, "I loved Uncle Gil."

When I said that my heart cried out to ask about Charles but had I said his name I would have wept. Auntie Meg would have wept too for her own reasons and how would that have helped?

"If we don't wash up," I said, "Mother and Dad will be here before we're ready, and you know your ladies won't be able to start the tea without you."

She stood up.

"Oh well" she said. "There's not more to be said then. We all come bang up against it every so often. Jock said it when I was last at Powell River."

"Said what?"

"He asked if you still startled people by being so much like Charles."

***

9

Chapter Nine

Summer, constant summer. Oh yes, the tropics enjoy the season they call winter. But it is not the same without the wind from the snow on the mountains. Charles was so right when he told me that. Sometimes I look at Jimmy, amazed that he has never told me once that he missed the snow on the mountains. But he was right to tell me the break would be easy, with London first and even a honeymoon in Paris before Malaya and the war that forced us south to Australia. By that time my babies had taken over. A home for them was my first concern in Sydney. First there was Lisa and then Barbara and finally the adoption of my adorable waif, Henrietta. Not that I could show them off in Canada until the war was over and then there was only Mother and Auntie Meg. Nothing was the same because my father and one brother had joined Uncle Gil and my next brother Donald was in Japan. The family was different and neither I nor my little girls fitted in. We were overwhelmed with Peg's children and the children of Wilf and Harriet. Returning to Australia was almost a relief when our leave ended. Mother and Auntie Meg promised to visit but somehow the time was never right for such a long journey. They are talking now of coming to Egypt, longing they say, to see the antiquities.

I long for them too. Jimmy has never once invited his parents which is seen by some as a bad facet of his character produced by the second world war, but it is not. He does not miss his family any more than he misses the snow on the mountains

.

"I take my Canada with me wherever I go." he says patting my cheek with affection.

***

The depression deprived us of the yearly camp at Cedar Cove. I like to think it was the depression although it may not have been. It may have been that my parents used the depression as an excuse for not going any more, after the trouble there last summer when Charles was married to Pat, and Greta to Tony Johns.

But Auntie Meg Gilbert loved Cedar Cove more than any other member of the family, except perhaps me. Towards the end of the depression she bought a block of land, sold for a song, high up on the hill above the Cove on the high side of the road. She could not afford to build a house on the land for several years but in the meantime she pitched a permanent camp with two wooden tent platforms and a tiny permanent kitchen made of corrugated iron which could be locked up and used as a store when the camp was not in use. All Auntie Meg's family were grown up, so she often asked me to go with her for the weekend at the start of summer as she established camp. She was gradually clearing the land under the great pine trees that stood in majestic glory on the site. She was a wonderful gardener; a profusion of flowers grew almost immediately around the little kitchen. The view from the top of the block behind the tents was magnificent so there was one Saturday when we built a bush house, three or four of us, and then, tired and dirty, went down to the Cove for a swim before our evening meal. I remember there was a crowd of people on the beach when I walked along the sand but I did not look at them. I was only interested in the cool sea and, throwing down my towel, ran straight in and began to swim far out toward the raft. There was a splash behind me and I swam forward as swiftly as I could exhilarated by the bouncy feel of the swell of the waves beneath me. A streak flashed past and beat me to the raft, pulling its long length up onto it before I could touch. When I looked up there was Jimmy Millar, hugging his knees and grinning at me.

"Hello Kit" he said." I saw you as you went into the water. Where have you been all these summers?"

I hadn't seen Jimmy for nearly three years and was amazed how tall he was.

"You've grown yards" I said.

"And you've shrunk." Jimmy said. "But you can still swim. I'll beat you to the rock."

"No" I said "I'm only staying a minute then going back for supper. We've been working all day building a bush house up at Auntie Meg's. The others are not even attempting to swim this far. The lazy things are splashing around the shore."

Jimmy said "I came down with a crowd for a bonfire tonight. Will you come?"

"But I don't know your friends. How could I?"

"I'll introduce you. The more the merrier."

I thought to myself that Jimmy Millar had become more confident in the last few years. I had heard he was at university. It must have brought him out.

But I said, "Oh, I couldn't Jimmy."

"I didn't bring a girl," Jimmy said, "I never do."

I digested this piece of information and then, being human and female, said:

"Why ever not?"

"I've just been waiting around."

I felt a bit mean. During the depression boys couldn't afford to take girls out on dates, especially boys who were going to university. And Jimmy Millar wasn't the kind who went around with a crowd. Maybe he didn't have the money to take a girl to beach parties.

"I see. It's tough with the depression, isn't it."

"I said I was waiting around for a girl I wanted to take to the bonfire, what's the depression got to do with it?"

It had never been any use beating around the bush with Jimmy. He just didn't get it.

"I just thought that you might not have the money to take girls around."

"On account of the depression?"

"On account of the depression."

"That's a lot of nonsense, Kit and you know it."

"Really, Jimmy what a thing to say. I suppose you think everybody has as much money during the depression as they had before it. You must be very lucky indeed."

"I'm just the same as everybody else, neither lucky nor unlucky. Money's just hard to earn that's all. You still have to earn it if you need it. And it's got nothing to do with taking a girl out."

"It has so."

"That's the same silly attitude my parents had about going to university."

"I hear you go nevertheless."

"Sure, I go. I have to go to be what I want to be."

"And what's that?"

"A tropical medicine research scientist."

"A what?"

"You heard me and anyway that's beside the point. We weren't talking about what I want to be."

"Jimmy Millar, I never knew a boy like you! You haven't changed a bit."

"Now we're getting somewhere."

"Are we?" I said. "Only far enough to see that you are bound to get what you want even during the depression."

"That has nothing to do with it. I can't afford to wait until the depression's over, that's all. I told my family straight and I'm telling you."

"Well, all I can say is that you are lucky your family can afford to keep you."

"My family can't afford to keep me, and I don't ask them to. I pay my way at home, and I pay my fees and I can pay to take a girl out if I want to. I work."

"I see" I said. "I'm sorry Jimmy."

Jimmy stood up and all six feet of him towered above me on the raft.

"I don't tell everybody," he said, "but I'll tell you. I work in the cannery."

"The cannery, but I thought it was only..." I bit my tongue.

"Only Japs? Well, you're right. Mostly it is only Japs because they don't care about doing dirty work and they can stand the stink of the place. I haven't noticed that they like it any more than I do but they stand it, and they eat, depression or no depression. They need good supervisors in the canneries, and they pay well for it. So they took me. The first summer they taught me the job and now I'm trained the money's good. I earn what I need."

Jimmy poised himself for a fleeting minute on the edge of the raft and then dived in. When he came up he swam to the edge of the raft and stuck his head over the edge and looked at me. His black hair was plastered flat with the water and his dark eyes under the straight brows were as penetrating as a hawks and yet somehow beseeching.

"Oh Jimmy" I said, "It's true, in some ways you really haven't changed a bit for all your higher education."

With both hands he hung on to the side of the raft.

"Listen Kit" he said "When I come out of that cannery I stink to high heaven of the scales, the guts and the stale blood of the fish. I'm greasy and oily and I degrade myself taking that job alongside a gang of Japanese whom I get along well with and like and who treat me like a brother. My parents and my brother and sister are ashamed to mention that I can go to university because I spend all summer in a cannery. The reason I got into the water was so as to be clean enough to ask if you would still go out with such a guy?"

"I wouldn't give it a second thought" I said.

"Well!" Jimmy said, "Charles always said that in a crisis you would give a double answer."

"I meant" I said sweetly, "that the fact you worked in a cannery would not worry me in the least, provided of course that you took a soapy bath before you arrived at my door." I looked straight at Jimmy Millar and couldn't take my eyes away. A tiny pulse began to beat like a flutter in my throat.

Jimmy pulled his eyes away first. He sighed. "Charles told me something else I remember too" he said.

"Did he?"

"Yes. He told me to watch out in case I was a one-woman man. He said it was a dangerous thing to be. I'll race you to the rock." This last without looking at me again.

"No Jimmy. I must go back; the others are walking up the beach. They must be wondering. Supper will be ready." I slipped into the water from where I sat. It simply was not in me at that moment to stand up and dive. Jimmy swam off to the rock with a slow steady crawl. He stopped a little way off and turned to wave. Then he swam steadily on.

I was not surprised to hear his voice later that evening. I sat on the edge of my bed in the tent and marvelled at the deep sound of it. I knew he would come after supper before the moon had risen high enough for the bonfire to begin.

"Good evening" Jimmy said to Auntie Meg, "I've come for Kit."

***

There was a Church Social the following Friday night. At every such social a friend of my father's sang and I had promised to accompany him on piano. On Monday morning I phoned Daddy's friend at his office and asked him to get somebody else. He was surprised. So much so that he found an occasion to tell my father. Daddy said to me:

"You're not coming to the social Kit?"

"No, I have a date."

"It's not like you. You promised."

"They'll have to find somebody else."

"Bert likes you to play for him. He's a bit upset. He said you didn't even give him any reason."

"Daddy why should I? He thinks he just has to ask. I'm always the one they make use of."

"Kit!" said Mother.

"Then what is it? What made you change your mind?"

"I'm going out with Jimmy Millar."

"Jimmy Millar. I see. But you knew you had the social Friday night. You could have gone another night."

"No, only Friday. On Saturday morning Jimmy goes to the cannery."

"The cannery," Mother said. "What cannery?"

"The one where they can salmon out at El Beach."

"But I thought that only..."

I said quickly, too quickly.

"That only Japanese worked there. Jimmy works there to earn the money for the university."

"It seems an odd sort of job for Jimmy Millar."

"A job is a job these days," Daddy said. "I don't know that the kind of job is all that important."

"It must be rather hard for his family to take." Mother said.

"That's not important at all." I said. "All that matters is that Jimmy gets the education he's entitled to."

Mother looked at my father. They were not used to me taking a belligerent attitude. They could have reminded me that not very many young people were getting what they were entitled to during those years. But my father said instead:

"I haven't seen Jimmy for some time but I remember that summer he seemed a determined sort of boy."

Mother said, "Your Aunt told me that his parents were worried about him. It seems he goes round with a fast crowd, Kit."

"Did she?" I said.

"Yes, they belong to some socialist society at the university and they say they are atheists."

"That's because they are scientific." I said.

"Is that what Jimmy's doing?" my father said. "Science?"

"Yes, he's going in for tropical medicine research."

"It sounds impressive, but it's a bit out of your line isn't it?" Daddy said.

"I don't see why?" I said.

"Because you know nothing about it or the kind of people who go in for it. It doesn't seem to go with poetry, music and social service and the kinds of things you are interested in."

"Maybe it's time I knew a bit about it then." I said. "It's a scientific age we live in."

"Well, be careful," Daddy said. "Be careful Kit."

***

If Charles had been poetry and dreams to me, Jimmy Millar became achievement and reality. To most people love is poetry and dreams. This may be because, for the majority of the human race, life is a practical grim business and passionate love, especially in its first awakening gives a feeling of wholeness, a possession of achievement which in ordinary circumstances is elusive. Love is nature's way of maintaining a balance in life. Jimmy was exceptional to me because he seemed to be all the things I was not. Life offers no security to a dreamer, no positiveness and very little straight forward determination. In spite of not being able to believe in these qualities I admired them tremendously in Jimmy. More than that, I built them up in him even as he built up their opposites in me.

By Christmas of that year I was absorbed by Jimmy. My whole life had altered course and swung into the strong force that was Jimmy's ambition and future. There was plenty of room for me to grow and expand in this area, and neither of us ever doubted this to be my rightful place. Jimmy wanted everything that was a part of me, my music, my verse, my social activities. There was plenty of room untouched by these aspects of life in Jimmy. He accepted me as a whole. If I wore a blue dress he liked me in blue, but appeared to find me equally satisfying in my old trench coat if that was the garment I found suitable to wear. With Jimmy I never found myself compared with girls who were glamorous or highly intelligent. From the time of our first date I was just Jimmy's girl. In the beginning I was nervous of the new society of eager questioning minds I connected with through Jimmy's friends at the university. Then I observed that Jimmy knew enough of the required answers for both of us on the technical side and sat back and beamed with pride when I ventured a remark or an opinion that was philosophical. I found that Jimmy was respected for what he was and had no desire to be accepted on any other basis. What was good enough for Jimmy was good enough for me.

Nevertheless, I had moved into a new world. Science had meant no more to me than a large awesome word in the dictionary. Now a door had been opened and my mind was newly stimulated. I began to see where Jimmy was going and why. When I thought about it there was inside of me a little grateful acceptance that I was going there too. That I was being taken on the adventure, and that the adventure was Jimmy's responsibility seemed to me perfectly natural, for such is the nature of first love, when the path is straight as far as the youthful eye can see.

"I love you just as you are" he said often to me, "soft and sweet. I need you soft and sweet, poetry, music and sadness and all."

It was as if he knew the steeliness in him needed some sort of balance to keep it workable even though he would have laughed at the suggestion. He allotted to me all attributes separate from his own in a strange almost conceited fashion, with no doubt at all that I could handle them, as if they were worth handling with no interest or pressure from him, and no more more than he expected pressure from me in what concerned him: his scientific and economic commitments. He would say odd things to me. Once after sitting quietly listening to me play Beethoven he commented:

"You know just which music to choose, when a man needs music."

"What does Beethoven make you think of Jimmy?"

"Beethoven. I wasn't thinking of Beethoven in particular. Just that you seem to choose the right thing at the right time."

"But what does music make you think of Jimmy - not me in particular? For instance, when we went to the concert last week."

"I took you to the concert because you wanted to go."

"But didn't you enjoy it. You said you did."

"Of course I enjoyed it. If I didn't enjoy music, I wouldn't ask you to play for me, would I, even if I went to a concert only to please you?"

"Wouldn't you ever go to a concert just to please yourself?"

"If you weren't around I might. You know, as a sort of second best."

"But just for the music, for what it says to you?"

He laughed.

"I might have known, you wanted to ferret out my emotional reactions while listening to music. You're a tartar for what goes on inside! Well, let me see. During the concert the other night, while that violinist with the long hair was playing something or other, two things struck me. One that the fellow himself was an escapist and had picked a satisfying way to escape insofar as he had the satisfaction of working at a defined discipline plus having the adulation of people to whom he gave relaxation in their leisure time."

"Jimmy!"

"Let me finish. The second thing I though was that music is good because it reminds the scientific mind that science is no use in itself but only in respect to the infinitely various human beings it caters for. That's what I thought, does that satisfy you?"

"Yes" I said reluctantly, "but I wish you just loved music."

Jimmy stood up and put his arms around me where I sat at the piano.

"I love you" he said, "and you love music. It's the same thing isn't it?"

I buried my face in his chest and said, "No."

When making love Jimmy was very gentle. He ran his fingers through my hair and my breath pulsed in my throat over the beat of his heart.

"Well, it is for me anyway. I couldn't cut music out of you even if I hated it which I don't. How could I? I just have to love the music along with you. When I have you, I have music too. That's how it is, I guess. Just the same honey, I wish you'd get off that piano stool."

He eased me up and we slipped together into the comfort of the large family armchair with the restrained passion of the home living room whispering, between kisses, of the bliss which awaited out two separate selves when we finally united as one.

****

Christmas arrived. The days stole past the cold into new warmth almost without my conscious recognition. On the wonderful days we spent alone together sitting side by side on the warm sands of the beach that spring and summer we never went beyond ourselves,

Jimmy and I, we two together, our present happiness, our accepted future.

Often, I took a poetry book along in my bag to read while Jimmy studied. There were times when the sheer joy of the day and the nearness of Jimmy forced me to read some passage aloud to him, wanting him to share how perfectly it expressed our love, our being together. He would put down his own book and look at me while I read, his face absorbed and contemplative. When I stopped reading he would take the book out of my hand and kiss me or else he would put his head on my knee and look up at me, his eyes teasing and tell me to read him another poem knowing very well that I would not. Only once in a while did he comment on the poetry.

"Read that bit again" he said once.
"You weren't listening" I accused.
"Go on read that bit about what love is made out of."
I read the little bit of Kilmer again.

"Love is made out of ecstasy and wonder
Love is poignant and accustomed pain
It is a burst of Heaven shaking thunder
It is a linnet's fluting after rain
Love's voice is through your song above and under"

"Jimmy you're not listening again"
"Yes I am" Jimmy said. "I like to hear you read, you look so serious and sweet."
"Oh Jimmy."
"Well, you do."
"It's because the words are so beautiful."
"It's because you are so beautiful when you read it. And so sad."
"Sad?"

"Whenever you read poetry you look beautiful and sad."

"I suppose it's because poetry is sad Jimmy."

"I know, that's what I don't like about it."

"But it expresses life and life is sad."

"I don't think it is" Jimmy said. "It's what you make it. If I have any-thing to do with it, it's not going to be sad for you."

"I don't mean personal sadness. You know I'm happy. If I wasn't I don't suppose I'd be able to bear to read sad poetry."

"You'd have to give it up then because it all seems pretty sad, melancholy stuff to me."

"Looked at that way, Jimmy all good literature would be sad, but it isn't really. It's just that it accepts life as it is and still finds all the beauty in it."

"You're too deep for me" Jimmy said and ruffled my hair.

One day on the beach I read him one of my own poems pretending I was reading from the book in my hand.

"Listen to this Jimmy."

He lifted his head waiting.

"Convinced I stand of the certainty of love
Inevitable as life, infallible as death
Determined to believe that love shall last
Declared supreme and honoured with each breath.
Assured I rest in heart and high above
Unfailing proof rides forward. My love glows
A vision all triumphant, beyond the threatening blast
Where doubts' persuasion as a tempest blows.

Even as youth stands straight at manhood's door
Fist on the handle, foot firm on the floor

Feeling his childhood slip, his shoulders bare
Accepting the mantle age shall be proud to wear
Justified in believing himself to be
A man complete; so sure is love to me."

"Well" Jimmy said. "Those are strong words. Not a bit like you usually read to me. You certainly delve round in the musty shelves of the library."

"Jimmy!" I stood up, overcome suddenly with a strange new emotion which overwhelmed me.

I ran down the beach. Jimmy caught me easily and took me in his arms. We never mentioned the poem again.

***

I look over the balcony into Shariz Ahmed Kismet Pasha. A donkey cart is pulling up in front of our building. A bespoke piece of furniture, I had ordered is about to be delivered. As usual I am redesigning a room, re-arranging furniture. It is another bookcase and I have had to move almost every piece of furniture in my den to make room for it.

A giggle rises up inside of me as I realise that once again I have moved, to yet another pride of place my wonderful carved and awkward box, that first real present from Jimmy which accompanies me everywhere I go. What a time I had that Christmas morning, fitting it into my young girl's bedroom.

***

After our first date when I fell out with my Father over the church social, I planned my week around Jimmy. When I went out with him the day was dedicated and I refused to allow any other thing to interfere. Apart from that my life went on exactly as usual. But by the second Christmas, as well as the weekly date there were almost daily telephone calls, and the family found Jimmy there for tea every Sunday. Also, I stopped going to evening service. It was not that Jimmy refused to go to evening service with my family. It was just that we couldn't bear to give up the time we had to walk and talk.

I said to Jimmy "Are you an atheist?"

"I don't know if I am or not" Jimmy said. "Are you?"

"No." I said, "I believe in God, or anyway in something that I think is God."

"God, meaning good?"

"I think so Jimmy. Yes, what's good is God?"

"And how do you know what's good?"

"Well usually when you look at things there's a good side and a bad side and you can choose."

"It's not that easy. The more you know the harder it gets and the closer the bad gets to the good. I can see how when you think you are choosing the good you could choose the bad."

"But if you think you are choosing the good that is the good for you."

"No, if you choose the bad it is bad, even if you thought it was good."

"Oh, Jimmy."

"Sometimes I think that's the trouble with this world. People choose the bad, thinking they are choosing the good."

"Well, I think if there was a God, then He must be good, then people ought to always choose the good."

That Christmas like thousands of other young people I had two weeks work in one of the big department stores while Jimmy had found himself a job in a warehouse for the whole Christmas holidays. The Friday before the holiday, after late store closing he was waiting to take me for coffee. I had his Christmas present, the first gift I had ever given him, in my purse. A first gift is always hard to choose and for a month I had been thinking about this one. Now that I was sitting opposite him I felt I could not have chosen anything more ridiculous and less suitable. When I was away from him I thought I should get him something that a girl would give a boyfriend that she really had not been going with very long and with whom she had made no future plans. When I was with him I felt that we had been going together for years and that our whole life was one plan made for the two of us together. The gift was a strange little token somewhere in between.

Jimmy said, "You know what I would like to give you for Christmas, don't you Kit?"

I said nothing.

"Well, of course I can't. I haven't the money and I haven't my degree. I suppose your father would think I have a nerve to think of it even. So I won't. But next Christmas I will."
"Alright Jimmy." I said "I'll still be here."
"You better be" Jimmy said.

The waitress put the coffee down and we wished her a merry Christmas.

"You aren't getting a present yet" Jimmy said, "I'll be bringing it over Christmas morning."
"But I thought you were coming at 5 o'clock for dinner."
"I am" Jimmy said, "but I got to thinking that I want to see my girl first thing on Christmas morning and so I will. I'll be good and go away while you have your tree and come back later with the rest of your relations.

"Oh Jimmy, you are mad. Your mother will think you're crazy."

"Do you want me to come? Yes or no?"

"Of course I do."

"Then I'm coming."

***

In the little pile of Christmas cards waiting to be opened one of the typed envelopes held a brief note that in the emotional perceptivity of the last hour coming home with Jimmy filled my eyes with tears. It was an unsigned message on a large, folded sheet of typing paper.

'I am passing through on my way to San Francisco - must see you for a coffee - 3:30 Spencer's main door.'

Greta's writing, which I had not seen since her formal thank you note for the petticoat, had not changed from the small, neat script of childhood. Not once since her marriage to Tony Johns had she written. Auntie Mary pretended she knew where Greta was and none of the family denied her whatever consolation she drew from the pretence. We knew a present had come from Greta twice each year, one on her mother's birthday and one for Christmas. I could say nothing but only hope for Auntie Mary's sake that Greta had seen her mother or wanted to send her mother a message through me. We only spoke of Greta in the past tense at home.

I arrived to meet Greta a little breathless, feeling as if I was cheating my family. There are some things you have to do, and this was one of them. To meet her at all had been difficult, arranged instead of my regular lunch hour. My feet were aching but I had not dared risk offending a floor manager with hundreds of applicants anxious for even the final day of my job. Greta was sitting where she said she would be. Her eyes were very bright and she held an enormous bag of parcels in her hand. She gave me a quick hug and brushed her cool face briefly against my own. A lump strangled my throat and I could not speak.

"Earrings" Greta said 'I see you wear them now. As a matter of fact you are looking very smart today. You wouldn't have a date tonight would you?"

I blushed in relief because I had my very special date.
Greta ignored the blush, continuing her woman of the world conversation in a sharp artificial voice; not condescending yet unnatural; not familiar yet without intimacy.

"And who's the young man?"

I longed to tell her the wonderful thing that had happened to me. I wanted her to know but I couldn't seem to find the words to start to tell her
.

"Jimmy Millar."
"Jimmy Millar! Are you serious?"

I had not wanted it this way at all. But I was hurt and I struck back.

"Yes, we are serious." I said.

Then I saw she had not meant it that way at all. For a long moment we looked at each other, the camp of that distant summer surrounding us, folding us inside the half-moon of the beach. There had been, at the beginning of that summer, no barrier between two girls on two camp stretchers watching the shadows play on the canvas above them. Suddenly there were no barriers now. Greta said:

"Two more from that summer. You and Jimmy Millar. I can't believe it."

I was more than hurt, I was incredulous.

"And why not. After all we did go around together all that summer."

"With Charles. Now if you'd said Charles!"

"Charles! He's a cousin. He's years older than I am and he's married!"

She looked suddenly deflated, the momentary excitement draining out of her face.

"I only meant you had so much in common with Charles. Jimmy was so different, not like the rest of us somehow."

"That's true" I said coldly "he's more intelligent. He's going to be a scientist."

"Yes" Greta said, "he would be something like that."

I drew myself up, blind with a cold fury:

"Really, Greta you hardly knew him at all."

She dropped her eyes before the anger she saw in my face.

"That's true. I'm sorry Kit. Anyway I hope you work it out better than Charles and I have."

I suppose I must have unconsciously feared how love might work out for Greta, and I had been afraid for Charles from the very beginning. But I couldn't speak, nevertheless. There was nothing I could say. Greta lit another cigarette and carefully blew two perfect smoke rings through pursed lips.

"Well anyway" she said bitterly, "I am not intending to give up yet, like Charles. He has walked out on Pat and their little boy, but he's a man. I can't walk out" her voice was calculating and hard. "But one thing I'm not going to do and that is live around here anymore. Tony has a job in San Francisco and I'm going. I'd rather die than stay here."

There are questions I felt you cannot ask. How could I say to Greta 'What are you saying about Charles' or 'have you stopped loving Tony' or 'didn't Tony ever love you at all?'

"Does your family know?" I asked instead.

"No, and they never will" her voice and her eyes were defiant as if she found it necessary to dare me not to tell them. "I haven't been home to tell them."

"Oh Greta."

"And if you're wondering how I know about Charles, well I'll tell you. He told me himself yesterday."

"He's here?" I cried, "You've seen Charles!"

"I met him yesterday. He's staying with friends but he didn't say who. It was funny that we two should meet, the two family black-sheep both running away."

"Oh, don't be silly Greta. Why on earth should Charles want to run away. It's ridiculous." But he hadn't telephoned. I hadn't heard one word from him.

"Because he is going to desert his wife and and doesn't want Pat to know where to find him. She's at home with her mother."

"Then he must have had some very good reason."

Greta said, "Oh, no doubt."

"Didn't you ask him?"

"No, I wasn't talking to him very long. We simply established the fact we were both in the same boat and then we talked about you."

"Me?"

"Who else, you being the only one either of us wanted to talk about."

"And did you tell Charles you were going to see me, Greta?"

"I told him I had written you a note about today and I asked him if he wanted me to give you his address."

"And did he."

"Oh no. As far as that goes. I don't think Charles ever liked me much, let alone trusted me. He just said, 'oh that's all right Greta, Kit will know where I am.' That is why I thought..." her voice trailed off.

"Thought what?"

"Oh nothing."

"I haven't seen Charles since the first year he went to the Island. He sent me some books. But I haven't heard since."

I stopped because I couldn't tell Greta that I had written two letters to Charles and had not had replies; that Mother and I had sent presents to him for the baby and received no letter of thanks. I didn't want Greta to know that my family was furious with Charles and that I refused to discuss him at home out of loyalty and out of pride.

Greta opened her handbag and took out a little parcel wrapped in Christmas paper and silver ribbon.

"Greta" I said. I felt I was going to cry.

"Don't get sentimental." Greta said, still not looking at me, "I know you couldn't buy me a present. I wanted to say thank you again for the yellow petticoat. It - well it made all the difference - in a kind of a way it was the only wedding present I wanted although I didn't even remember about it until it arrived. All I wanted was to marry Tony and I'm very glad that I did. Whatever happens I'll always be glad that I did. Even if I hate San Francisco, I'll still be glad."

"Why should you hate San Francisco?"

"Only because it isn't home. I expect I'll be miserable sometimes."

"But Greta you'll have Tony and a nice house and you'll make friends. You'll see."

Unexpectedly Greta said, "You were always the one who wanted to travel, not me."

"And I hope I shall" I said. "I certainly don't want to marry some old stick in the mud and stay here forever."

"You could stay single and take off by yourself" said Greta.

"How would I ever earn enough money?"

"Rob a bank" Greta said and looked at me.

We began to giggle. We laughed until the tears sprang to our eyes and we couldn't stop even when a fat tear rand down Greta's nose and splashed on to the table. It made us laugh all the harder. A strange man with glasses turned around in his seat at the next table and stared at us. This was too much for Greta who burst out laughing aloud and stood up at the same time. I stood up picked up my present and the large shopping bag and followed Greta towards the lift. By the time I caught up with her, she had taken out a compact and was powdering her nose. When she had finished she closed her purse with a snap and took the shopping bag out of my hand. Before I knew what she was doing she kissed me. Then she said.

"Actually, I always wanted to give you your first pair of earrings, but it doesn't matter. Now don't thank me and don't follow me."

The lift man called "Down." Greta rushed into it. I stood there and watched him close the door.

On Christmas morning my brothers stormed my room. I sat up in bed remembering Jimmy.

"All right, I'll start breakfast. But I want the bathroom first."
"Okay, come on."

They raced down the stairs and I reached for my clothes and made for the warm bathroom. When I came out dressed, Davy's high, shrill voice came up to me.

"But I heard a car at our house. Yes I did. There it is and Jimmy's in it. Jimmy's in it."
"Don't be silly." Mother's voice said. "Jimmy isn't coming until five o'clock."
"It is so Jimmy And he's got two Jap boys with him and they are getting something out of the back of the truck they're in."

This was too much for us all. We rushed, one after the other, to the living room window.

"Gee!" Davy said. "They're getting a box out. A great big box, as big as a..."
Mother said, "That will do Davy."
Davy protested, "I was only going to say it's as big as a trunk. It is so too."

How right he was. Jimmy and the two small Japanese had gently lowered an enormous parcel wrapped in brown paper to the roadway and were proceeding to pick it up with Jimmy at one end and them at the other, each taking a corner. Gingerly they began to walk up the slippery path to our front door. The boys rushed to the front door and I, feeling the colour rushing to my cheeks, was compelled to look at my parents. My father's eye was on me and his look quizzical but he said nothing.

Mother said, "Is Jimmy moving in Kit?"
"I don't know." I whispered.

My face must have been a picture for that wonderful Scottish humour which flooded so freely in my mother's veins got the better of her and she exploded into hearty laughter. For a minute I was cross that she should laugh at Jimmy and then I laughed too. There was a resounding bump at the foot of the stairs. Mother and I stood there hopelessly, holding our sides. Suddenly Daddy's voice said.

"For heaven's sake, pull yourselves together you two. Here they are."

I gulped and turned my eyes towards the door. Jimmy was backing in, bringing with him a fair amount of mud and frost from the road on his feet. He backed in far enough to get the huge parcel in as well as the two smiling faces at the other end. Gently they lowered their burden. Jimmy turned around. I shall never forget the look of him at that moment. His cheeks were glowing red from the frosty morning and his dark eyes shone with a happy, deep glow under his black brows and ruffled hair. He seemed enormous beside the two Japanese and the eager shining faces of my little brothers. He smiled straight at me and for a moment I thought my heart would burst.

"Merry Christmas, Kit." he said and turned to greet my parents. Then he said, "I would like to introduce my two friends Ioki Munoda and Ako Suzuki."
The two Japanese bowed and grinned.

I said "Hello. Do come in. I'm so glad you came; Jimmy told me about you this summer."

I turned deliberately to my parents; in a way I suppose I was challenging them.

"Ioki and Ako are two friends Jimmy was working with this summer at the cannery." My father said, "Come in boys. You must be very cold. Mother will make us all a cup of coffee." Ako said, "Thank you very much, sir. Just a minute. I will close the car."

He turned and went out, followed by Ioki. At the door he turned and said to Davy, "Want to come too?" Davy said, "No thank you." In his polite voice. "I'll see you when you come back. I want to see what's in the box."

All our eyes returned to the box in the large sheets of brown paper. Then all the eyes turned towards Jimmy.

"There's nothing in the box Davy." Jimmy said. "It's for Kit. She can put what she likes in it." He looked at me then and in his eyes was that spaniel look, hopeful and devoted.

"A box with nothing in it." Davy exploded.

"It's a special box." I cried and ran forward to hide my face in the wrappings. I simply couldn't look at my parents at that moment. "Help me undo the paper Davy." I knelt beside the enormous parcel "Come on Jimmy you help too. The knots are awfully tight."

Davy said, "Gee whiz!" but he wasn't allowed to continue. Daddy said. "Go and get a knife Davy." Davy went, mumbling to himself.

It was a wonderful teak chest, old and exquisitely carved with shining, worn brass hinges. I ran my hand softly over the polished figures on the lid. I could not see them clearly for the film of tears that suddenly filled my eyes. For a horrible moment I thought I was going to cry.

My oldest brother said in an awed voice "It's a glory box"

Davy said, "What's a glory box?"

"It's a box that girls put things in when they…, well things they want to keep."

"Gee!" Davy said. "It's a bit big. Girls don't have things big enough for that. It's like the pirates put their gold in."

Jimmy had been sitting on the floor beside me. He rose up to his feet and his voice seemed to fill the room above my head, for he spoke without realising into one of those pregnant silences.

"Then I'll put Kit in it shall I Davy?" was what he said.

I hear Mother pull her breath in slightly and then Dad said:

"How about that coffee Mother? The boys and I will help you bring it in. Come on boys."

"What about the tree?" Davy yelled.

"It will wait." Daddy said. "Like a lot of other things, it will wait."

Davy made for the front door, "I'll go and get Ako and the other boy. They're taking a long time." He ran out and banged the door after him.

Jimmy sat himself down on the box and put his hand on my hand. "Well, I guess I brought it too soon, Kit. You see I just didn't have enough money for a ring and anyway I can't really give you that until I get my degree and well, Ako's father has this shop and he said this box was a real beauty…"

"Oh, Jimmy it's so beautiful. It is a glory box isn't it, Jimmy?"

"Well yes, it is but maybe you don't get glory boxes until you're really engaged?"

"You usually don't. But I don't care. I love it. It's the most wonderful present I ever had."

"I don't think your father liked it. I guess I should have asked him if I could give it to you this Christmas."

"It doesn't matter Jimmy. I was going to tell him anyway."

"He must think I'm pretty sure of myself, bringing a glory box."

"Well, aren't you?"

"Yes, I am."

"Well, it's all right then."

"I guess he still feels robbed, just the same."

There was a rattle of cups in the dining room and then Ako's voice speaking to Mother. Davy must have brought the boys through the kitchen door.

My Father talked to the Japanese boys while we drank our coffee and Mother deliberately talked to Jimmy. I passed the food apprehensively and wondered what would happen about the box. I was trying to persuade Ako to have another piece of Christmas cake, while avoiding my Father's eye when I heard Mother say to Jimmy in a voice purposely loud enough for my Father and me to hear:

"I think before you go Jimmy, you had better help Dad get Kit's present upstairs to her room. With the crowd coming tonight I can't spare the space for it beside the Christmas tree."

I put the cake plate too suddenly on the table and ran out through the kitchen door and up the stairs to get my bed made and a space ready to receive that box. Davy's voice covered my retreat as he yelled out in his excited shrill voice:

"Well gee, if we all have to carry that big pirate box all the way up the stairs let's do it or or we'll never get our presents round the Christmas tree."

I tore to my bedside and began to pull off the blankets. I was hurriedly putting them on again when I heard my father's footsteps on the stairs. Somewhere beyond him a shuffling had begun which I knew would mean the ascent of the teak glory-box. I leaned over my bed smoothing the bedspread as my father came to my door.

"I suppose you have accepted the pirate's chest as Davy calls it. You want it and all that goes with it up here I take it."
"Yes Daddy."
"You didn't tell me you were ready for a box."
"I couldn't before last night Daddy, and I didn't get a chance this morning."
"I agree with Davy, it's a pirate's chest, listen to it."

I was listening. Thump, thump, it was coming up, step by step. My Father said:

"It will take a bit of filling Kit."

There was something in his voice that brought a lump to my throat. I turned and threw my arms around him, rubbing my face against his chin.

"I know" I whispered, "I'll start with the pink satin petticoat. Remember?"

He didn't answer but patted my shoulder instead. Then we both stood aside to make way for the glory box which had reached the top of the stairs.

In the Christmas basket there was a small parcel of books wrapped in brown paper and string. I receive it after Jimmy had gone home again and left us to the family Christmas tree. My father always handed out the presents one by one with ceremony and this one he had kept until the last. It was addressed to Miss Eleanor Jane and he knew it came from Charles. I took it from my father's hand avoiding for the second time that day direct contact with his eyes.

The boys were absorbed with their presents. Daddy sat down having finished his job and Mother, folding tissue paper said pointedly:

"It came yesterday, Kit, by special delivery from one of the bookshops in town."

I said nothing at all, my fingers working feverishly with the knots in the string, my shoulders tensed and my heart pounding. There were two books, "Poems from the Chinese" and "Laotse - Translation". I knew then where Charles was and where he was going. I also felt then that Christmas day was spoiled for me because I could not tell.

Mother said. "Well Kit, I suppose we must leave our presents and get busy in the kitchen. There will certainly be a lot of hungry mouths to be fed before this day is finished" She sighed.

'I've put the turkey in the oven. I suggest that you and I get on to the vegetables while Dad starts on a few sandwiches to feed you little monsters for lunch."

"Alright Mother. Shall I tidy up here first?"

"No, leave the boys with their spoils" Daddy said. "I'll do it later."

So we went to the kitchen, the three of us, and I didn't feel like Christmas. I felt like that sad day of summer three years ago when I had started to grow up. This Christmas the process had 'taken over' again. I felt the stretch of it and ached. First there was Jimmy to be protected and now there was Charles to be defended; Jimmy because he wanted to marry me and Charles because he wanted to deny marriage.

Mother said, "Kit, have you seen Charles?"

"No, I haven't. Do you want all these sweet potatoes peeled?"

"Yes. Those books he sent you came from a downtown store."

"He could have written to them and asked for the books to be delivered the day before Christmas."

My Father said: "Oh for heaven's sake Mother. Stop beating about the bush." He turned to me and the tone of his voice was unusually unpleasant: "I think, Kit, that if you know where Charles is you had better tell your mother."

I swung round towards my mother, my eyes full of angry stinging tears.

"I told you I have not seen Charles. What are you picking on me for just because he sent me some books. He always gives me books for Christmas. What has Charles done that there is all this talking about him all the time?"

"He's just disappeared, that's all, just disappeared a week ago, left a note for his wife to say he was going and went. So the poor girl has had to come home with her baby to her mother and father. It's a disgrace."

"It's a disgrace she ever married him." I said.

"At the time" my mother snapped, "you said yourself it was what Charles wanted and it doesn't become you to be rude to me my girl. Your Aunt Meg is in a pretty bad state about all this. Pat's people are onto her about it as you can imagine. Of course, she asked me if you had any idea where he was and I said I was sure you hadn't heard from him for months. I tell you Kit it was a shock to me when those books came. The hide of him sending you books and not a penny for his wife nor a word to his own mother."

"Why didn't you tell me before? Why didn't you say something? I didn't know."

My mother sighed. "You're not easy to talk to these days, living in a world of your own. I tried to tell you earlier this week but you're so touchy about Charles."

"I'll bet it isn't Charles fault. I bet it isn't."

"Don't be so ridiculous" my father said.

My father's spirit felt removed from me, distant. But it was withdrawn because of Jimmy. Charles had nothing to do with it. I knew he did not approve of Jimmy, who wanted his daughter as a wife, but he couldn't say so because he hadn't been asked. I didn't answer. I stood by the sink, sullen and miserable. I was alienated from them both. Daddy because he wasn't prepared for me to want to marry Jimmy and Mother because it was impossible for her to understand my attitude to Charles. So I burst into tears and rushed out of the kitchen up the stairs to my room. Closing the door loudly I sat in front of my window staring with hurt, glazed eyes at the distant mountain peaks. Nobody followed me upstairs, nobody called outside my door. If I wanted to sulk, I would be allowed to sulk alone. Mother and Father had others beside me to think of on Christmas day. After a few minutes I turned my eyes back into the room and they fell on the bulk of the Chinese chest. So I ran my fingers over the soft wood and, suddenly strengthened, went downstairs again.

When the phone rang Davy answered it. As he always got to the phone first anyway, it saved time on Christmas day just to leave him in charge. Mother was dressing and Dad stoking the furnace in the basement.

Davy yelled. "It's for Kit. It's Jimmy Millar trying to pretend he's somebody else."

"Hi." I said in the special voice I had for Jimmy.

But Charles voice said: "Merry Christmas Eleanore."

I caught my breath. The voice went on. "You got the books?"

"Oh yes, thank you."

"Then you know where I am."

"I think so."

"Can you get away today."

"Oh no - not a hope, too many people."

"I'm off tomorrow in the afternoon."

"Oh dear."

"Tomorrow morning, could you get out by ten say?"

"I think so."

"Alright - 10:30, spot we met the day we went to Chang's, remember?"

"Yes."

"Don't tell anybody Kit. It'll have to be a secret. I'll explain when I see you."

"Alright."

A glow filled me as I hung up the receiver. I thought, why haven't I seen Charles since I have grown up? I'll tell him about Jimmy and all the plans we have together. And I'll wear my new blue coat. Now I could enjoy Christmas day.

***

Charles greeted me, then pushed me back with his hand on my shoulders while he looked at me. He tucked my arm in his, which he had never done before. He was wearing a heavy trench coat which he had often worn, and I noticed that despite the familiarity of his clothes he looked handsome and peculiarly neat. I thought to myself that I had somehow caught up with Charles. It seemed as if the difference in our ages had shrunk. But when I sat opposite Charles at a little table in a drug store booth I could see that his mouth had harassed lines; his manner was nervous and the brown sports coat he wore was a well-worn friend. He smoked one cigarette after another while we talked.

It was evident that he saw something different in me although he tried to act as if he had seen me the previous summer. He started the conversation on a bantering note.

"Well little cousin," he said "you are quite grown up, I see. I would scarcely have expected such a difference. You have a certain quiet and indifferent elegance - you know like a woman safely in love."

"Well, I am"

"You are - are what?"

"In love"

Charles smiled a little and I noticed the corner of his mouth twitch spasmodically.

"First love is a beautiful thing" he said and stopped, his eyes on my face.

But I didn't blush. Instead, I smiled back at him quietly, so secure and confident in myself that I felt almost pity for him, the overwhelming conceited pity of the lover who feel safe for the one whose love has failed.

"It's the real thing Charles. First and last."

"Indeed," he said. "Do I know the lucky man?"

"Of course you do that's why I'm telling you. It's Jimmy Millar."

"Jimmy Millar!" But isn't he still at school?"

"He'll have a BSc in June. He's going back East for two years and then he hopes to go to London."

Charles relaxed and his mouth smiled a little again. "London is quite a long way away."

"I'm going too."

"You are - when?"

"Just as soon as Jimmy gets things settled, where he's to go and all. We planned it all last night. I'm going to have my ring next June when Jimmy graduates and then we thought we might get married and go abroad together. If we absolutely can't then I'll follow as soon as I can."

Charles said slowly. "I see. And how old may I ask will you be next birthday?"

"Oh Charles, you know perfectly well. I'll be twenty. Why?"

"Why, because twenty's too young, that's why. Far too young, especially for you."

I pulled my mouth in but didn't say a word.

"What does your father think about these wonderful plans of yours?" Charles demanded.

"He doesn't know. You see everything happened so fast yesterday"

"Yesterday?"

"Yes, you see I was going to tell Mummy and Daddy first but yesterday Jimmy brought the box."

"What box, I thought you said you were getting a ring next June?"

"Oh no - not a jeweller's box, Charles. Jimmy won't give me a ring until he graduates and has something to offer. This was a glory box."

Charles was watching me intently, his eyes closed a very little, even his hands were still. When I stopped my almost breathless whisper into the space between our heads in that empty cafe he moved his hand to his cheek and rubbed it, and from there back and forth slowly in a circular movement from his forehead to his mouth. I waited expectantly for his eyebrow to go up, but it didn't. Instead, he said almost to himself still looking at me.

"A glory box."

"Yes Charles, a glory box. You see, Jimmy got such a good chance to buy it from a shop owned by a friend's father. He wouldn't have had the chance again. It's so beautiful. You would love it, it's wonderfully carved, a real Chinese glory box."

"A glory box." Charles repeated. "A Chinese glory box. It isn't even funny."

He seemed to be making a flat unequivocal statement to himself. It was then Charles was like Daddy. He didn't approve. I stared at him, feeling the colour rush up in a warm humiliating wave from my neck to my cheeks. Charles lit another cigarette with a vicious strike of the match. The man behind the counter began to whistle and turned on the radio. Only then did I realize something was wrong. He had probably been watching us and decided he was eavesdropping at a lover's quarrel.

"Your father doesn't approve, does he?"

I hit back. "He doesn't approve of you. I had to sneak out to come today, I might tell you."

"My God, what's the matter. Does your father approve of you and Jimmy?"

"There's no need to swear Charles."

Then the eyebrow did go up, but I didn't like it at all.

"It doesn't matter whether your father likes it or not - is that it?"

"Daddy won't mind. It's just that I didn't get a chance to tell them first. He likes Jimmy. I thought you did too." This last was an accusation.

"I do" Charles said. "I do like Jimmy."

"Then what's the matter with you, Charles." I began, in spite of myself, to plead. "That's why I told you. I thought you'd be so happy for us. I thought you'd be glad."

"Why, to make three romances out of one summer?"

"That's exactly what Greta said."

"Did she?" He responded sarcastically. Then, "I need another cup of coffee."

He got up and walked over to the counter. When he paid for the two steaming cups, he asked the server to turn the radio down a bit.

"OK, sure" the boy said.

Charles put the coffee down in front of me.

"Now listen Kit" he said sitting down again, "don't talk, listen. Nobody has anything against Jimmy, get that straight. He's a good kid and without doubt an unusually clever one too and he'll probably turn out brilliant in his line. What is it by the way?"

"A tropical research scientist."

"All of that. No wonder you're carried away with it."

"I'm not carried away with his profession. Science is just his work. It's not his whole life."

"Isn't it? When did all this happen Kit, this romance?"

"This summer. I hadn't seen Jimmy for nearly three years before that - not since that last summer at camp. He's not the first boyfriend I've had you know Charles - not even the first one that wanted to marry me."

"I suppose Ray is broken hearted or hasn't he been told either?"

"You're being perfectly horrible Charles" but something in his face made me add - "Why?"

Charles sat forward.

"Why? I'll tell you since you've asked. Because you are you, a mix-ture of music and poetry and innocent naivety. That's worth some-thing to people like your father and me who have some idea what this damn world is really like. And we don't want to see your personality wiped out - that's all. You have the particular kind of personality that can be wiped out."

I was incredulous.

"And you think Jimmy will do that when he loves me?

"Not purposely of course not. He'll adore you. Come to think of it I suppose he always has. Has he ever had another girl?"

"Well, no, not really. You see he works so hard. He's much younger than the others at the university and all the spare time he has it takes to earn the money. He hasn't had much time for girls."

"I always thought he was a one-woman man."

I smiled thinking of Jimmy.

But Charles wasn't smiling. "I told him so once. I also told him it was a damn dangerous thing to be."

"He told me" I said.

"I meant it was dangerous from the point of view of the one woman. I'll bet he didn't tell you that? Oh, let it go, of course he didn't; he was only a kid, and I was having a go at him only he didn't know it."

"I love him, Charles." I said. "Really I do. It wouldn't matter to me what he was or what he did. I just love him, that's all. He loves me like that too. We didn't mean to hurt anybody else by not telling them. It was just that it happened too quickly for us."

"It always does," he said, "that's how it gets us all."

"Then you mustn't worry about Jimmy and me. We love each other and we'll be alright." I said softly, sorry for him.

"Research in tropical medicine. That's a pretty absorbing job Kit; it doesn't leave time for very much else."

"No. That's what Jimmy says. But then he says he only wants his work and me." I added shyly trying to put Charles at his ease again. "That I'll make up for all the rest for him. He knows he's got a big job ahead. I want to help him. That will be my part."

"And who'll make up for all the rest for you?"

"I'll have Jimmy, I'm terribly interested in his work too. There's such a future in it. After all it's a scientific age we're in and I'll have a part in it."

"You certainly will" Charles said. "But what about your poetry, what about your music?"

"Jimmy wants me to keep all my interests"

"Kind, I'm sure." Charles commented dryly. "You don't consider then that what you call interests could be a career or a life's work if they were developed by, shall we say – Jimmy?"

I laughed, "I can't imagine Jimmy developing poetry."

Charles spoke softly, looking down at the table.

"Kit, you know, don't you that there's no tropical research here. That there never will be. If you marry Jimmy you'll have to give up everything you love that is part of you, the snow on your mountains, the forests at your sea's edge, not to mention your family and your friends, your piano, without even contemplating any success you might have had here as a writer expressing the reality of your birthright."

"I hadn't visualised it quite that way Charles. That's how Daddy must be feeling. Poor Daddy. I hadn't realised how it would be for him. For Mummy it will be alright, I think. Underneath everything else she really wants me to be the wife of a man who has an interesting and successful career. She'll be proud of that. It's different for Daddy."

"And what about your own career."

I laughed. "Oh Charles. I don't have a career. And even if I did have, I'd give it all up for Jimmy even if he wasn't going to be a scientist and take me all over the world with him. Just think of the places I'm going to see. It will be like a dream come true."

Then we both remembered, and Charles looked at his watch.

"Time's nearly up." he said. "I'll have to go soon."

"But we haven't talked about you at all, only me."

"I didn't intend to talk much about myself. I only wanted to say goodbye to you. But I thought you'd still be here when I got back again, when things got straightened out. I forgot that you wanted to travel too."

"You're going to China, Charles?"

"I'll be back, inside a year."

"But it costs so much."

"I'm working my way by sea. Chang fixed it for me"

"From here?"

"The details don't matter. I'm going."

I forced the words out. "And Pat and little David?"

"Kit what did you say when the family told you what a dill I've been?"

"I said whatever you did, you had your reasons. And then I wouldn't talk about it anymore."

"Well," Charles said, "you were right. I have my reasons. I'm not running out on my obligations. I'm coming back. I have signed on for a return trip. As soon as I can I'll send money for Pat and David. Does that answer your question?"

"Not entirely Charles."

"It's all I can tell you now anyway. Someday maybe I'll tell you the whole story, but not now. There's no pattern to it now, nothing fits. That's why I must go away to think."

"Is Pat very extravagant?"

"Funny you should ask that, although I guess our whole family is talking rather than you in particular. Yes, Pat's a bit extravagant but don't worry about her on that account. She has a right to be. She has an income of her own from an uncle of hers who died in England. So, she won't starve."

"Does your mother know that?"

"Hell no. Didn't you know I inherited our strong Scotch family pride?"

"But Charles you haven't saved any money at all have you if you're working your passage. You haven't been home for a holiday since you were married, working in that mill all your holidays and Pat has been home regularly."

"I don't mind working in the mill. I'll probably work full-time in the mill when I come back as teaching is no longer my profession." Charles said and stood up.

It was so like Charles on our tramps to the lighthouse. He had finished the conversation. We walked out of the drug store and stood at the door.

"Charles, how will I know where you are?"

"We have chosen to be travellers you and I, my dear Eleanore, and travellers being pilgrims I expect we'll meet from time to time at some shrine or another. Don't worry your pretty head about me. Your mother's probably quite right. She knows Jimmy will look after you well. So you can add my blessing."

He bent suddenly and kissed me lightly on the cheek then strode off rapidly leaving me standing in the street. This time I did not follow. The cold bleak wind threw itself upon me with the stinging violence of ice, reminding me that it was winter, vigorously clutching at my coat to divest it of its warmth. The cold air slapped my face. Had I noticed how bitter the day less than an hour ago when I came to meet

Charles? It was winter indeed; bitter weather Charles had turned up the collar of his coat against. And somewhere Greta too had started her longest journey. Greta hated the cold. Perhaps she could avoid it in California.

It was winter but I belonged to summer. Inside of me summer glowed with such a warmth the winter wind could only redden the pink of my cheeks. We were four companions of one summer. Greta was gone and Charles, stooped against the force of the wind was on his way. I turned in the opposite direction and let the wind blow me as it blew itself away from my mountains towards the sea, towards the life of constant summer which I would share with Jimmy Millar.

*****

Jimmy lived at home with his family in a suburban house. Mentally he had left home as far back as the time I first met him, certainly long before I engaged myself to marry him. It suited Jimmy to live at home just as it suited him to work in the cannery in the summer. He occupied the third bedroom, vacated by his brother Tom, who left home to be married and work in Haney when Jimmy was fifteen years old. Jimmy pointed out to me that unlike Tom he had always paid board from his holiday work, a considerable sum in total. Married at twenty-one into a Haney business as partner to his wife's father, Tom had signed his own cheque as a guarantee to this father-in-law concerning his business acumen, a fate which had somehow appalled Jimmy and produced in him a periodic generosity far beyond his means. In my family generosity was so much a part of living that we took no notice of its importance. My father regularly bought out of his pocket treats and surprises. Mother and my aunts unloaded their baskets of produce on each other's kitchen tables and in the back kitchen of church halls with such regularity I scarcely ventured anywhere without carrying something. Outgrown clothes and new trimmings moved from house to house. I was used to no waste and no parsimony. Every occasion meant a gift, ten cents worth of jellybeans or a bunch of lilac. As children we only saved up money for presents. What we wanted ourselves we always hoped for; rarely indeed did we save for it. During the depression when Mother bought even the butter at Saturday morning bargain sales in the city, she thought it quite natural to send half a pound of it with her baking-powder biscuits to the Scouts Hall. If we had to save we did without ourselves, eating on certain memorably unpleasant occasions as far as I was concerned a dish of bacon flavoured oatmeal and fried onions with our vegetables or macaroni rissoles. The impression the oatmeal dish made on Jimmy who ate it with relish one winter night was considerable and underlined for me the moral stupidity of embarrassment because I knew the fare at Jimmy's house was constantly the best to the point of monotony. Jimmy's father was conservative in his food taste; his choice if often repeated was not meagre, his preference running to roast beef, steak and kidney pie, pork and apple sauce, and salmon, with chicken on Sunday. Jimmy did not so much ask me to dinner at his place, rather he would say, "Want to come for chicken next week?" or if it was Saturday supper to which his mother invited me, he would remark, "Roast beef and apple pie".

Jimmy shared more meals at my home than I did at his so before a year was out he had run the gamut of a new gastronomical experience and struggled manfully if politely for his share of the delicious depression fare my mother provided, baked beans and griddle scones, American dry hash, spare ribs, mutton stew with raisins, curried shank-bone with rice, browned mince-meat, potatoes with cheese sauce, home salted salmon from the barrel, vegetable pie, corn chowder, sausage meant turnovers, pickled plums, home-brewed raspberry vinegar custard with eggs drawn with naked arm from the icy brine in which they were put down when hens laid well in the summer; pancakes, bottled fruit dumplings, oatcakes, rolled-oat cookies, home-made bread, all these things which we accepted Jimmy savoured, his nose sniffing like a gourmet when he squeezed into his place at our kitchen table. The hot vegetable soup which was always in the huge black pot at the back of our stove was his special favourite. I had taken a cup of hot vegetable soup after school in the winter for as long as I could remember. Like porridge for breakfast my mother and her sisters believed in soup. In our basement were sacks of turnips, parsnips, carrots, potatoes and onions. With barley and bone these provided the soup. I don't know why it tasted so good, cutting up the vegetables was the meanest of my jobs, but I still enjoyed the soup. Jimmy adored it. On cold nights he even went so far as to sneak into the kitchen with me after a date to see if the stove was still on and the soup hot. But he liked sugar on his porridge, a luxury my father would never allow, his theory being that a sprinkling of grape-nuts improved the teeth while sugar was the ruination of them. A piece of buttered toast covered in sugar and sprinkled with cinnamon however was considered legitimate fare with cocoa at night. Insofar as teeth were scrubbed immediately afterwards before retiring to bed.

Jimmy's father was a serious man, disapproving enough in general conversation to remind me of Greta's father, a thought I discouraged actively as unfair and biased. My relations knew Mr Millar as a careful businessman who uncompromisingly supported the continuing Presbyterian Church. He and his wife were respected as good citizens of the narrower view. Jimmy's sister Bessie lived at home and worked in the local telephone exchange. The Millars, according to my family's opinion, had it in them to look after themselves.

From the very first occasion I was invited to tea, the Millars made me welcome. Jimmy's mother offered me kindness, his sister and father acceptance which I felt was more than enough to begin with for it was obvious that Jimmy, to his family, was already something apart. He lived at home, yet he did not belong.

Trying to ferret out the reason, I concentrated on a certain antipathy I felt between Jimmy and Bessie. With Jimmy, Bessie was too patient and long suffering, Jimmy too critical.

"It's all very well" Jimmy snapped one night as we left his house, "working for her poor heathen as Bessie calls them, but not when it takes so much of her time that she goes out looking like a scarecrow. Mother slaves away ironing her clothes. You'd think she could do her hair decently."

Bessie's hair had been screwed back in a bun that would have disgraced a washerwoman.

"She's probably not interested in clothes Jimmy" I suggested.

"I'm not talking about clothes. Her taste is her own business. I'm talking about her person. She used to be so particular."

"Do you think it's something to do with losing Alex Kershaw?"

"I think it's why she lost Alex Kershaw. I don't blame him."

"Well I do." I said hotly. "He went steady with Bessie for years and then in six months married somebody else, new to the choir. You told me yourself."

"If a girl hasn't got time to look after herself, how's she going to look after a man and a family?"

"That's selfish Jimmy."

"Sure it's selfish. I am selfish according to my family and Bessie is unselfish, dedicated to helping the unfortunate. In the end I bet you Kit, I'll do more for the unfortunate than Bessie ever will. Bessie and Mother and Dad too for that matter keep on talking about saving the souls of the heathen. If you ask me any heathen would rather have his life saved by a selfish doctor who puts himself first than have his soul saved by an unselfish missionary type who looks miserable and wants to take away all the things that make his simple life happy."

"But there are wonderful missionaries, Jimmy."

"No doubt. But I bet they're self-respecting and tidy themselves up first before they start on the heathen. I bet they don't sink to the level of the poor unwashed and lose their own centre. A good missionary would do more by example than anything else anyway. The heathen would look at a self-respecting missionary and think that being a Christian must be all right if it made a man upright, well-dressed, well-fed and the master of his own fate."

"Jimmy, you didn't say all this to your family did you?"

"Of course I did. It's true. It's time Bessie took hold of herself. She used to be a swell girl and now she's just running around in circles between the Missionary Society and prayer meetings. You'd think she'd catch on. She's the only girl I know of her age that's so silly!"

"You must have made them terribly angry, Jimmy."

"I did not. I wish I had. They were horrified and shocked and long-suffering. They think I've been contaminated by the University. They'd probably like to kick me out so I could return as a prodigal son. It's too bad I'm self-supporting as well as a scholar, not to mention engaged to marry a good girl as they call you. It leaves them rather helpless, doesn't it?"

"I wish you weren't so hard on them. They love you, Jimmy."

"That's nothing to do with it. They don't trust me because I don't think the way they do. Bessie and Dad think they've got all the answers and Mother copies them. Mother really is unselfish, and they both take advantage of her. She needed a new hat and I gave her the money for it so Bessie brought up the poor Armenian's and Dad said he'd given up the idea of a new suit so Mother put the money in the church box. My money, that I earned working with the poor Japanese they despise so much!"

"Oh Jimmy, don't be bitter. They try to do what they think best."

"They don't think, Kit. If they did they'd realise that the real Christians, the few there are of them, took an Armenian orphan home to live with them, years ago. It's all very well for you Kit. your father invited Iko into the house and gave him Christmas cake. Iko is not welcome where I live or any other Japanese either. And yet all you hear about over the meal-table is missionaries and the poor heathen and all Bessie does for them. The truth is I've had it."

"The Minister at our Church is just as bad, Jimmy."

"Then all I can say is it's a wonder you go to Church."

"I don't do much since I've been engaged to you Jimmy." I said archly in an attempt to change the subject but he didn't smile.

"The sooner I get out of that atmosphere the better." he thundered. "It interferes with my work. My god, I hope I get the scholarship."

I was of two minds about the scholarship. If he got it, his prospects would be enhanced. But it would take him away to Eastern Canada for two years, away from me. I had a feeling that his mother felt the same way, preferring Jimmy should marry me and settle down after his graduation. A university degree was the ultimate honour she could accept. That it should be merely a starting point was beyond her imagination. I was selfish. I wanted Jimmy's physical presence. She was fighting subconsciously against the inevitable loss of a son who had outgrown her. Jimmy's father might be narrow and bigoted. My father, a good churchman, had hinted as much and I accepted his word scarce knowing the true meaning of bigoted as concentrating on the religiously narrow. Bessie I had hoped to love as Jimmy's only sister, the nearest to a sister I would ever myself possess. Jimmy discouraged me about Bessie. He was disgusted because he had lost her, because she had taken a job instead of matriculation and religion instead of life. Jimmy knew his occupation had moved him out of the orbit provided by his parents. He expected me to realise this and adjust myself accordingly on pleasant terms of uncommitted familiarity. I discovered it really did not matter at all to Jimmy whether his family liked me or not or I them. This was to me an astounding contradiction. I wanted my family to adore Jimmy.

I thought no man more handsome than Jimmy Millar, a head taller than I, lean-hipped, nose and chin firmly defined in his serious bony face; heavy brows, black lines over his snapping eyes; lips straight and firm except when his wide smile sweetened with humour the furrows that swung round his cheekbones and melted into the tiny crows-feet wrinkles at the bridge of his nose. Many of the boys I knew were still soft-fleshed and beardless with the tanned spotted complexions of fair skinned northern peoples. Jimmy was gypsy in comparison, his hair black, his eyes coal-shiny, his skin tight-stretched and so sun-susceptible that tan bloomed from gold to amber without his slightest effort.

We were, generally speaking, a fair-skinned family, subject to white cotton shirts over our bathing suits, red nose, freckles and sun-burn cream. Being pink and white to Jimmy's bronze, I decided I could not abide fair men. Romance for me lay surely with the dark and handsome breed. Not that the family saw anything unusual in Jimmy's colouring as cousins such as Charles were dark enough. One and all they did their best to keep me earthed.

"You sure can't miss his nose and chin" Donald commented once when I grew too enthusiastic. "If that's what you mean by a strong profile."

I regarded Donald with the distaste and contempt reserved by youth for those close on their heels yet younger, but withheld further comment just in case. Davy had grown fond of Jimmy back in our camping days and during the early period of my engagement seemed to be filled unexpectedly with a sort of admiration, a restraining awe.

"Jimmy sure must have brains." he announced one day to the as-sembled company. "He's no good at sports but he's still got hard mus-cles and his head's so big I bet he couldn't buy a hat any place."

"That will do Davy" mother said dryly.

"Well, gee, I bet he couldn't! His head sure is as big as a pumpkin, Ma."

"It is not" Donald squashed Davy, "or else you haven't seen many pumpkins. Nobody's head's as big as a pumpkin. You exaggerate everything."

"I have so seen pumpkins at Halloween. I've seen great big pumpkins haven't I Ma?"

"Just you shut up Davy" I snapped, sensitive and shaky. Adverse discussion about Jimmy at that period tended to bring me close to tears.

"Well, gee whiz, I only said Jimmy had a big brain. What's wrong with that. Anybody'd think you owned Jimmy Millar. How can anybody have a big brain without a big head I'd like to know."

"Unfortunately you seem to have neither Davy" Mother said. "So no more will be said, do you hear, not another word."

"Oh alright" Davy moaned "only you mustn't let Donald say I never saw a pumpkin."

Wilfred, the Adonis of the greater clan, was witheringly nice about my engagement to Jimmy.

"Oh well, it takes all kinds to make a world so I'm happy for you my sweet." (My sweet was his latest term of endearment for ladies). "Besides you can't have everything. If you go for brains I suppose you can't expect looks and sports too - it wouldn't be fair, now would it? A university degree or a sports career, one or the other, I say!"

There was not much doubt which Wilf preferred.

"And you certainly won't be getting the university degree, Wilf" Peg said sweetly.

She was very impressed and told me she thought Jimmy was very good looking in a strong sort of way which was gratifying and which sentiment I found I could agree with wholeheartedly.

"Do you think Jimmy's good looking?" I demanded of Mother in a burst of anxiety after one of my first tiffs with Jimmy, during which I discovered a certain new prominence manifested in his chin.

Mother, I remember, was leaving for town and looked at me above the modest dignity of her best tailored suit which she wore with the style and confidence usually inspired by a new garment. I think often of how well my mother and her sisters wore tailored suits, feminine blouses with good brooches at the throat, elegantly re-trimmed hats and spotless, darned suede gloves during the depression years. Their suits were almost a uniform of the determination that defeats adversity. Unfortunately suits did not suit me.

"Your Jimmy" Mother said with deliberation, "has a good face for which I am grateful as a mother should be about the man her daughter chooses. His eyes are set well apart and his features are not weak. There will come a time, I have no doubt, when he will look distinguished. He has the figure, the head and the brain for it. That's enough Kit. To ask for more is no mean form of vanity which I hope neither you nor Jimmy will suffer. I'm not one for discussing looks which by and large the Lord gives us, not ourselves."

"Men say some pretty ridiculous things" I observed dramatically. "Jimmy for example says I'm beautiful when I'm wrong."

"You're both blind as bats at the moment which is as it should be, I suppose. When he really sees you angry and you really see him stubborn it will be time enough to worry. Meanwhile you're not a bad-looking couple if I do say so myself, I who ought to have more sense than to encourage such conversation. See you've the dinner on in time and for heaven's sake Kit, attend to your room and your ironing before you get your head into a book. I have my doubts sometimes that you'll ever manage a home, engaged and all as you are, and I can't see Jimmy expecting less than the best from you."

"He'll get a few shocks" I said airily relieved and cocky again and still not a little annoyed at Jimmy.

"That he will" Mother said, "when he wants his socks mended." We smiled at each other intimately and almost immediately embarrassed began to laugh.

I don't know if Mother ever knew how the warm rich humanity of that simple statement of hers remained in my mind to bolster me up when Jimmy really seemed intolerably, ridiculously and irrationally stubborn. 'Blind as bats' I would think and laugh, seeing him suddenly handsome which would make him think me beautiful. Laughter, being infectious, is a grand prelude to loving.

The self-confident assertion and determination of Jimmy's acceptance of his right to education and his chosen profession impressed every member of my greater family filling them with a kind of willing respect. The knowledge of his mental capacity had of course preceded his re-appearance into our family circle. The less commendable aspects of higher education were admitted but granted only a secondary importance. Jimmy typified educational progress in a democratic society which was desperately sick. He was the rags to riches boy for whom free higher education was contrived and it pleased my family to see him calmly asserting and taking advantage of his claim. They saw a degree as the prize of those whom the Lord gave the brains to receive it. They saw Jimmy as one such and would have been personally affronted to see him fail. They did not discuss with Jimmy the profession he had chosen or the subjects he studied, yet they let it be known among friends and acquaintances what status would be achieved by the young man I was to marry. My feet of course were to be kept on the ground. It was candidly assumed I knew nothing of science. A scientific word from me held the disapproval of heresy, in case I transcend the average, begrudging me the use of intelligence. Not that I minded at first, basking in the reflected glory, overcome with pride.

It was only after Jimmy went East for further study, when I wanted to co-ordinate quotes from his letters into my conversation that resentment replaced the efforts that I made towards compensating myself for Jimmy's absence. Deprived of Jimmy's company I was forced to revert to family normality which excluded even a reference to my future means of support. A new kind of sorcery was pretty much what my family thought of pure science. Applied science had limited acceptance. Jimmy's world was as distant as the moon from even my father.

"You accept aeroplanes" I once accused Daddy, quoting Jimmy. "You accept radio and the telephone and x-rays and cars and electricity which you didn't have when you were young. Some scientist was working on those things long before they became reality."

Inventors were responsible and inventors were another sort of genius. It was no use to suggest that inventions were a build-up, a series of modifications and experiments on a given assortment of accounted data. It was always James Watt and the tea kettle and better for ordinary people to attend to their own business. 'Wonders will never cease' covered nearly every situation. Inspiration, sudden and complete gave humanity something new which was avidly accepted and exploited, not something which was already there that co-operation, patience, accumulated knowledge and scientific method had analysed and reproduced in sequence. There was this new thing: science and miracles. Scientific method was unknown, the evolutionary principle godless because in the popular mind of my youth science was anti-religious. To choose science was to leave church. I said to my father:

"Science is growth Daddy, going forward making life better for everybody. I don't see why people think science and religion don't go together."

"Religion has defined the ideal life. Science does not. It just goes on discovering new ways of producing things. I don't say life isn't better, but it seemingly results in indiscriminate production. Guns or medicine, whatever turns up."

"Yes, but if you have both religion and science then you have the ideal plus the new discoveries."

"It doesn't seem to work that way. Science is impartial and just goes on and on regardless, after achieving practical results and forgetting the chief end of man. God and Christian ideals don't seem to come into it - just one invention after the other for its own sake, good or bad."

"Most is good wouldn't you say Daddy in the long run?"

"I don't know dear. I wouldn't like to say. I can't help thinking the inventions might get out of control."

"They needn't if men keep high ideals."

"As long as scientific progress doesn't get a strangle-hold and replace everything else."

"But why should it?"

"Because men are a greedy lot. They want what they see. I don't know why it should be but I think it will get going at a gallop and leave everything else trailing behind in the dust."

"Jimmy's work will help cure those horrible diseases that kill thousands of people every year."

"Is Jimmy doing it because he wants to cure these people or because he wants to find out why they die and beat the cause of their death? Is he putting the people or the disease first? If his interest is in beating the disease, he'll go on to beat another disease and then another for the sake of science. In another field a scientist will go on and on making lethal weapons, also for science sake, and another will be making new materials for people to buy whether they need them or not. Another will develop better radios even when the transmission is perfect. Science becomes for scientists, an object in itself whereas religion gives a level discipline for living for every man."

"Science requires the most rigid discipline."

"Mental, for physical and material progress. Religion is spiritual discipline. It pulls people up by the personal measuring rod of morality.

"But science is not immoral, Daddy."

"Morality doesn't seem to come into it at all as far as I can see. What they call pure science seems to be outside morality, divorced from it, unconcerned, carried out for its own sake then handed over for any sort of use, greed or good."

"It needn't be. Scientists are good men, not wicked men. They didn't cause the depression. None of them are gangsters."

"They're not concerned with the depression either nor with eliminating the gangsters or studying Bolshevism nor with the Church or morality in general for that matter. Their only concern is science."

"That's a dreadful thing to say Daddy."

"Well, yes, I guess it is. I guess the world is too big a mess even for scientists to cope with. I have no proof to say a scientist can't operate personally according to his religious principles like the rest of us. You know more about it than I do Kit. I hope you're right about the good science is doing for humanity."

He always ended any conversation with kindness allowing me to keep my illusions. Besides his heart was too big to keep anyone out of the kingdom of God because of a profession, certainly not anyone his daughter loved, not the member of any profession in which his loved ones had an interest. He begrudged me nothing the future might hold that was good, but his reasoning warned him that the future held the brooding possibility of increased godlessness. The church in its corruption had been thrown out of Russia and civil pandemonium and acrimoniousness had replaced it by the state, through murder and violence after a century of festering hate. To my father it was like a repetition of the French Revolution, a bursting bubble of stinking horror between man and man, a reenactment of Dickens in the 'Tale of Two Cities'. What church could have been worse than this holocaust of inhumanity? Socialism was to him inherently Bolshevism, any church better than no church at all. I inherited from my father a hatred of violence. He preferred the depression that slowly broke his spirit to war in any form. The gangsterism in Chicago appalled him so that he could scarcely bring his tongue to speak of it. My father was a man who, when arguments and reasoning failed, stood still and turned the other cheek. He impressed upon me when I was very young the odd fact that as far as he could read there was not one line in the New Testament that justified the Crusades. As children, no Crusade literature appeared as our bedtime story.

The years have thrown up intimate conundrums unperceived in childhood. Never once did my father call himself a pacifist. My mother's family openly fought for what they thought was right. I wonder now if my father ever needed to discover any means to attain the ideals for which he stood. He belonged to no association, was a member only of the church and the church choirs in which he sang. He would not even agree to becoming an elder. "The Minister is a little narrow, Mother" I heard him say one time he was asked. It was not a hurried decision he made for his name came up for election with persistent regularity. In retrospect I see his outlook as perhaps socialist in the early and best sense. Yet Fabianism amongst those in whom he knew it appalled him. He told Jimmy it was a step or two away from Bolshevism, a statement pronounced at our dinner table that made Jimmy pull in his lips over an unuttered reply and fill his mouth with extra bread and butter lest he be rude.

"The way your father shies away from any limited or narrow view makes you fall into the trap of thinking he knows more than he does."

Jimmy remarked later. "Really I don't think he know anything about the Fabian Society or what its members stand for."

"And you know everything" I snapped back.
"No, I hate politics and keep my nose right out. But I do know Socialism isn't Bolshevism. There's all the difference between intellectualism and anarchy. I suppose the truth is your father doesn't know much about either. He could have done with a good education though, Kit."

Torn between two worlds as I was, I agreed with this latter statement of Jimmy's. But now I think perhaps it was better that Daddy was how he was, not even a teacher like Charles. Pure science is intellectualism and the products of its corporate mind have been amalgamated with anarchy. My father lived with only intuitive suspicions and apprehensions of the future. Nazi concentration camps, refugees in millions, the flights of dive bombers above the homes of children, Hiroshima and cold war fear were yet to become irreconcilable facts. Do penicillin, aureomycin, radar and television make up for this? He would not have thought so. His world was essentially the wide world, encompassed by the love of God to be lived through earning an honestly made living that provided time off to spend with one's children close to nature, on the beaches. Improvements in motor vehicles intrigued him, but speed for its own sake was going too far. Radio, like the gramophone was fascinatingly novel but in music personal performance was the superlative. Modernisation of the home was, for a mother's sake, a blessing but camping and gardening was the ultimate enjoyment for himself.

My father was as man of medium height who for as long as I can remember wore glasses. Behind the lenses his eyes opened wide and soft with kindness and some further quality in their depths, perhaps pity or sadness, which replaced that which showed dissatisfaction in the eyes of other men.

"I've often wondered what your father thinks about me" Charles had remarked once. "Those sad eyes of his looking at me with a remote kind of pity. I don't even feel it to be personal pity for myself. Perhaps its pity for all the human fools put together."

"I wish you wouldn't say things like that Charles. You sound so bitter."

"That's how I feel. Acidic, callous and bitter. Would I be less of a fool if I shirked the truth. You know, Wilf said a smart thing, for him, in respect to your father. He remarked that he'd rather be blown to smithereens any day by your mother than looked at by your father because he felt that his own father and mother and everybody else in the family always looks back at him from your father's eyes."

"Sounds double-Dutch for Wilf"

"Does it? Think about it."

I didn't then but I do now. I often think about it. The eyes of my father are the only thing about him that I remember clearly. The recollection of his words comes after the presence of his eyes rests lightly upon me with the colourless grey opaqueness of rain. It does not matter what colour they were really, only the generous lucidity matters, two round smooth windowpanes that gave access to the steady ray of light within. Sometimes in desperation I have cried out from my heart to this dim light.

"What would you do now, tell me, what would you do now?"

The light does no more than beam out the pity, steadily without deflection and the pity refuses to flicker until I am suffused with a warmth that I myself must suffer, and all the other fools in the humanity that surrounds me. I have at times been in a pit of terrible darkness, past self-purification, and been drawn out and lifted up by my father's eyes, the immovably rock-stern profile of Charles, my mother's laugh and Jimmy's hands. It took me many years to discover that these precious things belonged to me.

At the end of August Jimmy boarded the train for McGill University. He had graduated with brilliance and I, basking in reflected glory sat beside his parents and swelled with pride. Before he left, he put a ring on my finger, and I gave him every promise that glowed in my heart. The ring was beautiful, the diamond small but perfect and beautifully cut. Jimmy had chosen it at Christmas and paid it off by July after a month in the Cannery.

"Now" Jimmy said, "You're my girl and don't you forget it."

"As if I needed a ring to know that. Are you sure you could afford it Jimmy. It's so beautiful. You won't have much money."

"Only the best for my girl" Jimmy said. "I suppose like everybody else you're thinking there won't be any big cannery money where I'm going. Just the same believe it or not I've got a job next summer."

"Oh Jimmy - next summer."

"Now don't say, you can't stand not seeing me for two years. Two years are nothing in our lives. You keep busy and think about me. Only one thing. Keep off too much poetry. I don't want you sad. I'll be back for you."

"And we will have our letters, Jimmy. You'll write often."

"Once a week, honey. Anything more will be just extra. Once a week will be for sure. I know I can do that. I'm not going to promise what I can't do."

***

After Jimmy had been gone for a year I found myself in the stillness of night remembering his hands, the long fingers tense and tender on my arm as if the slightest pressure, the merest contraction might somehow hurt me, as if my skin which he caressed was the petal of a flower. No matter what he said, his love had always been evident in the touch of his hands, in the nerves of his fingertips. Too many things were difficult to recall about love a year after Jimmy left. The pressure of forcing remembrance lost to me the moments that meant the most. I tried to relive them but I couldn't. They were so many they became diffused, so myriad the connection, so fragile they burst like bubbles and disappeared when I tried to re-possess them. Love is as distant as the dream state yet so intensely alive, so vital that there is not time to register impressions, to capture and record for all those future hours of waiting, the static times of longing when nothing counts but memory and every memory sobs in the heart. It was always his hands I would unexpectedly feel even when I forgot the features of his face, when my mind struggled impatiently to recall like a chorus the words he said. But I would remember his hands suddenly with unaccountable urgency and my eyes would fill with tears. This was all I had of tangible loving in those waiting days, remembering the touch of a man's two hands, feeling them crush my own and fall anxiously apart as if my fingers might break in two.

Life of course moved on. A year and a month after Jimmy's departure I celebrated my coming of age with a small family party which was all and even more than I desired. The highlight of my birthday was a pink satin nightgown to match my glamorous petticoat which told me in language more specific than words that my father was with me again in spirit. I needed this assurance for without Jimmy life in the midst of the depression had reverted to a phase of such flat mediocrity that I even avoided poetry since it, with the speed of a chopped onion and equal acidity, brought instant tears.

I had not dated except in company with the crowd for the ring on my finger foretold the answer to be expected to that kind of telephone call. In every other way life moved on as usual. The first few months were hard to bear but time went by as time must always do.

I wrote part of a letter to Jimmy every night and studied his weekly letter with such a deep concentration that in the first year every word increased in meaning until I discovered in his replies, how one can misinterpret the simplest things. After that I began to enjoy his letters, receiving from them without anxiety only their basic content, certainly enough because Jimmy, in contrast to myself, wrote carefully composed letters relating his activities almost analytically, so that if time failed him notes would do. Taken literally Jimmy's letters were Jimmy's life. After a while I began to see them as such and knew if they were different, things were not going as Jimmy wished them to.

After my birthday Jimmy wrote:

"I'm taking a room with Sykes. He's not the usual run and keeps decent house. Apart from his work, music is his outlet. I can't say I like his taste. He dragged me along to a chamber music concert. You'd like Sykes. Music every week. Williams' mother likes music and therefore Sykes. So we were invited there for dinner before the concert. I told you Williams' old man is the Botany Professor, quite a character - doesn't know the data himself and bites your head off if you don't give it to him. Quick enough, but tops in his line. So Sykes talked to mum, and I answered the Prof and Williams was happily reduced to case-history conversations with his brother, a lawyer home for the weekend. The atmosphere was peculiarly good - so much so that Sykes and I have been invited by Williams from Christmas to New Year. So you needn't worry about me. I'll be getting a good dinner. Better keep your music up Kit. I told Sykes you're pretty good and Sykes being the big-sheep-dog type ingratiatingly passed on the information to Mrs Williams. So you have a reputation now. Herewith enclosed the program of the chamber music concert. Sykes is into mathematics and he argued all the way home that music and maths have the same source. I'm not convinced."

In one year and after my birthday party, my aunts, cousins and Jimmy's mother had filled the Chinese glory-box. I put in the ginger-jar with my birthday presents and closed the lid. I wrote to Jimmy that the box was full.

"For God's sake don't start another one" he wrote. *"By the time we get married we will have enough to carry around without you collecting more tablecloths. We don't want a lot of luggage. Conditions are different where we hope to go. Houses are tropical and usually provided furnished. Even your clothes will be different. Phillips, who's been lecturing here from Malaya says you'll need cotton. The last thing you want to do is collect."*

He had sent me a little brooch for my birthday, like a ring of blue flame with a pearl centre. I told Mother and I think she was relieved. Life was a constant financial effort for her and she had bought towards my trousseau three lengths of materials she could ill-afford. I looked however with apprehensive longing at the row of books in my bookcase and the tremendous pile of sheet music in our living room. At a future date I decided to try re-packing the Chinese chest with a layer of books and music as a base. There were a few things in the glory box I had made myself which would make suitable gifts to other brides who knew they would be furnishing the usual kind of house. Among my contemporaries and relations the word went round through my mother that pots and pans were unsuitable presents for Kit.

That Christmas, the second without Jimmy, Davy had no envy for me, only masculine pity.

"Gee, all you've got this year is hankies and underwear and those d'oyley things, except for Charles."

Except for Charles who had sent a small square package of pure white Chinese silk tied with red ribbon. He had come home again and was working at the mill and living in a small town near Port Alberni.

Pat and their little boy David had gone back to live with him. Charles had been but once to see his mother yet all the family seemed happy about him again. He had done the right thing, the best to be expected of Charles, taking into consideration the peculiarities of his nature. But I had not seen him. He had not written to me. The previous Christmas he had forgotten me altogether. I looked at the silk with a jaundiced eye as if it were something Pat did not want. It was the first Christmas that Charles had not sent poetry. I wrote my thanks formally as to a stranger. There was no further correspondence.

To get closer to Jimmy in his absence I tried desperately hard to be friends with his mother and sister Bessie. But there was little common ground. Bessie grew more absorbed in a limited Christianity and left her father's church to join another which entirely disapproved of science. This created limitations when we talked about Jimmy. I felt she also disapproved of my bridge club, of the dances put on by our Church Young People's Society and the plays we produced to raise funds; in short, she suspected my motives attending the social activities our church provided instead of getting involved in the prayer meetings and evangelism which were her own special interests. I saw little enough of Bessie before her engagement and even less after it. I always felt guilty about Bessie as if I was somehow to blame for having known her so little. She was Jimmy's only sister and I had no sister. Had I known her before the break with Alex Kershaw things might have been different. Every second Friday I had tea with Jimmy's parents, but on these occasions Bessie always went to her meeting straight after her meal. I thought when she decided to marry Cyril Cook she would share with me the treasure of her glory box. I showed her mine one Sunday afternoon but she refused to open hers to me until the day she had her bride's shower a week before she married, during the third week of May. I was one of twenty people most of whom I didn't know. Mother and Auntie Meg were invited with me to Bessie's shower tea.

"She must have been embroidering for the last twenty-years." Auntie Meg said on the way home. So I knew that most of the things must have been made with Alex Kershaw in mind, which made me feel sadder and more guilty than ever.

Bessie was not a traditional bride and had no attendants except a married couple, a brother and sister in the faith who stood up with Bessie and Cyril and then signed the register. Mr and Mrs Millar and their eldest son Tom and his wife were there. Jimmy was away and glad to be so there was no invitation for me. I was terribly hurt and Mother and Daddy and all my relatives indignantly blamed Jimmy's mother for not standing up to Bessie. I knew Jimmy's mother stood up to nobody. She worked in the house from morning to night and agreed with everything her husband said. I suspected Mr Millar had latterly found that Bessie's views threatened the comfort of his own.

Jimmy's mother came to see me in the evening after Bessie's afternoon wedding. She was a little woman with a face shaped like Jimmy's. She had Jimmy's eyes, faded and watery at the edges. I remember thinking to myself that she must have been pretty and dainty when younger. Her hands and feet were beautifully shaped and small. She was kind and considerate to me and out of them all, only she knew I would be hurt. So she brought me a tablecloth of ecru linen, finely worked with self-toned cross stitch and pulled thread work, bordered with wide hand-crocheted lace. When she gave it to me, she asked to see again the things in my box so while Mother made tea I took her upstairs to my room. She sat on the white painted chair in front of the white desk Daddy had built in front of the window under the eaves where the roof sloped attic fashion. On my bed was a party dress of rose shot taffetas Mother had recently finished making for me. Mrs Millar's eyes fell upon the dress.

"What a pretty dress dear" she said, and I was embarrassed for her, knowing she would think I had planned to wear it at Bessie's wedding.

"It's for a friend's twenty-first tomorrow night" I said quickly, "Mother just finished it this afternoon and I pressed it."

"You'll be going without Jimmy then?"

"Yes."

"It's not very fair to you is it dear, Jimmy being so hard driving on himself, so ambitious he must go away from his home to follow this new profession. It's not what I hoped."

"He's very clever. I'm very proud of him."

"He was a gentle boy, a home boy I would have said but the determination of his father is even stronger in him. He'll go his own way, no matter. I don't understand it myself."

I twisted the ring on my finger.

"I do" I said, "the whole future of the world depends on science, Jimmy says."

"The whole future of the world is in the hands of God" she said stiffly. "His father says it is blasphemy in the boy to say otherwise."

"No" I said, "I don't think that. God made science. It's for good. It's for helping people."

She disagreed. "I would have been proud if Jimmy had chosen to be a doctor. I'd have been proud of that."

"It's the same in a way" I said, convincing myself for Jimmy had told me many times that it was not the same, not the same at all.

"He said himself it's not the same. I begged him to go for medicine. The principal in his High School too - but he would not."

"He must work where his heart it."

"He must work where God wills." she said. "You should tell him. He doesn't listen to me. Have you asked him to do medicine?"

"No."

"If you had he would have changed, no doubt. He'd change if you asked him now."

"Oh no, I don't think so."

"He would if you said you wouldn't marry him unless he did. He's promised to you. He's a good boy. He knows his duty to you even if he has forgotten it to his parents."

"I couldn't do that, Mrs Millar."

"You have your rights" she said. "Your right to a nice home near your folks, to a nice wedding with all your friends about you. You want to be a real bride. It's not right of him to ask you to give up all you want for him."

"He wants me to join him in London early next year."

"He wrote to me" she said. "He won't come home again this summer because of the cost. He'll work at the job as long as he can and then get to England at the end of August."

"Working his way on a tramp steamer he thinks."

"You'll not agree to such a plan."

"If he spends the money coming home this summer he won't be able to send for me so soon."

"It's not right he should send for you. He should come home and marry you properly. His father and I have told him so. Bessie wrote too and Tom agrees. We told him very plainly, Kit. I want you to know that. I told him your parents would not let you cross to some foreign part by yourself."

"Mother would come with me if she could afford it Mrs Millar. It's not possible."

"Then get Jimmy home and marry him here, dear. It's right that you should."

"He must be in England by October to take up the scholarship."

"Do you really think he needs to study more, Kit? To my mind and his father's, he has more than enough education. It's time he was settling down and taking his responsibilities."

"He'll need to study two more years after this year - at least."

"His father will give him no further support Kit. I'm bound to tell you that. If he comes home now we'll help where we can, but not otherwise. He would not be where he is now except for his father's patience."

What was I to say, knowing how Jimmy's determination had confounded his father year after year. Money earned at the cannery, coaching money, weekend jobs, warehouse loading to pay his fees. Yet until he had gone back East on a scholarship his father had kept him, and Jimmy knew it. I knew it. I suspected his father had reproved him for getting engaged before he had even fully paid for his board and keep. In their way Jimmy's parents had accepted me nevertheless, given me generous presents, cultivated my parents. They had convinced themselves I would be a settling influence, limiting Jimmy's ambitions to what they considered reasonable proportions.

"It's not God's will that a man should be over-ambitious Kit."

"He has to finish, Mrs Millar." I said. "He'll be unhappy if he doesn't. Jimmy has to finish what he starts."

"I see no end to it. He's my son but I am not a fool. You will be the one to pay. Are you willing to play second fiddle to science all your life?"

"I don't expect it will be like that" I said.

"No, I suppose you don't. The young never do" she sighed. "His father's done all he intends. I wanted to tell you."

Second fiddle! Second fiddle, I was thinking indignantly, arrogantly. Anyway, I would rather play second fiddle to a brilliant scientist than to a man like Jimmy's father, the manager of one section of a shipyard and an elder in an old-fashioned church or second fiddle to a converted bible basher like the man Bessie had married. What I said was hypocritical and smug.

"You'll be proud of Jimmy one day."

"I was very proud when he graduated from university."

"That was only the beginning."

"So it seems, 'Pride goeth before a fall and a haughty spirit before destruction.' Never forget that dear and don't forget what I told you when making your decision."

But my decision was already made. As Jimmy's wife I would travel the world. As Jimmy's wife I would back his career to the limit of my resources. Mother called to us that a cup of tea was waiting. We went downstairs.

"Poor woman" my mother said after Jimmy's mother went home. "She was ashamed about leaving you out of the wedding. Not that she had much choice, it seems. She was disappointed over Bessie's wedding. It was plain as the nose on your face, the disappointment. She wanted Bessie to be a bride like Alex Kershaw's wife was. Instead she had no ceremony, not of her own denomination. She was telling you no doubt. You were a long time upstairs."

"It wasn't that she was telling me Mother. She wants Jimmy to come home instead of going on to London."

"Aye, I can understand that."

"Well, I can't. How can she expect him to give up the chance he'd worked for all these years."

"There's his obligation to you Kit" Mother said. "It's a long time to ask a girl to wait."

"I'll go to Jimmy as soon as he can send for me" I said.

My parents were silent. I knew they wanted Jimmy to come home for a white wedding in our own church. I was after all their only daughter.

Daddy said: "Mother tells me Ray is taking you to the party tomorrow night. Is that quite fair?"

"He asked me" I said. "I couldn't very well refuse. I wanted to go to Beth's twenty first. She's one of my best friends."

"I could have run you over" Daddy said.

"Ray would only have asked to bring me home" I snapped.

"I'm sorry for Ray" Mother said.

"Look Mother" I protested. "It's only like Bessie Millar going around with Alex Kershaw until he got married to somebody else. Now she's married somebody else. Ray and I are good friends. He's had another girl since I went out with him."

"A lot of people think he's carrying a torch, Kit. It's not fair to the lad with you engaged to Jimmy. I wouldn't like the Millars to hear of it."

"Fair, fair!" I cried. "Nothing is fair. Jimmy's mother says Jimmy isn't fair to me if he doesn't come home and I'm not fair to her if I don't demand he comes home. I don't think it's fair to interfere with his career. It's not fair if Ray takes me to Beth's party and not fair to Beth if I don't go. It's not fair to Ray that I'm engaged to Jimmy and not fair to Jimmy if I go out with Ray. Worst of all I know it's not fair to you if I go away to marry Jimmy and not fair to Jimmy if I don't. What am I going to do?"

"Calm down" Mother said, "the woman has upset you. There's no ned for any fuss at all. I suppose she saw your dress up there. I told you to hang it up."

I didn't answer.

"So Jimmy has told his parents he's working his way to London" Daddy said.

I nodded.

"He'll get on, that one" Mother said. "I thought you said if he got the grant his fare would be included."

"There's an allowance that covers his fares. He wants to save it towards sending for me. He'll have what he earns this summer as well."

"What would you live on in London."

"He thinks we could manage on the allowance. He will have to board somewhere anyway."

"He thinks two can live as cheaply as one, is that it?"

"It wouldn't be for long. If he gets the job on the boat in September, he'll have a bit of money saved and then he'll see how things go and what it's like in England, how much things cost. Then if everything goes well I could leave after Christmas to get there in the Spring."

"In the Spring, that's less than a year Kit."

"I know but we won't see each other this summer. It seems a terribly long time to me."

My father said: "You're young enough."

But my mother was more practical.

"Now Dad" she said, "we faced this when Jimmy went back East. Kit is set on marrying Jimmy. She's had time to change her mind if she was going to and I see no sign of that. If the lad can manage to support a wife I see no point in making him wait alone in a strange country any longer than necessary. Kit and I can get ready by the spring. You can see for yourself she's neither the one thing nor the other as things are now."

My father lit his pipe using about twenty matches.

"I'd like your mother to go with you." he said finally.

"Well I can't and that's that" Mother said, "so stop worrying your head about it."

"You always wanted to see the Old Country" Daddy said.

"Aye and one day no doubt I will. If Kit doesn't get back. I'll go to see my grandchildren and Meg along with me."

"I'll get back" I said. "Jimmy says the tropical research men get home leave every two years."

"Do they now" Mother said impressed, "that's something to look forward to, isn't it Dad."

"It would be wonderful if you could come abroad to see us with Mother" I said to Daddy.

He sucked his pipe, knocked it out, staring with mild disappointment into the bowl.

"Hand me a pipe-cleaner will you" he said. "Oh, I don't know. Capilano Canyon is good enough for me or a trip by sea to Bowen Island."

"Oh Daddy" I said.

"Have you thought how you'll go Kit?" Mother asked.

"Via Panama, Jimmy says. One of the Empress boats is going from here about March."

"That boy will look after you" Mother said with satisfaction, "and since you've set your heart on him it's just as well. I wouldn't want to see you running round the wicked world with a man like your cousin Greta got, nor for that matter with anybody as erratic and unreliable as your cousin Charles."

"I think Jimmy should come home and take Kit with him" Daddy said.

"I'd rather it that way and so would you, Mother and you know it. It's what Kit wants in her heart too. Did Mrs Millar ask you straight out to ask Jimmy to come home Kit?"

"Yes she did."

"Then you write and tell him he's not to worry about your fare. I'll pay it."

"Oh Daddy - could you? If I get that job on the Island I was offered I'd earn quite a bit towards the fare myself."

"I'll manage somehow" he said, "don't you worry."

My mother was silent but her eyes were suddenly filled with tears.

"If I can get the job, it will be worth giving up work at the Centre. It will be all of July and August and two weeks at the end of June. They also said one week to tidy up in September on full pay."

"But what are your chances?" Mother said, "If you leave to come home to marry Jimmy in August."

"I wouldn't tell them Mother. I would just work as long as I could and then leave. They'd have no trouble replacing me."

"That's not quite honest Kit" Daddy said.

"But Daddy from the middle of June to the middle of August is over a hundred dollars and I will have my keep and probably tips."

"It may be very hard work Kit."

"Oh I don't know. In rushes it might be. I would be in the shop and only serving when people happen to come. The dances are only on Saturday nights and Mr Jones said he takes the money at the door. I would only have to help Mrs Jones get the hall decorated and serve the supper."

"What did you tell Mr Jones, Kit?"

"That I would have to write to my fiancé about his plans and then I would let them know by the end of this month. He said he would particularly like to have me. He wants somebody reliable; that's why he asked at the Centre."

"Charles is somewhere near there" Mother said.

"Oh I doubt if I'll see Charles" I said. "The timber mill is not that near the lake. Only tourists come there and people who have week-enders."

Because of the proximity of Charles I had, until that moment, almost dismissed the whole offer but now nothing mattered, nothing except getting Jimmy home to marry me.

"Weekenders from Alberni."

"But I won't go into Alberni, Mother. As you say the job will keep me pretty busy. Besides I didn't like Pat and I don't think she likes me. The only possible day would be Sunday and that's impossible, the shop is open then too.

"Why?" Daddy said.

"Sunday is a busy day, Mr Jones said. But they give their girl free time off Monday or Wednesday afternoons. There's no church there anyway."

"I see" Daddy said, "it's a place for the idle rich."

"Americans come for the fishing."

"I suppose that's why Jones wants a reliable girl. I'm not so sure about you taking it Kit. It's hardly your kind of job."

"I want it" I said. "I'll write to Mr Jones tonight and then I'll write to Jimmy."

"Take your time" Daddy said. "Write to Jimmy of course but give yourself time on the other."

But from that moment I didn't want time. I wanted the job, and I wanted Jimmy. I was sick of waiting, sick of standing by in the half-light. The sooner I married Jimmy the better. As suddenly as that I made my decision. It was May. By the end of August I would be a bride. At the end of September I would be in London, Mrs James Millar a married woman in my own right. I took my father's advice in reverse fashion, deciding to secure the job first before I wrote to Jimmy. Mr Jones telegraphed his reply asking me to be at the lake by the tenth of June. Delighted I wrote to Jimmy and began to make my plans. The world appeared rose coloured for the future Mrs James Millar, who had stepped out from the shadows of nonentity into a new life packed with promise.

I made my plans right up to the final Saturday, the day I was to sail across the Straits of Georgia to Nanaimo where I had a friend who would meet me, taking me home for the night prior to putting me on Sunday's train to the station nearest to the lake where Mr Jones would meet me. I had arranged everything down to the last detail. It was as if I had come alive again; as if a door had opened inside of me out of which I stepped as a new person, a woman in charge of her destiny, knowing where she was going and making plans accordingly. Final details of my wedding I did not discuss, telling my parents that the essentials were known: our own church and a small afternoon reception on an unofficial open-house basis, nothing was to involve unnecessary expense. When I heard from Jimmy we would finalise the date and the time. I noted everything in my room to be taken abroad with me and those things required for my job and leisure time at the lake. I listed my books and my music. I arranged temporary leadership for my girls' group, knowing my colleague would carry on when I finally departed. My piano pupils were handed over to other eager teachers. My mother fussed about my clothes, and I accepted her decisions with the proviso that she was only to alter and arrange but not unless absolutely necessary, spend. I explained to her as Jimmy had to me that it was foolish for me to take too much considering what our future life would be. We surveyed my wardrobe and decided what was necessary for the sea voyage. Little would be new but only I would know this. Mother and my aunts were slightly shocked at my attitude but admired what they called my common sense. My clothes were adequate and I knew it.

By the first week of June preparation for the beginning of my married life were so well in hand that I had moved out into the mainstream in an atmosphere of self-satisfaction and bliss. It seemed as if the indecision of my girlhood had left me forever. Life had at last become solely my future with Jimmy.

Then Jimmy's letter came.

"You will notice darling, I am a day or two late with my reply to your proposition. You can imagine how I was tempted to see you again before I hoped to and take you to London as my wife. You know how much I want

you. You probably did not fully realise when you wrote your letter that my plans were finalised here. The allowances of my scholarship are arranged and also my passage from Montreal on a cargo ship, the "Minto Castle" on the 2nd of September. This could not be better as I will have two solid months working and earning here in the university lab with Professor Urdo. This is a chance I cannot afford to miss, nor can I jeopardise my opportunity by even suggesting I work for a shorter period than two months. Between you and me, my opinion is that the job was arranged to help me. I think Professor Williams had something to do with it but as is usual in these things, nothing will ever be said.

"I had to talk to somebody so I talked to Sykes. He goes to England as well but not by my route and to Cambridge. Sykes considered you to be the victim of family pressure and when I thought about it I realised my own parents are probably more to blame than yours. I heard from them since I wrote to say I would not be coming home and hoped you would join me in London. You say in your letter how pleased my family would be to see me. It was dumb of me to have been unable to anticipate that Mother would come to see you. The truth is, Kit, except for you, I have no desire to come home. I'm not sentimental about home ties. I've only come as far as I have against the wishes of my family, not because of them. I know your family means a lot more to you than mine does to me. When I marry you, you'll be my home and all I want. That's a plain statement of fact. I want you and I want my profession. Places will always be incidental to me. Besides the kind of job I'll have won't ever be available at home. The climate's wrong.

"So darling, although there's nothing I'd like better than to marry you this summer, I think our original plan must stand. Leaving your people would be just as hard for you at the end of August as it will be next spring, but by spring I will know my way about London. I will have made my contacts and have a place for you.

"Thank your father for me Kit. It was decent of him to offer, but I doubt if he can really afford it. I'll book your passage and send your fare.

"Sykes says to tell you that by the time you arrive he will have arranged a week in London during which he will take you to one concert after another and that I can come if I must but that as he is never likely to find a wife for himself, not being the type, he won't care. Williams is going to Edinburgh, so you see we all made it, one way or another."

So they make it one or way or another. Sykes and Williams and Millar but not me. My proposition did not make it. I was merely the bride who would arrive when sent for. I was the one who would be allowed to come in the spring when things were arranged to fit me in. Skyes would help Jimmy make me welcome because he, unlike Jimmy Millar could not find a girl to do what she was told. It had come to this. Jimmy cared more for his profession than he did for me. I could wait, couldn't I? I had only been waiting two years already. What was a mere two years to a scientific career?

Sykes! He had talked it over with Sykes! Sykes had considered I was under pressure. Pressure of parents! Not the lonely pressure of love for Jimmy, not the agonising pressure of waiting between two worlds. Jimmy had talked it over with Sykes, but I could talk it over with no one at all. I could only sit like a stunned forest creature after the fire had passed. I could not even cry. After a while a full deceitful bitterness closed over my mind, blocking out anger as useless and reason as futility.

I had come in late and picked up Jimmy's letter from its prominent place on the mantlepiece. In the morning there would be questions. But the night was long and by the morning, the rings under my eyes were tale-telling of sleeplessness of the uncompromising, remorseless kind unrelieved by tears. Yet in the morning before I went to the Centre, I told my family casually, almost gaily:

"Jimmy can't say for sure at the moment. He's a bit jammed because he has been offered a lab job for the summer by his professor. I'll probably know for certain next letter."

But there wasn't going to be a next letter because I was never going to write to him again. I was going to a beautiful lake that lay like a jewel waiting for me under the summer sun. I was taking my prettiest dresses to wear at the dances and all of my poetry books to read in my own time at the lake's edge under the overhanging firs. 'A most beautiful place' Mr Jones said, as Charles had said and the Mill Manager. Charming to the customers, Mr Jones hoped! Speedboats and canoes and people - happy people; Americans with money. That was why Mr Jones had to have a girl he could trust. I could be trusted. Good, safe, faithful Kit, to be sent for when suitable! The lake was inviting, secretive, becoming, deep and green and beautiful. I was going there. I was going alone without family, without ties, by myself, to be myself, unmolested, without pressures of any kind whatever, where I knew nobody and nobody was waiting to look after me, to tell me where to step and what to wear. Nobody at the lake would know me well enough to tell me anything. A week after I came home I would be twenty-two years old.

"Kit where's your ring?"
"I'm not wearing it today. I think I'll have to have it altered. It keeps slipping around when I'm playing for the gym."
"Put a bit of string on it" Donald suggested.
I turned on him with unpremeditated sarcasm. "String!" I said icily, "on my ring! No thank you."

By eight-thirty on Saturday morning my family had established me safely on the ship to Nanaimo although the sailing time was scheduled for 9 o'clock. My father carried my heavy suitcases on board.

"Are you taking your rock collection?" he asked as he put them down in a selected place.

"No, my books" I answered.

"But surely there will be a few books around that you haven't read."

"My poetry books and my notebooks."

"I see" he said, then after a moment's hesitation. "Kit if there's anything wrong don't you think you could tell us?"

"I will when I'm sure, that is if there is anything. So far there isn't. You know Daddy I'm just disappointed of course that Jimmy couldn't say right away that he would be able to come home."

"I wouldn't hold that against him Kit. As your mother says, he always has everything planned well in advance. It's a good characteristic."

I couldn't discuss it.

"I'll write as soon as I can Daddy. After all everything is arranged as far as possible until I come home again."

"Do that" he said, gravely, unconvinced of the verity of our conversational level. "Your Mother will be anxious."

"Oh, I'll write every day or so. But I can only let you know about the other when I know myself."

"Have a good time" Daddy said and kissed me goodbye.

"Mind the people now" Mother said. "Take your time with strangers - go slow!"

This was Mother's advice every summer so I smiled and squeezed her tight. She wanted to say more. I think she wanted to tell me specifically why I must mind people but there wasn't time so she was limited to her usual mother-bird advice: you can knock yourself about a little when you land on the ground but its other birds you must watch out for, different species of your own kind.

***

10

Chapter Ten

The noises of the Cairo day have increased to an almost insufferable momentum; the hum of a big city whose inhabitants are too many. Yet this is an ancient city and only superficially in a hurry. Individuals do not appear to hurry although there is a feeling of poverty, pressure pushing them each hour of the day. Those making the noise scarcely seem to matter. Egypt is so old.

It is almost noon and the air is heavy. I will leave the balcony, have my lunch and do the household accounts with Abdul so he can sleep away the afternoon. When he and Hassan have gone to the roof to rest, alongside their friend the doorman, within hearing of the lift bell, I too will rest but here, again on the balcony within sight of the Nile, and beyond its munificence, the domes and minarets that rise all the way to the souk and El Azhar and the Citadel. Tomorrow I must rouse myself and visit Khan Khalil, the great market to buy some gifts. I will visit my friend Muhamed Awad who will invite me into his inner sanctuary behind the beaded curtain to offer me jasmine tea. It is possible he will not invite me until some tourists enter his shop and when they do, he will charge them double or even triple his price for me. Three times if they are American tourists, but he is not the rogue I once suggested to him he might be.

"But milady," he droned. "Does it not say in the most holy Koran that those who have must share. And is it not true that in our time the Americans have most of the riches of the world?"

His shop is like Aladdin's cave, full of gold and silver, brass and copper, mother of pearl and is perfumed with sandalwood, ginger and myrrh.

***

My room at the lake was on the second floor of an immense log structure which contained the shop, the home and the dance hall. Steep stairs led up to my quarters from a small square hall between the single storied shop on the lake's edge and the double storied house. This hall, lined with padlocked storage cupboards had three doors, one which led outside was usually locked, one to the shop and one to the dining room of the house which was always open. It was amazing to me that the store and the dance hall should be built along the lake shore while the main room of the house, the over-furnished dining room should look out through one small window to the forlorn and dusty pier road.

The long thin room I was shown into smelled faintly of new pine boarding. Boasting three windows, one which looked straight on to the lake and two smaller ones, one also to the lake down the slope of the store roof while the other crossed the road to show the pine forest on its further side. The room which was furnished with the usual comforts, a bed, a washstand, a deal table and chair had a lock on the door. A little extra had been added; an old-fashioned basket chair with two cushions and the bedspread had obviously been newly made for my arrival.

Mr Jones was very proud of the room.

"Up until this year the young lady help in the summer had to have the children's room and my boy had a bed in the dining room, not very satisfactory especially on dance nights. We just got this finished."

"It's lovely" I said thinking how I could ask to re-arrange the furniture. "There's a view from every window. Would you mind if I put the table in front of the big window so I could put my books on it. I read a lot."

Mr Jones laughed. "Books eh? I thought you had rocks in your case."

He was a short man, thick set, a bit red faced and hearty "You just make yourself comfortable. Settle yourself young lady and come down for tea in a bit and meet the wife and kids. Mama's got them under control waiting to get a good look at you" He moved to the door then turned "Be sure and lock your door now. Mama always says you never know with a shop and summer people."

I hung up my coat behind a hessian curtain strung on a wire for a wardrobe and moved the table in front of the window looking out on the lake. How mysterious the waters were, unfathomable, primeval green crater depths in the forest with no known tides like the sea. The grandeur of nature rose up suddenly to envelop me like mist, stinging my eyes to tears with fear and strangeness.

"You won't mind having your dinner after seven?" Mrs Jones asked. "We eat at five-thirty for the children. Tom gives out the mail and then we eat. I'll keep your meal hot for you. You can eat in the dining-room. I'll just be putting the children to bed by then."

"I'd just as soon eat upstairs I think, if you don't mind."

I knew quite suddenly that was what she wanted me to say. I looked at her directly realising with wonder that I was doing so for the first time and that she was only half looking back at me out of the pale hazel eyes circled heavily above her cheek bones. In fact her gaze seemed to go through me with such vacuity that in embarrassment I almost looked away. In the back of my mind a situational similarity struggled momentarily for recognition. She looked like somebody I knew, that was for sure. Then my eyes fell on the pretty face of the little girl whom they called Dorsey, short for Dorothy I supposed, who had wide black lashed eyes exactly the same colour as her mother's, only shiny and expectant in her sweet four-year-old face. Dorsey was a beautiful child. Glancing again at the mother I saw she was equally pretty and I thought incredulously, not only pretty but young. Young! Tom Jones had begun to speak again and I realised he must be young too, not more than thirty perhaps. The little boy after all was only six. How odd. I'm probably within ten years of their age I thought but they don't seem to be my age at all. They're different, both young and old at once.

"All the other boats tied up, except for mine, the big motorboat that needs paint, belong to people who have summer places on the little islands you can see or on the far shore. When they come they leave their cars in the car park behind the dance hall and take their boats." Mr Jones was plying me with information and I listened, but my mind was also in some other timeless place trying to evaluate his wife.

"Your hair is so pretty" I said to little Dorsey, and her father answered with warmth and pride "They've got their mother's curly black mop, a blessing they don't quite realise yet." Above his red face his own sandy hair was thinning. He hasn't many looks at all, I thought. I hadn't noticed that before either. I glanced again at Mrs Jones but she gave no sign that she had even heard. Her husband noticed my glance. His voice cut sharply across whatever was her reverie.

"What do you say, Ilma, to taking the new member of the family around for a quick look outside so she knows the lay of the land? Out of season I open up from five to seven on Sundays, no mail of course but the locals come around and the permanent weekenders. We have about a half an hour now." He was talking to me again I realised but his eyes were on his wife.

"Ilma," I reflected "Ilma. It suits her."

Mrs Jones sighed again "You'd probably show her things better than I can" she said to her husband "I'm so tired today."

"I have to open these cases. Pero wants his amenities. He's leaving at 5am in the morning. He turned to me again explaining "Pero is our cougar hunter in these parts. His wife is a nice girl. She'll be around too, to meet you."

"Does he really shoot cougars near here?" I asked incredulously

"They don't come in this close anymore, too much company around here. The nearest he ever bagged one was at the mill, ten miles away and it was old and toothless. There's still a bounty on them though."

I saw Mrs Jones shiver, her eyes on her children.

"Why don't I just walk around by myself and look" I suggested "or perhaps the children would come with me."

"Oh no, oh no" she said quickly as if rousing herself. "I'll come. I forgot about the boxes for Pero. I'll get a sweater. We still need one when the sun begins to go down. Put sweaters on, all of you.

"I don't need a sweater" the little boy cried "It's warm out isn't it Papa?"

"Do what Mama says" his father snapped "And get your sister."

"I'll get mine" I said. The dining room cleared before I had left it.

Mr Jones unlocked the door from the hall and went into the store.

***

The next day I met the Tanners; the mother, father and son who worked like beavers all winter to grow rich in the summer. I liked the son whose speedboat would pull up every afternoon after lunch till the pressure of tourist trips kept him away all day. Then the speedboat pulled up at night. The big, natural, friendly, uncomplicated Bob Tanners of this world are a blessing to girls their own age. Understanding, they see companionship for what it is, friendship offered without strings, a joke shared without premeditation, a compliment offered without a price. From my first day in the store Bob and I gravitated towards one another as naturally as contemporaries should and so seldom do, two of a kind, two of an age.

"I'm Bob Tanner. Tom Jones said I'd find you here. What's your name?"

"Eleanor Jane, Known as Kit."

"Hi, Kit. What goes on after lunch?"

"I'll know that after lunch."

"I'm not offering myself, only my boat. Boats are to me what dates are to other guys. She's a beauty. I'm taking her out at exactly two o'clock. It is now a quarter to twelve."

"At two I'll have exactly one hour until three."

"The pier then. Be seeing you."

"OK. Who's that I wonder?" A motorboat was skimming like a bird about to dive bomb the pier.

"Alex" Bob said. "He's in Jones' boat. He's OK in case you wonder. I have to talk to him. Don't close the store by mistake. If you do you'll just have to open up again for him. He's like that."

"Does he always ram the jetty?"

"He never rams the jetty. It's only that he can't do anything without style. He was born that way. By the way, has Jim Thompson been in?"

"A little boy called Thompson came for the mail last night. I don't think they called him Jim."

"Jim's the father. I'll grab Alex."

He leapt down towards the jetty. And I watched him without being conscious that Mrs Jones had come into the store until she spoke.

"We'll close up now, dear."

"But a boat has just come in."

"It's only Alex. He'll eat with us." She closed the door of the shop, and together we went into the dining room. Tom Jones and the children were already seated.

There sounded a great banging on the front door of the store.

"I'll go," Mrs Jones said. "It's Alex."

"I heard the boat." Mr Jones remarked and got up. "The kids are hungry. You serve up, Mama. I'll see what Alex wants."

"There's plenty if Alex hasn't eaten."

"I doubt if he's eaten since yesterday," Mr Jones said as he went into the hall.

"Poor Alex," Mrs Jones said to me. "It's probably true, he never thinks about eating. We all feed him whenever he turns up from wherever he has been."

"Where does he go?" I asked.

She turned towards me then and I noticed two little spots of colour on her cheeks.

"We don't ask," she said.

When he came into the room the children threw themselves at him with shrieks of joy. But he stood above them smiling, and leaning over kissed the hand of their mother. Then he turned to me, waiting.

"This is Kit Marshall. She came yesterday, Alex."

He bowed above my hand which he took into his own. His fingers were very long and thin and spotlessly clean. He bowed so low that I noticed the mop of his unruly hair was pale gold, fair to grey and very curly. I was startled, but pleasantly so. I felt like a princess.

"Hungry, Alex?" Mrs Jones asked.

"Oh no, no. This ees not so. But I eat wis you of course - no man could find in his heart to refuse such cooking."

"Sit down, all of you," Mrs Jones said with staccato sharpness.

"I'm all served out in the kitchen."

I moved towards my chair. Alex was there before me. As he pulled my chair out his teeth flashed in a smile of incredible whiteness. Then he sat in the place set for him, but lightly like a bird poised for flight. When Mrs Jones brought in her own plate and put it down he was behind her chair in a matter of seconds. This behaviour in such a place might have amazed me, but I recalled that Charles knew this Alex whose manners had impressed Pat. Conversations flowed around me. I sat in silence remembering that weekend of which I would not speak.

Mrs Jones hovered about the men, passing food and drink, but like myself she did not speak. The men talked fishing all through the meal, ignoring the children in the room. Only when we rose from the table Alex, like an automaton pulled away our chairs. I was not allowed to help with the dishes, so I excused myself and went upstairs.

"Charming," Alex bowed as I went out. "You are charming. It ees good." He had not spoken a word to me during the meal.

When Jim Thompson came into the store he made a point of speaking to me.

"Bob Tanner told me you played the piano in the dance hall. Bring any music with you?"

"No, I didn't."

"No matter. I've got plenty. When will you come?"

"Come?"

"Home to my place. Eloise will be delighted to meet you and so will my boys. I only hope you can play French songs for the sake of Eloise."

He laughed and the store was filled with his mirth.

"I can manage French songs" I said, "Mr Jones says I'm free every evening after I've eaten at seven, Give me half an hour for supper."

"Let Eloise give you supper."

But I had not met Eloise except for a tantalising memory of that weekend with Charles and Pat. Was that name Eloise?

"After supper the first time." I said.

"Okay. Let's see. Saturday's no good. I'll come for you in the boat Friday night. That'll be good. Alex might come with his guitar and Charles will be there for the weekend.

"Charles?"

"Yes, Charles Gilbert. You know him."

I was startled into sounding ridiculous as I stammered "Of course I know him, he's my cousin."

Jim's expression seemed to alter, and I knew that his whole conversation, including his invitation, was based on my relationship with Charles. How could I have reacted so stupidly. However he smiled, this nice Jim Thompson and rescued me immediately.

"He's a rum one Charles. Never a word did he say. I thought he forgot when I saw him last week."

"He didn't know I was coming here. I didn't tell him. Is Pat coming too?" It seemed too much to hope.

Then for a moment I had a glimpse of the real Jim Thompson through his brown shark's eyes in his brown earthy face. He loomed up above me from the other side of the counter and I felt myself shrink to half my size.

"No" he said "Pat never comes even when she is not in Victoria. You haven't seen Charles for some time then. Understandable." All statements barked at me.

"No, but–" There were no excuses really. I could not finish.

"You want to see him?" Jim demanded.

"Oh yes. I should have written but I came so quickly. I couldn't decide until the last minute."

"You don't have to explain to me." Jim Thompson said softly. "It doesn't suit you to explain. You are like Charles. I'll ask Bob Tanner too. Perhaps you would like him to bring you. We can surprise Charles."

"Thank you, Mister Thomson."

"My friends call me Jim" he said. "You stayed with them once didn't you, before David was born when Charles was teaching?"

I nodded, surprised how much that weekend could hurt me even yet.

"I think Charles would like to be surprised. Friday then." He was such a big man the whole door seemed filled with his lumberjacket as he went out.

By Friday I realised that I should have known the lake would be a magnet for Charles if he were anywhere near. And of course we had all known he was working somewhere on the island. The lake was his kind of habitat in the same way that it was mine. Out of all my kindred I needed Charles because my heart was sore. It seemed inevitable that he should come to fulfil my need but facing the truth of this I also knew I did not want him. I was unprepared for what he would expect of me. Unfinished and spasmodic verse scrawled in a notebook, incomplete, often illegible were the only products of my mind; the great love affair of my life was under threat, and I could produce nothing but recriminations, self-pity and indecision. Altogether there was too little too answer Charles' questions.

I went to the Thompsons on Friday night prepared to put on an act full of bright affability without much speech. Until I found out, that is, where Charles was at and where his present aspirations, if any, were to be found. I would be like he was sometimes. Enigmatic was the word I thought of before I failed in the first round.

Eloise Thompson was small brown to Jim's big brown. Her eyes were deep-set and lustrous and the hair on top of her head was heavy and straight, worked in two braids like ribbons around her head. Her speaking voice had a husky quality which changed to the trilling sweetness of a wood-thrush when she sang French songs. She came down the path with Jim when Bobby's boat pulled in at the Thompson's pier. The four of us walked back together, Eloise and me in front and Bobby and Jim dropping a considerable distance behind. We stopped to wait.

"Talking boats" Eloise remarked" Always boats. It is terrible n'est pas?"

"Or fishing" I laughed. I liked her.

"Well, what do you think of my brown hut?" Jim asked when we stepped onto the porch. "Just what I would have expected" I answered unexplainably.

"See?" Jim said to Eloise. She smiled, put her hand on the door and opened it. "Charles" she called out "Surprise!"

From inside I heard Charles say "Kit, for heaven's sake!"

We rushed toward each other and when we met stood silent, my eyes successfully containing a sudden rush of tears.

"Oh Charles" cried my unenigmatic self, "how wonderful to see you."

"You little devil" - he answered and kissed me, French fashion on both cheeks. "Just how long have you been here?" And then he turned to Jim and Eloise and Bob and put me right in the place where I belonged. "Ever since she was a baby and would get lost, this one" he said indicating me in the crick of his arm "has been my favourite cousin. She writes like you, you know Jim, but not such mundane things as letters. Her aspirations are towards much higher things."

It was only then during the laughter that I noticed Alex sitting on the floor in an open-necked blue shirt with his back to an open fire.

"Hello Alex" I said. He jumped up then as lightly as a cat, bowed above my hand and flashed his teeth in a welcoming smile.

"Go with Eloise and see the boys" Jim invited. "We promised you would, and they promised after that to go to sleep. As good parents we insist you keep our promise as an example which, you may notice later, has not had the desired effect. We told them there would be a surprise. We had to since Charles qualifies as one of their heroes, and in spite of themselves they would have spilled the beans."

The Thompson house was built of half-log, unlined but draft proofed with streaks of white plaster in true log cabin style. The three little boys were in a room off the kitchen with four bunks, a huge table, two benches and an enormous built-in cupboard which was wide open and with room to spare. Another bedroom opened off the living-room with another door out to the veranda viewing the lake. The kitchen along the back was long and thin with copper pots gleaming and ladles shining French style among the fishing reels and gaffs hung each in its own place along the length of the inside wall. There was a hot black stove and at the far end, under and close to a window surrounded with red-checked curtains, the space was entirely filled with a great dining table covered with white oilcloth. Utterly different I thought from the Jones kitchen. And Pat's kitchen. As the thought flashed in the midst of Eloise cajoling the boys back into their beds, I realised I had only seen Charles in the Thompson living room and Alex and the open fire.

How many hours was I to spend in that living room that smelled of wood I was not to know. Not how I was to love and return to the memory of it and the company it held. Yet on that first Friday night the room engraved itself on my mind in a frame so perfect I have been able all my life to gaze into it again.

We were called back to the room from the kitchen by the voice of a violin which was quite naturally accompanied from the side of the kitchen stove with the voice of Eloise who simply stopped talking, smiled and opened and shut the wooden door, her lips forming words as she moved.

"Il était une bergère, Et ren, ren, ren, petit patapon."

There was not much light in the room, a hurricane lantern hanging near the front door and on an upright piano a small old fashioned kerosene lamp with an amber glass base. The glow of the fire spread to gold on the head of Alex and red on the face of Charles who sat on a couch covered with a rug of fur skins. Between them was a place for me and I slipped into it gratefully like a rabbit into a waiting burrow. Bob sat near the fire on a carved wooden stool, one of several around the room. What was in the room besides these things? I looked carefully around and, in the half-light, distinguished the long fireplace as hand quarried stone and the loaded bookshelves rough timber which somehow blended perfectly with the polished rosewood of the old piano. There was another couch under an Indian blanket and beyond the piano an Indian rug of immense proportions and colour covered the wall from floor to ceiling. The mantel, a great thick wooden beam above and across the stone of the fireplace glittered with a ridiculous shadow dance of carefully displayed treasures; a French-Canadian white wood couple carved to a size to be held in the hand; a copper plate and bowl; animals and ceramic birds and a French porcelain clock. Each had an appointed place between two antique brass candle sticks catching their own light.

Around me as I sat in that place all the accents blurred; Charles assumed the tones of Alex, Alex of Eloise, Jim of Charles. Velvet flutterings of words brushed past my ears as I picked up the conversation until, when I spoke, my voice could have come from the lips of any one of them.

"You mean a person is really something beyond the body then, just an occupier of a house that can be seen while the real person inside cannot. Because of the protection of the house, truth can be produced inside."

Only the voice of Charles was capable of the reply that flushed my unseen face in the shadowed light.

"There you are, she demonstrates my theory. She won't let anyone read her poetry of course, at least she never lets me so I don't know if it's good, bad or as yet indifferent. It doesn't matter, it's still what goes on in her head, in her special house. Thereby she assumes the same is true for everyone else. It makes no difference what she was taught at school. What she was at the beginning she still is. I used to worry about her, about a clot of an English teacher she had once. I thought he might have destroyed something in her. I was wrong. He couldn't destroy any more than I could encourage"

"Charles!"

"I simply mean, Kit, that what you are, you are. You haven't changed fundamentally since you were six. You lived inside yourself then and you still do now."

"Education notwithstanding" Jim said and laughed.

"Teachers notwithstanding Jim, but of circumstances I'm not so sure."

Alex spoke "You just said what eez inside she eez and not possible to change. That is lies. Ze inside can smash wiz many blows on ze outside."

"The inside can be killed outright or crippled or starved. That's circumstance. But the personality is not changed."

"You are a fatalist, Charles." Jim said

"Not quite. Do you know what I used to think? I actually believed the spark of genius was in everybody. That it was dormant in each individual child; that only circumstance hid it from view. That somehow, somewhere, something true was always there and that it was my mission to discover it and expose it to the light. I was mistaken; the order of things is different. Just once in a while, spasmodically, incalculably, out of thousands of human beings all climbing on each other's backs for a place in the sun, there is one that moves out in front. Nothing stops that one and nothing helps either except superficially. In fact, that one goes against society. The rest of humanity comes swimming along together trying to catch up with the one in front and swallow them."

"You make the system sound horrible" I said.

"Jim goes on about why I gave up teaching. I might as well have saved my breath as a teacher. Teaching hasn't made any difference to you has it, Kit?" He laughed a little in his throat." You don't believe me now do you?"

"No, it's not that Charles, I just can't accept your reasoning."

"So, that's how good a teacher I am. You don't accept my reasoning, not even you, my favourite cousin. You believe what you must because of what's inside yourself, what you want to believe you think is true, or what is true for you, you think you believe. Everybody is like you. Teachers make no difference. They simply pass on accumulated information by rote, tabulated and conserved since writing was invented."

Jim rescued me. "Oh come on Charles. Maybe not all but most of the information is tried and tested and improved for the benefit of the human race. After all a scientific method has been worked out and applied to knowledge of almost every kind that can be built on."

"Without discrimination; better medicine and better ways of killing; better ways of living and more ways to face death. All written down and passed on. All protected and hoarded. Good and bad, the highest and the lowest, bigger churches and bigger jails. As you say all scientifically handled now, each of us taking what his circumstances and his genes make him think will bring him happiness and personal success. But it still hurts to die and degrades the body to go hungry. You ought to know Jim. You opted out when you came here."

"Well, I guess I opted out of being a teacher." He stopped suddenly. "I suppose what I'm doing is explaining to Kit that the last thing you can be is a teacher if you don't believe in anything you teach."

"Have it your own way" Jim said, and I saw him glance at Eloise.

"But you wanted to be a teacher, more than anything else" I cried out.

"My mistake. I thought through passing out good information I could discover and develop personality. The reality is that masses of what is called information is passed on according to the system prevailing in the area. Usually it is a forced system and it can be good or bad. Students react to the system according to the constitution of their hereditary instincts which also can be good or bad."

"But surely a good teacher helps them make the best of whatever they have?"

"No. various circumstances plus the nearest school system brings out or covers up what's already there. Each hungry child goes after food in his own way. A child reads more books if his father has a library. Prodding, pushing and encouragement only lead a teacher into disillusion. I found that out and when I did, I quit."

"You've sure got it all worked out" Jim said dryly "Surely you must admit to some progress."

Something in Charles seemed to succumb. "Sure I do but on an individual level, rather a sort of unpredictable genetic arrangement."

Jim laughed. "Encouraged by education and brought out by education."

But Charles wouldn't give in on that. "No" he said, "in spite of education. Not even a genius has a chance in our schools nowadays, in fact the opposite; the nearer to genius the harder the adjustment to daily circumstance."

It sounded like my voice cutting in "But genius is recognised, Charles. What about the great composers and the scientists and poets?"

"Sure, after the genius is dead when his individually creative contribution is seized upon and incorporated, and often wrongly, into institutionalism. And after the life-force has gone out of the person who can no longer startle and frighten his contemporaries. Just take a look at the portraits of artists and philosophers, musicians and writers, even great statesmen. They all look as if they were forced into a tight restricting skin too small for them."

We had all been listening with minds in immobile bodies relaxed by the firelight. Now suddenly all the voices rose in unexpected defence of the poor genius!

"Ah yes Charles. Zee eyes burn out of zee sockets." Alex agreed.

"Trying to escape the physical restraints do you mean?" Bobby asked.

"Oui" from Eloise "You must have the body to live n'est pas? You must learn to use it so as you can do anything at all. Even this genius."

"Sure, and the genius has to have a form to work through and any form is a restraint, a casing. Ideas must be crystalised, I can see that and the control of it for a genius becomes a full-time occupation. That's where your teaching comes in Charles, learning the control early. A genius knows this instinctively, concentrates and lets the rest go." Jim said

Eloise finished for him "For the genius this is very difficult n'est pas?"

Charles, under siege retorted "so he starves."

"Not quite or he wouldn't produce."

"Look how many died young. And how many are never discovered. Call it the environment encountered or surrounding circumstances, call it anything you like, teachers can't make any difference."

"That's pure cynicism Charles."

"Oh yes, I know, and martyrs are never cynical. I suppose that's why they are dead before their ideas are accepted."

"They sow the seed and that's something."

"The seed was already there. Martyrs and geniuses try to coerce the growth because they happen to recognise the possibilities. Great idealists are always super-egoists and hard to live with. They insist on bringing out what's in them. All of us who are only ordinary people have ideas in our heads which we are perfectly sure of and yet wouldn't mention."

"Such as?" Jim persisted

"Well, since she would never say it herself, Kit's idea of God living in every little growth and every person instead of up in a heaven surrounded by the saints."

"Oh Charles" I protested "I never said that."

"I know you didn't, not since you were about six anyway. You know it just the same and you accept it, and you have always lived out the theory in your life but you learned early that it wouldn't do you any good to shout about it anymore than it would have paid you to disclose publicly a certain telepathic insight you displayed in respect to Rupert Thoms.

I stared at him aghast. "Is that what you mean?"

"Yes, that's what I mean. Take myself. I hate war and, believe it or not, under my cynical exterior I'm a super-egotist and wanted to shout my ideas. I thought school teaching a good medium but I was wrong. While the fathers of all the little boys and girls base the pride of their lives on being veterans of the glory of war the only thing I stood to gain was the loss of my job if I opened my mouth. The time factor is wrong. I'll probably have to use all my wits in some despicable capacity to avoid being slaughtered in the next war before enough people are prepared to wipe out the curse of mass killing."

There was a silence and a sigh from Alex. Into it Eloise also sighed. "Ah, oui alors." before she said "No, I bring café. You will 'elp me Kit?"

I stood up like a dreamer walking in sleep and followed Eloise gratefully to the kitchen. Alex's voice pursued us in a soft purr through the door. "Zee circumstances, my friend, always it is zee circumstances."

Eloise turned up the lamp hanging from its long ceiling hook until a steady glow illuminated every cup and plate on the dresser shelves.

"Alex I can understand" she said, "But your cousin Charles, is he always pessimistic like this?"

My reply was reserved, a politeness from a great distance. "I have not heard him speak like that before. I haven't seen him - much - since his marriage."

"Alors. Since the marriage, non? It is reason enough n'est ce pas?" And with premeditated clatter and bang she took down the cups. Then with poker in hand she noisily stirred the coals before choosing an enormous piece of wood for refilling the stove which she poked in with vehemence; her small body vigorous with the effort needed to jam it into the fuel box. As if in direct answer to this commotion in the kitchen the first tuneful notes of a melody on the violin stole out of the living room and swelled in depth as the full bow drew across the strings. A little secret smile played to match across the lips of Eloise. After a moment or two of the music to which we both listened like birds in suspended flight Eloise spoke again.

"Tonight you go back 'ome with Bobby, non? Charles, he stays 'ere. Tomorrow Charles will come to see you. "He is fond, as Jim says, fond, I see that. You will be gentle with him, no? You will. I know that. He is one unhappy man, inside is hurt bad."

Her words, spoken so charmingly between English and French enchanted me with the comfort of a fur collar keeping the cold from my ears. This small woman whose knotty work worn hands were as tiny and swift as swallows and whose eyes I had not noticed before. They glowed like coals under beguilingly long curled lashes and brought comfort to me like Auntie Meg. My heart melted toward this French wife of Jim Thompson as surely as his rough hands intended to coax her with his violin. He played well with the same well practiced touch his friend Alex displayed when he kissed a lady's hand. How strange to find these three people here with Charles who had so quietly allowed me into the circle of their lives. Picking up the plate of buttered bun I smiled at Eloise who had told me how to handle Charles, something no one else had ever been able to do.

Quite naturally, happily, I put down the bun and my coffee cup and walked to the piano. I began to play some excerpts: the Moonlight Sonata; the Appassionata; the Sibelius Romance; Palmgren's Sea;

some Debussy and just one Tchaikovsky song, To the Forest. All sat very still knowing that I played to acknowledge the song that held Eloise and Jim together; to replace the poems I had given to Charles and to ease the unknown heartbreak that seemed to ache in the breast of Alex Popolov. I knew that only Bobby was amazed. The notes fell like teardrops from my fingertips into the still room and beyond to the resting trees and the calm of the dark night. My heart dripped into the keys an offering to this mysterious place which had accepted me as I hovered unanchored and purposeless in time. I knew that after my own fashion I was trying to keep myself together; to keep from longing for the strong firm touch of Jimmy's hand on my hair, for certainly the breath of his presence was near enough. His strength stood just beyond the threshold, searching a way to come in to bind me forever into himself. As I played I was almost overcome with longing for Jimmy. And yet I was playing to be myself in a room with people who were in my orbit more than Jimmy; people whose individuality was cruelly real to the point of necessity. Except for Bobby Tanner who was waiting to speedboat me home. I lifted my hands from the keys.

It was only then I noted the little boys, sitting beside Bob in front of the fire in a sleepy brown of ruffled pyjamas. The little Thompson boys adored Bobby Tanner. Only he could have kept them quiet.

***

11

Chapter Eleven

Between the dirt road that ran to the pier and the Tanner's tourist cabins arranged on the far side of a cleared parkland was a strip of original primeval forest. It ran from the point where the road turned in off the main road, a distance of about a mile to the shop and pier and across the lake front back for perhaps half to three quarters of a mile. Rough mystical no-man's land of ancient spruce, hemlock pine and shrub pussy willow, it was a deliberately uncleared area where logs were left as they fell and ferns perforated along with fungi and mossed bark. The centre was dark and silent with heavy carpet of leaf mould and the accumulated fall of brown conifer needles and cones. Halfway along on the lakeside there was a high bank above the water languidly invaded by a pussy willow copse. I broke through this copse and discovered a sanctuary of moss and fern for myself where I could sit and watch the water, within call of the house yet hidden from view. Breaking away the inner leafless willow twigs and shoots that jutted up through the green brown backed fronds of the fishbone ferns I found a seat of moss and made myself a bower, shaded and sweet. There is no doubt whatever that when I arrived at the lake I was not only romantic but over-sentimental and invaded with a supremely egoistical sense of injustice, the unfairness and disillusionment of love. It seemed to me that only in nature could I find the exquisite solitude I needed for my contemplation.

Within a week I knew what was required of me in my job. At 8:30 each morning I was expected to breakfast with Mrs Jones and the children, Mr Jones having eaten at an earlier hour. From nine to twelve I was in the shop. Then came lunch finished in half an hour, even to the drying up. From then until three when I opened the store again my time was my own, as it was after seven when we closed and I picked up my evening meal on a tray which was always carefully prepared and waiting for me. On weekdays I took my meal to my room or to the lake's edge. On Saturday and Sunday I was needed almost full time. Mr and Mrs Jones worked in and out of the shop throughout those two days.

Saturday was a very busy day with all the preparations for the evening dance. As well as serving the customers I had the dance hall to arrange and decorate while Mr Jones waxed the dance floor. There was the supper to look after which Mrs Jones and I prepared and served on a long trestle table at the house end of the hall. The band played on a platform at the other end and part of my duty was to see they were satisfied with drinks. Cleaning up after the dance on Sunday morning with Mr Jones I often thought of my mother's efforts preparing for church and visiting relatives. Mr Jones was fair; after dance night he did not expect me in the shop until eleven although he opened up at nine. Just the same I tried to get busy tidying up the hall by that hour myself. In fact my duties ended before twelve when the dancing recommenced after supper. Two women came with the band did the dishwashing and I felt that if I stayed up late it was because I loved dancing and not because my presence was necessary. Dance nights were fun, decorating the hall was a Friday pleasure which excused me from the counter and on Saturdays and Sundays I sold souvenirs and postcards instead of weighing sugar and counting eggs.

I was happy in my new job; weekends were exciting and weekdays placid with time and a place for contemplation. I even began to discover a little time for writing since all days were engulfed in the beauty of my surroundings. Mr Jones was an easy boss and affable in the store once he knew he could trust me with the regulars' accounts. He had a rough way of teasing me a little in front of the customers but he never failed to let them know I was his deputy and my final word was also his. I tried to be very careful to make sure that what I did was indisputably his wish. Jimmy had told me that was how he had been so successful with his bosses in the cannery. As for Mrs Jones, she just moulded me into the family providing me with every need, although without intimacy. She seemed to live in a world of her own with her children. After the first week she ceased surreptitiously checking my room and never at any time did she comment on the books.

I was a little hurt at first but later felt grateful not to be asked if I had a particular boyfriend for I was not really prepared as yet to discuss Jimmy whose photograph lay face downward on the bottom of my suitcase and whose ring I wore on a gold chain under the demure cotton frocks with white pique collars that mother had run up as working dresses for me. While Mr Jones went out of his way to keep me satisfied, Mrs Jones was uncommunicative, apparently fearing I might assume even the smallest degree of intimacy. Yet she was always kind for which I was grateful. Neither of them interfered or questioned my time off and if there was somewhere I wanted to go or something particular I wanted to do, all day Tuesday or Wednesday was mine. By the time a month was up I felt at home by the side of the lake, liked my job, found Mr Jones a good employer although one who left me emotionally cold and unresponsive, while mystified by his wife Ilma who somehow kept me so distanced from herself and the children.

In the beginning it may have been this personal sensitivity to Ilma Jones that pushed me to discover my retreat. Almost every weekday the weather was fine I found an hour to spend on the moss with a book; often before two o'clock when Bobby had an hour free with his speedboat. I was secure in my hidden isolation for almost that first month and then my peace was shattered.

"Every day you come" the voice of Alex Popolov said. "Every day here to sit."

Startled I jumped to my feet. Alex was standing perfectly still at the lake's edge beside the bank, his face upturned almost level with my own.

"Leetle one" he said baring his startlingly white teeth in a smile " 'ad you been a fawn you would 'ave made not even an eye move. I would not have known, yes or no, you are there."

"But you spoke to me" I said recovering enough to have realised how silently he must have moved. With a tiny flutter of panic I wondered how long he had been there, if he had followed me and why.

"Even a bird would 'ave rested still" Alex went on.

"I'm not a bird and you frightened me" I retorted indignantly "why did you follow me?"

"There are many woodsmans but not so of woodswomans."

I couldn't help smiling. "I'm not a woodswoman" I said smugly.

"Then you are artist or poet. Or why this?" Alex answered with an all-embracing sweep of his hand. Flattered into an unexpectedly confessional need I told him simply "I come here to read and write and think"

"For privacy from zat house, I think. Come down eet is not for me to come up, eet is your leetle place."

I gathered up my books went out my back door and came around to join him at the water's edge. He was sitting facing across the lake. I sat beside him at a small distance.

"She wonders what it is you do" he said. "She thinks maybe eet is you meet my friend Bob."

I laughed, "So I do" I said, "but he comes for me to the pier in his boat, never here."

"I know. Still every day eet is here you come, she says disappear here. Is it not so?"

I could scarcely keep the growing anger out of my voice. "I don't bother anybody Alex. It just isn't anybody's business if I want to sit here by myself. And if Mr and Mrs Jones wonder where I am why don't they ask me? I would tell them."

"Of course," he said. "And of course you are angry wiz me. I am sorry. Eet is only I knew you were one who is loving this lake like me. I know so I watch."

"Spying on me?" I drew in my breath.

If he heard he took no notice, his narrowed eyes still focused somewhere on the opposite side of the lake.

"You do not understand" he went on. "It ees Ilma, she is not like you and me. She is frightened. For Ilma zee woods is zee terror. You do not see zis? You do not notice with zee children?"

"Alex why is it you tell me this?" I demanded, understanding somehow that he had not discussed speaking to me with Ilma Jones and that certainly Mr Jones had nothing whatever to do with the matter. He was in some way protecting Ilma Jones. My voice forced him to turn, I suspected unwillingly, towards me. His eyes were dreamer's eyes, veiled, unfathomable. I looked into them directly for the first time and knew the sadness of the man for what it was, so that I had to temper my question with another "Why don't you tell her there is nothing to fear in the forest?"

"It would not be zee truth. For her zee truth is this fear."

A strange sense of unreality circled around me. I tried to escape.

"All of this, Alex, has nothing to do with me has it? You know it has nothing to do with me."

"Ilma knows it is wiz me as it is wiz you, zee lake, zee forest. She ees afraid for us, afraid for you, she ees responsible for you."

"So she asked you to follow me?"

"No, no, this ees not so. She does not know I come. She would not 'ave 'ad me come."

"And she will not speak to me herself"

"This she could not do. I understan'."

"If you are asking me to give up coming here and only to sit where I can be seen I won't do it."

"I do not ask this."

"Then what do you ask?" I muttered petulantly for I was baffled again.

"I ask nothing" he said his eyes on the water once more. "I come to tell you this, not ask. Without a right there ees no asking, ees it not?"

I could not speak then, and there was no use to pretend so I too looked out at the lake in silence. Part of me comprehended perfectly, yet another side of my intuition was withdrawing from an explanation I did not want to hear. Before he felt forced to speak again I said softly "Does she never go out on the lake?"

"No."

"Or into the woods?"

"No."

"It's like half of life" I said

"Much less it is, she 'as." Alex said

"If she stood in the door and called, I would hear."

"If she knew."

"I'll tell her. I'll tell them both if you like just casually when I can"

Alex did not move and neither did I. He just began suddenly to talk quietly as if from a far distance.

"I 'ad a sister, older than my brother and me. She was sixteen. After my parents were gone she was like a mother to me. You understan' we were in zee country estate in Russia. My brother and me we wanted to play in zee forest. For me zee forest was zee best big thing in my life. She would not let us go. She had this fear. But I went, always eet was so. I went and she wept, and I loved her very much. But still I went even wizout my brother. For me zee forest was life. I was in zee forest when they came. They took my sister and brother into the forest and under zee trees they shot them dead. Zee forest gave to me life, to zee others death. I was only little you understan' when I found them, eleven years so I knew this fear. I knew eet well."

After a moment I said "You belong to the deep forest Alex, like Charles, But I only to the fringe. It is the view I must have, I know that." It was true but I felt like a conspirator when I said it, as if having given a favour I had been given a greater favour in return and somehow now it was up to me to keep some secret balance. Alex did not lift his eyes from the lake waters. "This is zee truth" he said "for each his own ees fixed."

The lake was very still and in its mirror an image began to rise in my mind towards the surface. Tensely I waited for the revelation it might bring. But a fish jumped from the shallow water and ripples swept out in ever widening circles. The image receded uncaptured. In this moment Alex rose and left me as silently as he had come.

Mr Jones was in the store that afternoon when his wife bought in the afternoon coffee. There were no customers.

"By the way," I said as casually as I could before she left, "I thought I should tell you I've made myself a little bush house on the lake just inside the forest. I hope you don't mind. Ever since I was a little girl,

I've loved a little place in the woods to read. My father helped with my first one. If you should ever want me just call. That's where I'll be."

Well, well" Jones boomed "You must have taken Peter Pan seriously. I must make a bush house as you call it for Dorsey. I never thought of it before."

My eyes were on Ilma Jones who was standing perfectly still looking down at her feet.

Her stillness was so real it permeated the space until she said:

"Maybe later. Dorsey hates the woods." Then quite suddenly she looked up into my eyes. "She's so little, yet" she said, only to me as if she were apologising. She was pallid and her lips trembled. I had an almost uncontrollable urge to put my arms around her to hide and comfort the naked fear that stared me in the face. Then I drew back, my intentions halted because I was remembering something, somebody, and the pain of that indefinable recollection stabbed my mind with a needle fear of my own, vivid and agonising. Did her eyes blur then with tears or was what I saw the falling of her heavy lashes. With a little gasp she fled past me, through the shop door into her dining room.

"Ilma's not at all well" Mr Jones remarked, his voice embarrassed.

"Maybe she should have a holiday" I said, "away from here, Victoria maybe or even further." I suppose I was thinking of Pat and that mill manager's wife. As Mr Jones stared at me his colour rose. Aghast at my impertinence, I bit my lip, aching with remorse and also fear. I, who had tried to be so careful to have said such a thing, to have become involved.

I need not have worried.

Mr Jones shrugged his shoulders. "You might have an idea" he said "although I doubt it. She loves the house so much she'll hardly stir out of it. Still, I might persuade her after the season."

He had only been embarrassed because his wife had run out. He had taken my remark as the suggestion of an outsider trying to cover an awkward situation.

∗∗∗

12

Chapter Twelve

Charles knew, and I know that Egypt had to be on my agenda even as China was on his. Charles speaks perfect Chinese. It was part of his usefulness during the war. My Arabic is less sure. I do not study enough. He would not be proud of me for languages. They, for him are a gift. For poetry, maybe. Perhaps there is another copy of my book waiting for me on the table.

It is late afternoon now and still I sit thinking of the ginger jar. Somehow, before I can open Charles' letter I must think things out, right back to the beginning. Until I am sure enough of myself to open it. I have always been like this; always known in advance certain needs for certain sureties and have learned to control them. So I know, today I must trace thoughts right through the two summers of my youth. Take them right through to the end.

The rest of the story will not be easy to remember. It will make me ache. I always ache with intuition without knowing why. I did not know why with Ilma and if I had, would it have made any difference?

Only this, without Ilma Jones I doubt if I could have made it through the war; made it all the way to Egypt via Australia.

***

How beautiful that summer was. I projected myself into it deliberately almost as if it was only to be something outside of me like a dream or an imagination. All the people were part of the atmosphere of the lake itself and the forest around it. It was a strangely exciting feeling for me to be closely acquainted with people without really knowing them at all, to live in this beautiful setting with fascinating characters like Alex and Jim, Eloise and Ilma, old Sven the lonely Swede and Pero the cougar hunter whom I would probably never see again in my life. I didn't really know about people then and the effect even a day's encounter can have on your life. I was transient, a bird of passage. Yet by the end of summer I knew very well the place into which I could always escape when reality overwhelmed me. Having love so close to imagination and dream I would have no further need to search for its habitat. There would always be this lake.

When Charles came he liked to borrow the beautifully crafted canoe, willingly lent by Alex Popolov for the excursions we enjoyed together on the lake. We would paddle an hour and then pull up for half an hour or so at some mossy spot where we could beach the canoe. Usually, our return was swift and sure of stroke to get me back to the store.

Charles came almost every weekend for Friday night at Thompsons and the couple of hours I could spare on Saturday. Or else he came for part of Sunday and went back to the mill with Jim on Monday morning. He preferred to avoid the dance on Saturday night for his own reasons and when he came on Sundays we took a thermos and sandwiches with us so that I could include my lunch time which gave me an extra hour away from the store.

We talked a lot on the excursions, as if finishing conversations which had begun in that other summer and needed completion in spite of the passage of five years. He told me a lot about China; things about war and hunger and disease that I had not suspected and could scarcely believe. He spoke facts with a dry certainty which I received with silence as beyond argument. He had been and he had seen, and usually what he had to say ended abruptly in his own silence of memory leaving no opening for any continuation of the subject.

Both of us skirted around the intimacies of our lives and both of us knew it. We deliberately kept the realities of our lives at a distance as far away as Charles was with China, Jimmy back East and Greta in America. We knew how close to the surface we were but neither of us would speak. One time after he finished telling me about a temple he visited in Henan I burst out:

"How can you bury a brain like yours in a sawmill?"

"The sawmill is merely a temporary circumstance Kit. Don't belabour me about it. I lost my brother Davey when I needed him most and I don't intend to lose his namesake for any reason whatsoever. He has to have time to grow, little David, and the mill is not so bad while Matt Mathews runs it."

"It's almost a haven isn't it" I countered.

He looked up sharply "A haven?" he queried "I earn my money; it's hard physical work and good money in a depression."

"That's what I mean, a haven for earning money when you need it, for you and for Alex and for Jim."

He stood up and looked down on me as I sat on the moss hugging my knees.

"Get up" he said "We'll go. You see me as I am, why I'll never know. But as usual I find it damn tempting."

And on another beautiful afternoon following a long silence he suddenly turned on me.

"I find you incredible. Something's gone wrong with you and Jimmy. I know that and yet you're not unhappy really. You can be puzzled, perturbed, concerned and you're intuitive way past normality; at least I think you are but you can't be unhappy, you're not unhappy! The cynicism you affect is pretence. It's a kind of mask to cover up the fact that you can't be really depressed like I get."

"I'm just more optimistic, I guess."

"No, it's not that. It's some form of faith I think. Either a person has it or they haven't."

"Oh really, Charles, just because something goes wrong with your romance or mine that doesn't wipe out romance."

"For me it does and for me life can only be what I feel myself. The life of other people must be pure conjecture on my part. I don't know what goes on in minds other than my own. No romance for me means that romance is out. I admit of course that others appear to enjoy romance, but I can't be sure. I can't feel the emotion for other people, I'm not a part of it. I can't admit happiness to be a part of somebody else's life if I don't feel it myself. But you can and it makes all the difference."

"Well of course it does. The possibility of happiness is swelling around us all the time. It's there. A breath of it can be captured even when everything seems to have gone wrong with personal life. It can't be denied no matter how miserable an individual feels. We cut ourselves off, Charles, yet the possibility for happiness is always there. It can be found in almost any circumstances. Your mother told me once that your father died happy.

"Well, I won't. I'll go out grumbling."

"About not reaching out and taking the share of happiness you could have held in your hand."

"You shouldn't say things like that Kit. Can't you see I tried that? You make me feel deformed, as if I have a faculty missing. Maybe I have. Maybe most of us have."

"Oh give it up, Charles. You make me feel like some sort of egotistical Pollyanna. Unless of course, maybe I am. Maybe lots of us are."

He laughed then but there wasn't much humour in his laughter. I knew he wasn't going to pursue the subject any further when he raised his paddle.

"A few maybe. All I can say is that you are lucky. The big majority of the human race find life a miserable affair.

***

The week before the last dance of the season there was no work at the mill and because Pat went to Victoria with David and Alex took Bobby Tanner on a four-day hunting trip, Charles gave himself a mid-week holiday much to the delight of the Thompsons. Alex gave him full care of his canoe. It was quite wonderful for me too. We went out on the lake every day.

On Thursday I took my day off. We went miles in the canoe, exploring every tiny bay and mossy knoll. The first tints of autumn were appearing as gold and scarlet on the sumac shrubs close to the moss where the sun struck the lake shore and the great conifers dipped branches into the water. There was a little breeze that sang a lapping music to duet the paddle as we passed by. Early on that day we began to argue, and we got back again on to the dangerous subject of our loves. There came a point when I accused Charles. We were resting after a late lunch under a giant fir.

"I don't think you were in love with Pat when you married her Charles."

"What did you say? What?" his words clipped like a pair of scissors. I repeated my statement though I had startled myself with it.

"You tell me that," he said. "You! You know I was in love with her. You were the one I told. You know I was in love with her."

"You did not tell me that. What you said was that you were fascinated and repelled at the same time. Those were your words. I ought to know. They made such as impression on me and I always believed everything you said."

"When I told you I was fascinated and repelled you knew I was in love, didn't you?"

"I thought you might be."

"You knew it." He made the statement a bitter fact.

"I was only fifteen."

"You knew it. You still know it. But now you deny it because you don't want to believe that's what love is. Fascination and repulsion, both at once so you often can't tell one from the other. You don't want to believe."

"It's not pure enough is it, not even romantic. You knew I loved Pat and you hated me for it. You made that plain enough on the weekend you came even though as you say you were only fifteen. You despised me for wanting Pat. Not Pat herself, she left you cold, but you thought I was despicable, that I'd let you down. It's true isn't it? You thought by loving Pat I let you down."

"By marrying Pat you let yourself down."

"Then what is it about Pat that makes you think I couldn't love her? Tell me that and don't skid like mother and say she seems so selfish. We're all selfish. And I don't want to hear that old cliche that some are more selfish than others. Some have to be and Pat seems to be one of them. So why? You tell me why." He was so angry all other sounds seemed to have stopped.

"She's your wife, Charles. You shouldn't ask me that."

"Don't hedge, Kit. You're the only one I can ask. For God's sake don't hedge. You've gone this far, finish. You've said I wasn't in love with Pat when I married her. It's been hell since. So what about that? If you know why, tell me. I want it said. Only you can say it."

As suddenly as it had arisen the rage drained out of him. His eyes filmed over and he turned his face away from me.

"If you won't say it I'll have to" he said quietly "She never loved me. I'm not sure she even loves David although she swears she does."

"Or her parents or anyone else," I said "She can't. Like you said, I don't suppose she can help it. I wish I could hate her Charles for hurting you like she has. I'd like to hate her. I really would but I can't."

"I can't either" he said

"But you don't love her either" It was one of his statements I made.

"No. Not anymore."

"You never did. Because there is nothing to love except that she's pretty. That's not enough for you."

"Pretty. You don't think she is pretty do you? She'd hate that. She has sex appeal you mean, her body is enticing, has a siren sort of allure. I fell for that, so let's be honest no matter how degrading."

"You didn't know, Charles."

"But you did?"

"That awful weekend. It seemed to me that Pat had manufactured herself to a set pattern she had decided on, that she could change her outward appearance like annuals in a garden because there were no trees with roots."

"Astute for your age."

"I was hurt. There was Greta that summer too."

"Don't tell me you despised Greta too for taking Tony Johns."

"I didn't despise you Charles. I could never despise you or Greta either. I loved you both and it was just that I felt everything was wrong. As if some malevolent fate stepped into that summer and mixed everything up. I even felt it was somehow my fault. You see if I had only been older or less childish for my age I'd have known Greta was falling in love with Tony Johns. I'd have met Pat on an equal footing and found out about her. Your parents might have talked to me more. I just felt helpless."

The whole of that summer came back to us then and sat there with us at the edge of the lake and we had to accept its presence in a sort of quiet communion.

Then Charles said. "You might have imagined yourself in love with me and then the cat would have been in the fire."

"Charles."

"I saved you that anyway."

"I'd have got over it."

"Would you? Being you I wonder. It was better you fell into Jimmy Millar's arms. He was your age, as far as girls were concerned anyway and just your size for a first love."

"He wasn't my first boyfriend and when I met him again and he was my love, you were horrible. You didn't approve."

"You were too quick for me, that's all, too sudden. Your engagement shocked me like my marriage shocked you. I went hollow when you told me. It was as if I was losing part of myself."

Ours eyes met then and clung together in a complete absorption that blocked out the sky. We leaned toward one another and then his arms tightened around me and his lips pressed down on mine. I felt the strength of him surge through my body and terrible burning assaulted the pores of my skin. I lay limp in his arms while his kisses fell with hunger and desire on my eyelids grown strangely still and my lips passive with expectation until the violence of his passion left us and he kissed my hair, my cheeks and my pulsing throat with increasing gentleness as if he held a fragile thing of porcelain or alabaster but scarcely a receptive woman of flesh and blood. My heart pounded with such force that my breath was jagged, pushing itself from my throat in uneven gasps. Then suddenly I was gentled against his breast. His words came to me as from some great distance and were as spasmodic and unpredictable as my breath and did not seem to belong to Charles at all.

"Oh my darling, my little sweet, you're soft, so soft. I love you. I have always loved you. I've been so lonely, so damn lonely. Your hair, see it clings to my finger. Don't move. Don't take it away Oh my beloved." Then he began to quote and I know every word "The forest flowers are faded all, Eleanore, Eleanore. I turn to thee as to a bower. Thou breathest beauty like a flower Thou smilest like a happy hour. I turn to thee. Eleanore, Elanore."

I came so near to myself again that I could open my eyes. Perhaps I struggled and there was no greed in Charles, no force that gathered to itself without scruple that which was not freely given. He let me come back from my ecstasy like a piece of thistle down tossed into the sky as the victim of some wanton wind.

Charles was sitting with his back against the fir trunk as he had when we ate our lunch; his long legs stretched out towards the water, his feet in old sandshoes pointing skyward. And I was there too as I sat back beside him in my blue gingham dress with the white peter-pan collar. Only everything was changed, and I sprang up to my knees, turned and sat backwards upon them staring at Charles, breathless. I didn't know what I felt or how. The inner self I thought I knew so well had been drained out of me. Did Charles, looking at me then, answer something in my eyes?

"I'm your cousin. I'm married. I know and I knew in time. But for God's sake don't you say it. Don't you ever say it. Promise you'll never say it. Promise." The urgency in his voice hissed like a cutting knife. Yet his voice was low and his eyes veiled, somehow withdrawn."
"Charles. Oh Charles. Of course I promise. It's only that I ..."

"Don't quite know what happened. I can tell you. You're lonely here, cut off from what you hoped for, from what you planned. You needed someone to make love to you. And I love you. In some damn peculiar way I always have."

"I love you too Charles."

"I know you love me, Kit. You love me like a part of yourself. It's hard not to build on a thing like that, not to thinks it's enough, not to put in more than there is."

"I wanted you to make love to me. I wanted it more than I ever wanted anything in my life. I still want you to. Can't you feel it?"

"Oh that." Charles said and stood up "Too many people try to spend the rest of their lives together because of that."

He put his hand under my arm at the elbow and lifted me to my feet. Then he searched for matches and with an infuriating deliberateness lit a cigarette.

"You had better comb your hair before we go back, Kit." he remarked. "I made rather a mess of it."

"And you're sorry" I accused bitterly.

"It happened" he said. "It had to happen sooner or later. I had to know."

"And now that you know, or think you know all that goes inside of me as well as yourself what do you propose to do?"
"Do?" asked Charles and answered himself. "There's nothing to do."

I thought to myself I should sob and run to him in tears. Then he would take me in his arms again and kiss me. He's mine, I thought, he's mine and I want him, I want him more than anything else. But though my blood was racing and my heart throbbing I knew I wasn't sure. I could not cry, and I could not throw myself into his arms. So I combed my hair and clambered into the canoe while Charles held it steady. There was scarcely a ripple on the lake under the paddle dip. The water broke away like quicksilver. The cedars dangled long fingers to be reflected in a cold still mirror. The wind we had with us before was still. I kneeled on the red pillow in the bow facing the way back. My paddle lay across the canoe balanced under the white knuckles of my two clenched fists. Charles who had taught me to handle a canoe with his own expert ease guided the swift birchbark toward its home base. I did not paddle and Charles did not speak. In the deep unbroken silence I remembered other journeys. Perhaps Charles thought of rapids he had run, turns in fast flowing rivers he had known… But the lake was placid and unperturbed. Neither did I speak.

But when we came in sight of Alex' landing I said clearly above the paddle dip.

"We might have had a house here like Jim and Eloise."
The canoe rested. I knew just how the paddle was raised.
"Or like Alex."
"You're not like Alex. You're like Jim, you love music and books and children and nature, outdoors like this, forests, fishing, canoes. Alex is a deep forest hunter."
"And you and I are pilgrims, my dear Eleanor. We would die stuck in one place."
"Oh, don't be so silly, Charles. You know perfectly well what I mean."
"Only too well" Charles said, "only too well."

He dipped the paddle again and we skimmed the lake surface as he swung the canoe away from its mooring where our rowboat lay, back toward the centre of the lake in the direction of the house where I had my temporary dwelling.

"I'll come back later for the rowboat." he said. "Jones won't want it will he?" I knew he wanted the canoe for himself for the time that was left before he went up to Jim's. He would go up the lake swiftly and reset in solitude.

"No, he won't want it. He never does. Besides it's early, earlier than I said we'd be back.

"I know"

"Are you going to stay until Saturday?"

"No." he said, "I'm going back Kit."

So I swallowed and gave up and even conquered the rush of tears that threatened my eyes. It was all so dreamlike anyway, as unreal as an imagination or a story one had read before sleep. Some part of my inner self supposed he was right. Charles was always right. But he wasn't quite finished with me yet.

"Kit, there's one thing. Oh hell, it's a stupid thing to say but if you should ever need me, you know if ever the second best is excellence, I'll be around somewhere."

"I'll never need you more than I do now. Don't talk about second best. It doesn't suit you."

"Leave it alone Kit, leave it alone. The role is one I recognise, not one I relish. Not today of all days."

"Today has been beautiful Charles! I'll never forget it. All of it right up to now seems like a wonderful dream. Everything that happened I wanted to happen. Everything, and I'm glad."

And I knew as I said it that I had wanted Charles to make love to me and that I had wanted more of Charles than the companionship of a favourite cousin. There was something in him that completed me. What was it he had said, that my love for him was a part of myself? It was not the love of two merging into one but one becoming whole. What sort of woman would I be now that I had become myself?

Would I accept myself, face a woman who had to contain the poetry of Charles without wanting the man that he was. Suddenly looking at my reflection in the water I felt despicable, like a person who has crossed a stream to safety by means of another's body stretched across the rapids. Everything Charles had given I had incorporated, absorbed and made part of myself.

So Charles could go away now and leave me satisfied, desiring no more. He would leave no hollow aching space that had to be walled round and avoided as Jimmy had. He was not all or nothing as Jimmy was. In the depths of my being he had made the poetry in me safe, safe against love, against life itself. With Jimmy or any other man my centre could be secure. As Alex had the forest, I too had my own place.

"It is I who am like Alex" I cried out to Charles "Alex knows it. You know it. It is only I who have been such a fool to not know."

If he heard he did not answer. But his stroke was easy until the paddle lifted and the canoe drifted gently toward the pier.

"Dear Charles" I said softly "You have given me the poetry. I'll always have you with me."

"It is in you Kit" he said

"But only you knew it was there. You forced me to see it. You have secured it for me."

"Then for God's sake hang on to it."

The canoe scratched lightly against the pier so that I had to put my hand out to balance the landing. Charles did not move as I stepped out of the bow. The pier and the canoe rocked crazily so that the waters of the lake splashed over my feet. Swaying I looked down at Charles who did not raise a hand from the paddle to caress the craft to stillness. His eyes as he looked up at me were misty with splashes of spray. Then he raised his eyebrow and smiled. I started to put my hand out in one of those inane useless gestures that mean nothing at all. With the same movement that raised it I let if fall and turning picked up my basket and ran up the pier.

***

There was a letter under my door, a thick letter addressed to me in a small precise script clearly defined in black ink from the fountain pen I had given (how long ago it seemed) as a first present to Jimmy Millar.

"Dear Kit,

You win. You have given no adequate reason why I must come home to marry you, but I will. At this stage in my career it seems a waste of time and money but if it's the only way to get you that's all there is to it. Some men need one thing to complete them and some another. I need you. Since you stopped writing I've been wandering around this town like a ship without a rudder. I may as well admit I've been through the usual emotional wringer but not being a naturally jealous type, my practical side came out. I re-read the spots off your letters, especially the last one and they still didn't make any more sense to me than the first time I read them. But the letters smell like you as I know you or if that is not a polite way of putting it, they are like you as my girl. When I read them you are here with me and that doesn't seem to me to leave any room for a rival. Besides I have convinced myself that I know you well enough to realised that if you had fallen for somebody else you've have told me right away. The only influence I could suspect might give me a run for my money was Charles Gilbert. You needn't get furious about this because I know that from the beginning Charles objected to my profession as a foil for your personality in a much more subtle way than even your father did. I not only like Charles but I respect his perspicacity as something special even though I find it impossible to understand his point of view. His relationship with you always baffled me so it crossed my mind that without my presence you might arrive at his way of thinking. However, as Charles is but your favourite cousin in the family doghouse for marrying somebody you don't like and hasn't had a mention in one of your letters since I left you, it seemed pretty far-fetched to drag him in. His chances of influence seem as remote as mine.

You might as well know that this letter is about as honest as I'll ever be. I had to get advice from a woman since you are a woman. Otherwise I feel I would go mad between watching the post and telling myself you had no damn right not to answer my letters. I haven't had much to do with women here, except for casual parties. All my friends know I'm engaged which hasn't made my position any easier. Anyway, you can like this or lump it, Williams' mother has been good to me ever since my first Christmas here so I went to see her and asked her straight out what in the plans I wrote to you could have upset a girl. Talking to Mrs Williams did me a lot of good but not in the right way you might think. She laughed so hard there was nothing left for me to do but join in. After a while she apologised for her mirth and said there was nothing wrong with my plans except that they were mine and that if there was one thing in their lives that girls insisted on planning it was their own weddings. She added out of kindness to me that under the circumstances she was sure you would come around. I said that if that was the reason, which I very much doubted, she just didn't know you. I told her that you looked soft on the outside but had a centre as stubborn as a mule. I was then brusquely informed that in that case, the sooner I got back home and married you before someone else did the better, because you sounded exactly like the kind of girl both her son and I needed. I don't say she wasn't right, but I was shocked dumb when she said it and in the interval it took me to recover my tongue she actually offered to lend me the fare, which of course I politely refused. I tell you this right now because if I don't Mrs Williams will herself, for the big news just out is that Prof. Williams is going to London next term for two years, which, incidentally, will set me up just where I want to be if I work like hell as one of his research students. When he's through with me I will be eligible to work in Malaya, the Eijkman Institute in Batavia, even in Cairo where the Sphinx you emulate that appeals to you so much is waiting.

Well, I have been working like hell day and night. At other times such as in bed and at breakfast, nothing seems worth the effort. Not that I'll let the work go but my heart's not in it Kit. So far I've changed nothing but whatever you say goes, so for God's sake, say something!

Yours as ever and forever
Jimmy"

Laugh, Eleanore Jane Marshall, called Kit, laugh, giggle your head off, stuff your fist in your silly mouth and cry genuine salty tears of humility and joy. You are alive again and ready for it. You are going to be married to Jimmy and go to London and Malaya and Egypt to make a home for an up-and-coming scientist with a future. You are going to live on your toes in a world with a brilliant future. You are going to cope with the mundane realities of travel and pounds, shillings and pence, the gas rings and bath heaters of furnished rooms. You are going to argue and love, give and take, hold out and give in. You won't be planning alone again. You won't be living alone. You will be sharing. Remember that, sharing. You'll be giving as well as taking. Jimmy's work is not more important to him than you are. You'll be sharing, you and Jimmy. Sharing and loving. Stop crying, you blind egoistical, foolish creature. Stop crying and write. You have just time to catch the mail. Write. This very minute put down what's in your heart. Don't wait. Don't think. Write to Jimmy and tell him you love him.

"Dear Jimmy,
Don't change your plans. I'll take the will for the deed. In two weeks I'll be leaving this job. I've loved being here and I don't want to go home again to put in more time waiting. It seems to me that the way you shared a worry

with your friend Sykes in Montreal need not be so different from living with me in London. You needn't worry too much about the time I'll have on my hands to be lonely. I won't be lonely ever again. There are hundreds of things I want to see and lectures I want to hear. London is a literary centre as well as a place for science. Jim Thompson, a friend of mine here at the lake says concerts are cheap in London, real symphony concerts Jimmy with artists who are the world's best.

I'll get on a boat, as soon as I can book passage after I get home. Mother and Daddy will understand. They have already begun a routine of weekly letters written by Mother and added to at the end by Dad. I'll write to them from overseas and describe everything I see. They'll love that. Your parents won't be pleased darling. They won't help you anymore either but they shouldn't have to help a man once he's married and they'll get over feeling bitter in time. We are grown up after all. We have to decide for ourselves. It's mail time now. I hear the post van arriving.

Dear Jimmy, thank you for your letter. I can't imagine any real life without you.

Yours with love and no doubt whatsoever.
Kit."

***

After I wrote to Jimmy it seemed to me that the spell of the lake lifted like mist from a valley. Only a consciousness of Charles remained with overwhelming compassion to ride with me on my highs over the next hours, before doubts began to work themselves into regrets that tended to magnify into threats. Those kept me awake at night reliving the last weeks. After a number of days I knew I was whole but I suffered the consequences. Moreover I would not hear from Jimmy again for at least another two weeks and that only if he answered my letter the very day it arrived. After so much silence would he want me still on the same terms? I had explained nothing. Would he be angry over weeks spent worrying that ended in such easy capitulation? Whenever I felt these questions coming on I would re-read Jimmy's letter and then start making lists. On twenty sheets of paper I went over the clothes I had, the books I wanted to take, the people I'd farewell, the arrangements to be made. I built up my future life in words on those sheets.

In the store I worked longer hours, stacking the cans of beans together in neat rows, paying meticulous attention to customer needs and the account books. If Tom Jones noticed any difference he accepted my efforts without comment. He took any work I did for him for granted, noticing nothing except a deviation from his regulations or a minute mathematical error; even these faults failed to arouse in him more than a slight sarcastic teasing.

Ilma flitted in and out of the shop and the house all that lovely summer. She rested when the children rested in the long sunny afternoons. Her routine, like her husband's and for that matter mine seemed laid out as part of the summer pattern. Like myself she ate the same meals, addressed the same people at the store. Only she went nowhere away from the premises. There had never been the slightest difference of opinion between us since the day I told her about my bush house. There was no intimacy either. Yet I felt that when I told her I was going to London to be married I would hurt her. So I couldn't bring myself to tell her. Instead, I wore my ring in the store.

"You have an engagement ring I see" she said, "you don't often wear it."

I replied deliberately "I've been wearing it around my neck; I thought I might lose it. It suddenly stuck me how silly I've been. If I did lose it Jimmy would buy me another one. We've been engaged for two years. You see at the end of this year we are going to..." She cut right across my sentence before I could finish it, before I could tell her. "How lucky you are to feel so sure." she said and walked through the door into the house.

I wanted very much to talk to her. Yet even on the busy weekend when I worked with her she covered her thoughts. Order was always maintained. I never knew her to be late with a meal or fail to have the children organised in time. The children laughed and played but never away from the house. If ever I thought to take them with me to walk or row to the Tompson's or the Tanner's, before I could ask I would discover my free time was their bath time or sleep time or they had been promised stories or a treat. The children belonged only to Ilma. It was uncanny. Ilma was as thin as the traditional wraith under the flowered dresses she wore. Beside her I felt extraordinarily sturdy, solid, simple and healthy for she so lacked these attributes as to make them uncomfortably conspicuous in other people. She dressed nicely all the time and wore a light lipstick carefully applied as the only make-up against the paleness of her face. One always felt the potentialities of her prettiness which had the quality of a glamorous butterfly in the final stages of metamorphosis when it is a compelling fascination to stand by waiting for the unfolding of the sticky wings is a compelling fascination.

Her speech, at least to me, had the same quality of promise composed of endless trivialities, yet with undertones of unrecognisable depths. I knew the week Charles left that I too would be glad to leave the lake to get away from Ilma Jones. She disturbed me as much after two months daily contact as she had on the day of my arrival. Yet I was so drawn to her. I wanted to talk to her, to tell her I was going to be married to Jimmy. I needed to talk to a woman, and she was the obvious one in my daily life, only a little older than I, just the next phase ahead of me in a woman's life. And I lived with her in her home. She provided me with every smallest service. At her request, sudden and anxious though it was, we were Kit and Ilma, though we both spoke of Mr Jones whom I never called Tom.

I wanted to talk to Eloise and Jim but felt constrained because of Charles. The day after Charles had taken Alex' canoe and swung it with vicious strokes down the centre of the late, Jim had been waiting for me to open up the store. He handed me three books: Sandburg, Countee Cullen and one called Poems from the French tied together with a piece of string.

"Before Charles left this morning he asked me to give you these books. He said they were yours more than his. When he came to us he expected to stay for a weeks' holiday. He went without explanation. I thought he was happy with us, happier than we had ever known him."
"He was"
"Did we offend him?" Eloise says its none of my business but I think you should know that I saw Charles pass our place in Alex' canoe yesterday afternoon. At six this morning he came back to us, packed his bag and asked me to take the canoe back and bring Jones' rowboat to this pier. He didn't even leave a note for Alex."
"Alex will understand."
"Will he? Well, I don't."
"It's just, – just that he wanted to see David."
"Is that all you have to say?"
"There is nothing else I can say Jim. Charles is Charles. He made his own decision. He went back to Pat and David."
"You know as well as I do that Pat isn't worth the little finger of his hand."

"She's his wife. He was in love with her when he married her and little David is his son."

"And you're his cousin."

I think I was crying inside but I wanted to be honest with Jim. As usual I defeated myself. A new strength in me now was grown-up enough not to cry.

"Yes, and I've loved him ever since I was a little girl. He has always been wonderful to me, more than a brother. He's the best friend I've ever had or am every likely to have Jim."

"And that's all?"

"All? What more could I ask?" I had been such a fool. Why hadn't I worn Jimmy's ring all summer?

"Nothing, I suppose" Jim said and turned on his heel and went out of the store.

I had made it impossible to go to Eloise and Jim and rejoice that I was going to London to marry Jimmy Millar.

In the end it was Bob Tanner I told on Saturday night at the last dance of the season. Fresh-faced and red-brown-skinned after his hunting trip with Alex he turned up glowing with life and natural good spirits.

"Gee whiz he's keen, that Alex," he said when we were dancing after supper. "He never misses a trick in the weeds. Got me back the minute he said he would."

"Don't tell me you were that keen on dancing, not more than fishing and hunting."

"Well," Bob drawled "it's the last dance of the season and the new schoolteacher from town is here. Quite a gal."

"Which you knew no doubt before you left."

"Sure thing, but no woman's more important than a trip in my boat. She went like a honey, simply purred along. Want a ride in her, she's at the pier?"

"You don't mean now?"

"Sure, why not? Suppers finished, what's to stop us?"

"Well, I could suggest the new schoolteacher. She's nice, not to mention the big brown eyes and red hair. The competition's going to be keen Bobby."

"She'll be all the more interested if I play hard to get. Let's go"

"I'll have to get a coat."

"And out of those shoes. I'll give you five minutes."

I went through the kitchen at the back of the dance hall to the door leading into the house and inserted my key. All the house doors were kept locked on dance nights. It was dark in the hall at the foot of the stairs, but as I started up a silvery light from the front door as it quietly opened suddenly lighted my way. I heard a little gasp as I turned. Ilma Jones stood in the doorway; one hand at her throat, the other swung somehow awkwardly behind her.

"Oh Ilma," I said "sorry. You startled me."

Her reply was a whisper. Clear, yet hoarse as if strangled in her throat.

"Going up already Kit?"

I found myself whispering back "No, just getting a coat to go for a little moonlit run in Bobby's boat. It's a beautiful night so we thought … "

"It's alright. Tom always stays until the very end before he locks up"

Starting up the stairs again I stopped and turned again. "Is everything all right with you Ilma? You're not feeling ill or anything?"

Again, her voice came up the stairs to me with the same clear urgency as if she were trying to be convincing against insuperable odds. I had remembered how early she usually went to bed and how even on dance nights excused herself before the supper was finished.

"I was just getting a bit of air. It's a strange night don't you think, very close even with the moonlight. I often go for a bit of air when I have a headache."

"Can I get you something?"

"No. Oh no. I'm going up now."

When I came down with my coat she was gone and the hall was in darkness. Outside it was indeed as Ilma said a strangely beautiful night. The air felt unnaturally exciting and the moonlight fell across the pier in streaks as the clouds crossed the sky rapidly driven before a strengthening wind. The boats tied up in formation along the pier had begun to bob up and down and bumped each other with little scratchings and scrapes. As we hurried down the pier a firefly and then a dragonfly hit me in the face driven by the gusty wind.

"Bet it storms before morning. The wind's turned round." Bobby said. "Good thing you got your coat. Alex said the weather would turn. He always knows."

"Does he?" I said and saw the canoe and fell silent. Alex had not come to the dance.

"God" Bobby said, and I knew he too had seen the canoe. I had never seen his face so concerned, so serious as when he turned to me.

"Get in" he said offering me his hand "We'll drift her. He didn't want to draw attention to the pier with the roar of his Evinrude., He sat facing me with his hand on the tiller.

"Why in the blazes does he have to leave his canoe there. Why can't he bush it?"

"Somebody might steal it."

"Don't be nuts. An Indian made it for him. There's not another birchbark like it on the Island."

"Just the same."

"Just the same, he didn't tie it up there."

"How long has it been going on Bobby?"

"I dunno how long, - that's what nobody knows."

"Poor Ilma."

"Why doesn't she leave Alex alone. She's married. She's got kids."

"I guess she can't, Bobby."

"What the devil happens in a case like this, that's what I wonder. What happens in the end?"

"I don't know. It's frightening isn't it? She's terrified. I know she is. She was standing in the doorway when I went to get my coat."

"Gee whiz, you poor kid, living with it. You know someday somebody's going to say something."

"It won't be me, Bobby. I'll be away in a week."

"Has Tom asked you to come back next summer?"

"No, he won't ask me. I rather think Ilma always wants a different girl. Anyway I wouldn't be able to come. I'll be in England."

"England?"

"Yes. I'm going to be married in London before Christmas."

"Well gee," Bobby said, genuine awe in his voice. "The women around here take some beating. Fancy sitting with that under your hat all summer"

"Oh Bobby. I haven't known all summer. I only knew for certain this week. Jimmy's back East studying and everything has had to be arranged to fit in with his post grad work and how well he did. We couldn't say until we were sure."

"Well gee" he said again "Congratulations and best wishes and all that. Why doesn't anybody ever tell me things?"

"Nobody here knows but you Bobby. I haven't told anybody else."

He leaned forward and kissed me lightly on the forehead.

"Good thing I've got my boat isn't it?" he remarked ruefully. "The way the women get snapped up in front of my nose."

I laughed "Sure is. Just the same I'd make a play for that schoolteacher if I were you. After all she's not a summery fly-by-night."

"Like your cousin Charles. I don't suppose you're going to tell me what he thinks of your engagement."
"Actually he's known Jimmy for years. He encouraged Jimmy. The three of us used to tramp from camp to the lighthouse together."

Bobby laughs shortly "I didn't think you would" he said "but that's okay. Mind if I spill the beans?"

"What about?"

"Well, you are leaving here to get married. What else? They'll all be interested, Mum and Dad and the others. Or do you want to tell them all yourself?"

"I guess I'd rather not have any fuss, Bobby."

"Is that why you kept it quiet until after the dance?"

"I suppose so. I don't know really."

"Well, I think the locals would like to know Kit. Not that much happens in these parts."

"Enough, I would have said"

"Hmm" he said "Well, I'll promise to be discreet."

He used a ridiculous emphasis on the last word and we both began to laugh since we were both young and somehow excited. Life for us was full of promise. We had drifted down almost to the Tanner's wharf and as we came abreast of it a couple of motors were turning over in front of the store. Sputtering they broke the moonlit silence with a roar, drowning out the motors of cars starting up on the road. Bobby swung his tiller around.

"Party's breaking up early" he said and looked up at the sky. The clouds were coming over, black and menacing and moving fast. A sudden sharp knifepoint of wind bit into my cheek and sent shivers racing down my spine. "Going to be a storm so they are all going home. I'll open her up and we'll have a quick run."

"No Bobby, take me back." I said in sudden panic "I'd rather."

"If you're thinking of Alex he's already away" Bob said. "I saw the canoe crossing as I swung around. I told you Alex knows the weather better than anyone else."

But I was shaking with a cold unreasonable fear. "Please Bobby, I'd rather go back. I'm cold."

He pulled the starter rope and the nose of the boat leapt into the air. It was scarcely two minutes before he choked off again and slid up against the pier. The last boat was pulling out.

"Careful there you wildcat" someone called out "Goodnight, goodnight." The cries were echoed by the loon across the water under the rising wind. "Goodnight, goodnight, So Long, be seeing you."

"Goodnight Bobby. See you tomorrow."

"Goodnight Kit. God bless."

The engine barked and the boat's prow rose again. Bobby is going to check on Alex I thought as I ran up to the house, unlocked the first door, locked it again, ran up the stairs, unlocked my door, and once safe inside stood with my back to it panting like a hunted deer. Because of the sounds I had begun to hear. But then what do you do when you can't run any further from sound, when you hear the thuds and the muffled sobs even more clearly from the other side of the wall beside your bed? Light the lamp? No, light the candle in the porcelain holder. Tell yourself it is none of your business and take your clothes off and go to bed. So I took my dress off and threw it over the back of the chair. Even with the candle it seems so dark, so terribly dark. It was dark because suddenly the sounds had ceased and silence is dark.

In my petticoat I went to the window, pulled the curtains back above the table and looked out at the last shred of moonlight in the enveloping blackness. Listening acutely I could hear the wail of the conifer branches beating wildly against each other under the force of the wind. I stood there and waited for the rain to drown the sounds that had begun again in the next room, the sobs again and the menacing grumble of a voice I could distinguish as belonging to Tom Jones. Then Ilma's

cry, almost a screech like an eagles' prey.

"No, no. No Tom. Think of the children." A piteous wail and a scuffling sound.

"Now get out, get out before I kill you."

The rain came down hard as the first drops stung the windowpane. Then the deluge, onto the roof, in the drainpipes, slithering away in waterfalls and rivulets, in cascades from the house to the lake. A peal of thunder, torrents again, splashing and drowning with water. The end of summer.

I thought I heard the banging of a door, an outside door and strained to hear anything above the sound of the storm. Beneath my window was the front door but there was no light and I could not see, even the shadows were obliterated and there was no trace now of the moon as the rain steadied into a downpour. Again I thought I heard a door bang. But I was not sure. I began to tremble. Listening. Until terror grew in me. Another door seemed to shut somewhere, it seemed to be upstairs now. Suddenly the terror in me was such that I could wait no longer. Fear is weaker than endurance, which is why we rush out under fire, why we beat at prison-guards with bare hands. I unlocked my door and stood trembling on the landing. There was silence on the stairs but a changed silence, a deeper, darker silence with the smell of the earth under rain. I don't know how long I stood until I realised the front door was open. If I ran straight down I could pass the dining room door and get out. There seemed to be no light at all but the dining room door seemed to be a menace. Tom Jones had hurt Ilma and what if I met him as I ran out? And I had to get out. That was all I could think of, that I had to get out in order to help Ilma. I had to get out and he would try to stop me. If I could just get out of the house I could get help. I slipped off my shoes and descended the stairs soundlessly, step by step, my hands slipping before me on the banister. At the foot of the stairs I bolted and ran out into the night, hiding myself against the wall of the store as far as its shelter could save me. I half expected to find Ilma crouching somewhere there and when I didn't find her could not decide which way she ran. She wouldn't have dared go into the forest, so it had to be up the road or down the pier to the lake. I think it was then as I halted with my back against the board wall that there was a lull in the wind gusts and the rain and I hear the oars of a rowboat, a distance from the pier.

Crossing the road I ran into the forest instinctively groping my way the little distance to my retreat in the willow copse. It was almost halfway down from the lake to Tanner's and I suppose I realised that I could swim from there to the Tanner's wharf. I could not have found my way through the forest at night, nor even could I have followed the long way, on the road, staggering on trembling shoeless feet under the blast of the storm. The thought of the store pier with its flooded empty rowboats shuddering aimlessly on their ropes appalled me. Also, I knew that from the pier I would have been wind-forced to drift to the centre of the lake, my arms helpless against the elements. But from the side of the willow copse the lake was protected by the point on which the willows stood. At the farthest end of the little sandy beach I slipped into the water and began to swim.

My first sensation was the soft clinging warmth of the water after the rain-coldness of the air; it lulled me as gently as my bed received me at night. But only at first. Then the wind assailed my head and made waves that blinded my eyes. It was only then that I wondered if I would be able to find the wharf and that there might be a light still somewhere at Tanner's. The current was with me, only the wind my enemy. Yet there was one terrible moment when I began to sink gasping for breath and fought desperately for life. I had swum too close to and was sucked beneath a tree that hung twisted branches into the water. I pulled myself up against the tree-trunk and clung. While I hung there the gale ceased momentarily and I heard somewhere far off toward the centre of the lake the dip of oars. Also in that moment I detected the glimmer of a light, the small yellow flutter of a lamp that must be Tanner's boathouse. There was a peal of thunder and the storm rained hard on me again.

Safety surrounded that light, distinguishing refuge from chaos with warmth and friends instead of fear. But my limbs refused to proceed toward it. I became part of the inertness of the fallen tree, a slimy, wet, backboneless creature attached only to the suction of terror with my teeth rattling in my pounding head and my half-clothed body shaking in the icy fingers of the leaves above the black cavern of the water. The lake in wrath and violence bubbled and boiled to the shrieking howl of wind, rising toward me like a witch to dredge me down. The darkness was like a live thing creeping closer to me whispering that I was lost and forsaken, useless against the faceless power that controlled the deepest waters. Murder was on the lake, and passion beyond redemption and pity controlled the Jones pier, but I was helpless, lost among the sobbing trees. For how long, one minute or five? How long is the brink of eternity where consciousness battles for existence against its opposite?

The water splashed up against my face, warmer than the rain perhaps, or colder than my shivering skin. I lifted my head from comforting hardness of the trunk to look again for the light. I knew quite suddenly it was Ilma the waters were looking for and not me. From a distant hill so high it dwarfed the lake to a gem of turquoise set in the gold of early morning I remembered the voice of Charles, clear and distinct. 'There is a difference between fear and pride, Matt. Kit doesn't frighten easily. She has nothing to fear from the waters.'

I slipped down and out into the lake with both arms rested and relaxed, with strength again and plunged forward through the turbulent water. My feet seemed a long way behind beating rhythmically like a small propelling meter.

Bob Tanner was in the boathouse and with him his father and Alex Popolov. I must have appeared as an apparition to them, a forlorn drifting phantom in a clinging white petticoat with a face drained of colour and dripping with water like my hair. They were struck speechless and then advanced toward me from the boat they were repairing in one combined movement of shocked anticipation, I think they would have suspected why I was there without me uttering a word.

"I swam" I said and swayed toward them in the boathouse door.
"Swam?" they echoed in unison and reached me. Mr Tanner recovered first, "Get that thermos, son. I think there's half a cup of coffee in it. And towel. Alex, - the towel, man, the towel."

But Alex didn't move, just stood still staring at me. I was only conscious of Alex, the others didn't matter.

"Ilma" I told Alex, "Ilma. I think she's out on the lake in the rowboat. I heard the rowboat again as I swam down."

Mr Tanner had put his coat over my shoulders and Bob had dashed back with the coffee but my eyes were still glued to Alex who stood suspended like a cat about to leap, his eyes little black pinpoints of horrible concentration.

"Did - he - hurt - her?" Alex made each word sharp and separate like a bell toll.

"I don't know what happened Alex." I wailed "I don't know. I only heard from my room. It was terrible."

"Bob" Mr Tanner said "Take Kit up to the house and get her some dry clothes and wake your mother. I told her I'd be late fixing this boat so she's gone to bed. Then come back and we'll get the boats out. You and Alex can wait then while I go up and see what's going on at the Jones' house."

Alex cut across his words sharply like a man fighting for breath.

"Where ees she?"

"I don't know Alex, I told you. It was so wild and dark I couldn't see. There was an argument and he threw her out. I know he did. I didn't hear any more." My voice trailed off, "- into all that rain and wind, into all that rain."

"Now just take it easy dear," Mr Tanner said looking over at Bobby, his eyebrows raised.

"Zee lake" Alex persisted "you said zee lake"

"Kit's upset" Mr Tanner said quickly, "Nobody could hear a rowboat on a night like this. The Jones are probably still at home. We'll see."

But Alex was like an animal trapped. Suddenly he sprang toward the door. Perhaps because he had lived the last two weeks with Alex, Bobby anticipated his intention and with a flying leap as unexpected as Alex', brought him down to the floor. They rolled over and over. Astounded, Mr Tanner moved forward and separated them.

"Are you two crazy?" he demanded.

"If he goes there Jones will kill him." Bob gasped. "He'll kill him Dad."

"No." Alex hissed "I'll kill"

"I've had enough Alex" Mr Tanner shouted "If I have to get help, you'll be run out of here like a dog. Kill? What are you talking about?" He closed the door of the boathouse with a loud bang. "Get this girl up to your mother Bob" he snapped "and get back quick. The sooner we get up to Jones' pier the better."

"Please can't we just get in the boat and go now?" I moaned "Please go now. I don't want to stay here not knowing. And we might find her if we hurry."

Mr Tanner looked from his son to Alex and back again to his son. Bobby nodded.

"She'll be okay Dad." So Mr Tanner agreed and said to me "You might as well get into your own clothes as ours and in any case you'll be just as wet again either way. The sooner we know what frightened you into this the better."

It was his father who steered the big launch up the lake against the storm; Bobby sat with his arm around me in the cabin and across from him Alex watched me ceaselessly trying to verify through me what he knew was true. I had seen eyes like his in a fox in a trap. His jaws were clamped shut but you felt that at any minute he might open them wide, but you couldn't tell as you sat there whether he would whimper or howl out his agony. So we didn't speak to him on that short run. The three of us sat in silence until the launch scraped the pier.

"Come along Kit." Mr Tanner said putting his head into the cabin. Bobby helped me up. It was still raining but I didn't feel it and Mr Tanner did not hurry. All was in darkness and at the veranda of the store he guided me into shelter with his big fishing flashlight. "Before we go in" he said, "If Mrs Jones did run away what made you think she'd go out on the lake on a night like this?"

"To go to Alex" I answered, "What else could she do?"

"Hide somewhere until morning or go to Thompsons or somebody else."

"She'd never do that" I said. "She's absolutely terrified of the forest."

"Come on" he said and we proceed around the house.

The front door was open exactly as it had been when I ran through it, driven back by the wind to catch on the latch inside. At the top of the stairs my bedroom door was swinging. The big torch in Mr Tanner's hand lighted the emptiness of the dining room and kitchen. We went up the back stairs. The door to the children's room was locked. Mr Tanner rattled the door and then walked on. I had only been twice to the big bedroom which backed on my own; when Ilma had been indisposed I had taken up a tray with tea. I had been amazed at the room, a sort of boudoir with rosebud chintz entirely unexpected in such a place.

The door was wide open now, the bed dishevelled, the bedside mat in disarray. Clothes and shoes were scattered on the floor. But what my eyes remained fixed upon was the knotted piece of rope with a frayed end. Mr Tanner drew in his breath and kicked the rope.

"She just might be with the children locked in." he said but his voice was without conviction. He no longer believed what he was saying. "Call the children" he said suddenly. "Call them. I'll pound on the door and you call them." Completely at the end of my resources I had to tell him. "No, not yet. I can't cope with them yet. I feel so sick."

"Come back to the boat again." He said kindly "We'll go and get Jim." Then we'll break in. I don't want to do it with only those two in the boat anyway."

I felt sick all the way down to the boat. I was so ashamed of feeling sick but I couldn't help it. I kept seeing the rope. Bobby came out of the launch to help me down to the pier. Together the three of them handed me over to Eloise. They took another boat with them when they left again with Jim. And they had agreed that Alex could pick up his own canoe. He was sane again and needed his canoe.

Before they left there was a strange thing that Bobby Tanner said to me. He said I was not to worry because I had done everything I could, in such a short time it amazed him. He said that when he arrived at Jones' pier for the second time after he had taken me back, he happened to look at his watch. It was only two hours since the beginning of the storm.

It was no use Eloise telling me to sleep, she was too wise for that. She simply stripped me of my clothes and dressed me in flannelette pyjamas, gave me a hot-water bottle and wrapped me in a blanket. After she gave me a drink and two calming pills she just made me comfortable on the pillows of her divan in her living room beside the fireplace. She stirred the dying embers of the fire into a roaring blaze with pinecones and kindling while I sipped the hot drink and watched her numbly. The rain fell steadily now as the wind fell and both of use listened to the boats on the lake purr past, their motor sounds fading into the distance. We didn't talk except that Eloise excused herself after I was settled. She would prepare coffee and bread for the men she said.

I think I half woke up when I heard her open the back door and recognised the rustle of oilskins as they were removed and thrown on the floor. Jim's boat had come back and it was daylight. I lay there hearing the subdued voices and the clink of coffee cups in the kitchen. As the voices droned on and on a kind of envy settled in me with the acute cynical despair of loneliness. Jim and Eloise, so close together in the kitchen. What had they done to be as lucky as they were? Why Jim and Eloise? Why not Tom and Ilma, Alex and Charles? Why should I lie waiting outside their intimacy for a word, a sign, an assurance? I needed so desperately a share of their strength. My head buzzed with their murmurings, my mind wavering back and forth unanchored in a tangle of names in water.

So that when Jim came in with Eloise I had lost track of time and place and for a minute I thought that Jim's enormous presence was my own Jimmy come from somewhere far away to rescue and protect me from myself, to dismiss with ridicule the impractical flights of my imagination, to reclaim intuition as merely unscientific co-incidence, to declare the eyes of a boy called Rupert normal. The eyes of a boy called Rupert, or a woman called Ilma Jones.

I think I must have screamed with recognition as Jim sat beside me on the couch such that he was forced to put his arms around me to protect me from a self that terrified me. With my face buried in his woolly sweater I heard myself crying out.

"I thought you would never come. Why don't you take me away from here." Then I turned away from him towards the wall muttering "It doesn't matter what you say, Jimmy. Ilma Jones - Ilma has Rupert's eyes, Rupert's eyes."

Eloise said softly "I gave her two of those pills, Jim. I thought they'd make her sleep." I heard Jim answer. "Jimmy is her fiancée, you remember. Bobby was telling me just now in the boat that she told him just tonight she is going to be married in London before Christmas. She was coming to tell us. She was so happy, Bob said; just had a letter to say her Jimmy had got the scholarship he was after. He's doing science at McGill. I'll have to go out again now Eloise. They'll be waiting for me.

I sat up straight then. My own voice back, suddenly alert and anxious, demanded answers.

"Jim, tell me what happened"

"Neither Tom nor Ilma have been found Kit. I got into the children's room through the window on the roof. They were both sound asleep. We know Tom went in the truck. He did not take them with him but he took the key apparently in case Ilma came back first or else he locked the door before the row in case she ran in to be with them. Apparently those kids have learned to sleep right through all the noise on dance night so nothing else would have wakened them. I did not disturb them. Old Sven is picking the lock now and he will stay until we get back. Mrs Tanner is going over. I closed your door, Kit. So far only the locals know. Pero is covering the back roads as well as ours. But if we don't find them soon the police will have to be called. You know that don't you Kit. So get what sleep you can."

"Poor Ilma, poor, poor Ilma. Where's Alex?"

"He's with Bob, searching the lake."

"The rowboat was gone wasn't it?"

"Yes"

"Don't tell Alex, Jim. Don't tell Alex about Rupert's eyes."

They stood above me, Jim so large, Eloise so small, staring down.

After a moment Jim said "Would you like me to send for Charles?"

"Charles? Thank you, but no, Jim. Charles has had enough as it is. He'd only know the truth about Rupert and that wouldn't help me, Jim. It wouldn't help me at all. He'd say I must learn to live with it like my mother said. Only Jimmy can help me. He doesn't believe in eyes or second sight or any of those things. Once I'm married to Jimmy everything will be fine, like you and Eloise. I want it to be like you and Eloise." And I lay down and turned my face away from them and closed my eyes.

The full light playing on the walls and ceiling in the house of Jim and Eloise produced fantastic patterns on the barbaric colours of the Indian rug above the piano. Streaks of fire and water, fluidity and destruction intermingled, faded and rose again in ochre and scarlet, orange, black and mottled grey all under-toned by and super imposed on the thick rich brown of the earth. Beneath the rug the piano was silent, absorbing into its keys the music of rain falling, falling.

But rain was not falling when I woke at noon. The sky was blue again and alive. How peaceful it is, I though as I opened my eyes; the piano is absorbing the song of the birds. Yet my head is heavy. I do not belong here. I am a visitor. This is the kingdom of Jim and Eloise. I think perhaps I am lost. I should be waking up in a nice bedroom above the Jones' store, but I am not. I should be a poet but I can't because Charles is gone. I can't be a pianist because I have given that up as well. Am I not Eleanor Jane Marshall about to go home to a loving family. No, that little girl is gone forever. She has grown up and is about to turn into a woman called Kit Millar. But can't quite. No, has not yet arrived. Is still lost.

"Eloise, Eloise."
"Yes darling, coming."
"Is Ilma found?"
"Oui, la pauvre."
"Who found her Eloise?"
"Alex. It was right that it should be Alex n'est pas?"
"Was Jim with him?"
"Bob, he was with him."
"Oh no, not Bobby. Not the only one left, Eloise."

"He is in this world, Bob like us, all in this world."

We clung together comforting each other, two women weeping beside a lake unfathomably deep, swollen with the waters of the night that had swallowed another woman. Jim found us like that. With him was Bob Tanner looking withdrawn as if part of his mind was concerned with depths he has not known before. As soon as they came in Eloise and I turned anxious eyes towards them accepting the futility of further tears.

"Tom's been found' Jim said 'Pero found him. He lost control of the truck in the storm and went over that little gulch. Pero went down and pulled Tom out. They got him to the hospital in time. They've just got back. Tom made a statement, Kit. You'll have no explanations to give."

"Me?"

They looked at each other, Jim and Bob. I looked at each of their strained faces and then Eloise.

"Poor darling" she said to me, her face a strange brown pucker of worry and tears. She turned to Jim. "That poor man, he makes a statement. What is it that he says Jim?"

"That as everybody knows he can't drink. After supper at the dance somebody made a crack about a canoe that upset him. When the storm threatened he cleared the hall and then got himself into a bottle of whiskey. Then he went upstairs and quarrelled with his wife. On his way downstairs he said he locked the children in to intimidate her. He remembers getting into the truck and then nothing until coming round pinned under it in the gulch. Pero verified the whiskey."

"He knows about Ilma?" I whispered.

"Yes, he knows."

"Does he know about me?"

They looked at each other again.

Then Jim said. "He made the statement Kit. He was asked if anyone else was in the house. He said not as far as he knew; that you had gone off in Bob's boat and had not got back when he left."

Then Bob Tanner spoke to make it easier for me.

"When the storm broke, Kit, we were down lake, below our place. There was a light in our boathouse, my Dad was there so we pulled in to shelter."

"A sensible normal thing to do" Jim added

"And my father came back with us, as you know. When the three of us walked up we were amazed to find the front door open, your door banging. You were frightened so we investigated."

"But Ilma? Ilma? What are you telling me about Ilma?"

"When she heard Tom take the truck out we think she tried to row down to our place to ask Dad to go after him."

I stared at them all. I heard Eloise draw in her breath. There was such silence in the room a crack of the fire startled us like a firecracker.

"You're saving Alex" I said "saving a place for Alex. Tom Jones will sell up and take his children and go away."

"Of course," Jim said "and with the money and the reputation to start up somewhere else. It has to be like that. For you too Kit."

"And Alex?"

Silence again, a reserved deep silence and all their eyes watching as still as a deer in a ticket.

"You're forest people all of you" I cried out.

"You see, Jim" Bob said "She does know. I told you it would be alright."

He turned to me and smiled, the rueful smile of a boy who had only just discovered what he really was going to be and was glad.

"We are going to bury Ilma over on the other side beside Sven's wife.

"But she hated the forest."

"She loved Alex. If she is there Alex will always have a place to come back to"

Suddenly Jim said "Kit why did you make Bob bring you back last night?"

"I was so frightened for her. Her eyes. They were like the eyes of a boy I knew called Rupert Thoms. He died - violently. He - he troubled me so much I thought I hated him. But it was, well just that I knew. Ilma troubled me like that. Only I didn't know. Perhaps until it happens you never do."

Bob said with something like awe in his voice.

"Like Alex. That's why he's so strange, why he goes to the forest by himself, like an animal. He told me last night that Ilma's eyes were exactly like his sisters. He had a sister in Russia who was killed, only he didn't know either until afterwards. He never knew where they buried his sister. Since he lost her he never loved anybody except Ilma. He'll know where Ilma is. It'll give him a place to come back to. The lake will hold him."

"Your lake, Bob Tanner" I said to him, smiling with a kind of relief, a swelling of inner gladness that the lake was also part of kind, uncomplicated Bobby who with his family would make a success of their tourist business and still maintain and protect the superlative beauty of its very particular landscape.

"It's different for me. I was born here" There was pride as well as modesty in Bob's voice. "Dad was thinking, maybe it would help if he made an offer for the store."

"Keep the fringe forest, Bob." I begged "Keep the fringe forest."

"Like a park" he said "but with a straight pedestrian walk through for the sake of convenience. I hereby offer free lodging whenever you want to come and stay. Meantime get a good sleep for heaven's sake. I'm off for a bit of shut eye myself. Be seeing you."

Later when the house was still, Jim Thompson came in with a hot drink for me, stoked up the fireplace with an overnight log and then surprised me by sitting down.

"Apparently it didn't occur to you to ask Charles what I was doing here." he said bluntly. "You accepted rather easily all those books and the piano, the violins and the French conversation. Did you think they grew naturally on our side of the lake?"

"No."

He smiled a little "But you didn't ask Charles. He told me you didn't. For some reason it came up in our conversation the night before he left."

"Actually I thought it was wonderful to find what you have here. I guess I just took it for granted that Charles would too."

"I'm a remittance man, Kit, only a proud one, too proud to take the remittance except for a little gift, a couple of thousand a year from my grandmother who died before I was even of age."

"Don't tell me anything, Jim. Let me remember you as Jim and Eloise, belonging together in this house."

"I can't, I think because of something in you which Alex recognises and Charles protects." He paused and I knew he was looking at me intently although I didn't look back. "And loves. Eloise came to England to sing in a night club in London. I was married, I played in a symphony orchestra and I was a partner in a family business established as long ago as the industrial revolution. My father was a staunch Anglican and represented his constituency in Parliament."

"You chose Eloise."

"Without reservation."

"Jimmy's like that. He knows what he wants, with no reservation."

"Then go to him the same way Eloise came to me, or don't go at all. No man is a shelter in a storm. We're all participants, Kit, men and women alike. Don't fool yourself. It wouldn't do for you any more than it did for Ilma Jones."

"She wasn't meant for life, Jim."

"You say that, and Alex says that. Maybe even Charles would say it. But I don't. I say she wasn't meant for the life she had. Even if she had died in Alex' arms. Everything would have been changed. She denied herself and thereby she denied life itself."

"You didn't have children when you met Eloise, did you Jim?"

He looked at me strangely for a moment but there was no change in him and I was glad he had kept the children he had in him to give to Eloise.

Then he said "It wouldn't have made any difference, no difference at all. Anyway, once you've found out what you need, what you really need I mean, you're bound to lose something else. I guess you know that. I could also make a speech on how life has a way of building up again. In our case it built up on love and a mutually repressed something in both of use that fed on our beautiful scenery rather than an inner city."

"Like Alex."

"Well, we have that in common with Alex; being nourished by nature. Only it's everything with Alex. With Eloise and me love comes first."

"So that you could do without the scenery but Alex couldn't. That's why he has to stay here, no matter what."

"Charles told you that I suppose."

"No. I don't think he ever mentioned Alex in that way."

"What? But he's exactly the same himself."

"Oh no Jim. Alex knows where he belongs but Charles is still looking for whatever he has to base his life on."

Jim looked at me intently.

"I hoped he had found it" he said gruffly and then grew embarrassed to have become more personal than he intended. He made me feel like a small child who had stuck a pin in his arm so that he was resisting the impulse to administer a smack. There would be no further intimate conversation. For all that I felt compelled to answer.

"No" I said dismally "Charles has to find his own freedom first."

Jim rose to his feet and towered over me. He really was a very big man.

"Well Kit" he remarked, like a lawyer summing up a case, "Poor Ilma couldn't stand up to life and Tom will have to start on about a hundredth part I'm afraid. Alex will be fine after a while. He has managed before. I guess Charles will work out what he needs to. You've had quite a summer Kit."

I looked up for what I knew to be my last question. "What about the children, Jim? What about those two little kids?"

"We think Tom will try to make a start somewhere else. He's a good storekeeper. He's been a bit of a rigid bully of a man but he's a good honest and efficient storekeeper. I don't think scenery matters much to him. In fact he might be better without it. We'll keep the children here between us until he's ready for them. And we'll make them a place to come back to in case either of them finds this lake an essential need, which is always a possibility you know. I suppose Eloise has told you a welcome awaits you too, anytime you like."

"Thank you, Jim. I love both of you. Goodnight now."

***

13

Chapter Thirteen

Every night just before the sun goes down and the gun goes off for the end of the fast of Ramadan, a woman has been singing beneath my balcony. Her voice is melodious and sweet and pure enough in the high notes for a place in grand opera. She sings the Koran and looks upward for alms. I always wave down to her, making sure she and no one else catches my coins. For I know that for that one night she will have no need to walk the streets and be abused for the price of a loaf of bread.

Where did she learn to sing like this? In what hovel does she, who has the voice of a lark, hang up the rusted black of her all-embracing garment? Once, long ago, was she so inspired by the waters of the Nile that her music is always with her? She is my serenade of Ramadan, my song of Egypt.

Coming up in the lift, my neighbour said, "I do hope Madam, you are not disturbed by the prostitute who begs at our door? It seems someone encourages her by throwing coins. Is your husband well, Madam?"

"At present he's at a conference in Beirut and will return on Friday. You are all in good health I trust?" He nods as the lift door opens and departs.

Will you come again tonight my songstress? Will this be another night you will gladden my heart?

***

Bob Tanner drove me to the coast and carried my luggage on to the steamer, found me a seat and farewelled me with a gracious abandon of kisses and chocolate. All the way from the lake to the sea we had been a boy and a girl enjoying with deliberate intention a day of rejuvenation, a bridge day between the past and the future which was so much ours we could build into it amazing sequences of possibility. Lunching at the Chalet Bob had said:

"Order salmon. When you come back I'll be fat and you'll be forty."

"You fat? You'll eat like a horse and look like a stick and I'll be fat and scared to eat at all."

"Either way salmon will be ridiculously common to me and you'll turn up your delicate lip at it after caviar."

"Wrinkling my red nose under an appalling hat."

"More likely speaking with an atrocious accent, very English – 'dear boy' and all that."

"You'll have six children and a cruiser on the lake."

"Here's hoping. Champagne laid on for visiting toffs at a price but same address, same lake."

In an autumn glory that could have been spring we drove over the mountain down to the sea in an open car that didn't go too fast, battered by the wind in our hair, to the ship gleaming white in the harbour. So now, having settled me aboard Bob handed me a little parcel.

"From Alex" he said. "He asked me to buy it and give it to you."

It was a carving of a deer. In a way the small gift represented all that lay behind me at the lake, every word we had not spoken, the symbol of a man whose heart was buried in a forest. To travel with me around the world with the Indian rug from Jim and Eloise and an

Indian doll and silver bracelet from the Tanners. All with the poetry books from Charles to join, from this summer, the Ginger Jar of that other summer, in the carved box of Jimmy Millar.

"I'll have to go now. So fare thee well, dear friend."
"Dear Bob. Thank you again for everything!"

Without another word we walked together to the gangway. He was ahead and I saw his startled look as he suddenly turned back to tell me.

"Well, blow me down. You've got a relation on board. She must have been hiding until now. Pat Gilbert. She's sitting on a deck chair farther up. I suppose she's waiting for me to blow. So, dear Kit, you won't be alone after all."

I could not doubt his word. He knew Pat Gilbert. In previous years she had sometimes come to the dance. She lived in a town where he knew everyone and everyone knew him. But I could not trust myself to look or to reassure him.

"Will you answer if I write sometimes from overseas?"
"Sure I will. I'll try to give a literate description of the local peculiarities. It's not my long suit but I'll try."
"You're sweet. Bye now."
"I'll remember that. I'm never likely to be called that again. The compliment is duly returned. So long."

He swung down the gangway. I waved to him as he strode down the wharf. Then I turned quickly but not quickly enough.

"Hello Kit."
"Hello Pat."

She was very chic in black and white linen, her hair long and smooth as a cap to her shoulders, her lips a scarlet streak in a fashionably white face.

"I want to talk to you. In fact I caught this boat to talk to you. Where do you prefer, inside or the deck?"

"The deck. I'll get my things."

"If you prefer. But you can go back. It won't take long."

"I can't very well leave them, can I?"

"Then I'll come with you."

She was deliberately menacing and smooth about it, unembarrassed as a star in the movies. She had been waiting and watching perhaps ever since I came on board. There would be no escape from her. Strangely enough, no matter what she thought I did not seek escape. Nor for once did I anticipate. Some time in my life it seemed to me this had been bound to happen; I would sometime be forced into an unfortunate position where I could not avoid an unpleasant conversation with Charles' wife. Now, at the end of a terrible week was as good a time as any other. Now, as the ship drew away from the pier and we sailed out of the harbour into the Straits of Georgia.

Pat spoke in a kind of hissing whisper as she sat in an empty space in the empty alcove of seats Bob had found for me.

"Where is Charles?"

I said with truth "I don't know Pat."

"Don't give me that" she said "Tell me where he is. Because if you don't I'm going to tell the world all about you and Charles and your so-called working summer."

"There is nothing to tell"

"What kind of fool do you take me for? I know about you and Charles. You and your innocent baby ways, your nice safe covering engagement to Jimmy Millar, studying afar off. I'll go to Jimmy's parents and break that up soon enough do you hear. I hate your kind of woman and I'll make you pay where it hurts most. Now you just tell me where Charles is, since he is not on this boat with you."

In a kind of dream I realised she had expected to surprise me with Charles but all I said was the truth again.

"I told you. I don't know where he is. I have no idea at all. I thought he would be at home with you and David. Charles hasn't been near the lake for almost a week."

"He's taken David" she said then, almost as if she believed me "He's gone and he's taken my son."

"He's Charles' son too Pat."

"Don't you say that to me. Don't you dare say that to me." she hissed. "He's not Charles' son. He's mine. He's my son."

I hear myself saying softly "What are you telling me Pat?"

"I'm telling you" she hissed back at me 'that Charles has taken away my son. My son. Mine and Tony's" That's why I married Charles. I had to when Tony married that silly blonde cousin of yours. Not that he wanted her really."

"I don't believe you" I whispered "It can't be true"

"I want David back. He's mine and I want him back. I'll give you twenty-four hours to tell Charles and if I don't have him back by then I'll put the police to it and the newspapers, the whole thing including the nice little affair you had with Charles this summer."

"I had no affair with Charles this summer."

"Charles is in love with you. He admitted it you might like to know."

"You accused him of it! Is that why he left?"

"Naturally I accused him. It was obvious. He was high and mighty and pure on your behalf but he didn't deny it. He couldn't be, could he?"

"So finally you drove him away" I whispered almost to myself, but she heard and because she was keeping her voice down for me alone the scene seemed more than ever unreal like a move sequence. Not that anybody was listening; it was a beautiful day and the passengers were out on the deck. She snapped at me.

"I drive him! Oh no. You came here and ran after him! I'm the wife remember. That's how I see it and that's how everybody else is going to see it."

I tried to argue with her "But he's my cousin, Pat. Why shouldn't I have seen him when I was near. I always have. And I was sorry for him of course." I added the last bitterly.

"How sweet of you. But I am not deceived by that line. You've always been crazy about him, ever since you were a dear little girl."

Her nastiness got through to me at last and I began to come out of the movie scenario where the real me seemed shattered. So that I stuttered:

"But not, - not in the way you mean" and then stopped. It had been so close to what she meant.

"Enough to know where he is though." she persisted "Now you can find him. I've humiliated myself all I'm going to with his family. I've asked everywhere he might be and been lied to. I've made up stories and run around like a little fool. Now you can do it. I'm going to my parents and if David isn't back tomorrow night I'm going to the police and the newspapers like I told you I'll put them straight onto you, and his mother."

At that point, before I realised what she was doing she got up and walked away with dramatic defiance toward the coffee counter.

Her footsteps were minced on her high heels reminding me of some movie I had no desire to recall. I sat still, appalled. But alive. Myself again. One by one all the events of two summers flashed by to possess my mind. Then, gradually I began to feel people taking attitudes; my mother and father wanting to believe my story because I asked them to but remembering too many things, even how quickly I left home for the lake and not wearing Jimmy's ring. I knew that Mother had never approved of Charles taking me around as he did; although she trusted him, had wondered why he courted Pat and yet had insisted on walks with me. I felt the questions my brothers would ask when I was out of hearing. I could anticipate Aunty Meg's distress and see Aunty Mary's eyes when Uncle Pete taunted her over Greta. And Greta? Would she one day be confronted with Pat and Tony's son? Would Tony want a share of David? Jimmy's parents were a foregone conclusion. Like other people they would say 'Cousins! Imagine! An affair!'

While I sat I thought of Jimmy being with me. Jimmy might accept my work but distrust Charles. What was it he had said in his letter? That the only influence that would give him a run for his money was Charles Gilbert. I began to shiver. For all this poor Charles would not even have David. Publicly he would be deprived of David. Publicly disgraced. A court of law would be bound to give the child to Pat. Better he knew from me than any other. Better if he hated me for telling him than he be told by anyone else. Surely, I thought there must be an answer to all this. I stared out the cabin window at the sea rolling gently and I guess I prayed in whatever fashion young women do. It couldn't have been very long before I saw Pat move. I found myself beside her in an instant. She stood still then and I surprised myself by using her own weapon of accusation.

"Were you lying for effect" I said, "or is it true what you said about Tony?"

She snapped back "Why ever do you suppose he took your silly little cousin Greta? Don Juan himself, that's Tony. If he had to be caught by marriage he might as well be big and romantic about it and be sure to get something pure and young enough to be unspoilt, as unlike himself as possible."

"You did the same with Charles." I shot back in fury at her callousness.

"She laughed "So that's what you think of Charles, unspoilt and pure. Dear me, and I'm thinking the same of you while both of you no doubt are thinking the same of your flirtatious blond cousin who took Tony."

I answered with weary complexity, the fury dying out of me, unequal to her viciousness. Besides I was out of my depth and couldn't tell where the current was taking me.

"Haven't you said enough Pat?"

"No" she said walking back inside where she sat down. "We're not there yet are we?" She settled herself. "I've always wanted to say a few words to you. Your kind of girl needs to have the puritanical nonsense knocked out of her." She was on the attack again. And strangely enough as I sat there listening to her unexpected statement, I reflected that I too had wanted to talk to her.

"You had lots of opportunities to talk to me this summer. Why didn't you come to the lake? You knew I was there long before Charles came for his brief holiday while you were in Victoria."

"Brief holiday. You don't know how many brief holidays Charles takes. But I do. I'm his wife, his neglected wife in the eyes of the world, my dear Kit. But that doesn't concern me. I don't want Charles. I want David. David is mine. Tony forfeited his right to him and Charles never had any. He's mine and I'll got to any lengths to get him back. So you see, my dear, you have been caught exactly where I want you."

It was a drama, like fiction and I was right in the middle of it. I answered her with precise clarity, surprising myself and without premeditation, as if in her film script:

"You aren't blackmailing me Pat. I don't even recognise, let alone admit the grounds of your accusations. Nor do I think you can hurt me personally one little bit. You are trying to get at my family by blackmailing Charles for falling into a trap you set for him yourself. In the eyes of the law as I see it, David belongs to Charles. He has his name. If you publicly prove that he doesn't, the poor little boy will be nameless. I can understand why Charles took him away, whether he belonged to him or not. He loves him. More than that, Charles would never hurt a child, let alone David."

"David is my son. Any court would give him to me. He needs his mother. Also I have the means to support him, I can prove Charles unstable and" she paused "unfaithful."

It was a sort of Anna Karenina situation developing only I seemed to be on the wrong side. But I persisted.

"Very well" I said "That's what you'll do if Charles does not give David back. What will do you if he does? Will you divorce him?"

Startled, she recovered herself quickly. "It seems I have underestimated you" she said "but I'm not falling into that one."

"I don't know where Charles is but I'm going to try to find him. When I do I want to give him a note from you promising to divorce him if he gives David back."

"On what grounds - infidelity?"

"I don't think so. Desertion perhaps."

I was as cool as a movie star myself. So much for a wonderfully real, well-nourished imagination.

"Don't be silly Pat. You don't want scandal for your family any more than I do. You don't want to spend your money either trying to prove what you can't because within a couple of months I'll be married to Jimmy Millar in London. And there's nothing you can do about that because Jimmy knows Charles well and is marrying me. He is not therefore inclined toward believing you. His parents would be horrified no doubt and my family shocked but capable of seeing the truth. As for Charles, he could not be more unhappy than he is or else he would not have run away with David. Surely you can see that it's better for David to have one parent and a secure name than a future such as he has now, rather than tossed about like a football in a court case." I stopped as suddenly as I had begun, breathless before I finished lamely "It's up to you."

She was staring at me hard, her black eyes little points of steely light and I stared back building up in myself the feeling that she wanted freedom for herself if not for Charles. Finally she blinked and responded:

"What proof do I have you will deliver the note if I write it?"

"None whatever. But you stand to lose nothing by writing it. After all you can't expect Charles to give David back with nothing in exchange. He has given everything he had to David. Surely if David does not belong to him he should be free to go back at least to the place where he started. And of course" I added "you'll be free too to do as you please as a divorcee."

"I have no notepaper." she said reluctantly, no longer sure of herself, so I pressed home my advantage in a way I wouldn't have believed possible of myself before the last week at the lake.

"I have and a pen in my purse. How many days have Charles and David been gone Pat?

It was a measure of my success that she answered immediately.

"He went off the day before Ilma Jones was drowned. When he didn't come home with David that night I thought he'd gone to the Thompsons. I thought since it was Saturday night I would get a lift up to the dance and confront him there but I found a note from him telling me he had gone for good and taken David with him. Then I decided to come to the lake to see you but Matt Mathews came to tell me about the Jones affair. He was really after Charles. When I heard you were staying with Thompsons I decided not to go to the lake. Jim wouldn't have let me in. And anyway I didn't tell Matt about Charles. I didn't want them to know I had started phoning around Vancouver until I heard you were going home today."

"And you knew David was safe with Charles! Are you going to your parents?"

"Yes. I'll go there for two days. I'll tell them Charles has David and will be bringing him back there. My parents are very fond of David."

I handed her a pad of writing paper and she wrote. I read what she wrote:

"You better let me make a copy for you in case you forget."

When I had she stuffed it into her elegant purse, got up and walked away. I put her five-line letter into an envelope and, with hope in my heart labelled it 'Charles Gilbert'.

From my mind's turmoil my eyes became conscious of the sea. The waves rose and fell, small whitecaps appearing and dispersing in rhythmic flows that gradually took over that erratic beat of my pulse. There had to be an answer again since I had gone this far. I had to find Charles.

"Take me to Charles" I whispered to my other self. "Take me to Charles."

"And his number one son" came the answer.

Chang. Mr Chang. After all this time could I find Mr Chang who would know where Charles was? I would go right back to where I met Charles on the day of the Ginger Jar. From there I would go on.

The coast was still a long way off. A middle-aged man in a striped blazer and greys sat down where Pat had been. This time I was safer, talking with a stranger who would carry my suitcase down the gangway.

***

Abdul asks may he bring in my dinner before the sun goes? I agree knowing well that he and Hassan will embellish the feast in the street below with that which I alone cannot consume. Nor will I ask how much he prepared, hoping perhaps I will have a guest to share. He is unaware that I have refused to dine out, that I have longed for this time of solitude, that I wished only to use the day and night to write and instead have been lost in reverie. O moon of Ramadan, I will wait until the gun goes and the revelling begins and all the little fires flare higher in the streets and the people around them eat and eat and eat. I will look down from my fifth floor balcony on all their ridiculous short-term happiness and know I belong to them.

Then I will go inside and read the letter from Charles Gilbert. Then perhaps, only then, I will sit down and write and when I do Jimmy will phone from his hotel room in Beirut to bid me goodnight.

***

Determined not to discuss tragedy with me in the street or in my cousin Peg's car (dear Peg, kindness itself married now, happily settled and expecting a baby around Christmas) my mother was matter of fact, bright and yet somehow overly affectionate, so much so that I felt undone when she met me, over exposed to sympathy after Pat. But the effect made me brittle and careful, withdrawn, almost sophisticated, so that Peg would say to her mother and all that bevy of my married cousins that it was unbelievable how I had changed, not the same girl at all, what an appalling thing to happen to a young girl, right in the very house she was living in, as bad as the Greta affair, as bad as Charles. But at the boat Peg was sweet and understanding.

"Welcome home, Kit. It's good to see you. I'm going to run you straight home with your mother. I won't stay because you'll have so much to talk about. I'll drop around again tomorrow."

"Thanks Peg. It's good of you to bring Mother in." I couldn't get to the car quickly enough. I bustled mother with such speed that at the car we had to wait for the porter to catch up with my bags.

"We've got news, haven't we Auntie" Peg said, giving Mother a lead. "Wilf's engaged!"

"Again?" I asked flatly, wondering if Pat had left the boat yet; if I'd get away without seeing her; not trusting her to be last off the boat; not trusting my luck to be rid of her even as far as home.

"Again?" Peg said, her voice staccato so that I was forced to look at her and at Mother. "He's never been officially engaged before that I know of. We're delighted all of us. We always thought he never really got over Pat, you know."

"Pat?" Had my thoughts precipitated her even into conversation?

"Yes, Charles' wife, you know." Kindness and solicitude dripping like too much honey on a single slice of bread.

"Yes, I know. He's had dozens of girls though, hasn't he? Is she nice, the new one I mean."

"That's it." Mother said. "It's such a surprise. You'll never guess. I thought it was so nice. They only got engaged three days ago, and he brought her round to see us yesterday. It was a surprise!" She looked at me expectantly and I felt mean, but still uninterested that Wilf had decided to marry three days ago. Three days ago - when tragedy struck the waters of the Lake.

The porter arrived and put my bags in the boot of the car. Mother got into the front seat beside Peg and I climbed quickly into the back out of sight of their anxious faces; to converse distantly from this temporary sanctuary. We got out of the traffic on to the road home.

"Now" I said to the backs of their heads, making a tremendous effort to help them because they were trying to help me. "Tell me more about Wilf. Do I know his fiancée?"

Mother gurgled "You certainly do! You'll be delighted. She hopes you'll be her bridesmaid, being such an old friend and Wilf's cousin."

"Who is it?" I said, hoping the exasperation would not sound in my voice.

"It's Harriet!"

"Harriet?" Did I imagine I screamed the name?

"Yes. She still lives behind our old place in the Avenue. She's a schoolteacher now and very smart and capable. She'll be wonderful for Wilf. He's much older than she is but it doesn't seem to matter with Harriet."

"No, it wouldn't matter to Harriet."

I began to laugh. Sitting there in the back seat of Peg's car my whole frame shook with unmerciful spasms of mirth. Wilf had ducked Pat and got Harriet. Harriet had arrived in our family! My Mother would help her, knit her baby clothes after she and the family had attended Harriet's big white wedding. She would have all the trimmings. She would make no mistake. It was a monstrous joke, in-credible!

They must have thought my laughter was hysteria, an uncontrolled release of the tension that had mounted up in me over the past week at the lake. I tried not to let them see how I bit my lips to stop the fury of my laughter peeling out like shaking bells in a tottering tower. I hoped they did not know that tears streamed from my eyes as I shook there, huddled in the corner behind my mother out of line of the rear vision mirror. It was so funny, so excruciatingly funny that I had come home to tell Mother there would be no wedding in our Church with myself as the centrepiece, the beautiful bride smiling at the long-awaited groom. Instead, Harriet had stepped in. Harriet who would have earned the money for the clothes for which she would need Mother's advice to buy. Harriet, who is marrying Wilf, the one out of all our family who would want the biggest show on earth and could pay for it out of the profits of his father's meat works. Harriet who had taken such pains to precipitate my adolescence would now settle down in domestic security, with all her certificates to fall back upon in case the meat business folded up, in case poor Wilf unexpect-edly failed to measure up. Harriet! Wilf was marrying Harriet!

Without warning, the laughter subsided in me as suddenly as it had begun and hiccoughs began.

"I'm starving" I said to Mother, "I'll be glad to have supper. I didn't eat on the boat. When will Daddy be home?"
"We'll just have time for a cup of tea and he'll come in."

I was glad. I had an urgent need to have him home. What had to be said, must be said, only once. The first story of the lake in one sitting before I slept and the second the night after I had found Charles, if I could find Charles, if he was where I hoped he might be.

"And the boys?"

"Donald did not get back, Kit. His boat gets in tomorrow." Donald had a summer job on a coastal ship.

"Has the job finished?"

"I'm afraid so Kit."

"Anything else come up?"

"No. I wouldn't talk about it to him Kit. He'll just have to wait like the other unemployed lads. He's not easy at home, but I'd rather have him home than on the roads."

"Did Andy win the tennis?"

"He did. He'll keep the cup now."

"He went back to school, right? You didn't say in your letter."

"Aye, he went back. There's a number like him. The principal is taking them on a bit further, like ready for university you know - a bit of the first year. Then for Andy there's the sports."

She didn't say but not for Donald, but I knew. Donald was the one who wanted to go to university. He was a special type. He wanted it all or nothing.

"And the girls?" I said.

"Oh yes, Andy's the one for the girls, the devil."

There was no need to ask about Davy. At sixteen he was still at school. Like Andy he had sport too.

"I've other news too" Mother said "that I'm sure you'll be delighted to hear. Just before I left, Mary phoned. She's had a letter from Greta. She's living in Los Angeles now and she's expecting. Now what do you think of that?"

"That's good news" I said with dull acceptance, "good news indeed!"

In the morning my family took pains to let me sleep. In my own room, so comfortable, so welcoming under the eaves sleep had come easily to me and I rested untroubled, unhaunted and tranquil until I woke at ten. As soon as I was wide awake I knew what I had to do. Completely dressed for the street, I confronted Mother, who had closed herself noiselessly in the steamy kitchen. She was making jam.

"Why Kit, you're all dressed up."

"Yes, I have to go out, Mother. I have a last errand to do for one of the people at the lake. I want to go right away to get it over with, so I can be myself again, before everybody begins to phone and call round to see me."

"You didn't say last night."

"I know, but it won't take long. I'll be back as soon as I can."

"But where do you have to go?"

"Oh, just to the city, a restaurant in the city."

"A restaurant, that's strange."

"Not really. It's easier by far than a private address."

"Your father could have gone for you."

"No Mother. There are some things you have to do yourself."

"Alright dear. But Meg and Mary have already phoned."

"If anybody else does, tell them I'll phone back, that I'm next door, anything. When I come back, I'll be clear of the lake."

"I hope so. It was a terrible thing to happen to a young girl. Your father was against your going. I should have backed him up."

"I'm glad I went" I said. "Don't you worry. I'm alright."

If she was unconvinced, she didn't say. She left her jam making to have coffee with me and kissed me goodbye, grateful to have me home again. I left her to find Charles. Charles by himself might have been anywhere but Charles with David was something else. David was a small child, a tiny boy less than five years old, not a baby yet old enough to notice where he was and wonder why. Charles had no car and I suspected very little money. He might have taken David to his mother, but obviously he had not done that. The other home he had was Chang's and David could be hidden there, unobserved to a point of complete oblivion.

To find Charles I must find Chang's, a restaurant hidden away in Chinatown where young girls should not go alone, in a street where women might be accosted, even at high noon. But I had no choice. I got off the streetcar and walked to the door of the Hudson's Bay store where I had run into Charles on the day of the ginger jar. Then with blind instinct and the furtive speed of a hare ahead of a hunter I went down one street and then another, into Chinatown.

***

14

Chapter Fourteen

This room! How have I come here into this sanctuary, this habitation of art and incense. Such wealth is here; how is it I can hold this richness, touch it with my hands, the frail smooth luminousness of jade, pale ethereal pink like the underside of a flamingo's feather, a streaked translucent yellow of a tiger's eye, the green of the newest fern in the forest. The goddess Kwan-Yin, of mercy, not white which is emptiness, nothing, but a three dimensional white, all-embracing, transparent. The aura of stillness in this room, thick with rich carpet like a lake, blue edged, lotus-centred; sheltered with silk, before the door an enormous screen, peacock-studded, crimson satin flower-clustered under the tree of life where a window might be the altar here. Painted scrolls, ebony-backed chairs, dragon carved, immobile with dignity, a great gong of soundless brass, reminiscent of clamour, but silent, subdued into fellowship with Kwan-Yin and the yellow jade Budha, the smallest presence of all, in the most sanctified place, so that the very benevolence of its minuteness, dominated my eyes.

This room is someone's soul, a personal temple. What am I doing here resting on one of these chairs, a screen in front of the door through which I came in from a passageway of lanterns?

I am waiting for the door to open, for Charles to come. While I sit in this silence Mr Chang will find Charles, will bring him to me, into this peace which had pervaded my consciousness. The trembling of my limbs has ceased. I have drunk of the nectar from the bell of the flower which is the soul of Mr Chang and dried the tears which burst like spring water with relief at the sight of him, his hands folded veinless and white as two plucked pigeons, his almost hidden eyes, opaque, absorbing my fear.

Without touch, with impersonal courtesy I heard his voice address me, even as his great bulk rose between me and the other eyes beyond him in the restaurant where once long ago I had dined with Charles at the beginning of that first summer.

"Miss Eleanor, cousin of Charles, whom you have come alone to find. This way please. Be so kind to follow me."

I stepped back and he proceeded me up a flight of creaky narrow wooden stairs. Behind me as I followed, a young Chinese man stood immobile like a shadow watching our ascent. It did not seem to matter that Mr Chang should see the misery of my face washed blank with tears.

"Has he gone?" I asked, "the boy who brought me here. I was lost."
"He will not speak" Mr Chang said and opened a door and beckoned me inside. "Walk down the hall of lanterns. At the end is a door. Enter and you will not be disturbed. I will send Charles."

No questions, no answers, dim light from the strange exotic ebony and silk in myriad butterfly shades of colour throwing fantastic patterns on a row of closed doors on one side of the passage. No sound but my feet clip-clopping on the hard floor. At the end my noisiness silenced, my tears dried like the sobs in my throat from a place deep within myself, my fingers aching to touch a tiny figure carved in jade; my back upright against the fury of a dragon carved upon a chair.

"Kit."

"I've brought you a letter Charles" As simple as that, no explanations, no recital of the hard way I had come, of being lost and found again. No query where he had been or why. I did not rise and he did not sit. I took the letter from my purse and he took it from my hand. But he made no move to open it.

"Why did you leave the lake?" he said.

"Ilma was drowned. There was a storm. Alex found her and she's buried now beside Sven's wife on the edge of the forest."

"I'm sorry Kit." he said. "I haven't read any papers. I had no way of knowing. What has it done to you Kit? You're different. What's happened to you?"

"What happened wasn't in the papers Charles. A notice! Lake Tragedy, Mrs Ilma Jones wife of Tom Jones, mother of two children, lover of Alex Popolov a Russian living on the memory of a sister murdered in front of his eyes, who played the violin with a British aristocrat who left England to marry a French cabaret singer, who looked after the girl who should have known in time that the eyes of Ilma Jones were the same eyes as the eyes of a boy called Rupert who died violently."

"Kit, oh my God" He dropped to his knees then on the beautiful Chinese carpet and buried his face in my knee. "I ran away and left you, my God."

"I sent you away Charles. As far as you were concerned there was no alternative. I chose Jimmy Millar."

In the silence the eyes of Kwan Yin were gentle but Charles rose to move restlessly around the room.

"Why have you come" he said at last. "Why have you sought me out. You know what I am. You didn't come to make me feel despicable did you? The truth is self-evident."

"I came to ask you to give David back. The letter I brought you is on the floor."

Even as he stooped to pick it up I sensed the terrible violence of the anger in him. He tore the envelope open and as he read his shoulders hunched and stiffened under his tweed jacket until the muscles of this neck stood out in ridges, dark blue in the strange subdued light of the lamps. He turned away from me.

"So Pat blackmailed you. You had to come."

"I had to come Charles, but not because Pat blackmailed me. The reason you have the letter is because I blackmailed Pat into writing it. The divorce was my idea not Pat's. I demanded your freedom in return for her son."

He turned slowly his eyes on the letter in his two hands. His voice when he lifted his head to speak was cold as steel.

"Why? You don't want me. Why should you demand my freedom for my son. Because of Jimmy?"

"Do you think I'd want Jimmy on these terms Charles?"

"Do you think I want freedom on these terms?"

"Jimmy is an adult. David is a child."

"All the more reason. He's all I've got."

"I could say the same about Jimmy. But it wouldn't be true. I knew Jimmy wouldn't pay the slightest attention to anything Pat could say but I wouldn't marry Jimmy if I thought he was all I had. Do you think I want to be a millstone around his neck, a bloodsucker making him provide everything, giving nothing in return?"

He was staring at me while I spoke his eyes suddenly narrowed, his brows down.

"What's happened to you Kit" he said. "You're so different. I never heard you talk like this before. What's changed you?"

"You have, Charles. If anyone had changed me, you have. You're the only one who's had that power for years and years. I'm so grateful Charles. I might have gone away a child. That's why I want to go knowing you're free. Free to go to China or anywhere else you want to go - decently free Charles, free inside, not tied and hunted. If you give David his chance, you'll be really free. Can't you see that Charles?"

"You're asking me to let David live with Pat."

"No, Charles, no. It's not that he should live with Pat but with himself. His chance to be himself - later when he grows up, to know himself."

"That's why I took him, what other reason could I have."

"You don't know who David is, Charles, you can't be sure. All you know is that Pat is his mother. Your doubt will confound him. Good or bad he will know Pat for his mother but because you don't know what you are he will not know what he is either. He will love you and not know because you will not know. If he grows up with Pat, you will be more his father, than you will be if he grows up with you. When he is old enough he will face only a divorce situation, an incompatibility that had nothing to do with him personally. He will remember you Charles. If you keep him he will seek Pat. Your only chance with David is your freedom."

"Do you think she'll bring him up? How? I ask you. How?"

"With her parents in that impersonal, large empty house of theirs. She'll impress him as a smart and beautiful mother. He'll be sorry for her in the end because she'll tell him nothing."

"How would you know that? You haven't lived with Pat."

"Do you think she'll tell David what she did to you? She'll blame you for the divorce, and probably me, but never herself. To do that she would have to admit that Tony Johns turned her down, chose to marry Greta, a girl of seventeen, rather than herself. Even if David loves her blindly, he will have a chance to be himself, Charles, the chance to judge as himself, to wonder about you and his mother. He'll be safe to develop nurtured, educated in a regular school. You'd know he was there."

"Do you think he would have no education with me? No food? Do you Kit?" Tears in a man don't fall, they swim inside eyes like doomed water drops in a bubble, prisoners that beat themselves into dissolved oblivion but never escape.

"Oh dear, Charles, you'd do so much for David that in the end you'd strangle yourself as well as the poor little boy. Cut yourself free, you must for your own sake as well as his. Let yourself go free Charles, free to start again. Go to China again free."

"No man is free. I wouldn't be free in China. I can't be free of David. I can't be free of you. Freedom is non-existent. Stop talking about freedom. It's a deceit!"

"If I came to China with you, would you give up David?"

Dropping to the chair beside me Charles seized my shoulders violently, staring at me intensely until there came into his face an unfamiliar expression of open candour that changed his face so that I knew from that moment on and forever how pitifully masked are the normal faces of men.

"You love Jimmy Millar" Charles said turning to face as I did the alcove of the little Buddha "I know you love Jimmy Millar. For your life you must have Jimmy Millar. Why do I pretend? David must have his mother. To take either of you would be to live with a sacrifice, a hostage to appease my passions. It's appalling how disgusting love can be isn't it? Don't cry Kit. I taught you myself, as you can say, how to cut free of me. You are the best pupil I will ever have. Maybe a good teacher is proven by what he learns from those he teaches. You don't need me anymore now Kit. You're right, there is a kind of ultimate personal freedom. Somehow you've reached it and handed it on to me. I don't know what I'll do with it yet but thank you just the same for the relief of knowing it's there. The dreadful thing is that I've been wanting to teach without knowing ultimately learning is a personal thing. I wanted to teach you poetry and philosophy and then go all the way with how to live and love as well."

I put my head against his shoulder and hid my burning aching eyes in the roughness of his tweed coat. His arms encircled my shoulders gently and he lifted his free hand to stroke my hair, while his voice went on muted, absorbed in the melancholy like an obligato by a violin.

"I've been trying to replace you with David. I wanted to teach him how to build a canoe, stalk a deer, fish for salmon, what to think, who to love."

"You have given me so much Charles" I whispered. "You have so much to give!"

"You said that once before Kit - so much to give - well giving is free - or else it isn't giving - it becomes bargaining. Don't ever bargain Kit!"

"I came to bargain."

"No, you came to give. Leave happy because of that. When you get home phone Pat and finished the chapter. Tell her tomorrow at ten David's holiday will be over. I will deliver him where he belongs and depart."

"Oh Charles, where will you go? What will you do?"

"I'll go away and observe and ponder my freedom, but I won't compromise with it. I'll hold it in both hands like wine in a goblet and drink to the dregs."

"I won't know where you are."

"You'll know what I am. I know what you are: like me you are a pilgrim only you're starting your journey the natural way, not spewed out like I am in violence. You won't travel my way; I'll fight but you'll flow. Maybe it's the difference between a man and a woman. I don't know. But I'm glad, Kit. You'll go with me always now."

His arm tightened around me with an almost imperceptible pressure. The movement through its submissiveness and control was poignant with longing so that in overwhelming sympathy my body melted towards him and my breath, caught unprepared in my throat, choked back upon itself and mingled with the sudden pounding of my heart. I knew what he would say, must say and when he did, I would respond. I was woman and Charles was man and between was the great mystery, the incalculable possibility, that ultimate unity which is perfection. Delicately balanced, the moment hovered, intangible, unforgettably sweet. Unable to speak, suddenly intense with a new and unmistakable ecstasy that stirred like quicksilver in my veins, I know not only the words which Charles would speak, but I could feel his lips just how he would shape them; as if for that one strange second of life I was Charles, as if I had known some previous primeval existence in his company, been twin to him in the same womb. I was closer to him than skin or bones or flesh, I was his life-book and he was mine. Beyond passion in some ethereal place of kinship I heard his voice above my hair:

> *"The forest flowers are faded all*
> *The winds complain, the snowflakes fall*
> *Eleanore, Eleanore*
> *I turn to thee as to a bower*
> *Thou breathest beauty like a flower*
> *Then smilest like a happy hour*
> *I turn to thee"*

I broke away from him, exalted.

"We're the same Charles. We are each other's self like two halves of one. Only we didn't know before. We've been trying to make a union and we needn't do that. It's done for us already. It doesn't matter what we do Charles or where we go. We're like twins. We don't need to be together because we're the same."

His eyes glowed into mine, luminous with recognition.

"What I can't do you must" he whispered. "What I can't be, you must be. You look so radiant Kit. I'll always know how happiness looks and be glad. I'll fight it out somewhere Kit, but in the end we'll come to the same place."

"I'll be on the fringe of the forest. Alex knew."

"His kind always does. That's why their pull is so strong and dangerous. But Jimmy will sail right down mid-stream into the new world. He'll go fast. You know that don't you dear.'

"Yes, I know that. But not too fast. That's what I learned this summer. He'll wait for me."

We had come so far together Charles and I in that moment that he was able to smile in that endearing rare way of his that shot one eyebrow up with unexpected humour.

"I always said he was a one-woman man."

"He hasn't time to be anything else, thank goodness. Can I see David before I go Charles?"

"No. Go happy. The telephone, like Jimmy is the best kind of scientific invention, through it you can say what must be said without the terrors of physical contact. But promise me Kit that you'll talk to him some day when he's older, when knowing has begun.

"I promise."

"I'll take you home now."

"Take me only as far as our meeting place Charles, our corner where we met the day you brought me here and Mr Chang gave me the ginger jar five summers ago."

We went out of that room of antiquity, past the silken screen that for decades longer than the years of our lifetime sustained embroidered peacocks strutting in richer purple and gold than the struggle for life had ever provided them and where silver cranes beside them do battle. A tiny Buddha in Ming yellow jade sat motionless on the ebony stand in eternal silence. The carpet deeply embedded with the lotus muffled the sound of our feel as we opened the dragon carved door to go into the hall dimly lit with the elaboration of lanterns. The outside door swung inwards as we passed to go down the first flight of bare unpolished stairs. Even the open restaurant door provided no obstacle on our way down towards the street. Beyond the door we became dimly aware of the hum of voices and the clatter of man refuelling the earthly machine that contains his vagrant wondering soul. I did not look but I know Mr Chang was just beyond the portals ensuring our descent, his hands pressed together, his eyes enigmatic, his heart beneath the black folds of his voluminous earthly robe, at peace.

In the street, the group of Chinese still stood excited and voluble against the boarded wall. Their voices rose and fell like the boom and tinkle of bells.

"There must be a new bulletin up" Charles said, steering me past, "the Manchurian War, you know, that's all they talk about. There will be a war in Spain too - a freedom war."

"Charles!"

"Why not. We're into freedom, aren't we, you and I? You produce and I'll protect - it's two sides of the same thing."

"God be with you Charles."

"Blessings on your offspring Eleanore Jane."

***

Abdul has brought me my dinner on a tray. It is beautifully presented, and I wonder why he feels he must use my best dinner service just for me during Ramadan. The sky is flooding into red sunset and Abdul's white teeth shine a huge smile in the half-light. My eyes fall on the tray.

There is the ginger jar. The ginger jar all stuck together, carefully pieced and matched except for a couple of tiny holes where the cracks will never meet. I smile and thank Abdul who must have spent all his sleeping time mending, for I know he will not sleep all night.

"Allah be with you Abdul." I say, "Go now and enjoy the feast." As I sit down I remember the sugar doll he bought for me the first year the children were coming for Christmas. He bought her on the very day we had guests for dinner and his arms were too full and he dropped her on the pavement. Hard sugar she was, three feet high and so beautiful in her garish red and pink and green and yellow clothes and her halo of gold and tinsel so that he could not resist her. He brought her to me almost in tears, poor sad sugar doll, crumpled into pieces held together with clothes.

'Don't worry Abdul,' I comforted him. 'We'll mend her.'

And we eventually did. She would come out again in all her splendour for this Christmas and the next.

Yes, Abdul was aggrieved. 'But milady' he moaned, 'when she fell into the gutter, before Hassan and I could pick her up, a beggar swooped down and seized the biggest piece of sugar and ran off with it shouting Allah is with me! She will never be whole.'

'Nor will any of us ever be.' I thought as I picked up the ginger jar and held it in the palm of my hand.

I was ready for Charles' letter. I knew before I opened it he was coming to see Egypt with me. The surprise was that he was bringing David with him.

*****

About The Author

ABOUT THE AUTHOR

Kathryn Purnell was born in Vancouver, Canada in 1911. She travelled by sea to Australia with her family as a young woman. During the voyage she met and later married Australian scientist William (Bill) Purnell.

Kathryn embodied the soul and spirit of a creative writer. She maintained an intense interest in everything around her, the natural and spiritual worlds, the everyday and the eternal, diverse countries and their cultures, as well as the human condition (of which she had an uncanny understanding). A gifted educator, she was an inspiration to many aspiring writers to whom she taught creative writing. She believed intensely in the need to encourage women writers, the constraints on whom she felt herself at a very personal level.

Bill Purnell's work in the early years of UNESCO as head of its Science Cooperation Division took Kathryn to Paris to live in the immediate post war years, then to Cairo and later Jakarta. She travelled widely in Europe and later spent time in South Africa. Her husband's ill health compelled the family to return permanently to Australia in the late nineteen fifties. It was particularly in this period of her life, with the common pressures of maintaining a family, supporting a husband in his professional life and finding time to create, that she felt most strongly the constraints and limitations placed on the female creative spirit by the societal practices and beliefs of the time.

But create she did, both poetry and prose work. She also spent much of her time teaching aspiring writers, mostly women. Active in the Society of Women Writers, in 1998 she won The Alice Award, a biennial award for long-term and distinguished contribution to literature by an Australian woman. Other awards included the State of Victoria Short Story Award and the Moomba Short Story Prize both in 1966/67 and The Society of Women Writers Poetry Prize in 1972. In addition to poetry, Kathryn left a fine legacy of prose writings, much of which is now being published.

ALSO BY KATHRYN PURNELL

PROSE
Play of Shadows
In an Urban Forest
The Augustinian Correspondence
Honey Eyes
Apollo in January
Sam in July

POETRY
The King Walks in the Orangerie
Safari
Pandora
Harpsichord of Water
Otway Country
Fairy Trees: Poems for the Fitzroy Gardens